Rush the Edge

BLUE DEVILS HOCKEY #3

S.J. SYLVIS

For my autoimmune girlies.
I see you <3

RUSH THE EDGE

USA TODAY BESTSELLING AUTHOR

S.J. SYLVIS

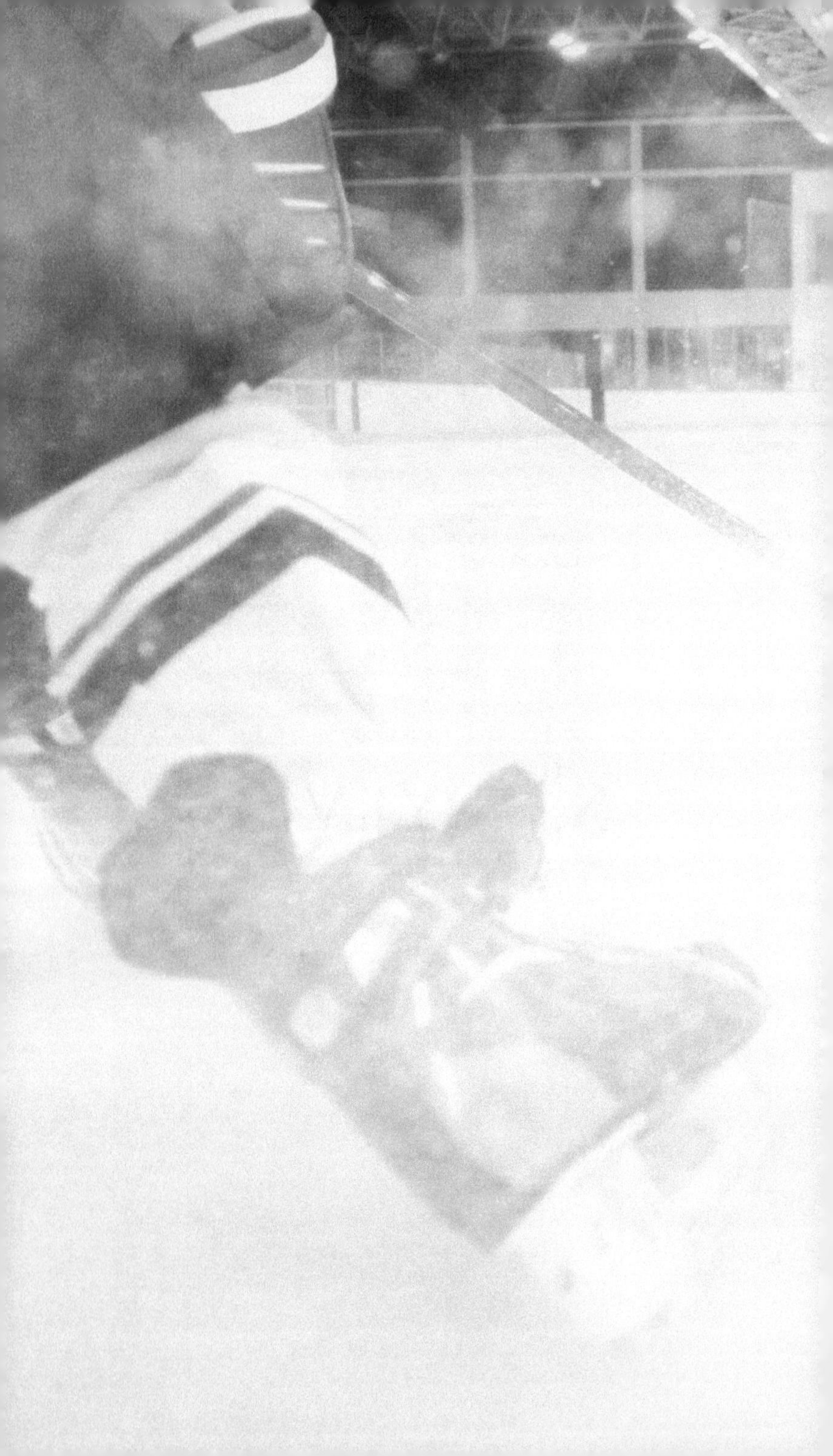

SIX YEARS PRIOR

KANE

YESTERDAY, I woke up with one secret.

Today, I woke up with another.

I lie in my best friend's room, on the extra mattress given to me by his parents, and pretend to sleep. River thinks I've been here all night, but little does he know, I spent it in his sister's room down the hall.

It was risky to go to her, but when my world is spinning out of control, who's to blame me for needing a fucking lifeline?

Daisy Sullivan is the only person in my life who is able to look beyond the mask and know what I'm feeling, no matter how hard I deny it.

That time I got an F and was almost ineligible to play hockey my sophomore year? She knew it ate away at me and stayed up past her bedtime for a week straight to help me study through our bedroom windows. She'd write a problem on a dry-erase board and hold it up for me to solve it on my own. That was when I fell in love with her smile.

Then there was the time one of my ex-girlfriends cheated on me with some guy from the rival school. It stung—probably not for the reason everyone assumed—but Daisy, even as sweet as she is, *accidentally* tripped in the lunchroom with her orange soda and spilled it all over Abby's head. All it took was one flick of my eyebrow in Daisy's direction for her to grin like a little rebel and for me to slip a little further past the line that River drew between us.

She's off-limits, forbidden for me to even think about like *that*.

Everyone, including her parents, considers me to be like another big brother to her. Daisy hasn't needed a lot of rescuing over the last few years, but it isn't just River's responsibility to protect her from guys who only think with their dick or keep her out of wild parties where she doesn't belong —it's mine too.

The problem is that I'm not threatening guys or whisking her away from parties with too much booze for her sake...but instead for mine. It's the only time I allow myself to be selfish when it comes to her. I trick myself into believing that I'm doing it for her sake.

What a fucking joke that is.

I peek an eye open as soon as I hear the shower turn on. There isn't much time, but I fling the blankets off and head down the hall as quietly as possible. My heart drives against my chest with wild anticipation as I reach Daisy's door.

I open it and slip inside.

Daisy sits up quickly, her pretty strawberry-blonde hair in a perfect mess. My entire body comes to life at the sight of her, heart and all. After having her beneath me last night, I see her in a completely different light.

She's nothing but sweet with a line of freckles on the bridge of her nose and a summer glow against her cheeks, but last night she was sexier than I could have ever imagined. The quiet, hot noises she let out as I touched her where no guy ever has will be on replay in my head for the rest of my life.

I stand with my back against the door in nothing but the same sweats I pulled on after she'd fallen asleep in my arms. She's wearing my T-shirt—something she'll have to give back before anyone sees her wearing it.

"Morning." I grin at her because I simply can't help it.

The drama from the last couple of months with my mom and the court seems a little less heavy standing in Daisy's room. I don't know what last night meant to her, but all I know is that I don't want it to be a one-time thing, even if I am leaving for one of the most competitive junior hockey leagues in a few hours.

"Hi," Daisy squeaks as a blush spreads across her cheeks, and my stomach flips.

I take a few steps toward her, and she remains unmoving with her blanket pooled in her lap.

"How are you, uh..." I run a hand through my hair. "How are you feeling?"

She has to be sore, right?

I know it's normal for girls to bleed after their first time, but it still made me feel guilty.

Daisy shrugs shyly. "Good, I think."

I glance at the clothes I peeled from her body last night, still in a heaping pile on her floor. "You sure?"

Her breathy laugh pulls my attention back to her, and she nods. Suddenly, she grows serious, the amused twinkle in her eye vanishing. "How are you feeling?"

She isn't referring to what we did last night, because, obviously, I'm fucking fantastic with her taste still lingering on my tongue. No, she's talking about my near panic attack from spilling the truth to her about Miles and how I shouldn't have been the one stuck in a tiny room with detectives offering me deals to keep me from suffering behind bars.

I slowly take a seat on her bed and place my elbows on my knees. I stare at her bedroom floor. "I'm better."

She breathes out a sigh of relief. "Good."

I turn my attention toward her. "Because of you."

She tries to brush me off with a shake of her head. "I didn't do much. I just listened."

I chuckle. "You did more than that. You somehow always know how to ground me."

A soft smile curves on her face, and for the first time since being drafted to the juniors, I have reservations. It's a competitive league, one where every single player has to play their best to be called up to the pros. We practice a shit ton and travel constantly. Where does she fit into all of that?

The parting of her lips scatters all my thoughts. "The distance will help," she adds quietly. "Your mom will come around eventually, and hopefully Miles will remember that you nearly sacrificed your future for him, and it'll keep him from making poor decisions."

I snort. "I don't know about that."

"Well, then, I guess it's a good thing you'll be far away from here," she jokes.

Our eyes catch. Panic surges through my veins, and I involuntarily grab onto her hand. "What if I don't want to be far away from you?"

A worry line appears in between her eyebrows. "What?"

My heart starts to race. The pressure begins to cave in on me, just like it was last night before I came to Daisy. "What did last night mean to you?" I ask, desperate to know what she's thinking.

Daisy's blue eyes widen. There's something deep within them that I can't read. I give her hand a squeeze, but a moment later, she pulls hers away, leaving me with an open palm and a stomach full of worry.

"Kane..." Daisy bites her bottom lip. "Last night was... amazing. But..."

A nervous laugh tumbles from her mouth, and I take it as a warning to get as far away from her as possible. Call me a pessimist, but I know she's going to stick a knife right in my heart.

I stand abruptly and peer down at her. I pull down a mask that even she can't see through. "So, what? You just wanted to use me to take your virginity?" I ask with a bite to my tone. Hurt slips onto her features, but I ignore it to the best of my ability. "Just like my brother used me to take the fall for a crime I didn't commit?"

Daisy gasps. "That is not fair, Kane."

She shakes her head and throws the covers off her legs to stand in front of me. We're a foot away as I tower over her smaller frame. My ears ring as she stares up at me.

"You're leaving today," she says.

I stay silent.

"And you're...you." She crosses her arms and lowers her voice. "Not to mention, River's best friend."

I furrow my eyebrows. "I'm...what?"

She huffs. "Are you really going to make me say it?"

I mimic her stance and cross my arms.

"Fine," she snaps quietly. "You're a player, Kane. You've been with tons of girls, and now you're about to be halfway across the United States with so many of them throwing themselves at you. Last night was..." She glances away. "You know there is no future for us. You're about to go do big things and achieve your goal—something you weren't even sure you'd be able to do, considering the last few months. There's nothing left here for you."

Except you.

My hands shake with the need to grab her and kiss her or, better yet, punch a fucking wall. Her refusal slices away at the last bit of *good* in my life, and she's right. There is nothing left here for me.

I reach forward and grab the hem of my T-shirt hanging loosely on her frame. I pull it up and over her head then bundle it in my hand with a firm grip. One last look is shared between us, and as much as it kills me, I turn angrily and stride out of her bedroom.

There's a knot in my throat that makes it hard to swallow. My lungs scream for air, and my heart screams for her.

But after last night, I'll never listen to that thing inside my chest ever again.

One

DAISY

"WHAT ARE YOU DOING?" My older brother has one eyebrow raised while he stares at me in my lotus position.

"Meditating," I answer before closing my eyes again.

Deep breaths.

In through my nose, out through my mou–

River snickers. I peek one eyelid open and see that he's smirking.

"Stop it," I hiss. "You're ruining my calm aura."

River chuckles and rubs a hand over his scruffy face. "Sorry, but since when do you meditate?"

On steady legs, I hop to my feet and cross my arms. "Since I had to drop out of college and pack up my entire apartment and move to the arctic."

I'm tempted to kick the half-packed cardboard box at my feet just to prove a point.

"Chicago isn't that bad," he says. "They have…"—he thinks for a second—"hot dogs."

"I can't even have hot dogs," I argue.

River makes a face. "Oh, right." He shrugs. "Sucks to be you."

I huff. "Jerk."

He grins, and I feel my lips wanting to turn up at the sight.

River and I are close in age, and though we're in our twenties now, we still act like we're children. If we ever go anywhere with Mom and Dad, we're forced to sit in the backseat together where he pinches me, and I punch him.

It's our little bit.

Despite continuously arguing and teasing one another— usually him teasing me—we have a great relationship. If I'm ever in a sticky situation, it's him that I call, not our parents.

Mom is anxious most of the time, but Dad is as chill as they get. That's probably why they've been married for so long —they're perfect for each other.

"Mom has called me three times today." I place some more books into the box and start to close it.

River takes over, shoving my hands out of the way. "She's called me four times, so I win."

I roll my eyes. "I don't know why she's so worried about me moving up there. You'd think she'd be happy."

"You know how she is. She worries about you."

"Maybe she should meditate," I joke.

River laughs as I toss him the packing tape.

"How did you get her to calm down?" I ask.

I wince at the sound of packing tape echoing in my empty apartment. River taps the box a few times before resting his arm on it. "I reassured her that I have friends in the area that can watch out for you and help you if I'm busy with my residency."

Silence fills my tiny apartment before I smile. "So you lied? Because I know you don't have friends."

River gives me a look. "I do too."

I roll my lips. "Whatever you say."

"Just because I'm at the hospital more than anywhere else doesn't mean I don't have friends," he argues. "And you're welcome, by the way."

"For?" The list is endless.

My brother scowls. "For letting you move in with me."

I throw my hands up. "That was *your* idea!"

If it weren't for the connections he's made within his residency, I would have never even considered moving to Chicago.

"It's within walking distance to Dr. Gibson's office too."

Right. The entire reason I'm heading to the Windy City.

"How are you feeling?"

The worry slips out of River when I don't answer right away. His hands freeze with a piece of tape stretched across a box.

"I'm fine," I say.

River, knowing more about Lupus than even myself, is well-aware of my particular triggers for flare-ups. Stress is a big one, so moving to a completely new city without a job and only a halfway completed college degree is worrisome.

If I ever want to get back to having a semi-normal life, I have to continue to manage my Lupus on top of finding a job and continuing to work toward the target. I had dreams and goals, all of which came to a screeching halt with my diagnosis.

Not to mention, I have to balance the financial aspect of it all.

I can't expect my brother to pay for the apartment on his own, and though our parents have always been there to help, I feel like a helpless child allowing them to continue to support me.

It'll be fine.

I need to figure things out on my own.

"You sure?" River asks, pulling me back from the edge of insanity. "You know what stress does to you."

"I'm *fine*, River." I hold up my pinky. "Pinky promise."

He squints. "We haven't made a pinky promise since we were, like, six."

"But I kept it," I argue, smiling.

River leaves my pinky hanging and goes back to packing boxes. "I sent word to my friends to see if anyone knows of any job openings for you."

I purse my lips. "But you don't have friends."

"Shut up, or I'm getting you a job at a hot dog stand on the side of the road."

I laugh silently because he *would* do something like that.

The rest of our time is spent listening to music, packing boxes, and dodging our mother's phone calls.

"You ready to go?" River asks after finally taping the last box shut.

I freeze. "For...?"

He grins. "For your going-away party."

My eyes light up. "Going-away party?"

River snatches his keys off the counter and tosses me my jacket. "You think Natalia was going to send you off without a proper goodbye? You clearly don't know your best friend well enough."

Natalia was my roommate in college before I had to drop out.

We've been best friends since.

"Let me guess..." I smile and zip my coat. "The Bex?"

River snaps his fingers at me, and I follow him out of the empty apartment.

The Bex was the ultimate hangout spot during college,

and although we're at least forty minutes away, I'm not mad. I might even get a basket of fries to end the night, knowing damn well they'll probably make me feel sick come morning.

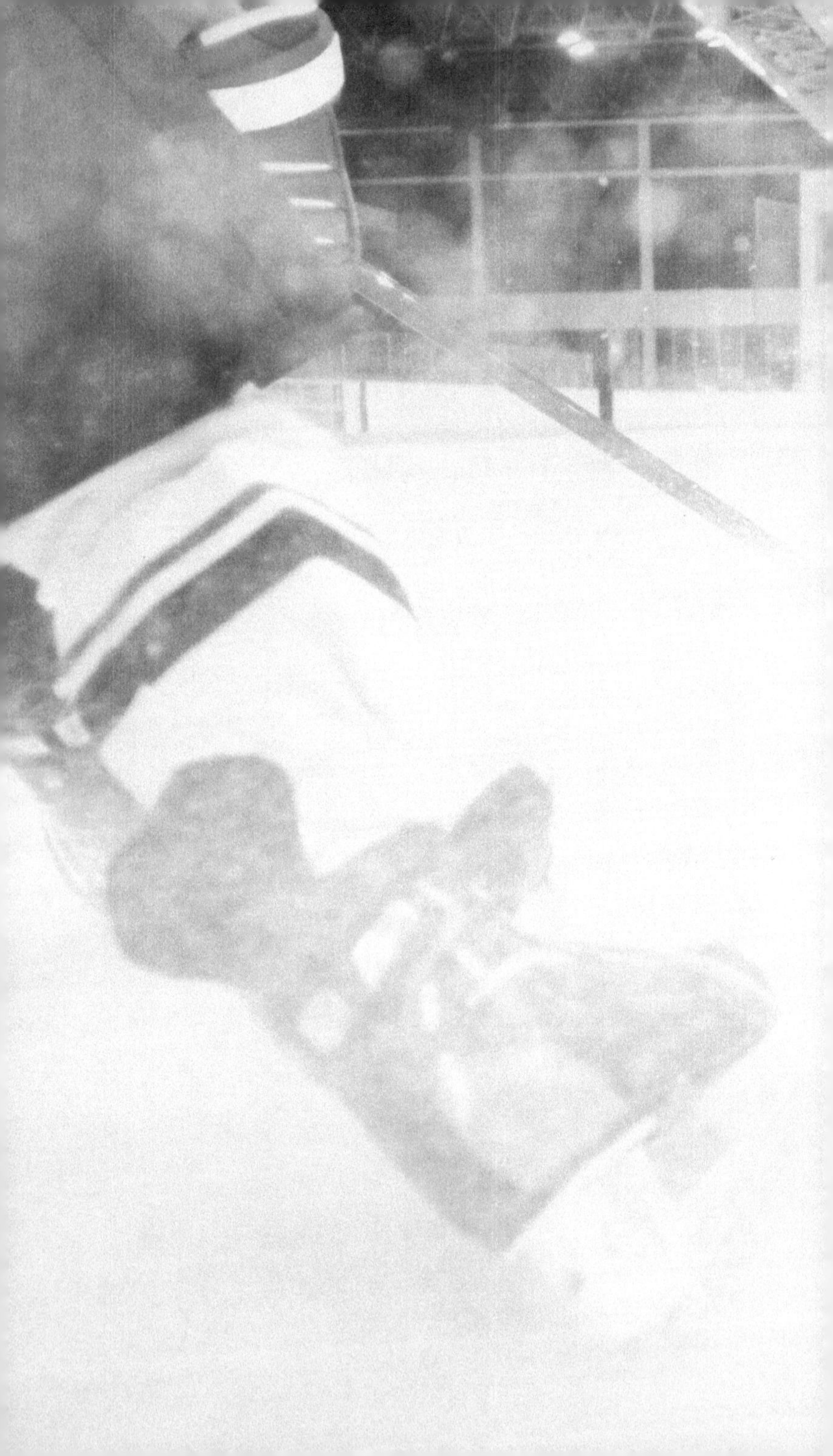

Two

KANE

I'M one of the first ones out of the locker room. After the practice we just had, I'll be lucky if I can even walk to my car. Probably won't stop me from going out later, but right now, my quads are twitching with exhaustion.

I swipe my finger against my phone screen and see a few texts asking me when I'm heading to the bar from my teammates and a couple from River. Ease slides into my tense shoulders when I don't see a text from a random number. It's not unusual to go months without a text with nothing but a dollar amount, but each day that goes by without one, I breathe a sigh of relief.

Instead of fucking around with a text back to River, I slide into my car and call him.

"What's up, man?" he asks on the second ring.

"On my way home from practice. You're not at the hospital today?"

River always was the smartest of our friend group, just like I was the most athletically inclined. Our senior class voted me the most likely to be arrested, which was their little joke after I *was* arrested, but they voted him most likely to become a doctor one day, and they were right. After completing his bachelor's in half the time it should've taken someone, he's in his first year of residency, and it turned out he was sent to the same city I play hockey in to complete it.

River snorts sarcastically. "You need practice. That last game sucked."

"Fuck off," I snap.

I'm still irritated that we lost our last game and that I wasn't able to get a hit in when one of their players started getting mouthy with Volkova. Not that the grumpy vet of the team needed me to step in and fight for him, but if he wasn't going to do it, let someone that will, you know?

"Hey, listen…" River starts off slow, and my hackles rise. "I have something to tell you."

A certain someone pops into my head, but I quickly banish her like I've been doing for the last several years. River eventually caught on that I didn't want to talk about Daisy or care to know how she's doing, but with his tone crawling with apprehension, I become fully engaged.

"I'm getting a roommate."

I furrow my brow. "Uh, alright?" *Why the fuck do I care?*

River lives in the apartment below Malaki and me, so unless his roommate is planning to throw ragers the night before our games, I really don't give a shit. Now, if he wants to throw ragers on our off nights, then *cheers*.

A steady breath leaves me when I realize there's no talk of Daisy or anything like that. I sit back in the driver's seat with my car idling and turn on my heated seat, hopeful it'll ease the throbbing in my legs. "You worried I'm going to force your new roommate into my game superstitions or something?"

"Now that you mention it…" he jokes.

I shrug, although he can't see me. "Better warn him. You

know I don't make the rules. If you're up, and it's the night before a game, we do what we need to do."

"You're fucking nuts," he laughs. "Wait...are you still stepping left skate first when getting on the ice for warm-ups?"

I remain quiet because, yeah, of course I am.

"I bet you're still wearing that hair tie around your wrist during games too. Aren't you?"

My jaw clenches with the subtle reminder that comes with said hair tie, yet I still wear it.

"Alright, that's enough. Did you really just want to tell me about you having a new roommate? Because I don't care," I say.

"It's Daisy."

I choke on utter fucking denial.

My heart skips a beat.

I grip the steering wheel tightly even though my car is in park and swallow the bitter thought of her. I act unfazed—like I've had to do each and every time he's brought her up—and repeat what he's just told me. "Daisy is moving to Chicago?"

Please tell me this is a fucking joke.

"Yeah, and I'm helping her out a little until she gets on her feet. Thought it would be a plus having you in the apartment above in case she needs anything and I'm at the hospital, you know?"

No. I do not fucking know.

I can assure you that Daisy Sullivan will *not* be calling on me to help her with anything. It's been years since I've come face-to-face with her, and I'd bet my life that she remembers our last encounter as well as I do.

Before I can say anything that would deter River from having his sister move into the same apartment complex that we live in, he's rushing off the phone.

I sit in silence for so long my legs grow numb. Four texts have come and gone, asking if I'm heading out for the night.

Part of me would rather go home, pull my laptop out, and look for a new place to live, but the other part of me knows I can't do that. I still owe Malaki for all the rent he covered when I couldn't—thanks to my inability to deny certain people.

And deep down, I secretly crave to see her face again, just so I can refresh the hazy image of her inside my head to fuel my loathing for another six years.

She was the girl I was never supposed to look at, let alone touch.

Except, I did, and I haven't been the same since.

Three

DAISY

"THIS IS FUCKING ABSURD, DAISY." River pokes his head through my pothos plant and stares at me in between its luscious leaves. "This thing belongs in a jungle."

I gasp dramatically. "I'm impressed that you know these types of plants do thrive in jungle-like atmospheres."

"I was making a joke," he mumbles.

I quickly unbuckle my other two plants from their seatbelts—something else River thinks is absurd—and look toward the skyscraper that I now call my new home.

The street isn't as busy as I thought it would be, given we're not far from downtown, but even if it was, River said no one ever uses this entrance anyway.

Holding my plants up high so they don't drag, we enter the elevator, and River presses 30.

The second-to-last floor? Great.

"What's the top floor?" I ask jokingly. "A penthouse for some fancy millionaire?"

He laughs, but it's an awkward type of laugh, like he knows something I don't.

I eye him closely. "If you tell me that Mom and Dad are moving to the 31st floor..." I let my sentence trail because it really wouldn't surprise me at this point.

"Yeah right," he laughs. "Dad will never leave his yard. He's spent most of our lives perfecting the grass."

I glance at my plant babies. *Runs in the family.*

The elevator doors open, and I'm greeted with my reflection on the shiny floors. I've looked worse, but my strawberry-blonde locks are extra frizzy and wild thanks to the Chicago humidity.

As soon as River opens the door to my new, fully furnished apartment, my jaw falls. Holy *shit*. This makes my old apartment look like it belongs on a Craigslist ad that reads "rental apartment for someone desperate."

It's not huge by any means, but it has fancy lighting and high-end appliances. My last place had a toaster from the 1900s, and the fridge squeaked every time I opened it.

"Um. How much did you say the rent was again?"

River places my plant on the counter and spins to stare at me. "I told you I'd cover the rent."

I shoot him a look because I'm holding my plants. Otherwise, I'd cross my arms and stomp my foot. "We are splitting the cost. I'm not moving in here for my big brother to take care of me."

He scoffs. "But why? I would if it were me."

"Because!" I say while walking over to the counter. I grab the pothos that he brought up and stride over to the window to place it on the little table for some indirect light. "Then it's too easy. Now that I'm in remission, I want to get my life back on track."

He doesn't understand.
No one does.

"As soon as I get a job, I'm helping with the rent."

River points to the overabundance of plants in his kitchen. "Maybe sell some of these godforsaken plants."

I'm offended. "No."

"Fine." He turns for the door...to gather more of my plants. "And relax, I snagged an interview for you next week."

"An interview?" I run after him as he heads toward the elevator. "If it's a hot dog stand, I swear to god..."

He puts his hands in his pockets. "A hot dog sounds good right about now, doesn't it?"

I ignore him and press L for the lobby. "If it's a hot dog stand, you're not getting free hot dogs from me on pure principle."

If I can't have one, neither can he.

"Relax." River nudges me with his elbow. "It's not a hot dog stand."

"Then what is it?"

He thinks for a second, his green eyes searching for something...*like a lie.*

Worry starts to itch my skin, and my neck grows warm. "Did you score me an interview out of pity?"

Against better judgment, I don't like to tell people about having Lupus.

It's an invisible disease, one where I can appear perfectly fine on the outside but feel awful on the inside. Questions arise, along with skepticism, and I've found that it's easier to live with it silently rather than explain.

I follow River out to his car and grab a few boxes, while he hauls twice as many into his arms. I stack one of my plants on top of his heavy load before we head back to the elevator.

"I didn't tell anyone about you having Lupus, so chill."

I breathe out a sigh of relief.

"I can keep a secret," he adds.

I glance at him. "Well, you did tell Stevie I broke up with

him because his breath was awful, even though I swore you to secrecy, so excuse me for double-checking..."

River stops halfway in the lobby and gapes. "That was in sixth fucking grade, Daisy. You're still holding that against me?"

I shrug. "Until you make up for it, yes."

"I'm letting you move in with me, *and* I've gotten you a job interview. I think I've made up for it." He presses the button to our floor, and I rest against the back of the elevator. I can hardly see anything over the boxes, but I know he's probably scowling at me.

"That's right. The mystery job."

"Yeah, about that..." he says.

The door begins to close, but at the last second, I hear a ding, signaling that someone is stepping onto it.

I guess no time is better than now to meet some of my neighbors.

"Speak of the devil..." River chuckles. "Pun intended."

What?

I try to see past the boxes, but all I can see is River leaning in for a bro-hug type of deal. A few slaps on the back later, and then the person is pulling away.

It isn't until I hear his voice that I freeze with shock.

The blood drains from my face as fast as the boxes slip from my shaky fingers.

Oh my god.

River and Kane snap their attention to me while I stand with my back against the elevator wall with two boxes full of botany books spilled beneath my feet.

Shit.

"Kane," I mutter, hardly able to say his name.

Kane Barlow, my brother's best friend and the boy who took my virginity, stares at me from across the elevator with what I know to be animosity covered up by a cocky grin.

"Hey, neighbor." His grin deepens. "Welcome to Chicago."

———

I'm in utter shock, and I fear both of them can tell.

Kane has changed over the last several years. His muscles are more defined, his jaw edgier with some scruff along his skin, and unfortunately those changes make him even more attractive than before.

He adjusts his backward hat before bending to help River pick up my botany books.

Say something.

What should I say?

Do I ask how he is?

Do I pretend like I don't care how he is?

"Move your foot, you klutz." River flicks my calf, and I jerk my leg backward.

"Oh, right," I blurt.

I quickly crouch down on the elevator floor and hastily gather my books to plop back into the cardboard boxes. My mind is moving one hundred miles per hour, and the one question that pops into my head zips out into the stuffy space without so much as a warning.

"Why are you here?"

Kane's hand freezes on one of the books. He slowly raises his chin, and our eyes lock. My lungs squeeze tight, as if he's reaching inside my chest and crushing the life out of me.

Kane and I were close at one point—maybe even closer than he and my brother—though River was oblivious. What started off as teasing turned into subtle flirting and a close bond I haven't found since. But that was a long time ago. Surely he doesn't still hate me, right?

"He lives here," River answers for Kane, and I pray he

can't tell that I just died a thousand deaths. "With another guy from the team."

"Excuse me?" I say in shock.

I quickly stand upright, ending my stare-off with Kane.

River gives me a funny look. "I told you I had friends in the area." He nods to Kane while folding the box. "I assumed you knew that Kane was one of them, considering he plays for the Blue Devils."

"Well, you know what they say about someone who assumes..." I fake a smile.

I had *no* idea he played for the Blue Devils, because the second Kane and I went our separate ways, I pushed him out of my head. I knew he made it to the pros, but I refused to watch any of the games in fear that I'd catch a glimpse of him, and then I'd have to start all over again with forgetting about him.

I silently laugh.

Who am I kidding?

It would be a miracle if I could forget about Kane Barlow.

He's the type of guy that lies quietly in the deepest parts of someone's memories, only coming out to play at the *worst* possible times.

The elevator takes fifteen years to reach my floor, and when the doors open, I fly out of there like a bat out of hell.

Kane and my brother are talking amongst themselves while I try to act normal. I hate surprises, especially the kind with devilish eyes and a hatred for me.

With a hefty breath, I square my shoulders and fumble with my keys to open the door.

Kane, who is now holding the two boxes I was holding, walks past my brother, who has left us alone to answer his phone—which is likely our mom on the other end.

Kane leans close to me, but I make no effort to acknowledge him. "Need help?"

"No." I press the key into its rightful place.

He snickers under his breath, and I look at him out of the corner of my eye.

"Not what you said the last time I saw you," he mutters.

My face grows warm.

He's referring to when I asked him to take my virginity.

Memories of us in my childhood bedroom zip into my head like a wrecking ball, and I now suddenly understand Miley Cyrus on an entirely new level.

My hand stalls on the key, and I finally come face-to-face with him. The hairs on the back of my neck stand up, and I sweat in places I didn't know existed.

Kane's lips lift with a grin, but I can see right through his friendly facade. "Look at us," he whispers. "Neighbors. *Again.*"

Four

KANE

WHY IS SHE HERE?

I was too blindsided to ask River when he dropped the news that Daisy was moving here. Even now, after I've digested the idea of her, and we've seen each other again, I'm still on edge.

When River and I reunited after a few years on different paths, things fell right back into place. It felt like no time had passed at all.

That is *not* how it feels with Daisy.

I'm a man now—well, sort of. Most of the team would disagree, thanks to the trouble I cause on *and* off the ice, but I'm more of a man now than I was six years ago. So tell me why I'm twisted on the inside with her being near? I've pushed Daisy so far out of my mind that I'm surprised I even recognized her when I stepped on the elevator.

But I most definitely did, and it's taking more effort than I'd like to pretend I'm not doused in irritation with her big brother around. Daisy and I have always seemed like we had a brother/sister type of relationship. But on the backside of that, it was something that I can't put a name to. Then add in the last day we were together, and it's a fucking storm of angry emotions.

"That's what you're wearing?" River's lip twists with disgust.

I quickly pull my attention to the hallway that leads to Daisy's new bedroom and land on her.

Hell no.

I'm with River. She needs to change.

If my blood ran hot at the sight of her, everyone else's will too.

"Yeah?" Daisy, with her sun-kissed strawberry-blonde hair pulled back into a sleek ponytail at the nape of her neck, glances at her outfit. "But thanks for making me feel self-conscious." She rolls her eyes and snatches her purse off the counter. "It's like high school all over again," she mumbles.

I snort because I'm a dick. Her baby blues flick to mine so fast I *feel* them. I raise an eyebrow, challenging her to say something, but she quickly backs down and turns away.

That's what I thought.

"Let's just go." She turns and leaves me and River in the dust.

River shakes his head and rolls his eyes in my direction. I go along with it, but I have no idea what he's thinking.

Does he think she looks bad in her outfit? Or is he thinking what I'm thinking?

Tight jeans that hug curves that weren't quite developed when we were teenagers and a sweater that is half falling off her shoulder, showing nothing but soft, smooth skin. Her hair pulled back doesn't help either. The only thing it does is draw attention to her slender neck, perfect for sinking my teeth into.

I hate that she's so goddamn perfect.

Irritation crawls up my spine.

After all this time and multiple women in my bed, I still find Daisy tantalizingly alluring.

I hate it.

I hate *her*.

River is oblivious to the fact that I can hardly look at his sister without clenching my teeth...but she's not. The shock on her face in the elevator was a window to the fact that she remembers our last interaction just as well as I do.

"Do you even know where we're going?" River asks, pulling Daisy back by the elbow to stop her brisk walk down the sidewalk.

She has no idea where we're headed, but that doesn't stop her from stomping like a brat to get far away from me.

I pause for a split second.

A sick smile curves against my mouth that River doesn't notice.

We *were* going to the best pizza shop in town. But I have a better idea.

"I'll lead the way," I say casually.

Euphoria's Edge is the last place I want to go. I don't frequent strip clubs often, but when I do, this one is low on the list. Emory has all but banned the team from going to his wife's previous place of employment, The Cat House, but Euphoria's Edge serves food, so it'll do.

We're nearly there when River asks where we're going.

I peer over my shoulder at him and do a damn good job of pretending Daisy doesn't exist.

"You'll see." I manage to keep my face from showing any sort of amusement.

Their footsteps behind me come to a halt.

"Why did you stop walking?" River asks Daisy.

My stride never slows, even as my mouth begs to curve. I

keep heading for the glowing red lights of Euphoria's Edge while keeping my wits about me.

"Kane!" I stop abruptly from Daisy's shrill tone.

Gravel crunches under my shoe as I spin. "Yes?"

She crosses her arms over her annoyingly perky chest.

Did those grow during our time apart?

"Where are we going?" Each word drags out of her mouth slowly.

I level her with a bored stare. "To get dinner."

River glances at the sign above my head and bursts into laughter.

"This is a strip club!" Daisy narrows her pretty blue eyes at me, and I can't help but feed off of it.

I shrug. "They have great hamburgers."

"Does it come with a side of crabs too?" She angrily laughs at her own joke. "I'm not going to a strip club for dinner. Pick somewhere else."

I place my hands in my pockets and rock back on my heels. "I didn't realize you were such a prude."

Her jaw drops, and the angry little glare she sends me puts a fire in my blood.

River laughs from beside her. "I can honestly say I've never been to a strip club with my sister..." He heads toward the door. "But I guess there's a first for everything."

"I am not going into a strip club with my brother!" she snaps.

"You act like I haven't seen you getting half-fucked by some frat boy before." River snorts. "Consider this payback."

Excuse me, what the hell did he just say?

Daisy stomps her foot and stares after her brother. "I didn't know you were there! That's not fair."

I can't seem to get the image of her being fucked by some guy out of my head while they continue to argue back and forth. My shoulders tense with something I refuse to acknowledge, and I quickly head for the door to the club.

The burger may taste like cardboard, but at least I can stare at the topless women dancing while I eat instead of Daisy and her pretty glares in my direction.

Five

DAISY

KANE BARLOW IS *STILL* GETTING under my skin even years later.

Who goes to a strip club for dinner?

No one.

No one does that unless they're eating something other than food for dinner.

The only reason he chose this place was to annoy me. He probably still assumes I'm a goody-goody, which is what the boys used to call me back in high school. River Sullivan's little sister: the quiet, good girl. I was the girl with her nose in a book, rolling my eyes at all the popular boys who took turns making out with the head cheerleader during the parties that my parents made River drag me to.

They never wanted me to be left out, even if I was underage at a party with copious amounts of alcohol and no adult supervision.

I sigh and bite into a carrot stick while watching one of the strippers grind against an older male in business attire.

We make eye contact, and I freeze mid-bite.

I feel like I'm encroaching on the scene.

Like, shouldn't they get a room?

"This burger tastes like shit." River shoves his plate away and looks at Kane for a response.

I roll my eyes. Of course it does! Kane didn't come here for their spectacular burgers. He came here to make me uncomfortable.

Another glance at the live sex scene in front of us, and yep, I'm uncomfortable.

"Yeah." Out of the corner of my eye, Kane leans farther back into the booth, seemingly relaxed. "It was better the last time I ate it."

"Probably not the only thing you ate," I mutter.

River laughs at my quiet joke, but Kane doesn't. Instead, he leans forward and places his forearms on the table that separates us. "You're right about that."

I turn and meet his eye, unable to hide the disgust on my face. "Being a man-whore isn't the flex you think it is when you're whoring around a strip club, Kane."

River blows a breath out. "Damn, sis. You're on fire with the comebacks tonight."

Kane's annoyingly hot mouth turns up on the side, and something tightens in my stomach. "You sound jealous."

I scoff. "Jealous?"

The only thing I'm jealous of is that burger on his plate. Even if it tastes like shit, my mouth still waters at the sight of it.

River decides right then to get up and go to the bathroom, leaving me and Kane all alone.

Thanks, big bro.

I look onto the floor and watch the girls earn some serious tips while pretending Kane isn't breathing down my freaking neck. The booth cushion bends when he scoots closer to me, but I continue to pretend he doesn't exist.

"Yeah...*jealous*," he repeats. "When was the last time anyone *ate* you?"

My cheeks burn.

"The summer before I left for the juniors?"

He did *not* just go there.

Unable to stop myself, I turn and meet him face to face. My belly fills with heat when I stare into his ocean eyes. His features are so much more defined since the last time I saw him —a steely jaw and high cheekbones with the same faint scar right above his left eyebrow from being hit in the face with a hockey stick in the tenth grade.

I won't admit it out loud, but god, he aged well.

The longer we stare at one another, the more uneasy I become. My thoughts spin, and everything blurs.

"Well?" he asks. "Am I right?"

"What?" I think I just blacked out.

A sly smile slides onto his face. "Summer...before I left?"

My nostrils flare with irritation as my traitorous eyes drop to his mouth. That sharp tongue of his slips out past his lips to wet them, and I grow warm. He knows I'm well aware of what he's referring to, but I can only pray that my face remains unreadable.

I shake my head and lean a little closer to him. He stays in the same spot, not backing away even an inch. "You really think the last time I had a man's tongue in between my legs was that summer night years ago? With *you*?"

One long blink is all I get in response.

He's so hard to read. Too much time has passed.

The tension rises, and my pulse quickens. Neither one of us are willing to back down, a challenge brewing between us, but as soon as my brother slides back into the booth, we're forced to break apart.

And just like that, things are back to being *normal*.

One decline of a stripper offering my brother a lap dance later—*thank god*—and I'm scooting out of the booth to head back to the apartment.

Kane paid for the meal, and I wanted to refuse in the worst way because now I feel like I should thank him. But to be honest, I'd rather chew my own arm off than show him gratitude after dragging me to a strip club for dinner.

When we get back to the apartment, I opt for the stairs because I can't stand to spend another second keeping my composure intact with Kane near. River looks at me questionably, and I quickly make up some excuse about needing to stretch my legs.

"But we just walked to and from the restaurant," he says.

Restaurant?

He means *strip club*.

I pretend to be deaf and hustle to the stairwell. The door slams and echoes throughout the empty space, which gives me full permission to finally breathe for the first time all evening.

My shoulders drop when I look up.

I'm going to die trying to climb these stairs, but hey, at least I won't have to deal with Kane and his feigned smiles that turn into scathing glares when my brother isn't looking.

One step down, a million more to go—

I freeze with the creaking of the door.

It opens slowly, like I'm in some horror movie.

"Running away, are we?" Kane muses.

I take that back. I *am* in a horror movie.

With a slow spin, I lock onto him standing halfway in the doorway with a cocky grin on his face.

"Why would I do that?" I ask.

I mentally prepare myself for a rude remark, especially since River is nowhere in sight, but instead, he rolls his eyes impatiently. "Do you still know how to ice-skate?"

Confusion fills me. "Yeah...why?"

Kane's face twitches with humor, and then the door begins to creep shut as he backs away.

"Wait! Why?" I blurt, making him pause.

The only answer I get from him is a devious smile and a quick wink.

Which does *not* sit well with me.

———

The only thing that pulls me out of bed is the thought of a matcha latte with my name on it. I switched from coffee to matcha a year ago because of its health benefits. I'm not sure it has really helped, but now I'm obsessed with matcha, so there's that.

After swirling a design into the cup with my oat milk, I head over to my plants.

The morning sun peeks between the two skyscrapers across the busy street, sending a stream of warmth directly onto my jade plant. With my finger, I rub the smooth leaf and smile with my mug pressed against my lips.

So far, Chicago isn't *terrible*. I have floor-to-ceiling windows, and although I thought I'd hate the city scenery, it's kind of pretty. The apartment is spacious, leaving plenty of room for me to move my plants around when needed, and with River being at the hospital so often, I hardly remember that we're roommates. Of course, there's the apartment above me that causes my anxiety to rise with its occupant, but I've done an excellent job at avoiding Kane.

I move over to my hibiscus plant and slip my finger into the soil, testing the moisture level. As soon as I pull my hand away, there's a knock on my door that startles me so much I spill my latte.

"Shit!" I blurt.

I drop my attention to the green stain on my silky robe. I annoyingly roll my eyes and sigh.

Another knock vibrates against the door. I stare at it with irritation and grit my teeth. I keep a hold of my mug as I stride over the hardwood in my fuzzy slippers toward the door.

Another knock.

Okay, seriously?

Without so much as looking through the peephole, I whip the door open with force.

It takes half a second for my annoyance to rise to another level.

Kane, who I thought was still traveling back from his away game—which I only know about because I googled their game schedule—leans against the doorjamb casually in his Chicago Blue Devils hoodie.

He checks me out from head to toe and then lazily moves his gaze back to my face. "You ready?"

"Ready to smack you?" I ask. "Always."

He scoffs before striding right into my apartment as if he owns the place.

I gape at him. "Excuse you?"

He ignores me and starts to move his attention all around the apartment, clearly in search of something. His tight features relax when he eyes my phone. I stand appalled as he picks it up and enters my password—something he has seemingly remembered from years ago.

I make a mental note to change it, right along with a reminder not to open the door without knowing who's on the other side.

"What on earth do you think you're doing?" I place my latte down and rush him to steal my phone back. "You can't just barge into my apartme–"

It takes my eyes a few seconds to scan the texts on my phone, but when I read the message from River, I gasp.

"Interview?" I exclaim. "I don't even know what the job is for!"

Kane clicks my phone off and flicks his chin to my bedroom. "We leave in ten, Daisy-Petal. Hurry up."

There's no time to argue with him or to call my brother and belittle him for not preparing me for my job interview.

I stomp off to my room with Kane resting his hip against my counter. "Make sure to change out of your robe. You have green shit on it."

My jaw clenches tightly, and I slam the door a second later.

Six

KANE

RIVER SAID DAISY NEEDED A JOB, so I found her the perfect one.

Through her bedroom door, she asks me what the interview is for, but I prefer to keep it a surprise. I'm not even ashamed to admit I'm looking forward to seeing her face when she finds out.

Am I being a bully?

Yeah, probably.

Do I care?

No.

It could be worse, which is something I have every intention to remind her of. Something else I need to remind her of is that I'm doing this for River, not her. She either takes the job, or she can find herself on the stage of Euphoria's Edge for money.

A quick mental glimpse at that visual and I'm suddenly cracking my knuckles.

"Two minutes," I shout toward her bedroom with a little more anger than I meant.

My cheek lifts for a second at her curses floating underneath the gap between the floor and her door.

I turn and glance around the apartment, noticing all the subtle changes now that it isn't just River living here.

It's like stepping into a fucking garden.

I count the plants near the window in the living room and shake my head before turning around and eyeing five more across the room.

Jesus.

After taking a seat on the couch, I lean forward and swipe one of the books off the coffee table.

The Green Witch.

I snort.

"That's fitting," I mumble.

"What is?"

I pop my head up and see her standing there in an outfit that is unneeded for the type of interview she's about to attend. Her tight black skirt hits about mid-calf, showing off her strappy black heels that click over the floor. Her hair is pulled back into one of those sleek buns that highlights her delicate features, and there are her lips. They're painted red, and I *hate* that they have me seeing double.

I'm able to mentally shake myself out of the trap she has me in and tap into the annoyance that amps up when she's around. "The title of the book." I toss it back onto the coffee table. "*The Green Witch*." My brow crooks when she glares at me. "You get it? *Witch*." The insult pops out of my mouth with irritation.

"Yeah," she snaps. "I get it."

Back when we were younger, her sweet smile used to get me all riled up.

Now, it's those blue eyes rolling in my direction.

Offending her is slowly becoming addictive.

"You ready?" I stand up before she even answers.

Daisy throws her hands up. "I don't know! Am I?" She glances at her outfit. "I have no idea how to dress because neither you nor River will tell me what the interview entails."

I head for the door. "That's because River doesn't know."

Her heels tapping against the floor stop abruptly. I pause and glance over my shoulder at her.

"Am I interviewing to be your maid or something, because *no.*" She crosses her arms, and I hold back a chuckle.

"As if I'd want you in my apartment." Plus, Malaki and I do a good enough job at keeping the apartment tidy.

She pulls back as if I've slapped her. "What is that supposed to mean?"

"It means I don't trust you," I say, wanting to wound her.

A look of hurt flashes across her face, but she quickly covers it up with pursed lips and silence. She starts toward me again, and I hold the door open for her to go first. I have the thought to stick my foot out to trip her, but I'm not one to hurt a woman, so I remain still.

I do, however, keep her pinned with a heavy stare until she moves past me. Instead of watching her hips swing from behind, because I refuse, I glance to the little table near the door.

A medical pamphlet catches my eye, likely one of River's, and I stare at it until I know there's enough distance between Daisy and me.

I head toward the elevator after she steps inside, except she presses the button before I even manage to shut her apartment door.

Her cheeky smile is the last thing I see before the elevator closes, leaving me to wait alone in the hallway.

I narrow my gaze. *Brat.*

I keep my face smooth and unreadable while Daisy's lips slowly part at the sight of the hockey arena. She slams my car door shut with a little too much force and glares in my direction, likely wanting me to explain.

I won't, though.

Leaving her behind me to gape, I head toward the doors with my hockey bag slung over my shoulder. Practice isn't for another two hours, but I would love nothing more than to feel her wrath after she realizes what her job interview is for.

She can take it or leave it.

It just depends how badly she wants a paycheck, I suppose.

"Why are we here?" she asks as she trails behind me.

Her heels click just as loudly against the pavement as they did in her apartment.

"Well, I'm here for practice," I say. "You're here for an interview."

"An interview at the hockey arena?" The clicking of her heels stops. I'm sure she is conjuring up the types of jobs that she could be interviewing for, but I doubt any of them are correct.

"I am not going to be an ice girl, Kane!"

I chuckle. See? Far from the truth.

"What's wrong with being an ice girl?" I peer over my shoulder at her and feign innocence. "They clean the ice in between timeouts. You said you still know how to skate."

Her red lips form a scowl. "That's not all they do, and you know it."

"Those are rumors. They don't fuck the hockey players..." I pause. "Not all of them, anyway."

"But the inclination is there! I'm not walking into a hockey arena just to be labeled a puck bunny. No thanks. I'll find a job elsewhere."

With a huff and so much attitude it could fill the entire parking lot, she turns and attempts to stomp away, but her heel gets stuck in a crack in the pavement. Out of reaction, I reach out and wrap my arm around her waist, pulling her flush against my front.

Fuck.

My chest tightens when she turns her head and fans her sweet breath against my skin. I look into her soft eyes. I always thought she had the most honest eyes. The truth bled through them every time we were alone, but now that I'm older and wiser, I refuse to fall for them again.

Time stops as I continue to gaze down at her face, but I quickly take control of the moment and immediately release her after she steadies in my grip.

She turns with a blank expression and brushes her hands down her outfit.

"The interview isn't for an ice girl, so quit being a brat and get inside before you're late." My voice is harsh, but that's the only way I can dismiss whatever the hell I just felt with her in my arms.

Daisy doesn't make a single peep until we're in the elevator and heading to the conference rooms. A shaky breath leaves her and floats out into the tight space we're stuck in.

I'm sort of glad the interview is so early.

I don't know how I'll explain to the team that she's off-limits without them assuming she means something more to me than she actually does. With the number of times I've fucked with them about their girlfriends or fiancèes by making some lewd comment or implying innuendos, I'm certain at least one of them will turn the tables and do the same to me.

Only, I have no real claim over her.

I wouldn't even consider us acquaintances at this point.

More like enemies.

"Go on." I flick my chin as soon as the door opens. "They're expecting you in suite two."

"You're not coming with me?" she asks, looking down the long hall before glancing back at me.

My lip hitches. "You need me to hold your hand, Daisy-Petal?"

Come on, give me one more eye roll for the road.

As if she can read my mind, she refuses to give me what I'm craving. Instead, she sticks her tongue out in between those red lips and defies me further by flipping me off and disappearing down the hall.

When the elevator closes, I sink back against the wall with sudden exhaustion.

The only thing that's keeping me going is picturing her face after she realizes the job I've scored for her.

River asked for my help with his sister, and he surely got it.

Seven

DAISY

A GIANT BLUE Devil head is staring at me from the middle of the long table in the empty conference room. I stay a distance away—it's sort of creepy—and shift my attention back and forth between its devil horns.

This is weird, but okay.

I jerk at the sound of the door opening in the corner of the room.

For a second, I thought Kane might have made up that I had an interview or, at the very least, sent me to the wrong room.

A short woman with curly red hair stops at the sight of me. "Oh! You're early! I'm Cindy! You must be Petal Sullivan?"

"Petal?" I repeat with confusion.

Ugh. Kane.

Cindy sticks her hand out after making her way over to me. I take it gingerly. "It's Daisy Sullivan, actually."

She laughs. "Oh, that Kane! He's such a jokester."

I fake a laugh alongside her.

That's one way to describe him.

It wasn't like I expected Kane to forget about me and our quick and painful parting in the years we've been apart, because it's not like *I* had. But it would have been nice to have prepared myself to be sharing an apartment complex with him and our bound-to-happen run-ins, especially if I'm about to be working at the same arena he plays hockey at.

I could at least have had an arsenal of comebacks ready to go whenever he throws some insult at me.

But no.

I was just thrust into hell with Kane as my own personal devil.

Blue Devil at that.

Speaking of.

"Um..." I point at the mascot head that I *swear* is staring at me. "What exactly..."

Cindy, dressed in a blue pantsuit matching the colors of the mascot perfectly, clasps her hands together. "You like it? I thought it was fitting for the interview!"

Fitting for the interview? What does that mean?

If I ask her what the interview is for, I'll seem unprepared, which is unfortunately the truth. So instead of asking any more questions, I play along and smile at the giant head before she takes a seat near the end of the table with her blue folder.

"Okay!" She is clearly a cheerful person if her tone has anything to say about her. "Here are the basic requirements for the job. Just read through those, and then if you could initial each one, indicating that you master the skill, that'll get us started."

I grab a pen. "Sure."

Cindy pulls out her phone and starts busying herself with it while I read through the requirements.

- Must be in good physical condition
- Must be able to ice-skate
- Must be able to dance and/or perform basic movements on the ice.

What the hell kind of job is this?

"How tall are you?" she asks without looking up from her phone.

My mind is running circles. "Um, 5'5"."

"And your weight?" *What?!*

Cindy shakes her head. "You know what, we will just get you measured. There is no way you're going to fit in it with the current sizing."

I place the pen down on the table slowly and blink a few times to get my thoughts straight. I read through the rest of the requirements and eventually drag my eyes back to the top of the paper.

Required skills for Blue Devils Mascot

I nearly fall out of the chair.

Mascot?!

The Blue Devils mascot?!

I flick my eyes to the Blue Devil head in the center of the conference table. My heart pounds with anger as I picture myself putting it on to sneak into Kane's house to murder him.

"I'm not sure if Kane told you, but we're in desperate need to fill this position. The other guy just up and quit in the middle of a game."

Gee, I wonder why. It's almost like he got tired of putting on a costume to skate around an arena with thousands of hockey fans screaming at him.

"I was told that you are in desperate need of a job, which

seems to work out perfectly. Our schedule is already set, so you'll know your hours ahead of time, except for a few random events here and there."

My first thought is to decline the job.

The mascot? Really?

But the need to prove to Kane that his little joke won't affect me far outweighs the embarrassment of putting on a smelly, sweaty costume for a living.

I glance at the devil's head again.

Kane set this interview up, thinking it would piss me off. It's becoming clearer to me with each interaction I have with him that the boy I once gave my everything to has turned into a man who wants to watch me burn.

In that case...

"If you're willing to hire me, I'm yours."

Cindy breathes out a huge sigh of relief. "Wonderful!"

I smile sweetly, but on the inside, I'm filled with mischievous glee. *Fuck you, Kane.*

His plan of pissing me off is backfiring. Now, I'm not only living in his apartment complex but I'm also going to be at his place of employment too. I sure hope he enjoys seeing me around.

"Are there any sort of medical issues I need to be aware of? This job isn't as strenuous as playing hockey, but I can assure you that it isn't easy to put that thing on and skate."

Silence fills the large room with her question. Cindy's soft eyes wait patiently for me to answer her, hope clear as day on her face.

I swallow the unease and choose to fill her in because it's unsafe not to. If something were to happen, or I have a bad flare and can't come to work, she needs to be aware.

"Well..." My voice is bumpy. "I have Lupus." I glance at the Blue Devil head and continue on. "It's an autoimmune disease and the entire reason I've moved to Chicago. One of the best specialists is here, and he has his own infusion clinic." The words tumble out of my mouth quickly. "I'm currently in remission, but if I were to fall into a flare and become ill, I may have to take a few games off."

Hopefully that won't happen.

I pride myself on the steps I've taken to keep my health intact, and I don't expect to stop now.

"Oh," Cindy's voice softens. "I had no idea. Kane didn't—"

I interrupt her. "He doesn't know. It's not something I broadcast." Plus, why would Kane even care? "It's easier to carry on with life and try not to let it control me. I should be fine," I try to reassure her, just like I'm constantly doing with my mom. "But I want you to be aware."

"I appreciate that." She reaches her hand out and softly pats mine. "And it can be our secret. I'll give you my personal number too. That way, if something happens and you can't make it, I'll be able to find a quick replacement for the evening."

I exhale, relief settling into my shoulders.

After removing her hand, she places a stack of papers in front of me. "Let's start filling these out, and I can fill you in on a few other things you'll be required to do as the mascot—media shoots and things like that."

I nod and grab the pen to start completing all the paperwork.

Halfway through, she tells me the salary. Regardless if Kane set this interview up to be a dick, the pay is much more than I expected. With the funds, I'll be able to help River with rent, afford any new medications or infusions if needed, and save up for my future that has felt out of reach since I became sick for the first time.

Eight

KANE

"FUCKING SHIT." I throw my broken stick off to the side, pissed that it snapped right before I was going to send a puck flying into the net.

I skate over to the bench and take the stick that's being held out for me. It doesn't feel right. It's not taped the way I like: black tape, toe to heel, fifteen loops around the blade—any more or any less and I can tell.

Another one of my quirks, but if it helped me get to the pros, then I'm not sure anyone has the right to say shit about it.

The puck slips against my untaped blade, and I growl quietly.

Practice is almost over, but we have a home game in three nights, so the more honed we are on our own ice, the better.

We're *this* close to making the playoffs—something this team has yet to do since I joined.

"Whoa." Malaki skates close and stops a few feet away. "Who is *that*?"

Rhodes, one of our veteran players, growls. "I swear to god, if I look over and you're talking about Sunny..."

"Sunny is old news, Grandpa. No one wants your nanny," Malaki says.

I chuckle and try flinging another puck down the ice. Somehow, Emory, our goalie, blocks it without even looking like he's paying attention. *Fucker.*

"I want your nanny." I wiggle my eyebrows and grin. I say it just to piss him off.

"Shut the hell up, Barlow."

A few of our teammates laugh as they skate toward the bench. I stop flinging pucks down the ice and glance at Malaki. "Alright, I'll take the bait. Who are you talking about?"

"Her."

I spin on the ice, and my expression falls.

No.

Maybe if I pretend she doesn't exist, everyone else will too.

"You know Cindy," I say. "She organizes all the media shit, like our interviews."

And other things...like dealing with new hires.

Surely Daisy didn't actually accept the job of being the team's mascot.

Then again, I've never known Daisy to back down from something. She may throw a fit, or begrudgingly do whatever the task is, but she doesn't give up easily.

"Uh-oh..." Malaki chimes in through my thoughts.

I do a damn good job at keeping my attention away from Cindy and Daisy. It looked as if she was giving Daisy a tour of the arena, which isn't a good sign.

Malaki sticks his twig forward and stops me from skating. "Are you hiding something?" He eyes me with a shit-eating grin.

"Since when do I hide shit? You live with me, for fuck's sake."

Something I wasn't keen on, but when I found myself in the hole because of Miles, Malaki was the only one I felt comfortable turning to. He became my roommate and got us caught up on the rent until I could replace all the money I'd loaned to my brother.

Loaned. What a joke.

With a loan, you get paid back. Miles will never pay me back.

Malaki moves his stick out of the way and skates alongside me toward the bench. "Since now. You're really going to act like you don't see that foxy little thing walking with Cindy?"

Don't react. Don't react. Don't react.

My grip on the stick tightens, and it takes everything in me not to bare my teeth.

Which is completely insane.

Our only night together as something more than her brother's best friend and my best friend's sister was a long time ago. So why am I still so fucked up over it? Why do I still hold such a grudge over what she did to me? The sting of her rejection is as fresh as it was back then, and every time I look at her, all I can remember is laying it out on the line for her to throw it all away.

Irritation runs up my spine with the thought of her making Chicago a home.

I refuse to let that happen—starting with making sure she doesn't get involved with any of these fools. The last thing I need is for her to be around even more than she already is.

"I see her," I finally acknowledge Malaki, but I keep my tone bored.

His eyebrows shoot up to his forehead before he smooths his face. "Ah. You know her..." he notes. "Who is she?"

I glance toward the stands again, and thank fuck, she's gone.

With a shrug of my shoulder, I turn away. "We grew up together."

"Oh?" Malaki is full of sarcasm. "Is that so?"

I shoot him a death glare. "Don't fuck with me."

His lips twitch, and I take that as my cue to head to the locker room. If I don't, I fear I'll accidentally punch him in the face and start a brawl with my own team.

"I'm not fucking with you." He catches up to me quickly. "I've just never seen you get riled up over anything other than hockey."

"I'm not riled up." I am fully riled up.

He chuckles and passes his own locker to continue badgering me. "So you two grew up together? Why is she here?"

My heart rate climbs. "She's River's sister," I snap.

Malaki's face lights up. "*That's* River's sister? Our new neighbor?"

I grind my jaw, and he throws his head back to laugh on his way over to his locker. I swear I hear him mutter something under his breath about how the tables have turned, but I'm choosing to simmer myself down by taking my gear off.

I decide to skip the shower because I need space and air. We have one of the largest arenas in the league, but knowing that Daisy is here makes it seem small, and before I know it, I'll be catching her sweet swaying hips slipping around every last corner.

After making it to my car, I slide inside and exhale a few times to calm down before grabbing my phone. I deleted Daisy's number years ago, during a drunken rage, but it was senseless. Everything about Daisy is permanently engraved into my brain.

I dial the number I have memorized, and it rings once

before going to her voicemail. I hate that my chest constricts with her voice floating through the speakers. It's the same damn one she set up when we were teens.

I quickly type a text after reluctantly resaving her number.

ME

Ignoring my call? Classic. I'm ready to go. Where are you?

DAISY-PETAL

The fucking mascot…really?

I wish I had stuck around to see her face during the interview.

ME

Is that code for thank you? Because you're welcome for getting you a job.

DAISY-PETAL

Actually, it's code for I hate you.

Good. I hate you too.

My car comes to life, and I relax back into my seat. If it were anyone else, I would have left them stranded by now. Don't get that wrong, though—I'm not waiting around because of her. I'm waiting because of River. If something were to happen to her, and it was my fault, I'd lose the only family I currently have left. The Sullivans may not be related to me by blood, but they stepped in when my family practically disowned me. We don't talk as much as I'd like, because I couldn't deal with the constant reminders of Daisy, but I know that if I need someone, they'd be the ones to rely on.

ME

So I take it you didn't accept the position?
That's a shame. I was looking forward to
seeing you in that costume.

She texts back right away.

DAISY-PETAL

Of course I took the position. I need a job,
and if Cindy is willing to work with me if I
ever need time off, what more can I ask for?

It doesn't come as a surprise to me, but it still sends a line of dread down my spine.

ME

Time off? For what? To make out with all
those plants in your apartment?

DAISY-PETAL

Leave my plants out of this.

I want to laugh, but I refuse.

ME

Hurry up. My car is idling.

DAISY-PETAL

I don't need a ride.

My gaze flies toward the other cars in the parking lot. Which one of my idiot teammates decided to offer her a ride home? I'll slash their fucking tires.

I exhale loudly. *For fuck's sake, chill.*

ME

You're moving into the arena just to get
away from me? You shouldn't have.

DAISY-PETAL

That's a good idea.

I'm becoming impatient.

ME

Where are you?

DAISY-PETAL

I'm about to turn the corner to Roosevelt St.

Did she...walk? In downtown Chicago? Knowing her, she probably has a trail of men following her, and I don't mean the good kind in business suits with Rolexes on their wrists.

I drop my phone and shift into drive.

DAISY-PETAL

Gotta go. I need to use my map. Thanks for the job that you most definitely assumed I would not take. I'll see you on the ice, Barlow 😊

My hands grip the steering wheel tightly as I tear out of the parking lot.

Nine

DAISY

I SMILE to myself as I walk down the busy streets of Chicago. My feet hurt, but I don't let that deter me. Granted, I won't be able to walk to and from the arena after working as the mascot, because I'll likely be too fatigued, but right now? It feels pretty damn good not to rely on Kane.

He didn't think I'd take the job, but I've got news for him: He's not going to bully me into hating it here. It's not like I'm going to up and move away just because of his insults and unexpected hatred toward me. I'm here for a reason—many reasons, actually—and none of them have to do with him. Not that he's privy to that information, but it's not like I'm here because of him. It's a total coincidence that my health has led me to the same city he's residing in.

The job, though...that's all him.

A slight chill wracks through me from the gust of wind, and I find that ironic considering I was thinking of Kane at the same time. There's no coincidence there. He's cold—especially toward me.

"Hey, pretty girl."

I quickly look to my right and stare into the eyes of a rugged man with a crooked grin. My mouth forms into a half-smile because though I'm not rude, I am leery.

"Are you lost?" he asks, glancing at the map on my phone screen.

I shake my head and continue to walk past. "No, I'm okay. I've got my map."

Before I know it, he's walking in stride with me. I peek at him and watch him check me out, head to toe. My stomach flips, and my finger hovers over my phone screen with the thought of calling Kane. But then, a rush of defiance flows through my veins. I'd rather drop-kick this man in the balls than call on the past for a little rescue mission.

"I can help you get to where you need to go," he says, continuing to walk beside me. He attempts to grab my hand before I can rush out my refusal.

I move backward and put space between us. "I appreciate it, but I'm fine."

My pace starts to quicken, but I've lost track of where I am. I pull my attention back to my phone and see Kane calling me. After hitting ignore, I realize that I've missed my next turn.

Shit.

"You can go this way." The man's hand lands on my arm. He begins to pull me toward a dark alley that belongs in the next *Purge* movie.

I put the brakes on. "I'd rather not get kidnapped."

Does this guy really think I'm going to follow him into an alley? I mean, I do have some blonde to my hair, but not all blondes are stupid, okay?

The man's laugh is gruff, and I wouldn't be surprised if he pulled out candy and tried to lure me with it. Now, if he had a plant or something, then maybe I'd consider it for a second.

"I'm not going to kidnap you, honey."

My nose scrunches. "Honey?"

He thinks for a moment and places his hand on my arm again and gives it a tug. "Baby? Sweetie? I'll call you whatever you want to be called."

"How about you call her nothing." Like a bullet to my chest, I stop breathing.

I hate the relief that comes with the sight of Kane, but it's hard not to be thankful, considering the man drops my arm and puts distance between us. He shrugs with feigned innocence. "Hey, man, she was lost. I was just helping her."

Kane's dark gaze slides to me, as if he's asking me to confirm the guy's alibi. One second passes and then another. He flicks his chin to his car, and I begrudgingly drag myself over to it because if I have to make a choice between Kane Barlow and Creepy McCreeperson, I'm choosing Kane, even if he hates me.

He remains in the same spot, a yard away from the man. I glance at his flexing fists by his sides and a protectiveness that I haven't felt in years sweeps over me.

"Kane," I say, half inside his car.

A faint growl climbs from his throat as he watches the man turn and head down the alley—without me. As soon as Kane catches my eye, I dip down into the passenger seat and shut his door.

I'm only able to escape his scrutinizing glare for a few seconds before he's slipping into the driver's seat to stare at me disapprovingly.

"I didn't realize you'd still be naïve after all this time..." His reprimand lingers in the interior of his car like a stench I can't escape from. "Especially since I was the one who took your innocence."

I'm able to keep the shock off my face as I slowly turn in my seat and face him head on. Our eyes crash, and the air is swirling with our heated anger. "I am *not* naïve," I say angrily. "And was that you who took my V-card? I couldn't remember who it was."

He scoffs so loudly his hot breath hits my face. "You couldn't forget about that night even if you tried, Daisy-Petal."

He's right. Because trust me, I've tried.

"Don't call me that." I cross my arms over my heaving chest and turn away from him.

"Why? Does it bring up some memories for you?" The tone of his voice strikes a nerve.

"Probably the same ones it brings up for you," I grumble.

Kane pulls out onto the road with a chuckle. "That would require me to think about you, so no, it doesn't bring up any memories for me."

"Is that so?" I only half-believe him.

He pulls into the parking garage for the apartment complex without answering me. I practically fall out of his car trying to get to the elevator first. Unfortunately for me, he catches right up with his chuckle hitting the back of my neck.

I press against the wall of the elevator to get away from him, but he doesn't let me off that easy. He turns and stares right at me. I avoid his gaze because I know he's trying to make me feel uncomfortable, but as the seconds pass, I start to think I would've been better off with Creepy McCreeperson.

Kane stays ramrod straight with his sights set on me as I watch the number of floors increase. My heart beats so hard it's weighing me down.

I move toward the door when we're one floor away from mine, but then, the elevator jerks, and I almost fall into him.

With one finger on the red *stop* button, Kane reaches out with his other hand and steadies me around the waist. Everything, including my breathing, comes to a halt. I tilt my chin, and our eyes collide.

"What are you doing?" *This can't be good.*

A shallow swallow moves down my throat with the distant memory of us in my childhood bedroom, hidden behind a locked door with secrecy. I remember every single part of him, down to the tiny, faint scar on his forehead.

His hand tightens on my waist as he pushes us both toward the door. My back hits the cool metal, and he traps me there with not only his arrogance but his weight too.

I'm suddenly caged in between his arms and forced to meet his intimidating glare.

"Let's get something straight, Daisy-Petal." Kane's neck moves with his Adam's apple bobbing, and my nostrils flare from his overwhelming, spicy scent. He smells like ice, cologne, and...the past. *He smells like him.* "The only reason you're still in this complex is because of River, and the only reason I set you up with that interview is because River had asked if I knew of any job openings."

I dig deep for my confidence and level my chin. "The real reason you set me up with that interview is because you assumed I wouldn't take the job."

He shrugs. "I should have known better. But don't get this twisted in that pretty little head of yours...I don't want you around. You're River's little sister. That's all you are to me, just like before."

I take a page out of his book and pretend like I'm unbothered by his words.

My jaw becomes sturdier when he drops his gaze to my mouth, waiting for my rebuttal.

"Funny..." A quiet, sarcastic laugh flows in between us. "I remember the day I said something similar to you... It sure seemed like I meant more to you then."

His eye twitches. "That was then. This is now. I don't want you to think that I want you here for any reason other than River. If that means I have to help watch out for you, then so be it."

There's a burning hole in my stomach that gets bigger the longer he keeps me caged in between his arms. It's so hard not to be swept off my feet with his masculine scent filling my senses and his dark-blue eyes staring down at me. "Fine," I finally say.

"Well, then." Kane nods. "Glad we got that taken care of."

Annoyed that he still has me trapped and is continuing to waft his warm, minty breath in my direction, I blurt the next thing that comes to mind. "Since you got your business taken care of, now it's my turn..." I exhale heavily, and his nostrils flare.

I hate that he's so attractive.

I can't help but trace the outer part of his steely jaw that leads up to his mouth with my eyes. I try to keep my gaze away, especially when his tongue slips out to wet his bottom lip, but it's like torture.

To make him as uncomfortable as he's making me, I press closer to him, erasing all the space between us.

He refuses to move, which is typical.

"Get on with it, Daisy-Petal," he grits.

I keep my composure, not allowing him to see the sadness that was left from our sudden end. It wasn't like I wanted to watch him go, especially after I gave him a part of me, but that's not something I ever intend on telling him. "I just want to make it clear that I didn't even know you lived in Chicago until you walked onto the elevator."

He laughs in my face. "I find that hard to believe."

A hot slash of annoyance slaps against my cheeks. "You think I kept up with you after that night? I didn't have to follow up on you to know what you were doing, Kane." I force a smile onto my face and take the knife he just put in my chest and shove it into his by bringing up one of the last things

I ever said to him. "How many notches are you up to on your bedpost?"

A twisted grin creeps onto his mouth, and it stuns me for a second. He leans in even closer to me, our faces so close that his nose brushes mine. Something warm coils in my stomach from the touch, and it's then that I realize Kane Barlow still flows through my blood just as potently as he did years prior.

"Too many to count."

He winks at me right before the elevator jerks again. I fall forward, and our lips almost touch. Kane is quick, but he isn't *that* quick. The shock skips across his face just like it does on mine.

As soon as the hallway comes into view, I escape the heated space and run to my apartment. I'm still fumbling with my key when the elevator shuts again. I turn and stare with my back pressed against my apartment door.

I slowly slide to my butt and shake my head at the heat he's left behind.

Even when he's insulting me and I know I should put space between us, I don't. Instead, I find myself craving his attention, just like I did when we were kids.

Ten

KANE

MY KISSING IS aggressive on a normal day, but with the way Daisy has been running laps inside my head, it's war-like at the moment.

The woman with hips for days moans into my mouth, and I quickly pull away and drag her toward the doors to the apartment complex.

It isn't often that I bring a woman back to the apartment now that Malaki lives with me, but there's a certain appeal to it, knowing that Daisy is one floor below us. It's sort of a little *fuck you* to her, even if she's unaware of my doings in my own space.

"How many notches are you up to on your bedpost?"

Her voice in my head replays over and over again. I picture her sweet face, in search of the tiniest hint that the idea of me fucking some other woman irritated her like it did when River mentioned her and some loser frat boy from college, but she was stone cold.

I did exactly as she expected as soon as we parted ways.

She wanted to paint me out to be some hungry guy only interested in meaningless sex, then that was exactly what I'd be. Maybe if I was the typical jock she said I'd be, then I'd get it through my head that I never deserved her to begin with.

"Wow," the redhead giggles as I pull her over the glossy floors toward the elevator. She isn't as hot as I thought she was at the club, or maybe I just think that because Daisy is still fucking with my head. "This place is *so* nice."

She giggles again.

It's fucking annoying.

I lean forward to press the button to my floor but accidentally press the floor below me. Daisy's floor.

Goddamn it.

Get out of my fucking head, Daisy.

I growl quietly and press the right button. My sloppy date thinks I'm making noises for her.

"You don't have to wait," she whispers seductively. "You can touch me now." She presses the emergency stop button that puts me right back to thinking of Daisy.

The redhead...Amy? Amanda?...jumps into my arms. I catch her with ease, though I sort of want to drop her. She starts grinding herself against my dick, and I let her, hopeful it'll harden me up. I press the emergency stop button again to resume the ride up to my apartment so we can move this to the couch.

Not my bed.

Never my bed.

With the woman's back against the far wall of the elevator, I plunge my tongue down her throat to show her who's in control. Or maybe it's to rid Daisy from my thoughts. Her head flings backward, and she makes way for me to suck on her neck.

I nibble on her skin until the elevator door opens. I dig into my pocket for my key but stop as soon as I hear a subtle gasp. I break away with the taste of salt on my tongue and peer over my shoulder.

Ah, fuck.

I quickly realize that the elevator opened up on Daisy's floor because I'd subconsciously hit her floor instead of mine. It takes one whimper from the woman in my grasp for Daisy to smooth her features. At first, she was shocked, but now she just seems bored.

Which irritates me.

I smirk while pressing my hips into the warmth coming from in between the set of legs wrapped around my waist. I catch the slight narrowing of Daisy's eyes, but that's when I notice the bags underneath them.

Was she asleep?

She must notice my internal pause, because she quickly crosses her arms and shoots me a teasing look.

"Hey, neighbor." She's acting awfully cheerful. "I dropped your package off upstairs. The mailman accidently brought it to my door instead of yours."

I squint at her. *What?*

"So sorry I opened it." She giggles, and fuck me if it doesn't remind me of summer nights back home. "I didn't realize it was yours until I saw that it was cream for gonorrhea."

I stiffen.

This fucking brat.

The woman in my grip freezes before she slowly loosens her legs. "Uh, what?"

I turn to her to try to convince her that Daisy is lying, but there's nothing I can say that'll make her stay now. She presses L for the lobby and puts obvious distance between us, as if I'm going to give her the STD by sharing the small space with her.

I glare at Daisy and her twinkling, little glint.

"Oh, you two go ahead," she adds. "I'll just catch the next elevator."

The door begins to shut, and she sends me a little wave.

Before it closes altogether, I shake my head at her.

Game on, Daisy.

———

The next day, I wait outside of Daisy and River's apartment, knowing she'll exit soon because she has to head to the arena for a fitting—something Cindy let me in on because she clearly thinks Daisy and I are on much better terms than we actually are.

That may be because I acted as if Daisy was like a sister to me when I scored her the interview, but what Cindy doesn't know won't kill her.

The door swings open, and I hurriedly shove off the wall with my hockey bag in tow.

Daisy stops abruptly, her shiny strawberry-blonde hair swinging behind her shoulders. She takes one look at me, confusion flickering against her soft features, before she shakes her head and acts as if I don't exist.

She presses the down button and puts her back to me.

I run my gaze down her backside—something she notices in the shiny elevator door. She lifts an eyebrow, and I try to play it off by leaning forward with my mouth right beside her ear. "Ready for your fitting?"

To my surprise, she doesn't even flinch. I get a whiff of her perfume, and it goes right to my dick.

Honey.

She smells like sweet honey.

Daisy strides onto the elevator, presses L for the lobby, and slips off to the right, whereas I head for the spot I had my date pressed against the night before. With the doors closed, the space gets tighter. Daisy's fingers clutch her oversized bag, and her white teeth clamp onto her glossy bottom lip.

"You know you initiated war, right?" I ask.

Ding.

Ding.

Ding.

A little noise sounds with each floor that the elevator descends on. It's a nice break in the loud silence that's currently screaming at me.

Finally, Daisy stops pretending I'm not inside this small space with her. "War?" she repeats, without looking at me.

I stare at the side of her pink cheek and put my hand into my pocket. "Just wait until you bring some guy back to the apartment," I warn. "I'll end it before it even gets started, just like you did to me last night."

Her sweet laugh slows my world for a second. "How will you know when I bring a guy back? Are you going to start stalking me?"

When. Not if.

I rarely feel jealous. There isn't anyone I've had in my arms that I wouldn't willingly give up a moment later.

But when it comes to Daisy...

The protectiveness I still have over her isn't as fleeting as I'd like for it to be, even with our past.

"I'll know," I say with confidence.

Little does she know, I have access to the camera in the hallway.

The elevator door opens, and she walks out first, heading toward the front doors instead of the parking garage.

Daisy, who looks much livelier today than she did yesterday evening, sends me a breath-stealing smile over her shoulder. "Seems like you've forgotten that I know how to sneak a guy into my bed."

I'm struck with silence from her bold statement.

And here I thought she'd never bring it up again after we had words the other day.

She turns and disappears into what looks like an Uber, leaving me to drive to the arena alone.

I'm competitive by nature, and if we're keeping count, that's twice Daisy has won our little sparring battle in the last twenty-four hours, which is just fucking unacceptable.

Eleven

DAISY

I FELT TERRIBLE YESTERDAY, but today, I'm a brand-new person.

That's the thing with having an autoimmune disease. Some days you are fine, and other days, you're just *not*.

I went to Dr. Gibson's office yesterday for some routine blood work to make sure my Lupus is still at bay, and apparently, my body was not a fan of that. Nausea got the best of me, and then it was made three hundred times worse when the elevator door opened to reveal Kane mauling some girl's neck.

Heat swept my lower belly, and nausea rolled through me.

That's why I reacted the way I did.

With River at the hospital again, I ordered some necessities to get me through the night if the nausea continued, but instead of stepping onto the elevator to meet my delivery driver downstairs, I got a front-row seat to a porno.

Ugh.

He said my little stunt last night initiated war, but doesn't he realize we've been in a constant war since the moment we met years ago?

Only now, we're fighting to get away from one another instead of fighting to get closer.

"There she is!" I perk up at the sound of Cindy's voice. She's a friendly face compared to Kane's and the grumpy Uber driver with the eyepatch.

"Hi." I smile.

"You ready for this, Blue Devil?" Cindy pulls me over to the center of the visitor locker room floor, which is what we're borrowing for the fitting since the team is on the ice for practice.

"As ready as ever," I lie.

I glance at the huge Blue Devil head on the bench and cannot believe I'm about to be the team's mascot. I still haven't filled River in because he'll find it hilarious, and I can't deal with that right now.

I'm sure Kane will manage to get a video of me falling on the ice and send it to him anyway, so I won't have to worry about it.

"Oooh, lucky me," I mutter as I pull the top of the costume on. "My own Blue Devil jersey."

The woman taking my measurements snickers. It doesn't take long for her to get everything pinned in the correct spots. When she's done, I slowly eye the Blue Devil head again before making my way over to it.

I can't help but burst out into laughter a moment later as I stare down at it.

Am I seriously taking this job just to prove a point? The pay is good, but is it really that good?

Cindy and the seamstress both turn to look at me like I'm crazy, which at this point, I think I am.

I grab the head, expecting it to be a lot heavier than it is, and slip it onto my shoulders.

It takes all of three seconds for me to burst out into laughter again. It echoes around the bobbling devil head, and I laugh so hard I clutch my stomach.

"Someone please take my photo for my best friend," I call out.

Natalia asked me how Chicago was during our FaceTime call yesterday, and when I send her this photo, she'll understand my reluctance.

I pull the head off my shoulders after I hear the shuttering of the camera, my hair a wispy mess. "This is too funny not to share," I say with a laugh.

"Funny or not"—Cindy shows me the photo, and I laugh harder—"I am so thankful to have filled this spot. You're literally saving my ass. I was afraid I was going to have to do this."

"Well..." I smile. "I guess you're welcome."

After pulling the outfit off so the seamstress can sew it for tomorrow, Cindy and I go over some of the details before handing me a pair of skates.

"Size eight, right?" she asks.

I nod and begin trying them on.

It's been a while since I've ice-skated. I'm certain I'll be fine, but a few practice rounds might be beneficial, especially with my joints aching a little more than usual today.

"Do you mind?" I nod in the direction of the ice.

Cindy glances at her watch. "Practice just ended. It's shorter the day before a game, so the ice should be yours."

Thank god.

Carefully, I make my way toward the arena. The closer I get, the stronger the crisp ice scent is. A pinch of nostalgia hits me, and I smile to myself with the reminder of evenings spent in the stands with my parents, watching River...*and* Kane.

Kane was the one who taught me to skate, which is really just annoying now that I think about it.

The moment my skate lands on the slick ice, energy zooms

to my heels and travels all the way to my hips. There isn't a sound to be heard except for the tiny hash marks I'm cutting into the rink. I start off slow, allowing my body to remember the feel of it, but it doesn't take long to skate the outer edge of the rink.

Easy peasy.

I can do this.

The nice thing about being the mascot is that no one will even know it's me.

Except for Kane...but he doesn't count.

"Uh, who are you?"

I do a half-turn and make eye contact with a tall guy wearing a Blue Devils practice jersey.

"The new mascot," I say.

The guy breaks into a grin, and the closer he gets to me, the bluer his eyes become.

"The new mascot?" He skates a circle around me. "Yeah, right."

I can't blame him for being skeptical. It is hard to believe.

"I'm serious." I put my hands on my hips. "I just wanted to get a feel for the ice before tomorrow's game."

The guy tosses his stick back and forth in his hands and stares at me incredulously. He peers back at the bench where the goalie is climbing onto the ice in full gear.

"Who's this?" he grumbles, seeming annoyed. "Ice girl? Sorry, but we need the rink to ourselves."

I blanch from the assumption. "I am *not* an ice girl."

"Oh. My bad," he calls over his shoulder as he skates to the net.

"She said she's the mascot," the blue-eyed guy shouts in his thick accent.

"Yeah, *okay*," the goalie shouts back. "I don't really care, Lars. Get your girlfriend off the ice. I'm not staying here all day to help you."

"I'm not his girlfriend!" I yell, heading off to the side.

Lars skates alongside me with ease. He's easily a foot taller than me.

He bends down, his helmet not even strapped on the bottom, with a smirk on his face. "Do you want to be, though?"

My mouth opens to decline his offer, but a familiar presence makes himself known, causing me to pause. Lars's eyes get larger, like he's surprised that I'm considering it.

I'm not, but it's fun to pretend with Kane listening in.

The last thing he wants is for me to mess around with one of his teammates, even if he won't admit it. I wouldn't stoop that low, though I'm sure he would if the roles were reversed. He's made it obvious that he's done exactly what I thought he'd do when he left for life beyond our small town.

"No, she doesn't," Kane answers for me, pulling both of our attention to the bench.

Kane, still in his hockey gear except for his helmet, skates onto the ice and makes his way over to us.

My heart skips a beat when our eyes meet. For some reason, I feel as if I've been caught doing something wrong, but Kane has no place in any decision I make when it comes to my romantic life.

Not that I am focused on that part of my life right now, but if I was, he doesn't get to have a say.

"I can make my own decisions, thank you very much."

Kane snorts right before he flings ice up in between us. I quickly try to move out of the way of the cold shavings, but I'm not that comfortable on the ice yet, and my legs slip right out from under me.

It is wishful thinking to hope that Lars's arm is wrapped around my waist instead of Kane's, but I recognize his touch as if it's my own. Heat races to the part of my lower stomach that he's touching. Skin on skin. It burns.

"You can't even skate on your own, let alone make decisions on who to fuck," he says in a grumbly voice.

Lars interjects. "Who said anything about fucking? I was going to take her on a date. That's what you do in Sweden, unlike you, *horas*."

Kane's grip on my waist grows tight as he puts me back on my feet. "Did you just insult me?"

Lars taps his stick on the ice in frustration. "I saw her first."

Is he fighting over me?

My gaze skips to Kane, and I freeze. His devilish lips tip, and I know *exactly* what he's going to say before he even opens his mouth.

"I already had her...and sorry, I won't allow you to have my sloppy seconds."

Blistering anger sweeps through me. I try to move out from beneath Kane's hold on my hip, but he's too strong, and I'm not steady enough on skates right now to escape. Lars skates away after we make eye contact and begins sending pucks into the net with the grumpy goalie blocking the shots.

"Let go of me," I hiss.

Kane chuckles. "No."

I cross my arms and stiffen my entire body in hopes it'll make it harder on Kane as he tries to pull me off the ice. It doesn't, though. The only thing it does is illicit a curse to fly from his mouth as he hauls me up into his arms and down the hall where the visitor locker room is.

"I see that you're still a stubborn brat," he mutters before opening the door and shoving me inside. The mascot head is still in the center of the bench along with my bag, but Cindy and the seamstress are gone, along with the rest of the mascot costume.

"And you're still a jealous asshole," I sneer.

"Jealous?" Kane's hands go to his hips in disbelief before

dropping his head. When he pops back up, his blue eyes are burning with something I can't name. I feel it everywhere, though, brushing over my flesh like electricity. "I'm not jealous, Daisy. Fuck whomever you want, just no one on the team."

An undeniable spark zips through me that I've only felt once before, and it's taken me until right now to realize just how much I've craved it. No one has come close to giving me a taste of exhilaration quite like Kane Barlow. I'm not sure how, but he has always managed to make me feel so at ease and chaotic at the same time.

I became addicted to it several years ago, and like a fiend, I'm craving it all over again being alone with him.

"Why not?" I flutter my eyelashes and purse my lips. "Afraid you'll overhear something that'll sound a little too familiar and give you a reminder of the past?"

Why am I pushing his buttons on purpose?

Kane's jaw flexes, and I hate that I'm proud of myself for getting under his skin. I almost drop my guard until he quickly advances on me. I'm not fast enough to dodge the bullet. He backs me all the way to the wall before grabbing both of my arms and trapping them above my head.

Breath vanishes from my lungs as I stare up at him.

"You think you're so clever, don't you, Daisy-Petal?"

I give him a closed-lipped smile, even if my heart is beating straight out of my chest. The undeniable pull that's always been between us is back with our closeness, and I have the urge to press against him just to see what he'll do.

Kane's eyes drop to my mouth, and I flush.

"I remember the tiny little freckle you have right below your left hip bone..." his voice scrapes against my skin like a jagged piece of glass. "And the birthmark you have on the inner part of your right thigh..." Kane moves closer and my legs spread apart on their own.

I need to jerk out of his grip or do something, *anything*, to act as if he isn't making my heart rate spike. But I'm stuck like glue.

How did I let him pin me here?

A shaky breath falls from between my lips, and his nostrils flare before he steals back the last bit of my control.

"I don't need reminders when it comes to you," he admits. "I just don't want you fucking my teammates, because I don't want you to screw with their head like you screwed with mine."

Kane's grip against my arm tightens, and I wince when he hits the tender spot from yesterday's blood work. He notices the catch in my expression and immediately lets go. Distance increases between us, but I still can't breathe.

Silence fills the locker room when he angrily pushes open the door and leaves me alone.

I look back at the Blue Devil head and sigh shakily. I attempt to lower my blood pressure, but in the end, I accept it for what it is.

A loss.

"We lost that one, huh?" I ask the immobile head.

I wouldn't even be surprised if it nodded back.

Twelve

KANE

THE NIGHT BEFORE A GAME, I'm practically crawling out of my skin.

No one expects it. I keep everyone at an arm's length, so they only get the aloof version of me, the one that acts unbothered, without nerves, especially while on the ice.

Sure, I let my temper fly, but that isn't much of a surprise to anyone in the league.

To know that I have an entire routine the night before a game because I'd do anything to win would be a total mind-fuck to the press. I rarely let anyone in on my habits. Malaki learned the hard way, walking in mid-jumping jack, which is exactly why he isn't home right now. If you're present during my night-before-a-game regimen, you have to participate.

I don't make the rules.

I apparently don't make the rules when it comes to Daisy either.

The music thumps loud, but it's still not loud enough to drown out the thoughts from earlier in the locker room.

I can't believe I let her get under my skin like that. I may have won our little tiff, but the lasting effects of having her so close are lingering. It pisses me off and excites me at the same time.

After discarding my shirt to the floor, I turn the music up even louder. I have the entire apartment to myself with Malaki out, and with River on night shift, I don't care how loud it gets.

It won't bother anyone, except Daisy, which seems like a perk if you ask me.

And chances are, after earlier, she won't dare knock on my door to curse me out.

Or will she?

Fuck, stop thinking about her.

"Thirty-one, thirty-two, thirty-three..."

With each drop in the bass, I do another jumping jack.

One hundred and thirty-three. Every night before a game.

Some of the drills, or *"superstitions"* if you're in the mood to piss me off, have disappeared over the years, but there are a few that have stayed, like the jumping jacks, stepping onto the ice with my left skate, the hair tie around my wrist for games, and the way that I tape my stick. Those are some of the oldest ones in the book, and I'm not sure I'll ever be able to stop them.

Whether I feel as if I have proven myself or not.

"Forty-three, forty-four..."

A bead of sweat drips over my nose as I stare out at the skyline. The skyscrapers are half-lit, looking more like golden stars than buildings. The city grows more awake as the evening goes on.

I wonder if Daisy is even home.

I growl.

Maybe it's time to reintroduce an old tradition just so I can get her off my mind.

I scoff mid-jump.

Going to the club the night before a game is never a good idea, and I never frequent the same woman twice, so if they ever give me their number, I trash it immediately.

The bass drops again, and I focus on the jumping jacks.

I mentally go over some of the line changes we made for tomorrow's game and run through the plays so intently that I almost don't hear the rattling of my door from across the apartment.

There's a fleeting sense of exhilaration with the thought that it may be Daisy, but surely she doesn't want to come face-to-face with me after earlier.

Swiping my shirt off the floor, I wipe it over my sweaty browline and drape it over my shoulder. Without looking at who it is, I swing the door open. Color me surprised when it's none other than Daisy standing there in what I assume to be pajamas. There's a line of anger in between her eyebrows that's fucking adorable as she pairs it with her mouth set in irritation.

"Are you kidding me?!" she shouts.

No bra?

I pull my gaze from her nipples poking through the thin T-shirt she's wearing and bring them up to her face.

I pretend I can't hear her over the music. "What was that?"

The bass is still pounding through the penthouse, and another bead of sweat drips down from my hairline, traveling all the way to my chest. Daisy trails it with her eyes before seemingly becoming angry with herself. Her blue eyes flash with something so enticing that I find myself giving her my full attention.

"Some of us work tomorrow, ya know!"

"Obviously!" I shout. "What do you want?"

Daisy stomps her foot like she's five before she pushes

through the door, bypassing me in the process. I'm too swept away by the tiny shorts she's wearing to stop her. Instead, I stand near the open door and watch her navigate the large space.

She pauses with her back to me, those thick strands of strawberry-blonde hair falling behind her shoulders. I let the door latch behind me, something that sends a naughty little thought into my head, and follow after her.

This is fucking up my entire night, yet I can't seem to care.

Suddenly, the music cuts off.

"Ugh! Finally!" Her shoulders fall before she spins her attention around the room, locking onto the spiral stairwell that leads to upstairs.

For the briefest of seconds, I let the dirty thoughts play out in my head. I picture myself leading her by the hand to my bedroom and tossing her onto my bed to fuck the attitude right out of her, but then I suddenly remember who she is and become angry that she's in my apartment, messing with my head along with my evening.

I have a routine, and she isn't a part of it.

Not anymore, anyway.

I refrain from running my hand through my hair with frustration because there's no way I'm letting her know that she's ruffling me. "What do you want?"

She turns toward me, and my eyes fall right to her chest again. "What are you doing up here? Having a fucking rave?"

My mouth twitches. "No."

"Let me guess..." A soft sigh freeflows from her mouth, and I can tell she's trying not to look at my bare chest from the way she's drilling a hole in the wall behind me with her stare. "One of your game rituals?"

She remembers?

When I don't answer her right away, she laughs. Her arms

move to cross over her chest, hiding those perky little buds from me. *Thank fuck.*

"Well?"

I flick my attention to her raised eyebrow. "What?"

"Where is she?"

It takes me a moment to catch on.

She thinks I'm fucking someone. Of course she does. Even back in high school, I was desperate to make it seem like I wasn't lusting over River's little sister, so I would bury myself in between other girls' legs every chance I could.

Thinking quickly on my feet, I pull away from the archway and make my way over to her. Being extra stubborn when it comes to me, she refuses to move. In fact, I'm not even sure she's blinked. When I get close enough, I lean into her space and stare *right* at her mouth. "I'm lookin' at her."

Her arms fall, her eyes growing large. I drop my gaze, and I get a glimpse of her hardening nipples, which completely fucks with my head.

"I am *not* sleeping with you to fulfill your stupid superstitions!"

Although I was kidding, there is a bite of disappointment that comes with her refusal, as if we will ever end up in that position again.

"Relax, Daisy-Petal." I back away from her because I need space. "I've grown past that."

I swipe my water bottle off the coffee table and chug it. She eyes me with suspicion, narrowing those pretty blue eyes in my direction.

"You're not superstitious anymore?" she asks.

I toss my water bottle onto the couch. "Oh no, I still am. Fucking someone the night before a game was no longer bringing me good luck, though."

Her lips part. "Oh."

I watch in silence as she glances around my apartment

space. My place is much bigger than hers, having double the number of rooms.

"So what were you doing, then? Because it sounded like you were..." Daisy's sentence trails, and if I'm not mistaken, there's a pinkish tint to her cheeks.

"Sounded like I was what?" I poke.

Our eyes catch, and I watch the words come out of her mouth with ease.

"It sounded like you were fucking someone."

My teeth clench. I'm not sure why that was hot coming from her mouth, but it was.

I tilt my head. "And you thought to come up here and interrupt me..."—I pause to let my words sink in—"mid-fuck?"

Daisy opens her mouth, clearly appalled, but I keep going because it's simply too much fun watching the thoughts play out over her features.

"What were you going to do? Ask me to stop fucking some woman? Tell her about that mythical STD cream that was delivered to your house by accident?"

Daisy's eyelashes flutter as she tries to come up with something, but I press a little more, simply because I won't be satisfied until I see her cheeks ripen with color.

"Were you hoping to get a glimpse? Or were you hoping to join?"

There.

Her eyes turn a shade darker, and those pretty cheeks stain with a blush. I can't tell if she's angry, embarrassed, or turned-on.

She's out of her mind if she thinks I'd let her join.

I wouldn't share her, even if it was with another woman.

Fuck, what?

"You are so irritating," she seethes.

I grin. "So are you."

Her eye roll makes me wild.

When she tries to stomp out of my apartment, bare feet and all, I panic. I quickly follow her and foolishly latch onto her wrist.

She widens her eyes with shock, but I'm committed now.

"Where do you think you're going?" I ask.

She peers up at me like some innocent little doe. Though, I know she isn't as innocent as she used to be.

"Back to my own apartment…" She lets her words trail. "Keep the music down this time."

I force out a laugh while I tighten my grip on her wrist. "You're here…the night before a game. You know what that means."

She gives me a dirty look that completely eggs me on. "I am not letting you fuck me, Kane."

I'm quick on my feet. "I don't want to fuck you." I tug her closer and catch her gasp on my chest. "But you'd let me if I wanted to."

Her jaw drops. "I would not!"

She's probably right.

With her wrist still trapped in my grip, I lead her toward the floor-to-ceiling windows that overlook the city. "Jumping jacks."

The memory plays out right in front of her face. I watch it like my favorite movie.

"You're still doing jumping jacks the night before a game?" There's the tiniest spark of amusement within her question.

"Yep, and we're at forty-three. So get to it."

Thirteen

DAISY

I NARROW MY GAZE. "You are insane."

Kane's lip pulls up at the side, and my stomach dips. "Let's go, Daisy-Petal."

I wish he'd stop calling me that.

I teeter with the idea of telling him to go screw himself and heading back to my apartment, but there's something kind of sad about the fact that he's up here all alone, carrying out his crazy superstitions the night before one of his games like he's that same eighteen-year-old boy I grew close to years ago.

So much has changed, yet things still feel the same.

"Ugh." My shoulders fall. "Fine."

Kane's blue eyes light up with excitement, and it shouldn't please me that I'm the reason it's there.

Get a grip. Kane is a total asshole who has a vengeance against me.

"That's my girl." He winks at me.

I'm warm all over, and that is *not* good. "I am not your girl."

Kane smirks, and then the music cuts back on. His large apartment is surrounded by Marshmello's beat and my wildly beating heart. I angle away from him because I'm not wearing a bra, and although I'm part of the itty-bitty titty committee, I still have *some* bounce.

My lungs start to get tired after thirty jumping jacks, but I ignore the sting in my chest because there is no way I'm letting Kane see me struggling. I'm not willing to let him in on the real reason I'm in Chicago, because he doesn't deserve to know anything about me.

This is my thing, and he has no part in it.

"Keep going," he encourages.

He's jumping with ease. His muscles flex with every jump, pulling my eyes to his abs like a magnet. Kane has always been blessed with a toned body, but now that he's in the pros and works out daily, his muscles are honed to perfection—a full eight-pack, rippling back muscles. Even his back strains with strength.

Stop looking at him.

I pull my attention away and put my best effort into the remaining jumping jacks.

My hair is beginning to dampen with sweat, and by the last few, I'm hardly doing them at all.

I press my back to the window and slowly slide down to the floor.

Kane stands over me with his hands on his hips. "You okay?" There's barely even a rise in his chest, whereas my lungs are screaming for air.

"I'm fine," I choke out.

"You can sit on the couch, you know."

I scoff as best as I can. "I don't know what you've done on that couch. I'm good here."

He rolls his eyes and heads to the kitchen. I shut my eyes, level my breathing, and will myself not to think about how hard he's judging me right now. One of the first things I'd noticed before I was officially diagnosed with Lupus was how tired my muscles felt when doing the simplest of activities. Unfortunately, even though I'm in remission, they are still weaker than most.

"Here."

My eyes spring open, and the rest of the air in my lungs disappears. Kane is crouched down in front of me with his blistering blue eyes, holding out a water bottle for me to take.

I grab it hesitantly, fearful he'll steal it before I get my grip on it, but he doesn't. The cool water coats my throat. He watches me closely as I drink half of it before he takes it back and screws the lid on.

A couple beats of silence pass between us before he slips down beside me and rests his back against the window too.

What is he doing?

"Don't even think about making a pass at me," I bite out.

I'm on edge with him this close. He's acting...neutral, and it's confusing me.

"When was the last time you exercised?" he snorts.

Okay, never mind.

"Earlier." I look over at him and grin coyly. "With Lars."

Kane's eyes flare with irritation before he drops his gaze to my cheeky smile. "Nice try." He pulls his knees up to his chest and drapes his arms over them. "He won't touch you after I warned him."

"Mmm. You sound awfully confident. Are you sure about that?" I ask.

I should really stop trying to get a rise out of him.

Kane pulls away, but I still manage to catch the annoyance on his features.

"What other superstitions have you kept up with since high school?" I ask.

I'm curious.

That's all.

I am not trying to put us on an even playing ground.

After a few seconds, he shrugs. "Not many. Jumping jacks, taping my stick. The normal stuff."

Normal?

I rub my sore legs to give my hands something to do. "What about your mom's smoothies? Do you still make those before a game?"

Before a game, his mom would blend together a smoothie for extra energy and good luck. He and River called it their game-day smoothie. It was filled with organic yogurt, ¼ cup of oat milk, a cup of fresh blueberries, a cup of fresh strawberries, one banana, and some chia seeds.

He answers abruptly. "No."

I stop massaging my thighs at the sight of his flexing jaw.

"Why not?"

Kane turns toward me slowly. Our eyes catch, and if I were standing, I'd likely lose my footing. There is something so haunted in his gaze that I feel it like a ghost brushing against my skin.

"When was the last time you saw me at my house, Daisy?" His hoarse voice sends a pain into my chest.

To be honest, each time I came home, whether it be for the holidays, college breaks, or when I got sick, I avoided his house like the plague. I wouldn't even glance in that direction in fear that he'd be home for a split second to visit his mom and brother.

Kane's neck bobs with a gruff swallow when I don't answer. "I haven't been home since I left for the junior league."

Confusion pulls on my head like a puppet. I keep my mouth closed instead of letting my lips part with shock.

"Your mom is still icing you out?" I whisper. *No way.*

Without answering, Kane hops to his feet quickly and swipes his shirt off the floor. "I'm going to shower," he says over his shoulder. "You better be gone by the time I get out, or I may have to prove to you that I was right when I said you'd let me fuck you."

I scowl at his bare back as he jogs up the stairs with ease to his second floor.

Instead of sending a biting remark his way, I slowly climb to my feet and make my way over to the door. It doesn't take much for Kane to get under my skin, but I'm not one to kick a dog when it's down.

Fourteen

KANE

I'M ON EDGE.

My leg shakes up and down as I sit on the bench in the locker room. I glance at my stick, checking out my handiwork. I count the fifteen loops and make sure the black tape is smoothed as best as it can be. I've done all my crazy lucky rituals, and yet, I still have a knot in my stomach.

We get the go-ahead from Coach and stand up to take the ice. The closer I get to the arena, the more my muscles tense. *What the fuck is wrong with me?* I'm never like this when it comes to a game. Hockey is a salve to me. It's my calm, even with how chaotic and aggressive it can become.

Daisy pops into my head, and I grit my teeth. I shove the thought of her bouncing breasts from her pitiful jumping jacks clear out of my mind and continue down the line. There's a stack of pucks on the ledge right beside the bench, and as soon as I take the ice—left skate first, *obviously*—I swipe at them. The tower crumbles to the icy floor, and the crowd roars.

Cool air brushes against my face as I zip around. The calm finally begins to settle over me, and I come back down to earth.

Until I see *her*.

It takes everything in me not to come to a complete halt.

I can tell that it's Daisy in the mascot costume, because she's way smaller than the previous person. Her skates peeking out from beneath the Blue Devil legs are tiny, and she barely comes to Lar's shoulder.

If he doesn't get the hell away from her...

I shouldn't be jealous, but I am.

If anyone asks, I'll blame it on being protective.

If she asks, I'll deny the fuck out of it.

My stick is light in my grip, and I play around with a puck at my feet. I wind backward and send it flying at Lars, purposefully coming close to our little mascot too.

They both look at me, and honestly, it's hard not to laugh knowing that Daisy is inside that thing, even if I am irritated.

Lars rolls his eyes, but I catch the half-smirk on his face as he skates toward me.

"Will you relax?" He does a half-turn while a puck bounces against his stick. "We're on the same team, ya know."

"Stop pissing me off, and I will relax," I say matter-of-factly.

He dips down to the ice and begins to stretch. I flick my gaze to our mascot and send her a scathing glare when I see that she's staring at both of us. As if she's caught, she spins and skates off to center ice and raises her hands, which makes the crowd yell even louder.

"I'm not trying to piss you off," Lars adds mid-stretch. "I was making sure she was okay, because you sent those pucks flying, and she nearly fell."

It's not his responsibility to make sure she's okay. It's mine.

My nostrils flare with the thought.

It's *not* my responsibility.

I skate in the opposite direction of Daisy with anger trailing me. It's fucking with my head that she's on the ice, in *my* space.

I just need to pretend it isn't her. It's simple. She's dressed in a ridiculous devil's costume; I can't even see her.

I glance to center ice again. It doesn't matter if I can't see her. I can feel her.

I'm cagey at the thought of her sharing the ice with me. It's fucking with my game-day mentality, and I really don't like it.

I'm unfocused, and I'm never unfocused.

Skating quickly, I pull up beside her and send ice flying in between us.

"Get off the ice," I demand quietly.

Even with my gritty tone, I know she heard me.

"What?" Her voice is muffled, but it's still as sweet as a melody.

Acting as if I'm not standing here talking to the damn mascot, I play around with the puck and send it into the net past Emory. He glares at me. Mid-turn, I repeat myself. "I said get off the ice."

If she could, I bet she'd stomp her foot at me.

"I'm doing my job. The one *you* got me!" she shouts.

Mistakes were made.

I should have never set her up for that interview.

"Get off," I growl. "Or I'll make you."

Ah, fuck. That was the wrong thing to say. If I lifted her mask, I bet she'd be smiling like a real devil.

"You'll make me?" she repeats.

My shoulders tense. I grip my stick with so much strength I'm afraid it'll snap.

"We'll see about that." She skates away from me, but I

only let myself linger for a few seconds before trying to get my shit straight to play a game that we need to win for playoff points.

Focus, Kane. Fucking focus.

———

The game couldn't have gone worse.

For me, I mean. The team did great. They're the reason we won.

I didn't play as well as I typically do, and I know everyone could tell. Most of them will keep their thoughts to themselves, except for a few, like Rhodes and Emory. Rhodes, the veteran of the team, will probably grunt out an insult that'll piss me off, but I'll remain quiet because it'll be true.

"You good? Drink too much last night?" Malaki asks.

I glare at him. "I don't drink the night before a game anymore, which you know because you live with me."

He shrugs. "I don't know what you do when I'm not there."

Malaki's lucky not to be a part of my rituals, unlike Daisy.

"So, you just get wasted every other night then?" someone mutters.

Malaki starts to untie his skates without making eye contact with me. "Your game was off, so I'm just speculating over here."

Lars chuckles. "I know what's got the hothead all twisted."

I bare my teeth at him. He's getting on my last fucking nerve.

"If you don't shut the fuck up, I will knock your teeth out," I snap.

Emory sighs. "Same team, brother. Quit it."

I grimace at him while he sheds his goalie gear. He's just as testy as I am, only he got himself a pretty little wife, so now he's all sunshine and rainbows.

Malaki perks up with excitement. He turns toward Lars. "Oh, there's tea? Do tell."

"The mascot..."

They converse as if I'm not here, and if I don't block them out, I may actually do something I'll regret.

I fucked myself getting Daisy this job.

It's messing with my head, and it's putting a wedge between me and the game—something that is simply unacceptable.

Hockey is all I have left.

I'll be damned if I let anyone take it from me.

Even her.

I pop up from the bench, in need of a shower, but there's no time for that. The need to get shit straightened out before the next game is more important than the sweat drying on my skin.

"Where is he going?" someone asks.

"Hopefully to fuck the ma—"

I slam the door because I know the next thing out of their mouths is going to send me into a full rage.

I'll be foaming at the mouth before it's all said and done.

Fifteen

DAISY

THIS ITCHY COSTUME is not only smothering but it smells godawful too. Like feet and mildewy snowsuits from little kids playing out in the snow for hours upon hours. The combo is exactly what one would assume—*vomit inducing*.

I hold my breath as I spin around to face the mirror. Cindy scored me my own little dressing room, which doubles as storage for extra equipment. It shares a very thin wall with the officials' locker room, and after having a listen, I've learned that they gossip more than a bunch of college girls at a frat party.

"This stupid freaking thing!" I reach for the zipper and give it another tug.

It's stuck. *Great.*

Not only am I covered in sticky sweat, smelling like a musty gym bag, but now I'm trapped in this thing for the rest of my life.

Okay, fine.

That's dramatic.

But I'm most definitely not walking through the arena, wearing the bottom half of my devil's costume for people to learn who's underneath the giant head.

My fingers pull on the zipper again, but it refuses to budge. I sigh angrily as another droplet of sweat rolls down my cheek, falling to the floor beneath me. *It's fine.* I'll just die of a heat stroke in this room and go out a winner.

I laugh to myself so I don't cry.

With half the costume on, I call Natalia on FaceTime.

When in doubt, call your bestie.

"What are you—"

"I need you to come to Chicago," I interrupt her and pan the phone down to my body. "I'm fucking stuck in this thing!"

Natalia stares at me through the screen for a few seconds before her laughter echoes around me.

"Oh my god," she says through a laugh. "It isn't funny..."

I try to hide my own smile.

"But it is..." She laughs again.

"Natalia," I whine, "what do I do?"

She finally controls her laughter and acts serious. "Get a new job."

I can't do that. Kane will call me a quitter.

"Natalia!" I shout. "I'm serious. I'm dying of a heat stroke in this thing!"

With the back of my hand, I wipe the sweat off my hairline.

"Okay, okay." I watch as she moves through her apartment with her thinking face on. "Is there anyone else around? Anyone that you can ask for help?"

I bite my lip. "Only the refs."

She lifts her arched brow. "Are any of them cute?"

"Really?" I huff.

Her laugh cuts through my frustration, and I finally start to laugh too. "This is so ridiculous," I say.

"Comical, you mean? I agree."

I scrunch my nose. "Bye."

She laughs harder, and I hang up the phone.

My hands fall to my hips, and I stare at the wall that separates me from the officials' locker room. Eventually, I trudge over to the door and open it, allowing the bright lights of the hallway into my dim dressing room. The light covers my shiny, sweaty skin, making me look even worse.

It's not like I'm trying to impress anyone—the less people who see me the better—but I know exactly who's in the vicinity.

It's quiet besides the referees in the next room, who I'm assuming are about to leave for the evening, so with one hand holding up the top of my costume, I take my fist and gently rap my knuckles on their door.

It takes a couple seconds for it to open, and when it does, the referee's eyebrows crowd together at the sight of me.

"Uh, hi." I send him, and the rest of the men behind him a tight-lipped smile.

This isn't awkward at all.

"I'm so sorry to bother you, but..."—a breathy laugh leaves me—"my zipper is stuck, and I really don't want to die in this thing."

Plus, there is no way I'm calling Kane to help me.

The man blinks several times before finally speaking. "*You're* the mascot?"

I shift awkwardly on my feet. "Unfortunately."

He shakes his head in disbelief. "Wow..."

I hear the faint mumbling of a younger referee standing behind him. "I'm requesting as many Blue Devils games as possible."

Leaning to my left, I get an eyeful of him. He smirks at me, and my face warms.

I quickly spin around and move my hair out of the way. "Can you please hurry? I'd rather no one see me in this."

"Move over," the younger one urges. "I'll help her."

"No," the other, much older referee says.

"What? Why?"

"Because you sound too excited. Go stand in the corner or something."

I smash my lips together to suppress my laugh. "Thanks," I whisper.

"You're welcome," he says, fiddling with the zipper. "Next game, do you think you could take a few photos with my girls? They love getting photos with the mascots."

"Absolutely." I smile over my shoulder at him as he continues to focus on the zipper.

After a few seconds, he grumbles, "This is really stuck."

"We can always cut it off," my admirer suggests.

He clearly didn't go stand in the corner like my hero demanded.

I'm starting to sweat again.

I turn slightly in an attempt to hide myself from anyone who happens to walk down the hall.

"Here, let me help." A hand lands on my hip to keep me still, and I know for a fact that it's the other referee.

"No funny business," I chide, giving him a look.

"I'll be on my best behavior, devil girl." He winks, and although he's cute, this is not an ideal meet-cute.

"What the hell is going on here?"

My heart stalls, and suddenly, I'm chilled to the bone.

Both sets of hands on me freeze. I turn and lock onto a pair of dark-blue eyes that would stop anyone in their tracks.

"What does it look like, Barlow?"

It's determined: the younger referee has a death wish.

The older one mumbles a warning under his breath. "Wes…"

"Well…it looks like you no longer have jurisdiction over me." Kane is as cool and collected as ever. "There's no penalty box to protect you, Ref, so how about you take a step away before I start to think about the way you talked to me on the ice after your bogus roughing call and get angry all over again."

"Wes," the older referee says his name with more authority than before, and thankfully, it works.

The heavy hand around my waist disappears, and I let out a held breath.

"Calm down, Barlow," the rational referee says. "Her zipper is stuck."

Kane's jaw wiggles back and forth, but he must have much more respect for this referee, because he doesn't seem as lethal as before.

Not that he has any right to act all protective over me.

"I can take it from here, Jeff."

My mouth starts moving before my brain can catch up. "I think Jeff's got it."

Honestly, out of the three men in my vicinity, I think I trust Jeff the most.

Kane's hand slips around my waist, and I'm being dragged toward my dressing room. He shoves us both through the door and slams it shut.

As soon as he lets go of me, I glare at him. "What the hell is wrong with you, Kane?"

Only, he doesn't answer, because with the work that Jeff did on my zipper, my costume now falls to my hips, revealing much more of my body to Kane than I anticipated.

Sixteen

KANE

DON'T REACT.

It's just a pair of tits.

Nice tits. Not overly big, but at least a handful each.

Just like the rest of her, they've changed over the years—right along with her fiery attitude that I'd never had the pleasure of being on the other end of until recently.

Her hot glare is a form of flirting, if you ask me.

"Turn," I demand.

The little scowl she's trying to intimidate me with deepens when I don't give her the time or space to do as I ask. My palms find their way to her curved waist, and I spin her.

"What is your problem?" She peers over her shoulder at me, and even the slanting of her cheek is perfect.

"You," I answer with full transparency. "You're my problem."

"How so?" she shouts, frustration seeping out of her.

She tries to turn back around to face me, but I don't let her.

No.

I grip her waist again, and this time, I push her up against the door lightly and trap her there. Her gasp falls over her shoulder and down to my hand holding her hostage. "Are you trying to intimidate me?"

If I am, it's not working.

I have her pinned against the door with her back to me because I don't want to look into her eyes. They make me feel things I don't want to feel when it comes to her.

Like the protectiveness that swept through me when I saw Jeff and Wes touching her.

Or the raging jealousy that pulsed when Lars made a pass at her.

Or the fact that she's taking up space in my head while I'm on the ice simply because I know she may be watching me.

The pressure of being the best reaches new heights with her in my vicinity, and it's already so heavy that I can hardly unbury myself by the end of a game.

I finally answer her question with a clipped, *"No."*

"Then what are you doing? Because surely you're not helping me," she laughs sarcastically, and I suddenly remember how much I love her laugh.

God. This is not good.

My head is spinning, especially as I stare at the smooth skin beneath her bra straps. I have an alarming urge to grip her hair in my fist and tug her head back so I can have access to her neck.

My dick hardens at the thought, and being alone in this stuffy room behind a locked door isn't helping.

I react in the only way I know how to.

I get angry.

With her costume bundled in one of my fists, I pull it as hard as I can. The ripping of the fabric blends with my pounding heartbeat, and I watch as the frayed material falls freely from her body.

"Fixing the fucking problem," I seethe.

Unfortunately, I've created an entirely new problem. As soon as Daisy turns around in a wrath of anger, I get an eyeful of her standing there in nothing but her panties and bra. I know the image will haunt me for days to come.

Daisy's baby blues form into slits, but she's so shocked that nothing comes out of her mouth.

"No costume, no mascot," I say.

My chest swells with pride.

Now, maybe, I'll be able to play a decent game without wondering where she is and if she's watching me from the side.

I watch with a stone-cold expression as Daisy steps out of her torn costume. She kicks it toward me, landing at my feet. I make no move to look at it.

Daisy crosses her arms, mindlessly pushing her breasts up even higher. "I can't believe you just did that."

I cross my arms too. "Yes, you can."

She sighs loudly, and it pulls my attention to her heart-shaped lips. "Why does it matter to you if I'm the mascot?" she asks. "Oh, and in case you've forgotten, you were the one who got me the job."

"Because," I snarl, "it fucks with my head."

"How?!" She throws her hands up, and I wish she'd recross her arms, because at least it hides some of her body from me.

She didn't want you, Kane. Don't forget that.

The sting from that night still burns.

When I don't answer her, she hastily stomps over to her bag. She pulls out a pair of jeans and starts to pull them up her legs furiously.

I stand back against the door with my arms crossed, smirking at her flustered behavior.

Sure, I'm flustered too, but I've been shadowing my emotions for years. She doesn't have to know that I'm losing my mind while she's parading half-naked in front of me.

In nothing but her jeans and lacy bra, she heads for me.

Shit.

My dick says that she's winning this little war between us, but my head refuses to lose.

"How am I fucking with your head, Kane? I'm literally skating around in a ridiculous, giant devil costume." Her cheeks are red with frustration, and for a split second, I think about grabbing onto them and shutting her up with a kiss.

"I'm not even doing anything," she mumbles.

Doesn't she get it?

She doesn't have to do anything to press on my mind. She messes with my head by just existing. Daisy is everything that I could've had if I didn't take the wrong path. I was naive enough to think she would look beyond what was on the exterior, but it turned out neither of us knew each other like we thought.

There's a pulsing in my head that I can't ignore.

My blood pressure rises the longer she stares up at me with those pretty blue eyes, eyelashes fluttering every few seconds.

Don't let her win.

With quick reflexes, I have her pinned to the door again. A gasp flies from her mouth, and I want to catch it with my own *so* fucking badly.

"You want to know how you're fucking with my head, Daisy?" I ask quietly.

She turns her head to hear me, but the only thing it does is give me clear access to her slender neck. I eye her racing pulse thumping against the soft skin, and it gives me just enough energy to finish what I started.

My knee nestles in between her legs as I grab both of her hands and press them above her head. Her wrists are so tiny in my grasp that I can easily pin them there with one of my hands. The excitement it brings me to have her trapped should terrify her.

Look at her, caught in my clutches, just like I was caught in hers years ago.

"You feel this?" I ask, gliding my other hand to her lower back.

I pull her tight to my body, and a hot breath escapes her lips. "Do you feel the pull between us?"

Daisy gulps, and I stare at her mouth. I lift my hand and brush my thumb against her plump bottom lip so gently it tricks her into thinking I'm going to be soft with her, but that's not who I am anymore.

Her eyes widen as soon as my hand slips to her neck.

To my surprise, she doesn't pull away. Daisy's sexy little body is still pressed into mine, and I know she can feel how hard I am.

It takes everything in me not to rub against her.

I want her.

I still fucking want her.

My heart skips a beat, and I immediately pull myself away from those dangerous thoughts.

"Well?" I put a little more pressure on her neck just to get her attention. Once I have it, I skim my palm over every one of her curves, ending at her thigh. My fingers dig into the denim before I scoop her leg up and wrap it around my waist. I do what I say I wouldn't and push into her.

A raspy noise hits my ears, and I bury my head into the crook of her neck so I don't do something I'll regret.

Like kiss her.

My fingers sweep up her leg until I reach the curve of her ass. While palming it, I flick my tongue against the delicate skin along her jawline, and it pulls a faint whimper from her.

I clench my eyes.

You've made your point, Kane.

But have I?

I whisper seductively in her ear, "Am I inside your head like you're in mine?"

She doesn't need to answer me, because I already know.

There's heat pooling between her legs and pebbled bumps brushing my chest through the thin material of her bra.

"Do you feel me everywhere?" I run my nose down her jawline before pulling back abruptly to look into her eyes.

A hot swallow works down my throat.

If she asked me to fuck her right now, I would. But she won't. She's much too stubborn for that.

"This is what you do to me by simply *existing*. I don't want you at the rink anymore."

I drop her hands and back away quickly. I keep my expression blank in an attempt to hide just how much touching her tortured me. I was trying to prove a point, but I think I only made things worse for myself.

Daisy exhales like she was holding her breath the entire time. The room grows small, and it's so tight neither of us can move. Instead, we stare at each other like we're at a crossroads.

Stay on track, Kane.

Snapping myself out of the trance I'm in, I turn and grab her shirt from the pile of clothes and toss it to her. The cotton hits directly on her chest, thankfully hiding her breasts.

"Get dressed. If you're not at my car in ten minutes, call an Uber."

And with that, I fling the door open and stalk down the hall, praying that she finds herself a new job so I can at least play hockey without her playing her own game inside my head.

Seventeen

DAISY

A SMALL HONDA pulls up at the curb, and I check the license plate before opening the door.

As soon as I fling it open, I freeze.

Confusion hits me as I stare at a sleeping baby tucked safely inside a carseat.

"Oh, sorry. Do you mind sitting up front?" I bend down and meet the face of the Uber driver who looks to be my age.

I quietly shut the door, hopeful not to disrupt the little girl's sleep, and slip into the front seat.

"Reese?" I say my driver's name, double-checking that she's the right Uber.

"Yeah." She smiles shyly before flicking her blinker on to pull out into traffic. "Sorry about...the baby. My sitter fell through, and I can't really afford not to work." She glances in the rearview mirror. "Thankfully, she sleeps well in the car. She won't scream or anything."

"Even if she was screaming, I'd much rather catch a ride with you instead of Kane." I sigh angrily. "He is...ugh...I don't even know!" I cross my arms and fume in the front seat. "I knew he was just trying to get in my head, and I can't believe I let him."

As soon as I turn toward Reese, I slap my hand over my mouth.

Kane has me so twisted that I forgot I'm in a car with a random person—someone who clearly isn't a licensed therapist if she's trying to make extra money by Ubering late at night with a baby.

"I'm so sorry," I mutter quietly through a laugh. "Ignore me."

Reese smashes her lips together, clearly trying to hide her amusement. "It's okay. I've been there and done that..." She glances in the rearview mirror again. "Gained a little something from it too."

I peek behind me at who I assume is her daughter. She's quite honestly the cutest thing I have ever seen with her footie pajamas and purple binky half hanging out of her mouth.

"She's adorable," I whisper.

The lights of the dash show off her mom's softening gaze. "Thanks. She forced me to grow up a little quicker than most, but she's worth the late nights and odd jobs to make ends meet." Her shoulders drop a smidge, and there's a sadness in her tone.

"Are you from here?" I ask, wanting to get her mind off the sad topic.

Does she have family to help her? I get the hunch that the baby's dad isn't in the picture, but I'd like to think that if I were to get pregnant, my family would help me in any way they could.

Though, I know not everyone's family is good.

Take Kane's family, for example—a brother who is selfish beyond belief and a mom who holds a grudge.

She shakes her head. "Are you?"

"No. I just moved here a couple of weeks ago. Hence why I'm spilling my guts to a random Uber driver." I snort. "I usually spill everything to my best friend, but she doesn't live here, so lucky you."

I glance at Reese again. With her dark hair piled on top of her head and warm eyes, she sort of resembles Natalia. Though, Natalia has much more of a firecracker personality than what I've seen from Reese so far.

She seems...soft...and sweet.

"Well..." Reese veers off toward the exit. "You're welcome to use me as your sounding board. My friends back home used to call me Mother Teresa because they said I had the best advice and made all the right choices." She laughs quietly. "Pretty ironic that I was the one of our friend group who had to drop out of college because I got pregnant...but whatever."

I shrug. "It's fine. Every—"

"—thing's fine," she finishes for me.

We both look at each other and laugh quietly, careful not to wake her daughter.

"I'm not exactly on the path I thought I'd end up on either," I admit. "I had to drop out of college too, and now I'm the mascot for the Blue Devils, so ya know..."

She taps on the brakes and shoots me a bewildered look. "The mascot?"

I shoot her a look. "Unfortunately."

"It's fine. Everything's fine," she mutters.

We share a smile, and it only takes me a few seconds to decide that Reese is as good as anyone to delve deeper into my thoughts over Kane.

By the time I come up for air, she's pulling in front of the apartment building with her jaw on the floor.

"I can't believe he ripped it!" She's just as appalled as me. "What an asshole. I am so tired of men thinking they have the upper hand."

"Right?" I cross my arms. "I cannot let him get away with it. He's bullying me like a child. We're not in high school anymore." I gaze at my apartment building with dread. Knowing Kane, he's probably brought some girl home and is having sex with her in the elevator again, just waiting for me to step onto it.

Reese's phone pings for another ride, interrupting our unexpected hangout session. "Oh, right. You gotta go." I grab the door handle.

"Wait." I turn toward her, and she's smiling deviously. "I have an idea to get back at him."

Her phone pings again, and her baby sighs wistfully in her sleep.

"Here." Reese pulls a receipt out of her purse and scribbles her number on it. "Text me your number, and we can meet up."

I latch onto the paper with desperation and tuck it into my back pocket, then I climb out of her car and whisper, "Be safe!"

Just then, her baby lets out a cry, and we both snap our attention to the backseat. Her binky has fallen out onto her lap.

In a panic, I reach toward the backseat and quickly pop it back into her mouth. She sucks on it for a few seconds before she seemingly falls right back to sleep.

Reese blows out a thankful breath. "Thank you."

I smile, and she quickly drives off.

I turn and stare at the apartment building door and pray that Kane isn't waiting for me on the other side.

———

I anxiously wait for Reese to hear her idea on how to get back at Kane. The coffee shop is right around the corner from Dr.

Gibson's office, and I have forty minutes to spare until my appointment with him to review my labs. I tap my fingers against my mug full of matcha until I see a stroller pop through the door.

I quickly move to stand up, but an eager man beats me to it, holding it open for Reese.

"Thank you." She smiles kindly, and unaware to her, he's practically drooling.

Reese is beyond beautiful—and her daughter is too.

"Hey!" I turn toward the stroller. The bright-eyed baby with the prettiest olive skin is staring at me with a toy in her hand. "Look at you! You're awake!" I scrunch my nose at her while smiling and turn toward Reese.

"She is so beautiful, Reese."

With admiration, she peers down at her daughter. "Thanks. Charleigh is my little ray of sunshine in the shit-storm I've found myself in." She laughs and rolls her eyes before locking onto the coffee I snagged for her. "Oh my god, is this mine?"

"No, it's for Charleigh," I joke.

Reese's eyebrows fold.

"I'm kidding," I laugh. "Yes, it's for you."

She quickly pulls the mug closer to her face. "Oh, it's still hot. I haven't had a hot coffee in..."—she glances at the stroller—"eight months."

Reese sips on the coffee before sighing wistfully. I'm not going to pretend I know anything about being a mom—a single one, at that—but Reese acts as if the cup of coffee is a million dollars. It makes me wonder how difficult her life is.

Either way, she wears the hardship well.

"Okay," Reese places the cup down and pulls out a tattered notebook. She cradles it to her chest and smiles at me. "I don't know if my idea will work, but since your costume is ruined, what if..."

The notebook flips open to a pencil sketch of a woman who looks a lot like me wearing a much-improved Blue Devils costume with skates on her feet, a devil-horned headband, and a trident in her hand.

"Holy shit," I whisper. "Did you draw this?"

Reese blushes while shrugging innocently. "I was a fashion major before I dropped out of college. I minored in marketing too."

I scan the drawing again, my stomach jittering with excitement. "This is amazing."

"I figured instead of fixing the costume, why don't you just get a new one? I researched the Chicago Blue Devils, and they've had the same costume since the team was established years ago. Their marketing needs some serious work." She sips on her coffee. "I have no idea if you're able to bring the idea to whoever is in charge, but"—she taps on the sketch—"*this* will amp up their marketing for sure. It'll pull in new merch too. The trident can be sold in their store, devils headbands for the little girls, and as you can see, the costume isn't overly sexual or anything. I mean, you'd still look hot, but it's respectful enough for the little girls to look up to you."

I nod through the entire explanation, thankful I have a plan for when I talk to Cindy. Explaining to her that Kane followed me into my dressing room and tore my costume to shreds so I would be forced to quit is going to make me seem certifiable and him unhinged.

Reese smiles over the brim of her mug. "Think Elsa but less ice queen and more she-devil."

I sit back with my matcha and beam on the inside. Showing up to the game like this will definitely send a message to my own personal bully.

Kane can take the costume out of the girl, but he can't take the girl out of the costume.

I pull out my phone and quickly text Cindy.

> Hi, Cindy! Could you meet up later? I want to talk to you about something before the next home game.

Reese and I take turns playing with Charleigh in between having our own conversation while I wait for Cindy to text me back.

My phone starts to vibrate with Cindy's name at the top.

"Hello?"

Cindy's exhale is so heavy I think I can feel it through the phone. "Please tell me you're not quitting."

If Kane had his way, I would.

"No! I'm not quitting. But I do have a problem with the costume...except, instead of repairing it, I think there's a better option."

"A better option?" she asks hesitantly.

I lock eyes with Reese while I speak into the phone to Cindy. "Can you meet up later?"

I grin at Reese, and she looks both excited and scared. I mouth to her, "*Are you free later?*"

A worry line works on her face, but she gives me a thumbs-up.

"Let's meet at the rink around 5?"

Cindy agrees, and I hang the phone up.

Reese and I lock eyes before bursting into girly laughter.

Charleigh makes a noise, and when we look at her, she's showing off her two teeth with a grin on her face.

Knowing I need to get to my appointment, I stand up to leave with Reese following after me but not before she downs the rest of her coffee.

"Don't forget to bring the sketchbook," I say, bending down to smile at Charleigh. "You're getting all the credit for this."

"That's really not necessary." Reese shakes her head. "I'm happy to help."

I shoot her a look. "It is necessary. I have to go run an... errand, so I'll see you at 5?"

She nods. "Do you want me to pick you up?"

"Sure." I smile.

"Perfect! See you in a few."

I wait until she heads toward her car with Charleigh and the stroller before going in the other direction toward my appointment. My stomach churns with dread the closer I get to the brick building in fear that my labs are going to show my levels rising from the added stress of moving.

Or maybe from the stress that Kane has inevitably brought me.

You don't understand how fragile your health is until it turns to shit within the blink of an eye, and your future is dangling like a soggy french fry in front of your face.

Eighteen

KANE

IT ISN'T OFTEN that an impulsive idea of mine works out, but the hockey gods must be on my side lately because I haven't seen Daisy since I crossed various lines in that stuffy dressing room with her.

Unfortunately, my head is spinning, but it has nothing to do with her.

I grip my phone and reread the text.

UNKNOWN

Kane, I've found myself in a less-than-ideal situation. Can you help me out?

How can one message make my chest tight with anxiety? I deleted Miles's number a long time ago because it changed so often. I was sick of deleting and resaving another, but I know when it's him, even if we go months without a conversation.

I place my phone on the bench beside me and start to lace my skates—the left one first, as always. The team is talking amongst themselves, Hart and Emory having an in-depth conversation about someone on the opposing team, but I can't be bothered to chime in because I'm trying to figure out a response to another piece of the past creeping up to haunt me.

My phone vibrates again, and I crack my neck.

Don't text him back until later.

UNKNOWN

I know I've said it before, but this will be the last time. I swear.

If I had a fucking dime for every time he's said that to me and I put it in an account for him, he'd never be in debt again.

"You ready?" Malaki sits right next to my phone to lace his own skates.

I angrily toss the annoying device into my locker, hopeful that I've cracked the screen so I physically can't respond to the text.

"I'm always ready."

He eyes me suspiciously, sensing my already angry mood.

I ignore him to grab my stick and black tape. Starting at the heel, I sink into a type of solace no one would understand as I begin wrapping it.

Fifteen times.

I smooth the edges methodically and embrace my inner quiet.

My nostrils flare whenever something other than the game starts to peer over the mental walls I've thrown up, but as soon as they're in place, I stand and head for the ice. My heart rams against my ribs as I stride through the tunnel. The arena comes into view, and I inhale deeply.

Home.

I find a puck after stepping onto the ice, the crowd clapping in the background.

I block the noise easily, like it's second nature. I fiddle with the black biscuit until I send it soaring into the net.

A few of my teammates are stretching, while others are skating around, getting familiar with the puck.

Rhodes is near the glass, talking to his daughter—who is admittedly the cutest pain in the ass ever—and her nanny, who I guess is his girlfriend now too.

I learned that the hard way.

It's fun to piss him off, though, so there are no regrets there.

Malaki skates over to me, and I do my best to ignore him as I bend down to stretch. One leg goes out in front of me and then the other. He follows my moves, and as soon as we make eye contact, he smiles like a fool.

"What?" I snap.

"I like the energy, man."

I scoff. "What energy?"

He begins stretching against the ice like he's starring in a pornographic video.

"Stop dry-humping the ice."

He points his glove at me. "That energy. You're more testy than usual. We're going to need it. Have you seen who the line ref is?"

Hopefully not the one I almost put through a wall the other night when I found him salivating over Daisy.

"Who?"

Before he can answer, the crowd starts to make a ruckus.

Minnesota must have taken the ice.

I stand and shake my arms out before cracking my neck.

"What the hell—" Malaki's dry chuckle snags my attention. "Who is that?" He pauses. "*Ohhhhh* no."

Not bothering to turn to see what he's staring at, I sigh. "What?"

"Uh…" Malaki's mouth forms a straight line, like he's trying not to laugh.

"I'm not patient enough for your bullshit," I mutter.

With a half turn, I see what has the crowd going wild. My blood runs hot, and if I wasn't so steady on skates, I'd have slipped and fallen.

I'm going to kill her.

Deep in my bones, I knew it was too good to be true. Daisy Sullivan is no coward. Why would I assume that she'd retreat after I ripped her costume to shreds? I should have expected that she'd have something else up her sleeve. She always did keep me on my toes, but *shit.*

I didn't think she'd do…this.

My vision blurs with anger, but the closer I get to her, the clearer my sight becomes.

Why does she have to be so alluring?

Daisy is the pretty lone flower in a field of men craving her attention. Devil horns and all, she's gaining the attention of every single person in the arena. The men want her, and the women want to be her.

"Let's give our new mascot a *huge* Blue Devil welcome!"

I glare at Cindy with her microphone and headset on. *Was this her doing?*

Daisy, who is dressed in a sort of figure-skater dress, does a simple two-foot turn on her skates with a wave of her devil trident. The apples of her cheeks shimmer with some type of sparkle, and she looks more like an ice princess versus a devil.

My heart screams inside my chest as I attempt to glare at her, but just looking at her softens something inside of me.

I hate it.

My teammates tap their sticks against the ice as Cindy hands Daisy the microphone. The urge to skate across the rink, fling her over my shoulder, and send her packing is almost blinding.

This is on national television.

When it comes to Daisy, I have to react precisely, when there aren't millions of eyes on us.

With one hand on the microphone and the other holding her trident, her sweet voice fills my head as well as everyone in the arena.

"Let's give it up for our Blue Devils!"

The crowd screams and claps, most of them rising to their feet.

I stay in my exact spot, likely melting the ice beneath my skates from the heat I'm feeling.

Daisy exchanges the microphone for blue foam tridents that Cindy gives her and takes off toward the glass. My breath lodges inside my throat when little kids come running down the steps with their arms stretched out wide for one of them.

Great, the whole fucking fan base loves her.

Even my teammates.

Ninety percent of them are standing around with their sticks loose in their grip and a haze covering their face—that haze being Daisy fucking Sullivan.

"Get to warming up," I shout on my drive-by toward our new mascot.

It snaps them out of their fantasies, and they go back to stretching. My jaw grinds back and forth while I watch Daisy attempt to throw a trident over the glass. One drops to the ice, and she bends over to retrieve it.

I stare at the perfect view of her ass.

Sure, there's a flimsy see-through piece of fabric there, but it does nothing to hide her body.

When she attempts to throw the trident again, she stretches herself as much as she can, revealing the mesh, skin-colored material along her torso.

My mouth runs dry when I get a side-glimpse of her breast. The mental walls I carefully built earlier to block everything out, except for hockey, crumble, blending right in with the ice shavings my skates are currently making while I rush the edge of the arena.

I stop abruptly when black-and-white stripes slip into the picture.

My least favorite referee appears beside her.

Wes.

My fingers tingle inside my gloves.

I'd love to punch his smug face, especially when he singles me out on the ice. Even more so now that he's hovering over Daisy.

The outer parts of my vision tint with anger when Wes's hand slips around Daisy's waist. He helps her throw a trident over the glass.

Don't do anything in haste, Kane.

I picture myself ramming into him so hard he smashes into the glass, but I can't do that.

I can't let my irritation over Daisy bleed onto the ice and ruin the only thing I have keeping me afloat.

A fuming breath erupts from my mouth as I reel myself in.

I stop right beside Daisy, my skates digging into the ice between us. If I went an inch farther, I'd have bumped into her. I would have saved her from falling on the ice, but I may have accidentally choked Wes in the process.

Lost opportunity.

"Look who it is...my favorite referee," I grit.

Wes smirks, knowing he's already under my skin. Daisy, on the other hand, looks startled. Her pretty pink lips part, and I can't stop staring at the blue shimmer on her high cheekbones.

"Nice outfit." I snort.

Her eyebrows cave but only for a split second.

The next, they're rising to her hairline with shock because I quickly steal the rest of the tridents out of her hand and toss most over the glass to various fans.

"It's not nice to steal things that don't belong to you," Daisy scolds me, yet she keeps her pretty smile on her face for the eyes watching us.

I play nice for the same reason she is and smile. "It's not the first time I've stolen something from you, is it?"

Her lips part as she sucks in a sharp breath.

Seeing her cheeks ripen makes my entire night.

Wes leans forward, but I cut him off before he can put his nonsense into the mix.

"Did you hear that, Stripes?" I slowly skate backward. "Shouldn't steal things that aren't yours."

His gaze slides to Daisy before circling back to me. I raise an eyebrow. *You get it? Leave her alone.*

Not waiting for his silent answer, I skate toward Ellie, Rhodes's daughter, and throw her the last foam trident. She screams with glee, and I wink at her.

When I turn around to head toward center ice, I catch Daisy climbing off the ice, but not before she gives one more wave to the crowd and a scathing glare over at me.

Nineteen

DAISY

I HAVE nine text messages waiting for me on my phone when the game is over. Luckily, with my new costume, courtesy of Reese, the zipper doesn't get stuck, and I'm able to slip out of it and head home before anyone can corner me.

By anyone, I mean Kane.

Or Wes.

For a second, I had the thought of bringing Wes home just to piss Kane off, because there is clearly some tension between them. I caught the implied threat from Kane when he told Wes that he shouldn't steal things that aren't his.

As if Kane owns me? *The nerve.*

But the second Wes started to terrorize Kane during the game, sending him to the sin bin a few times for unnecessary penalties, I decided against that plan.

I found myself fuming from the side. For one, I am not a toy, and for two, stop bullying *my* bully.

I scoff and toss my bag to the floor of my apartment.

How ridiculous of a thought.

Sinking onto the couch that I don't even think my brother has spent a single day on, I open my phone and start answering messages.

> **REESE**
>
> You looked so good! Did you make it home okay? I wish you would've let me give you a ride.

Reese, who I demanded take credit for the idea of my new costume, was paid by the Blue Devils, courtesy of Cindy, which meant she could afford to take a few days off here and there. I refused to have her pick me up tonight.

The other Uber driver grunted at me a few times, but I made it home just fine.

After texting her back, I move on to my next message.

> **NATALIA**
>
> I never thought I'd say this, but I kind of want to be a mascot now. 😂

> **NATALIA**
>
> Omg. You're literally going viral. LMAO 🤣

Am I?

I pull up social media and start to scroll.

My stomach ties with knots the more I look at the videos and photos.

A roll of nausea goes through me, and I'm not sure if it's from the sudden attention I'm receiving, the lingering thoughts of Kane glaring at me, or from the extra labs that Dr. Gibson wanted to take as a precaution.

My other labs were still within normal range, though more elevated than normal.

I've been more fatigued too, but given my new job, I think that's to be expected.

I move to my brother's text.

RIVER

WTF

RIVER

Please tell me you were the mascot before the outfit change.

RIVER

Is this the job that Kane got you? I hate that I didn't see this in person.

RIVER

I need photos.

RIVER

Never mind. I know Kane has a stash. I'll text him.

I roll my eyes. I'm sure Kane does.

ME

You're annoying

RIVER

The fucking mascot

ME

BYE

RIVER

Jokes aside, are you feeling okay? That's gotta be tiring.

I am tired.

ME

I'm fine. Being active is good for me.

I click my phone off and lie in silence.

My body is tired, and my head is pounding. Instead of making my way to bed, I stay on the couch and go over the game in my head. There was one little girl who looked at me like I was a queen instead of a mascot, and I'll admit, it was sort of sweet. The job isn't all that bad, and it really is good for me to be active. It keeps my muscles loose, and it's supposed to improve my fatigue.

The only con is Kane.

The scathing looks he continued to give me most of the night were hard to ignore, and the more I think about it, the more nauseated I become. To think I gave up flirting with the cute referee because I felt protective over Kane is absurd. It's like a slap to my own face.

With a huff, I sit up and glance at the Devil's mascot head lying near the door. The wheels start turning as I glance to the ceiling, knowing that Kane is just one floor above me. I swing my legs off the couch and head toward the devil's head and trident propped in the corner.

My immaturity rises to a whole new level, but Kane brings something out in me that has my thoughts spiraling. My blood boils when I think about him tearing my costume and threatening any guy who dares to look at me. Then I boil in other places with the recent memory of his hands on me inside my dressing room.

Ugh.

The new and improved mascot costume doesn't seem like enough to gain the upper hand.

This probably won't either, but at least it'll make me feel better.

I hold my breath as I wait for the elevator to open. When it shows up empty, I exhale and step onto it with the devil's head and trident trapped in my arm. The last-minute note I wrote is clutched tightly in my fingers when the elevator whooshes upward, pulling my stomach to the floor.

I bend over and clutch it as sweat starts to pool along my spine.

A wave of nausea hits me again, and I realize pretty quickly that I'm not nauseated from thoughts of Kane but because my body is tired.

The elevator door slides open to reveal Kane's door—the only one in the hall. I swallow my thick spit and drag myself over to it.

I bend at my knees and place the mascot head on the floor. I take the torn piece of paper with my quick-witted note written on it and stab it onto one of the trident prongs.

You don't own me, Kane. But maybe this will suffice.

Xo

Feeling proud of my handiwork, I stand up on shaky legs and dust my hands off. The floor moves beneath my feet, and I sway. My palm slaps against Kane's door to save my face from colliding with it before I abruptly back away and jam my finger against the elevator button.

Shit, hurry up.

Heat prickles my hairline, and my stomach twists. The hallway begins to close in on me.

No, no, no.

This wouldn't be the first time I've fainted, but no matter how many times I've done it in the past, there is no preparing for it.

I'm seconds from collapsing.

The elevator opens, and I dart inside. I turn and rest my back against the cool wall.

My breaths are ragged as I try to breathe in and out of my nose.

I need to lie down.

Before I'm safely tucked away in the empty elevator, Kane's door swings wide open.

He's standing there in nothing but low-hanging sweats and damp hair. After seeing my gift, he angles his sturdy chin toward me inside the elevator, and his blue eyes darken. I attempt to smile, but he disappears altogether when my vision blurs, and I collapse against the floor.

Twenty

KANE

WHAT THE FUCK JUST HAPPENED?

One second, I'm holding a ripped piece of paper in my hand from my own personal devil, and the next, I'm jogging to the elevator because the little culprit crumples to the floor right in front of me.

I shove my finger onto the elevator button over and over again and watch the number drop to the floor beneath me before seeing an up arrow. If I use the stairs, it'll take twice as long.

"Come on." I press the button again.

My mind is racing.

Is she toying with me to see if I'll come to her rescue? At this point, it wouldn't surprise me. We're clearly at war with one another, and up until now, I thought I'd win. But with the way my pulse is rising from watching her collapse, I'm not so sure.

I'm ready when the door opens.

I rush into it with adrenaline backing my every move, but she's nowhere to be found.

She *is* fucking with me.

I grip the note in my fingers and read it.

You don't own me, Kane. But maybe this will
suffice.
Xo

Nothing would suffice.

I crumple the note and throw it off to the side as soon as the door slides open on her floor, revealing her standing there with her back to me. I stalk toward her and snake my arm around her waist to spin her so she's facing me.

"You think you're so clever..." My words fade.

What I expected to see was Daisy's bright blue eyes burning with fire inside of them, ready to go toe-to-toe with me. But instead of seeing her flushed cheeks, I'm met with a pale face and cloudy gaze. There's a little worry line etched in between her eyebrows that has my own worry rising.

"Daisy?" I snap. "Stop fucking around."

Her legs give out, and I'm forced to pull her flush against my body. When her forehead hits my shoulder, I realize she's in a cold sweat.

I'm good under pressure, but seeing her like this has made me less agile and more jerky. I give her a little shake with my fingers digging into her biceps. Her head flops to the side, and I panic. My palm cups her cheek, and my fingers disappear into her hair.

"Daisy." I blurt her name again, this time less angry and more worried.

She seems to come to, her eyelashes fluttering. "I need..."

Her hands weakly grab onto my shoulders like they're a life-line. "To…"

I open her door and pull us inside.

"River?" I shout, hoping he's home.

"Not here," she mumbles, eyes still closed.

"What do you need? What is wrong with you?" I ask.

"Lay me down," she slurs.

I pick her up and cradle her to my chest. My heart pounds, and there's a ringing in my ears.

Without her consent, I sit down with her still in my arms to keep her steady. Slow, shaky breaths escape her mouth as she buries her head farther into the crook of my neck. One of her arms wraps around her stomach, like she's sick, and little sweat droplets dot her neck.

Instead of pestering her with questions, I remain quiet and try to wrap my head around the adrenaline rush I just got from seeing her in distress.

It feels so right to have her in my arms and so wrong to see her suffering.

Several minutes pass, and the sweat has finally dried on her smooth skin. Her breathing is less labored, and the pounding of her pulse has slowed.

"Do you need water?" My tone makes me sound bored, which is exactly what I planned. There is absolutely no way I am letting her know that her little show just affected me so much I can't even think correctly.

She shakes her head and exhales slowly.

"What do you need?" By asking her this, I'm forfeiting.

I might as well wave the white fucking flag.

You win, Daisy.

You fucking win.

"To stay still," she croaks.

I nod, more to myself than her, and lean farther back onto

the couch. I wish it irritated me to know I'm going to have her draped over me for a while, but it doesn't.

Eventually, Daisy seems to fall asleep.

I know this because she's managed to pin me like she's afraid I'm going to disappear. One of her arms wraps around my waist, and her bent leg gives me no other option but to rest my arm along it, trapping her just like she's trapping me.

At some point, I doze off.

I wake to the orange sun slowly rising over the skyscrapers that stand tall outside of Daisy's floor-to-ceiling windows. Her plants are lined up nicely against the glass, and I can't help but grin at the few clumps of soil on the floor between the pots, like she was messing with them recently.

Memories of her in the little makeshift garden come in like a tidal wave. That little sundress showing off her toned legs, no shoes, freckles from the sun on the bridge of her nose while she looked at me with those baby blues from across her parents' backyard.

I was so gone for her.

Grinding my jaw back and forth, I focus on the coffee table that my legs are propped on so I don't stare at her. If I had my phone, I'd text her brother right now and tell him about the incident, but it's upstairs in my own apartment.

Rushing to Daisy's aid without it gives me a great excuse to ignore the unwanted texts anyway.

Did I even shut the door after I ran after her?

I grunt quietly.

Probably not.

It doesn't matter, though.

Material things are replaceable.

She isn't.

I'd know, since I've tried replacing her since the moment I left.

I zero in on the notebook near my foot.

My eyebrow rises with mischief.

I move as discreetly as possible while sliding the notebook closer to the edge of the coffee table. Once it's hanging off the edge, I reach forward and grab a hold of it.

Daisy sighs softly, her warm breath brushing against my bare chest. I freeze until she slips into her slumber again.

With slow and steady fingers, I flip through the pages and snoop.

It's like high school all over again when River and I would sneak into her room to read her diary.

I found out things I wish I hadn't from that little polka-dot diary. It caused my first fistfight outside of the rink.

Collin Hennings. *Little fucker.*

The first thing I read in her new diary is **Tracker**.

Tracker? What is she keeping track of? All the ways she can irritate me?

I glance at Daisy to make sure she's still asleep before pulling the notebook closer to get a better look.

There are several symptoms listed with dates.

Fatigue, achy, loss of appetite, nausea.

What the hell is this?

I close the notebook and push it off to the side. My chest is tight with worry, and I'm agitated that I'm out of the loop. Maybe if I hadn't avoided home for the last several years or dismissed any talk about Daisy from River or their parents, I'd know what's going on.

A rough swallow moves down my throat while I drag my eyes over Daisy's delicate jawline. Her cute, button-like nose is the same from before, and those parted lips are a perfect shade of pink that I haven't let myself visualize in so long.

She was beautiful when we were teens, but her features are more defined now...just like these curves. I bet she catches the eye of every man from here to New York and back.

I grab her phone from the couch cushion and enter her password.

I scowl when I realize she's changed it. It only takes me a few attempts to get it right, because I know her better than she thinks.

I snap a photo of the page in her notebook, careful not to get her body draped over mine in the frame, and send it off to her brother.

> It's Kane. Want to tell me what the fuck this is and why I found your sister mid-faint a little bit ago?

A little bit ago, last night...he won't know the difference.

I place her phone on my chest and wait.

Daisy won't tell me what's going on with her—I know that for certain.

But her brother will.

Twenty-One

DAISY

MY HEAD POUNDS VIOLENTLY. I clench my eyes together and inhale.

Mmm. What is that smell?

I sniff again.

The scent is familiar, yet I can't name it.

With my eyes still closed, I lean forward and inhale one more time.

"Can you stop sniffing me?"

My eyelids fly open, and I'm left to stare at two very defined pecs.

Great.

I quickly analyze the situation. One arm is wrapped around his annoyingly toned torso while my leg drapes over his lap. There's something resting on my thigh that I can only assume is his hand and—

"Trying to come up with an escape route?" he asks.

There's no way out of this.

I barely lift a shoulder. "That or a plan on how to murder you and get away with it."

Kane's deep chuckle vibrates his chest. I finally get the nerve to peek at him, and all I'm left to stare at is his bobbing throat and stony jawline.

My lungs beg for air.

Space.

I need space.

I slowly begin to slide off his lap. My arm brushes against his bare skin, and his head snaps toward my movement.

He levels me with a dark glare. "Not a fucking chance."

His hand disappears from my leg, and he grabs my arm with a firm grip to keep me in place.

Something flares so brightly within his dark eyes that I flush with heat.

"I've got you right where I want you, Daisy-Petal."

My teeth sink into my lip. I pull back on my arm, but he's too strong for me on a good day, let alone a day where I'm weak.

Kane's eyebrow rises. "You're not going anywhere until you tell me what the hell that was last night."

I quickly go over the events that led me to the scenario I currently find myself in: tangled up with my brother's best friend who hates me.

Has he been here all night with me? In his arms?

I search the coffee table, remembering I'd left my notebook there.

"Where is my notebook?" I ask.

His mouth twitches. "What notebook?"

I sigh.

I do not have the energy to deal with this.

Sensing my irritation, he pulls it out and waves it in front of my face. His grip loosens around me, and I take the opportunity to scramble out of his lap.

The last little bit of air trapped in my lungs rushes out as I fall to my butt. "Oof."

Kane leans forward with a look of disapproval on his features, but instead of helping me to my feet, he just rolls his eyes in the most annoyingly hot way that I have ever seen and relaxes back onto the couch.

What does one do when they wake up in their enemy's arms?

Run. *Obviously.*

I carefully climb to my feet. My head pounds as I turn to head...where?

This is my apartment. He's the one who needs to leave.

Without making an idiot of myself, I smooth my features and spin to face him. "You need to leave."

Kane makes absolutely no attempt to even acknowledge me. In fact, he doesn't even look up from his...wait, that's my phone!

My hands fly to my hips. "Give me my phone!"

"Oh this?" He nods to the device in his hand.

"Yes! What are you doing on my phone?" I scoff. "Making sure Wes didn't try to swoop in and *steal* me via text message?"

Kane's grip tightens against the device. "He has your number?"

Of course not.

I shrug. "Maybe."

He glares at me, and I suddenly see why other players steer clear of him on the ice.

Finally, Kane drops my phone to his lap and rests both of his arms on the back of my couch.

"You can have your phone back after you tell me what's going on with you." He taps his fingers on the couch, like he's waiting for my explanation.

I'm not sure why he even cares, but either way, I'm not telling him anything.

I cross my arms over my braless chest. *I love that for me.* "Or I can just grab it from you," I counter.

Kane drops his chin and stares at my phone resting in his lap.

"Okay, Little Miss Confident, come and get it."

A challenge? Don't mind if I do.

I walk carefully, because I'm not so trusting of my balance after last night, until I'm standing right in front of him.

His sexy smirk drives me up a wall. My fingers itch with anticipation.

He remains unmoving with his arms still resting along the back of the couch like a smug asshole. Little flickers of his abs catch my eye that I try my hardest to ignore.

Although we seem to be at an impasse, neither of us moving, we're dancing around each other with buzzing energy.

The haughty look in his eye is all the push I need to get the job done.

I am not the little virgin teenager that he knew years ago. Dicks don't scare me anymore.

Even his.

One.

Two.

Three.

My arm stretches forward, and my palm slaps against the phone, but before I can curl my fingers around it, Kane flexes his hips and traps me there with his hand. There's a rigid outline that my fingertips brush against, and my thighs clench absentmindedly.

Shit, I hope he didn't notice that.

"Tell me what's going on with you," he grits.

I wonder if I could make him beg.

"Let my hand go, and I will," I whisper.

"I'm enjoying the placement, actually." He winks.

"With my hand on your dick?" I blurt.

He drops his attention to my boobs. "I was referring to your tits in my face. Did those grow over the last few years?"

I look down only to see my shirt gaping open from the angle. *Ugh.*

"It's apparent that you like them." I press on his hard length to make a point, but all that does is make his pupils dilate.

Suddenly, I'm swept off my feet and tossed onto his lap. My hands fly to his shoulders as both my legs wrap around his waist.

How the hell—

He's too swift for his own good.

"I have a hard-on because I have to take a piss, Daisy-Petal." Kane grips my hips, and for a split second, I think he's going to guide me back and forth against him. I completely ignore the fact that I *want* him to. "Surely you didn't think I was turned on because of your body being on mine all night."

My eyebrows knit together. "Of course I didn't think that!"

Kane smirks and raises an eyebrow.

Annoyed and unable to keep up with this charade, I push off him and stomp away.

His laugh follows me all the way to the kitchen, where I start to make my matcha.

"You win," I call over my shoulder. "I'm too tired to deal with you today, so if you could see yourself out, that'd be great."

His dark chuckle races up my spine. "I'm not leaving until you tell me what this is."

I glance toward the living room, and he's still sitting in the same spot on the couch with his back to me. His hair is a darker blond now, likely from spending all his time inside an ice rink instead of underneath the sun outside. He waves my notebook in the air, and my hand freezes with the frother still spinning in mid-air.

"Still snooping around in my things? Grow up, Kane."

I take my anger out on my matcha, frothing it so much it's a foamy mess by the end. Refusing to admit defeat in any part of my morning, I take my too bubbly latte and sip on it while mentally sending daggers into the back of Kane's head.

I feel much better this morning than last night, but I'm still not one hundred percent. I'm sluggish, and my limbs are heavy. Every time I blink, my eyelashes flutter too many times in their attempt to stay open.

Half of my matcha is gone by the time Kane climbs from the couch.

Just when I sigh in relief from his departure, he heads into River's bathroom with my phone still in his possession.

Ugh.

I exhale heavily and head to the cupboard to grab my vitamins. My hands ache even more than my knees do. The rigid cap of the bottle cuts against my palm when I squeeze the lid to open it up.

Growling under my breath, I try again and again until my hand is shaking.

Lupus: 1

Daisy: 0

I use my other hand to try to open the container, but it's even worse than my dominant one.

"Damn it," I mutter.

I should have taken my brother up on one of those infomercial gadgets that help elderly people open pickle jars after their strength is gone. It was a joke, but it would honestly come in handy.

"Give it to me." I jerk from the sound of Kane's voice at my back.

The vitamin bottle goes flying into the air, and Kane

catches it with a cat-like reflex. The cap is off within a blink of an eye, and he's handing it to me.

Is this a truce?

Instead of taking it, I ping-pong my attention between him and the opened bottle.

My hand stretches forward slowly, and he does nothing but stare at me with an unreadable expression on his face. My fingers brush against his, his abs flexing with the touch. He doesn't let go of the bottle. Instead, he peers at me in the same way he used to when we were kids.

"Are you sick, Daisy?"

KANE

DAISY'S EYES WIDEN, and I'm stuck with my hand on her vitamin bottle, frozen with the need to know what's going on.

River eventually texted me back, and what a dead end that was. He fed me some bullshit excuse about how she's sensitive over the topic and doesn't want him to tell anyone.

Since when does he care about what she wants?

Also, since when do I care?

I silently scoff. I've always cared, but since when do I show her that I care?

This is bad for my façade, but my heart is racing. The ringing in my ears is back, and there are too many emotions surging to be able to act like I'm unbothered by this.

"Daisy?" Her name slips through my clenched teeth.

Her gulp cuts through the ringing, and I focus on her mouth. "Yes."

The opened bottle of vitamins slips through my fingers, ironically, just like she did years ago.

She takes a step back as the pills scatter all around the kitchen floor like marbles. Neither of us make a move to bend. Instead, we just stare at one another.

It doesn't take long for the panic to surge. I lift my hand and aggressively run it through my messy hair. "What do you mean, yes?"

Sick? How sick and since when? Do her parents know? Does my mom know? Miles?

Does everyone know but me?

Daisy shifts nervously. Those perfect white teeth clamp onto her lip to nibble at the soft flesh. It takes everything in me not to reach out to free it. What seems natural to me when it comes to her isn't always relevant, considering we're enemies.

"I'm fine," she finally answers, though it isn't an answer at all.

Anger spreads like a wildfire. My fists clench by my sides. I teeter my jaw back and forth. "You practically fainted. You have a notebook tracking symptoms."

She sighs loudly, and it's a flame brushing against my skin.

I refuse to back down. "If you don't want to tell me, then fine. I'll find out one way or another, Daisy-Petal. Surely you remember how persistent I can be."

"How could I forget?" she mutters.

"There was once a time you told me all your secrets," I argue.

I told her all of mine too.

Her little nostrils flare. "Well, you left."

My muscles tense. "There was nothing left for me in that town...remember?"

Something flashes across her face, and it digs itself right into my chest. *Was that hurt I saw?*

"Tell me or don't, but I'll find out," I threaten.

She purses her lips, and the only thing it does is make me want to kiss her.

I glance at the clock on her stove. *Fuck*, I have to go to the rink—which, at this point, is probably a good thing.

Some of the vitamins crunch beneath my weight as I walk past her. A faint breath of relief leaves her when she thinks she's in the clear, but at the last second, my arm curls around her waist, and I pull her in close.

My mouth hovers over her ear.

She stares at me out of the corner of her eye.

"Have it your way, babe," I whisper.

I place her phone on the counter and walk out the door.

Daisy has no idea the man I've grown to be...because when I want something, *I get it.*

———

After seeing how indisposed Daisy was after last night's game, I assume she'll call in sick for tonight's game—if you can even do that as the mascot? Are there backup mascots? Substitutes? Hell if I know.

A twinge of guilt settles on my shoulders. The only reason she took this job was to prove a point to me. Is this a job she can even handle? Whatever happened to her wanting to open her own plant shop one day?

I have the notion to ask Cindy if Daisy is coming in, but what would that make me? Someone who cares?

Every few seconds, I glance around the rink. The stands are beginning to fill. Rhodes is off to the side, talking to his daughter through the glass while flirting with his girlfriend at the same time. I skate past and wink at Ellie. She throws up her little devil horns, and I force a smile.

As subtly as I can, I peer toward the bench in hopes I see another set of devil horns peeking out from behind strawberry-blonde locks. At the same time, Crew Hart, one of our newer guys from the trade, skates past and misses me by a hair. He's a damn good skater, so I know it wasn't a coincidence that he didn't ram right into me, but it gives me the push I need to get my shit together and focus on warming up.

Several pucks into the net later, I drop to the ice to stretch.

There's a group of girls behind me that are trying to get my attention, but my focus is elsewhere. *Where are you, little devil?*

A sick feeling fills my gut.

What if she fainted again?

I shake my head. River came home mid-morning. She doesn't need me.

With my glove on, I punch the ice and pair it with a growl.

"Well, that was stupid," Malaki says from somewhere nearby. "Save the punching for the game. The ice is our friend."

Out of the corner of my eye, I see that he starts to pet the ice.

I ignore him, but in true Malaki fashion, he doesn't get the hint.

"Where were you last night? I came home, and the door was wide open."

I grunt. "None of your business."

Amusement slides onto his face. "Were you with your little girlfriend?"

My brows knit together with anger. "You're pissing me off."

He grins. "I know."

I play better when I'm angry.

The entire team knows that.

In fact, Coach sometimes will tell me to keep the chirping up on the ice because he knows I play harder.

Rising to my skates, I swipe my stick off the ice and begin to take off.

Malaki is right behind me.

"Or..." His words linger, and he lowers his voice. "You weren't out at the casino, were you?"

I wiggle my jaw back and forth. "Did you go through my phone?"

Malaki's brow furrows. "Not purposefully. It was on the counter, and a text came in."

He comes from a place of worry, because he's the only one on the team that knows about my situation. After saving my ass, he deserved to know. But fuck, it still pisses me off.

The other team takes the ice, and the crowd grows restless.

"I wasn't at the casino," I snap.

With irritation backing me, I snag a puck from Hart and fling it to the top left part of the net, hitting the bar to pop in behind Emory.

"Nice," Emory says.

It was a nice shot, full of hot anger.

Malaki skates toward me again. "So you were with our little neighbor?"

"Whatever you're implying, stop," I say.

The last thing I need is even more thoughts of Daisy in my head right now.

Malaki grins, and it takes every bit of maturity not to trip him with my stick before he skates off. He turns and calls over his shoulder. "By the way, she just showed up."

I spin on my skates.

With that eye-catching shimmer on her cheeks, Daisy takes the ice with those foam tridents again. Only, this time, she manages to throw them up and over the glass to the fans without needing help from anyone.

Twenty–Three

DAISY

I SPENT THE DAY NAPPING, tending to my plants, which always eases my stress, and avoiding my brother, who can't help but dote on me when he knows I'm struggling.

Refusing to let my fatigue win, I pumped myself full of all the natural remedies I could manage in a day before slipping into my devil's costume and showing up for the game.

I waited until the very last second before making an appearance because I'm a big ol' chicken. I read through the texts between River and Kane that were left on my phone, and I'm happy to know that, for the first time in his life, River didn't betray my trust when it came to his best friend.

Take that, Kane.

Of course, it ended with a lecture from River that I should tell Kane about my diagnosis because he could tell that he was worried. I didn't have the heart to tell him that his best friend actually holds a grudge against me and that he only wants to know because he wants something to hold over my head.

Once the final period starts, I slip away and rest against a wall. Peppermint fills my senses, blocking out the smell of ice and sweaty hockey players, as I rub some more cream on my achy joints. There's a TV off in the corner, displaying the game, so I stand back and watch the Blue Devils put in the work.

By the time the game is nearing the end, my hands are sweating, and my pulse is racing. It's tied with two minutes to go. I pace back and forth, watching the second line jump over the wall and take the ice. Our goalie heads for the bench, pulling another player onto the ice to make it six on five.

Unable to watch from afar with the crowd roaring in the background, I anxiously rush toward the wall beside the bench. There are managers and security nearby, but with my devil's costume on, I stand in between them without question.

My bottom lip is raw from nibbling nervously on it.

The clock is rapidly ticking away.

The puck ping-pongs between the Blue Devils. Back and forth. Back and forth. And then, it flies in the air toward our net.

"No!" I shout.

The security guard glances at me for a second before we're both laser-focused on the ice again.

A hero comes out of nowhere in a blue jersey to snag the puck out of thin air with his gloved hand.

Number 3. Barlow.

He drops it down and skates viciously toward the other net, passing it back and forth.

"Come on, Kane!" I whisper-shout.

His stick winds backward, and just when I think he's going to send it into the net, he surprises me and the rest of the arena by tricking the other team. He passes it to the left to Crew Hart, and into the net it goes.

The goal buzzer sounds, and I shout along with the rest of the crowd.

I'd forgotten how exhilarating it is to watch hockey, especially when you're invested in it.

I'm invested because it's my job, though.

There is no other reason than that.

I quickly move out of the way when the rest of the team takes the ice to celebrate.

Two hands grip my shoulders, and I spin around quickly. Cindy is standing there with a huge smile on her face before she crushes me to her chest to give me a hug. "What a game!" she shouts into my ear.

I laugh. "I know!"

"It's so good to work for a team that is actually winning. Last year, we were shit."

"Darn, I thought I was bringing the team good luck," I joke.

She wiggles her eyebrows. "Oh, you are."

Cindy pauses with her hands still on my shoulders. She pulls me in, and her nose scrunches. "Why do you smell like a candy cane?"

"Oh," I half-laugh. "It's my joint cream. It's peppermint."

She sniffs again. "Smells good. It blocks out the scent of sweaty hockey players. Anyway"—she pulls me toward the bench when the guys begin to make their way to the locker room—"I need you to go on the ice and announce the players of the night."

"Huh?" My eyes grow large. "Right now?"

"Yeah, it's something new. I think the new mascot attire put a bug in our marketing team's ear, and now they're on a roll—not to mention the ideas that Reese has come up with. You two may just be running this place by the time it's all said and done."

God, I hope not.

Better yet...*Kane, you're fired.*

Cindy shoves a microphone into my hand and spins me toward the arena.

"We've already got the three players off to the side, ready for you to announce them. Do you know their names?"

On the inside, I'm a blubbering mess. Nerves settle in my lower stomach, and my legs suddenly feel as heavy as they did last night.

I move forward with Cindy shoving me from behind. I pull my chin upright when I see that Kane is staring directly at me.

Sweat drips down the side of his face, falling off the sharp edge of his jaw and to the floor beneath his skates.

"I know their names," I say at the last second. "I've got this."

Leave it to Kane to give me the confidence to pull myself together. It's not because I need him to calm me or anything. It's quite honestly the opposite. Watching him size me up is the push I need to prove something to him.

Maybe to prove that I'm fine, because after our tiff this morning, I know he's not going to give up that easily.

I skate onto the ice with the microphone held tightly in between my fingers. The arena is basked in various blue lights with a spotlight centered directly on me.

"Let's give it up for our three star players of the night!" I hold my trident up in the air, and the sea of blue-and-black jerseys stand and cheer.

My gaze slips off to the right. I don't have to look at Kane to know he's staring at me.

"First up is the guy with the winning goal: Crew Hart!"

Crew takes the ice and holds his hand up to wave at the crowd. He nods at me on his way past, and then he rushes off the ice for the next guy.

Malaki zips onto the ice after I announce his name and does a few circles around me with a grin on his face. His smile is contagious, so I find myself smiling along with him. He winks at me before heading off toward Kane, who just so happens to be scowling.

Figures.

"Last but not least, we have our very own Kane Barlow, who had the assist for our winning goal!"

The crowd grows even louder when he takes the ice.

Kane skates aggressively without even so much as a closed-lip grin. He's stoic, serious, and annoyingly hot with his scowl. He stops in front of me, taking me by surprise, and plucks my trident right out of my hand.

He takes off toward the glass and throws it over the edge to a fan.

What the hell?!

I manage to keep my expression smooth, pairing it with a fake smile.

It takes all my effort to remain poised when he doesn't stop there. As if he needs to gain any more fans, he drops his helmet to the ice, along with his gloves, and pulls off his jersey in a single motion. My jaw begs to slack right along with all the other women in the arena, but I clench my jaw tightly when I see what's on his wrist.

A thin black hair tie.

The same one he wore for every game his senior year of high school.

The same one he stole out of my hair one night after he and River rescued me from a party.

My thoughts run wild as he balls his jersey up in his hands and tosses it to a group of college girls who are no doubt fighting over it by now. I can't seem to look at them to find out, because Kane is zipping toward me with a devilish glint in his eye.

What are you doing?

My heart pounds so loudly I can't hear anything but the

whooshing of his skates toward me. He puts out his hand for me to take, and I stare at him for a split second before remembering that we're on national television in front of thousands of fans.

He's doing this on purpose.

I growl quietly, thankful the microphone is off now.

When our palms collide, heat coats my skin. He pulls me toward the opening in the ice, and I can't get away from him fast enough.

The second we're closed off from the cameras, I rip my hand out of his.

"What the hell was that?" I seethe.

I place my hands on my hips, and he follows the motion with a teasing glint.

"What?" He plays coy. "Me escorting you off the ice?"

"I told you I was fine! I don't need you to hover over me because of last night."

Kane lifts an eyebrow. "I wasn't trying to hover. I was told to do that."

A flush creeps up my neck and lands on my cheeks. My gaze cuts to Cindy, but she isn't paying any attention.

Kane pops his helmet back onto his head, stowing his sweaty hair away. "And prove it."

I pull back after glancing at the hair tie on his wrist again. "Prove what? How, with every interaction, you seem to irritate me even more?"

I have the sudden urge to pull on the elastic to snap it.

His mouth twitches. "Prove that you're fine and that you don't need me to...*hover*...over you."

The way he says *hover* makes me blush even harder. An image fills my head that has no business being there.

"That's why you're living with River, huh? So he can take care of you?"

"No!" I shout.

The more he talks, the more frustrated I become.

"And when he's at the hospital, working endless hours, he expects me to be there for you, doesn't he? He thinks you'll call me when you're sick and needing someone." Kane glances down the hall with a shake of his head.

"I don't need you to take care of me!" I drop my attention to my hair tie. "And give me back my hair tie!"

He laughs out loud. "No, and again, prove it."

When he begins heading toward the locker room, I panic. Is he going to start showing up unannounced? Watching my every move? Demanding that I rest or stay in when he suspects that I'm sick?

"Wait!" I blurt.

Kane stops walking but doesn't turn around.

"How do I prove it to you?" I'm hesitant, but I don't know that I can handle him being around even more than he already is.

"Meet me on the ice in an hour," he says.

Before I can question him, he's out of sight.

I turn back toward the ice and sigh.

Peppermint fills my senses as I lather myself again to hopefully prepare myself for whatever Kane has up his sleeve.

KANE

I ENDED ONE GAME, only to start another.

The arena has cleared out, the majority of the staff and team disappearing for the night to get rest before tomorrow's practice. I discarded the rest of my uniform and pads and traded them for gym shorts and a hoodie.

I've still got my skates on, which is the first thing she notices when she sees me sitting on the bench.

"You're gonna need yours," I say, checking her out from my peripheral.

Her bag falls to the ground beside me, and the scent of peppermint burns my nose. She sits down with a huff and starts to dig inside her bag for her skates. The grazing of her elbow against mine is subtle through our shirts, but my body is on high alert when Daisy is near. *Always.*

"What are we doing, Kane?"

I can't help but grin at her annoyed tone. It's just as easy for me to irritate her as it is for her to irritate me.

"You wanted to prove that you're fine, right?"

Our eyes lock. She nods slowly.

I grin. "Up for a game of strip hockey?"

The number of times I played strip hockey in high school is countless. River never let Daisy play, for obvious reasons. He'd kick her out of the rink before she even shed a jacket.

Daisy's lips part. "Are you serious?"

I lean back on the bench and spread my thighs. I gaze out onto the open ice. "If you manage to keep up with me and win, then I'll believe you when you say you're fine. It'll be a done deal."

"And if I can't keep up? Then what? You'll follow me around like a shadow?" She tightens her skates with so much force her fingers turn white.

I grip the bench. "Maybe. But I'd start with making you tell me what's going on first."

She mutters something under her breath about hating me, and I can't hold back my chuckle. Her head snaps over to me so quickly another burst of peppermint hits me in the face.

"I want something in return if I win." The attitude flowing out of her is damn near addictive.

"What do you want, little devil?" *Why did that sound like I was willing to give anything to her?*

Those baby blues flare with something I beg to touch, but then they soften, and her voice lowers. "I want to know the last time you talked to Miles."

The breath leaves my chest.

Her request is a slap to the face.

It's not like I was thinking about going easy on her and letting her win, but if I was, that question would have sealed her fate.

There's not a chance in hell I'll let her be privy to that information—not after what she did to me the last time I confided in her.

"Let's go." I stand and climb over the edge of the rink with a stick in my hand. I don't offer to help her, because the second my skate touches the ice, it's on.

It takes her a second to grab a stick to fit her height, but as soon as she does, she meets me at center ice.

I peer at her much shorter stance. Shimmer still covers her high cheekbones, matching the blue of her eyes. She's so fucking beautiful, especially when she smiles at me like she's ready to take me on. It irritates me even more.

"You remember the rules?" I place the puck in front of her stick. "You strip a piece of clothing if you miss the net. First one to shed all their clothing loses."

She pushes her hair behind her shoulder, giving way to her slender neck. The stick winds backward, and she sends it shooting off down the rink from center ice.

My teeth grind back and forth when she makes it.

"Lucky shot," I grumble.

Her girly laugh echoes around the rink, and I'm warm all over.

I take off and retrieve the puck, embracing the icy rink air against my heated skin. I can't decide if I'm enjoying the game or hating it.

I'm back to center ice in record time, thanks to having shed my pads. Daisy rests her chin on her stick and watches me closely.

With as much force as I can manage while staying accurate, the puck soars against the ice and hits the back of the net so hard it flies back out.

"One to one," I chirp.

She growls and takes off before I can to get the puck. Her hair flies past her face as she races back toward me.

"Right here." I tap my stick on the ice. "You have to make it from this spot."

Daisy lines herself up, and I can already tell she isn't going to make the shot. I bite the inside of my cheek to keep myself from correcting her stance and wait for her to miss.

"Ugh!" she mumbles.

It didn't even come close.

Our eyes collide. "Strip."

Her stick drops to the ice. I stuff my excitement down as she grips the bottom of her long sleeve shirt and slowly shimmies it up past the curves of her breasts and over her head. Underneath is a tight tank top that stretches across her body like a second skin. My mouth runs dry.

I quickly picture River's face to bring me back to reality. I know how it feels to be betrayed by someone you trust, and I'm not going to betray him by lusting over Daisy. *Again*.

With my stick, I pull the puck toward me and move to the same spot. My shot hits the net perfectly, because *obviously*.

"This isn't fair," she hisses on her way past. "You play this sport for a living. Of course you'll win."

"It's not about winning," I retort.

Her hand flies to her hip. "Then what is it about?"

"I'm waiting to catch you mid-faint again to prove my theory of you not being fine."

Daisy's eyes narrow. "This is stupid."

I chuckle. "Sounds like something a loser would say."

With all her mighty anger, Daisy winds up and shoots the puck from the other side of the ice, only to miss it by several yards.

I hold back a laugh. "Strip, baby."

She glares at me, and it's adorable. "Don't call me baby."

I place my back to her because watching her discard another piece of clothing will get my dick putting dirty little thoughts in my head just like when I had her at my mercy in that closet a few nights ago.

"There!" she shouts from across the rink.

I turn with the puck at my stick and do a double-take. My breath catches, and those dirty thoughts shoot right up from my balls into my head.

"Planning on getting fucked later? What the hell is that?" I point at her see-through bra with my stick.

I didn't think this through.

I never think things through when it comes to her.

"What?" Daisy glances down at her bra. "This old thing?"

This old thing.

This old thing?

Did she wear it on purpose? In case I cornered her in her dressing room again?

"Something wrong, Kane?" From across the ice, I can see her eyelashes fluttering.

It's almost as if she doesn't remember who she's playing against. I smirk and skate to her quickly. She panics at the last second and tries to scramble away, only for her to practically slip backward.

My arm snakes around her lower back, her bare skin scorching my palm in the process. "Oh, you want to play dirty?" I press her close to my chest and exhale into her face. "I can play dirty, Daisy. I'll have you stripped bare within seconds. Is that what you want?"

I wish I could read her mind. The wheels are turning behind her eyes, and the color on her cheeks comes back even brighter than before. I expect her to push me away and throw an insult at me, but as always, she surprises me. "I don't know, Kane. Is that what *you* want?"

I study her lips.

Those pretty pink lips.

I drop my attention to her cleavage pressing against my chest. The longer I look at her and feel her skin against mine, the more I notice her nipples pressing against the cotton of my hoodie.

This cat-and-mouse game we've suddenly found ourselves in is addictive. The pushing and pulling, the tugging and clawing. At this point, I'm not sure who's winning and who's losing.

"Don't push me to make a point, Daisy...because you know I will," I whisper.

She rolls her eyes, and it's nothing but encouragement for me. I tug her in closer. A breath whooshes from her mouth and lands on mine. I lick my lips, hoping to get the faintest taste of her against my tongue, in hopes that it'll be enough to get me to back down.

It doesn't.

My stick slowly slips from my other hand, and I graze her bare arm, watching little goosebumps race to her flesh. A shiver works down her spine, so I hold on to her tightly while gazing at her mouth. I creep my hand up her body, landing with my fingers tangled in her hair.

Her breathing is sharp and fast. "What are you doing?"

The majority of the lights above our heads turn off, and she gasps, pushing herself farther into me.

Fuck.

The faintest graze of her against my dick makes me weak at the knees. She's winning, and she doesn't even know it.

I try to remember the whole point of the game. I repeat her flirty threat in my head and remember how she insinuated that I'm the one who wants her naked and not the other way around.

I can play dirty and come out on top, but she's right. I do want her naked, and I think, deep down, I want her to need me in ways that have nothing to do with stripping her bare. It's driving me crazy not knowing what's going on with her.

I grip her chin with my thumb and finger and bring her gaze up to mine. "You're still so beautiful, Daisy."

Darkness surrounds us, but there's still a little bit of light filtering in from the bench. Those long lashes of hers flutter in disbelief, and I let out a raspy breath that I wish I were faking.

The truth is, she is still so beautiful, even if I am only telling her this now to get in her head.

"Kane," she whisper-warns.

"Daisy," I whisper back.

I've got her in the palm of my hand, thinking I'm playing nice when I'm filling her with all sorts of things that'll make her more likely to strip naked and lose. But...what would she do if I kissed her? Would she kiss me back?

There's a part of me that wonders if she's playing me like I'm playing her, but would that really be so bad in the end?

I lean in close to her neck, skimming my nose against her delicate jawline on my way. Her slow gulp catches my attention as I let my lips brush against her ear. "God, I've missed you."

Such a bitter truth.

"No you haven't," she says quietly.

"I have," I argue. "But I hate myself for it."

Surely she believes me, because it's the truth.

I place a kiss to the spot right below her ear, and we're pressed together so closely I can feel her nipples tighten as they strain against her flimsy bra. My groin tingles, and I let my mouth gently press against her neck again. *So soft.* My eyes shut, and I drag my hand up her back, my thumb grazing her spine.

I've never felt so greedy before.

Women give themselves to me with a single wink in their direction, and I willingly take from them.

But nothing comes close to this.

Being apart from her has only made things worse. Our chemistry has always been there, lying quietly under fleeting glances, but right now it's irresistible. The tension is tight but so fucking addictive.

"Kane." This time, my name is a plea. For what? I don't know.

I sink my teeth into her neck and unclasp her bra at the same time. My throat closes with desire as the straps fall over her arms. I quickly pull it the rest of the way off, tossing it somewhere on the ice.

A silky breath falls graciously from her mouth that I quickly become obsessed with.

I can't stop, even though I know I should. I'm pushing things too far.

"When was the last time you were touched, Daisy?"

I tug on her earlobe with my teeth while skimming my hand around to the waistband of her leggings. My finger plays with the top of it, and my eyes roll into the back of my head.

Fuck, I should stop.

"Not going to answer my question?" I tease, looking down at her.

I guide my fingers down farther, slipping into her panties. I'm twisted on the inside, a hot tug on every thought of touching her making it impossible to stop.

The goal was to get her naked and then declare myself the winner of our game of strip hockey, because between the two of us, only one of us is clothed, but things are taking a wild turn, and I can't seem to care.

My hand slips in between her thighs, and my heart stops.

Fuck. There is no stopping now.

I'm going to hell after this. Not only am I going behind River's back after I swore to myself that I never would again but also because, when this is done, she's going to think I only touched her to win. If only she knew the thoughts in my head, then she'd know that I'm not doing this to win our game but because I'm out of control.

Daisy Sullivan is my soft spot.

Instead of placing her on the cold ice, I pick her up and

skate us over to the bench. Her shaky, fast breaths fan over the side of my neck where her face is buried. After sitting her on the bench, I bend at the knee and untie her skates until they're sprawled on the floor beside me. I hook my fingers inside the waistband of the tight leggings she's wearing and slip them over her hips and down her legs.

"Kane—"

I shush her by dragging my fingers up the inside of her thighs. "By the looks of it, you haven't been touched in a very long time."

She tenses. "That isn't true."

It fucking better be.

I pause at the possessive thought that slips in. I need to get a grip. Unfortunately, that grip seems to be *her.*

My finger plays along the edge of her pussy, and I gaze at it like I haven't seen one in years. Her body begs to be touched as she wiggles back and forth in an attempt to get me to touch the spot that she needs.

I wish I could spend all night relearning her curves.

The thrumming in my chest is too hard to ignore. My dick throbs, and my mouth waters.

I want a taste.

Just one.

I glide one finger inside her warmth, and her hips meet me halfway. She's needy, and I fucking love it.

"It is true," I rasp, slipping my finger in and out of her while gazing at her body. The toned muscles of her belly move back and forth with her ragged breathing. I place a light kiss to the inside of her knee while getting her all worked up. She makes a noise that gives me a new high.

I have veered so far off course that I can't hear the warnings in the back of my mind.

Before I can talk myself out of it, my mouth replaces my fingers, and she coats my tongue.

"What are you—"

I silence her by tugging on her clit with my teeth. A whimper flows from her mouth, and she opens up wider for me. I've never tasted better. I lick and suck, eating her pussy so well she's curling her hips to meet my face.

It's hot and addictive, and I know that as soon as she gets off, I have to end this, or I'll do a lot more than bury my face between her legs. I'll fuck her so hard that she won't think of anyone but me ever again.

"Why does this feel so good?" she rasps.

Because we're made for each other. That's why.

Don't even go there, Kane.

She's so close. I graze her clit with my teeth and push two fingers into her, slow and steady.

Her pussy begins to tighten, and I quickly take my attention from in between her legs to her face.

Fuck.

My brain stalls.

Daisy coming is the hottest fucking thing I have ever witnessed. My fingers are soaked, and her whimpers continue the entire time she comes.

I can't get enough. In the middle of her orgasming, I move back to her pussy and lick up every last drop of her. Then, I lick my fingers clean too.

The rising and falling of her ribcage catches my attention as I come back to reality.

Our eyes snag, and I lose my footing.

You fucked up.

My jaw clenches, and all I taste is her.

I don't know how I got here, on my knees, with River's sister completely naked and spread wide open with a hazy look in her gaze, but fuck, here I am.

What did I just do?

After grabbing her panties off the floor, I hold them out

with my pinky finger. I casually run my gaze down her naked body in hopes it'll last me a lifetime.

"You're naked." I try to keep my tone even to hide how undone I am on the inside. "Which means I've won. So it's time for you to tell me what's going on."

Twenty–Five

DAISY

MY ENTIRE BODY FLUSHES. Embarrassment hits me so quickly I lose my breath.

"I won. Fair and square," he adds.

How could I be so stupid? So naive?

Forget the panties. He can keep them as his trophy.

I hastily swipe my leggings from the floor and quickly shimmy them back up my legs. Leaving my skates untied, I slip my feet into them and take off toward the ice. I head to my bra, and what do you know? My dignity is lying right beside it, mocking me.

My fingers fumble with the clasp, so I decide to leave it. After I've got my tank top and shirt straightened against my torso, I send a scathing glare to Kane. I skate over to the opening of the rink and rip my bag off the floor before flinging it over my shoulder.

He stands with my panties still in his hand and a haughty grin on his face. The shadows played tricks on my mind. They let me hide from the realization of who was actually between my legs.

Turns out, it's my brother's best friend, who is an even bigger dick than I thought.

What happened to the old Kane? The one who busted Collin Hennings's nose after he learned that he broke my heart? Or the guy who took the blame for shattering the kitchen window with a puck so I wouldn't be the one to get in trouble? Where did *he* go?

"All this just to win?" I cross my arms over my braless chest. "Wow."

Kane shrugs. "You pushed me to make a point, and I did."

My eyebrows rise. "And what point was that?"

I should take the look on his face as a warning. He shoves my panties into the pocket of his hoodie, and his annoyingly talented tongue slips out to lick his bottom lip. "That I can get you naked anytime I want. You play dirty, and I'll play even dirtier."

Kane stalks forward too quickly for me to get out of his way. He grips my chin and tilts my face to meet his. "Now it's your turn to keep up your side of the bargain. Tell me what's wrong with you."

I laugh sarcastically in his face and shove his hand away. He lets me back away but not without shooting me a warning glare.

"Why do you even care?" I ask.

Kane pops the hood of his sweatshirt onto his head. "If you're going to be passing out in my arms, I think I deserve to know why."

"Don't worry," I snap. "That won't happen again."

Kane becomes impatient. His hood falls backward as he runs his hand through his messy hair angrily. "Fine, have it your way. I'll just have to keep an eye on you, I guess. You got plans tonight? Because I do, and if I can't trust that you won't fucking pass out mid-elevator ride up to your apartment, then you're coming with."

"For fuck's sake," I blurt.

Kane eyes me angrily.

"Lupus!" I shout. "I have fucking Lupus, okay? It's an autoimmune disease. The whole reason I'm in Chicago is because River met one of the best specialists during his rotations, and if I ever want to get my life back on track, then I need to be able to have readily available resources like Dr. Gibson." I throw my hands up in frustration. "There! Now you know."

I'm fuming by the end of my rant.

Kane's jaw wiggles back and forth, but he remains quiet.

I'm so irritated by what he did to win our game that I refuse to sit in a car with him to head to the apartment complex, so I turn and stomp off down the hall.

"Here!" he shouts from behind.

Now what?

Is he going to throw my panties at me as a reward for telling him the truth?

I turn just in time to see his car keys flying through the air. They land at my feet, but I make no move to grab them.

"Take my car. I'm going out."

The need to refuse almost outweighs the exhaustion settling in my bones. But in the end, I bend down and swipe his keys off the floor. Before I leave, I see him skating out toward center ice.

He grabs my bra and shoves it in his hoodie pocket along with my panties.

I grit my teeth. I hate him.

———

It's been two nights, and I haven't heard a single peep from Kane. There have been no accidental run-ins or impromptu elevator meetings—with Kane, I mean. Malaki, who I learned is the other Blue Devil living with Kane, was waiting for me in the parking garage the night Kane had me take his car. He made up some excuse that he had just gotten home too, but after three random occasions where Malaki has shown up at the elevators, I have a feeling that Kane is having him keep tabs on me. River has been keeping an extra watchful eye on me too, thanks to Kane ratting me out for the little fainting spell I had.

Thankfully, River knows not to tell our parents. Otherwise, my mom's phone calls would be four times a day instead of two. But I wouldn't put it past Kane to call them.

Screw Kane.

Screw him and his hot mouth.

I sigh at my stupidity. The clarity I have while alone should be able to keep me afloat while he's in proximity, but everything changes the moment he's near.

I stare at the ceiling like I'm lovesick and wonder what he's doing.

"Ugh!" Irritation pulls me from the couch, and I head over to my plants.

"You'll never play games with me, will you?" I ask them while running my fingers over their luscious green leaves.

I spot a little yellow spot on one of the pothos. *Oh, so you do wanna play games?*

I move the plant farther away from the window, wondering if it's getting too much light. After plucking the yellowing leaves, I check the soil and give it a little more water.

"There, there," I say jokingly.

How I became a college dropout, living with my big brother in a foreign city, talking to my plants on a Friday night is beyond me.

Talk about pathetic.

If it weren't for getting sick, I'd still be living it up with Natalia on College Street, three shots deep and explaining the importance of photosynthesis to some frat boy who I'd forget by morning.

My phone pings with a message from across the room, and I assume it's her. She's probably thinking the same thing I am, though she's actually on College Street with all of our friends.

After placing my watering can down on the counter, I brush the soil off my fingers and grab my phone.

Who is this?

My pulse immediately races.

UNKNOWN

Hey, devil girl. This is Malaki. What's up?

Okay. It's official. Kane has burdened Malaki with checking on me.

This is ridiculous.

ME

Tell Kane that if he wants to know how I'm doing or what I'm doing, he can ask me himself!

Maybe this means he's too ashamed after what he did.

Yeah, right.

MALAKI

Actually, I'm texting you because I need your help with Kane.

I pause.

ME

Help with what?

I'm on edge after falling for Kane's stunt the other night.

Who can I trust? Kane's roommate asking me for help? Sounds like a scam.

ME

If this is another one of Kane's tricks, tell him I'll tell River all about what happened the other night.

MALAKI

The other night? Sounds juicy. What happened?

I pause before typing anything. Do I really want a text receipt stating what we did the other night? No. No, I do not.

MALAKI

Ah. So something happened the other night between you and Kane. That would explain things.

Now I'm invested.

ME

Fine. I'll bite. What's going on?

MALAKI

I can't get him to leave the casino.

My heart stutters. Kane? At the casino? There is no way.

ME

What's the address?

I change out of my sweats and throw on some jeans and a long-sleeve top. I rush out the door with no real plan on how to get to where I need to go, but one thing is for certain. If Kane is gambling, something is seriously wrong.

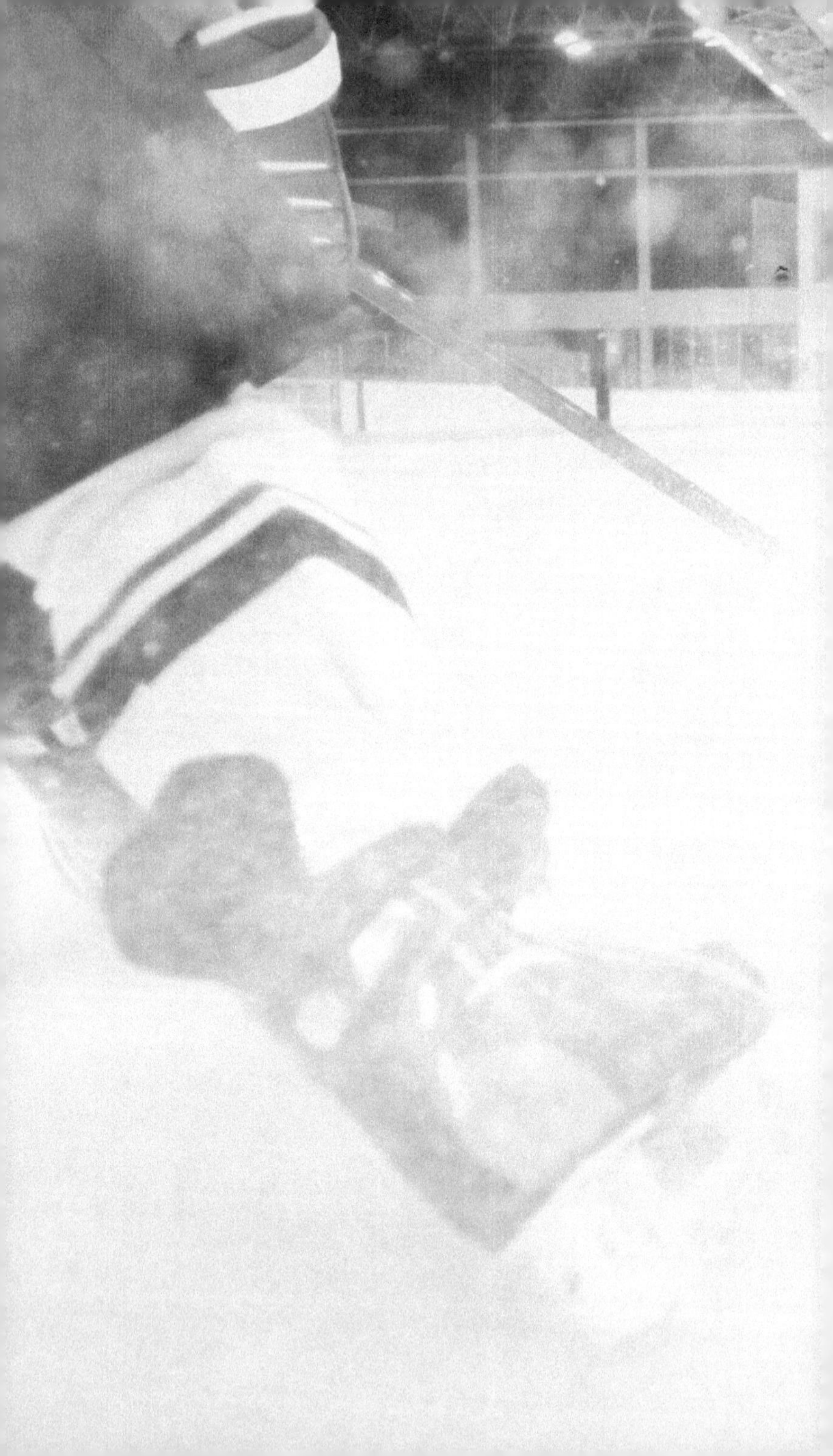

Twenty–Six

KANE

I **SEARCH** for my phone on the blackjack table while I wait for the rest of these idiots to make their wager. My vision blurs a little, and my hands are slow as I pat both my pockets.

Where is it?

All I want to do is reread the texts from River.

I scoff so loud the dealer glances at me with a furrowed brow. I should have the texts memorized by now because I've reread them at least fifty times.

River confirmed Daisy's confession and explained how difficult the last year and a half has been for her. Then he confides in me, as if I'm equipped to give him reassuring words of comfort.

"Stupid," I mumble.

Lupus.

Her immune system attacks itself, potentially damaging her organs.

My skin is crawling, and it has nothing to do with the

liquor rushing through my veins or the fact that I'm at a casino.

I study the man with broad shoulders past the dealer who has a woman with light hair pinned to his side.

Daisy?

I shake my head and right my vision.

Clearly, my buzz is starting to wear off.

I raise my finger at the cocktail waitress who's been eyeing me all night. She and the bouncer both glance at me every few minutes. They're either both into me or they're hearing little whispers in their ears from the men upstairs about how I'm going to rob them of all their money. Little do they know that I'm only here because I need to make up for what I gave away earlier, thanks to the real gambler of the family.

"Don't get another drink."

I peer over my shoulder, and Malaki is standing there.

"What are you doing here?" I ask.

"You invited me."

I did?

His face screws. "You're worse than I thought."

"I'm fine," I grunt.

I brush him off and turn back to the table. It's my turn. Thinking back to my cards, I glance at the dealer's card once more before flicking my chin. "Hit."

A darkness fills me when I take the card from him. Gambling runs in my blood, and I know better than anyone that it's a dangerous thing to play with.

"You're going to feel like shit tomorrow," Malaki warns from behind.

I shrug without looking at him. "At least I don't look like shit."

"Oh, thank god," he mutters.

Yes, thank god.

I grin while watching my opponents fall like flies. *I win.*

"Told you I'm fine." I smirk over my shoulder, except Malaki is no longer standing there.

Instead, it's some sort of magic trick, because surely, Daisy fucking Sullivan isn't actually standing at my back with big round eyes full of worry.

The longer I look at her, the more my skin itches.

Why is she here? At the casino? Dressed like she's heading to a baseball game or something? Ripped jeans, a long sleeve shirt, and an LA Dodgers hat. She stands out like a nun in a brothel.

Just look at her, commanding the attention of every male in the room. They're all wondering who this mysterious woman is in the middle of a hazy casino, hiding her perfect face beneath a baseball cap.

I've got an answer for them.

She's mine.

Anger scorches the soles of my feet as I stand up and turn for her. I'm a foot away when some older man with rings on every other finger hooks his thumb into one of her belt loops and pulls her into him.

The alcohol in my veins suddenly disappears, and I'm more focused than ever.

I faintly hear Malaki in the distance. "*Shit.* Stay here. I'll be right back."

Everything moves in slow motion.

The man pulling Daisy toward him. Daisy angling her chin to get a better look.

The never-ending slot machines stop their buzzing, and the place seems to empty. I grab the man by the collar of his suit and pull him toward me. "Let go of her." The lethal bite to my tone could be heard by a deaf person.

My heart pounds violently.

I suck in the smoky air of the casino and try to ground myself before I really lose my control. Two wrinkled eyes that his Botox can't even begin to hide swim with confusion. "Oh," he says, "I didn't know she was with you."

She's not.

Daisy's warm hand falls to my arm. It's soft and grounding. I love and hate it at the same time.

"Kane."

One word.

That's all it takes for me to cave.

I release my culprit slowly, lifting one finger at a time, leaving his wrinkled shirt behind.

"Come on," she begs. "Let's go. Please."

A hot thought flows through my head.

I like it when she begs.

What I don't like is the disappointment lingering in her dreamy blue eyes. My teeth work over one another the longer I stare at her face. *Why did she have to come here?*

"Go home, Daisy," I demand.

Beneath her hat, worry mixes with the shadows.

Before she can say anything, I lower my voice. "What are you even doing here?"

"I called her." I raise my glare to Malaki.

Never mind the fact that this is a form of betrayal, but he called her?

I flex my jaw. "You have her number?"

Since when does he have *her* number? Did she give it to him?

Shit, maybe I am a little drunk.

"Jesus Christ." Malaki presses my phone into my chest, and I quickly shove it into my pocket. "I grabbed her number from your phone. You've got that crazy look in your eye that you get on the ice, which is exactly why I called her to come get you to leave."

"You called her to get me to leave?" I laugh through the

anger. "Yeah, nice try, but I'm not leaving." I turn to Daisy. "Especially with her."

Malaki shakes his head.

I hope he chokes on his defeat.

Suddenly, he's tossing his keys to Daisy. "Here."

She catches them with ease.

"You get him home. I'll catch a ride with your Uber…" He turns to a random woman who I'm just now seeing.

"Her name is Reese," Daisy says. "And you better tip her well, Malaki."

"You get him home"—he nods at me as if I'm not standing a foot away from him—"and I'll give Reese whatever she wants."

Beneath the brim of her hat, Daisy crooks her eyebrow at me. Malaki's keys swing around and around her finger, and it's clear she's waiting for me to make a move toward the exit.

My blood sings with her attention on me, which is never a good thing.

I narrow my gaze, and she mimics me.

"I'm not ready to go," I say, just to see what she'll do.

Her nose wrinkles with disgust. "You're more than ready to go. Come on."

"Make me."

Why the fuck am I playing games with her? Again?

"Kane," she warns.

I smirk. "Daisy."

She sighs with annoyance.

I know I have her interest, because she glances around the casino like she's trying to come up with a plan to get me to leave. Little does she know, I'm not leaving until she begs me to.

"Should we play another game, little devil? Maybe you can redeem your loss from the other night?" I reach forward and grab a hold of her chin to tip her face for a better look. "Oh wait. You didn't really lose, did you?"

Daisy's cheeks burst with embarrassment. Or anger. Maybe both.

She slaps my hand away, and I can't help but chuckle.

Meeting one of my brother's high rollers tonight in order to pay him off might just have been worth it to end the night with Daisy scowling at me.

"You want to play more games, Kane?" Daisy shakes her head. "Haven't you played enough games for tonight?"

I pretend to think. "Not yet."

Daisy's nostrils flare. When her arms cross against her chest, I know we're about to go toe-to-toe. "Is your brother around here somewhere? Hoping you'll win back all the money he's probably lost again?"

She strikes a nerve, so I strike one right back.

I lean down and put my mouth next to her ear. "Go home, little one. I don't want you here."

By the way her jaw unhinges, I know I've pissed her off. I used to call her *little one* when River was around. I did it to irritate her, but it was also because it threw River off my trail. I couldn't have my best friend sniffing out my interest in his little sister now, could I?

"You let me know when you're ready to go, bookie." Daisy pats my chest a couple of times, right over my heart.

I follow her swaying hips all the way to her final destination, which just so happens to be near a group of men celebrating a bachelor party.

All but one of them takes a look at Daisy. I can tell they're making silent bets on who can score the pretty girl in the baseball cap.

I hate to admit it, but I think Malaki was right.

Daisy will get me to leave, or else I may end up in jail.

Twenty-Seven

DAISY

THE ENTIRE DRIVE to the casino, Reese and I conjured up a million and one plans on how I could tackle this issue.

The issue being Kane.

Evidently, I don't know Kane at all anymore, because the guy I once knew would never dare fall into the same habits of those who precede him.

Gambling?

How could he? After everything he's been through with his mom and brother?

Is this why he hasn't made it back home in six years?

My stomach twists. I'm not even angry that I'm standing in a crowded casino, breathing in thick clouds of smoke. Instead, I'm concerned.

I shouldn't be, especially after his conniving game of strip hockey, but old habits die hard, and though he's a man now, it's hard not to remember who he was before.

"Hey."

I perk up when a guy edges his way past my peripheral vision. I turn and slide a smile on my face. "Hi."

"What are you doing here all alone?" The guy looks me up and down as he smiles. "Are you lost?"

I glance at my outfit. I was in such a rush that I didn't care what I was wearing, but I'm clearly not in casino clothing.

I'm wearing a baseball hat. Could I look any more out of place?

Another guy steps forward. He's tall and handsome but way too sloppy for my liking. Amber liquor sloshes out from the top of his drink and spills onto the floor between us. "She's not lost," he slurs. His arm winds up around his friend's shoulders, and I think it may be keeping him upright. "She was on her way to my room before you stopped her."

His friend chuckles. "Even if you could score someone as beautiful as her, I don't think you'd be able to get it up right now, bud."

My cheeks warm from the compliment.

"Move over." Another guy with broad shoulders and a half-unbuttoned dress shirt slides in front of his two friends. I back up immediately because he's just as drunk as the second guy. "Want a drink, LA?"

"LA?" I move back every time he sways in my direction. I take the drink he hands me before he spills it on my shirt.

He points to my hat with a cheesy grin on his face.

Oh, right. Dodgers hat. Reese found it in the backseat of her car and placed it on my head in case I needed to be incognito while sneaking up on Kane.

"I'm more of a hockey fan myself, but I can get down with a girl who likes baseball."

Hockey fan? He'd lose his mind if he knew that Kane was a few tables down.

Who's actually probably losing his mind right now.

Or maybe not.

Maybe he doesn't care that I'm over here surrounded by a group of hungry men with a drink in my hand. If anything is for certain since coming to Chicago, it's that I still have no idea what's going through Kane's mind.

"Who said I only like baseball?" I ask.

"Ohhhhhh," the guys yell in unison. "She likes hockey?"

I grin.

I *did* like hockey, until I was all but forced to be a mascot.

"Who's your favorite team, blue eyes?" I turn toward the first guy only to see his expression shift.

My drink falls, and the casino spins. An arm slips around my waist, and I'm turned swiftly so I'm blocked from whatever is coming for me. My face hits the hard back of someone, and it only takes me a split second to know that it's Kane.

With one of his arms behind him, keeping me steady against his firm backside, the other is shoving the drunk guy off to the side where his friends catch him.

"What the hell—"

Silence fills the group.

"Holy shit. Are you Kane Barlow? The one who plays for—"

Kane stiffens. "Yes."

I attempt to free myself, but his grip tightens around me.

"And you almost knocked down my girl." He drags his words out slowly, as if he wants them to hear every last one.

The audacity.

"I am not your girl!" I hiss behind his back.

As if rehearsed, the group of guys leans around Kane and stares at me in disbelief.

"You're with Kane Barlow?" one of them asks.

I open my mouth, having every intention of calling Kane a liar, but then I get a glimpse of his sharp jawline angled toward me. "Say yes, and I'll leave right now with you," he whispers to me.

Why is he so good at winning these little games we keep playing? I remember a time when he used to let me win.

My head screams with a refusal, but then I remember seeing him at that blackjack table, and I just can't do it.

"Yes," I say.

"Well, why didn't you say so?" The group of guys scatters like marbles.

Except for one.

The same one who almost fell into me before Kane swooped in like a hero to save me—anti-hero, that is.

"Can I have your autograph?" he asks.

Kane's spine straightens, and the grip he has on me tightens.

He exhales deeply. "You almost crushed my girl, and you're going to ask for my autograph?"

My girl.

I both hate and love the sound of that. The smoke in this place must be clouding my thoughts because *what?!*

"Well, yeah." The guy snorts. "You're Kane Barlow."

Kane's laugh comes out menacing. "How about I autograph your face with my fist?"

"Kane." I tug on his shirt. "Stop it. I'm fine."

He scoffs at me. "I've heard that before."

Thankfully, the guy ends up being a lot smarter than I gave him credit for, because he takes off in the direction of his friends who have completely left him to fend for himself.

I let go of Kane's shirt as he steps away from me. I didn't realize I was holding my breath until air slips in between us. It cools me right away, but I'm right back to feeling warm when I find him staring at me.

I fix my clothing from being whooshed behind him. "Was that necessary?"

His lips flatten. "If I would've let it go on any further, I would have ended up in jail. So yeah, it was."

I'm mid eye-roll when Kane's fingers wrap around my wrist. He pulls me through the casino, as if I'm the one who needs to be dragged out.

I rip myself free from his grip when we end up at Malaki's car. Kane makes no move to get inside after I unlock it.

"Are you crazy?" A vein pops out of Kane's neck as he runs his hands through his hair angrily. "Were you going to take a drink of whatever that guy gave you?" He crosses his arms, his forearm muscles bulging with anger. "He could've been trying to date-rape you."

"Careful, Kane," I say. "You're starting to act like you care."

He snaps his head to me, and I jerk backward. "You're a damn fool if you think I don't care."

His insult is a slap to my face.

"A fool? How could I think otherwise after the last couple of weeks? You're so bent out of shape over the past and clearly holding a grudge against me, something that you have no idea about." I storm around the front of the car with fury and slide into the driver's seat.

Kane stands with his back to the passenger side. After a few seconds of trying to calm myself, I roll the window down. "Get in."

He spins around, the dust of the parking lot kicking up in his wake. The door flies open, and he begrudgingly sits down. The door slams, and I speed out of the lot in hopes I'll get us home sooner so we can go our separate ways.

There's so much tension between us I could suffocate at any given second.

Silence fills the inside of the car, and my heart aches with every angry beat. My fingers squeeze the steering wheel, and before I know it, I'm giving Kane an explanation that he doesn't deserve.

"I wasn't going to drink it," I snap.

He scoffs, like he doesn't believe me.

"Do you think I'm lying?"

He's staring at the side of my face, his angry gaze starting a fire on my cheek. "Wouldn't be the first time you've lied to me."

I stare at the blurring yellow lines out the windshield. The truth is on the tip of my tongue, ready to be unleashed just so I can stop this animosity between us, but what good would that do? It's not like it'll change anything. What's done is done.

"Don't act like you've never lied, Kane. Because we both know you have."

My claws descend when I sense the shift in the car. The tension lessens. Kane's tightly balled fist stretches out, and he places his palm on his thigh. "You lied to get me to take your virginity. That's called being selfish." He stares out his window. "I lied for someone else. There's a difference."

His version of that night stings, even if it is partly my fault.

"You think I'm a fool?" I turn into the parking garage and park. "Well, so are you."

Instead of getting out of the car when I turn it off, Kane leans back in the seat and gets comfortable. "Name-calling? That's what it's come to?"

I angle myself toward him, prepared to keep up with our arguing, but then I *really* look at him. His dark eyes, glossy from drinking, are hiding something within their depths that I beg to find.

My voice softens with a concern that I can't pretend I don't feel when it comes to him. "Gambling? That's what it's come to?"

His forehead furrows, and I can tell he's about to throw up some type of wall to block me. Instead of letting him lash out at me, I take a different approach.

Unpeeling my fingers from the steering wheel, I gently

place my hand on top of his. There's a spark of familiarity there that unburies itself from the back of my mind.

Instead of flicking my hand off his, he lets it stay, which only confuses me.

He's so hot and cold, but I'm not taking the moment for granted.

"Since when do you gamble, Kane? After everything?" I ask.

He slowly turns toward me. The hatred we've found ourselves in is slowly disappearing inside the small space we're tucked away in.

"I didn't go there to gamble," he admits. "I was..." His explanation lingers, and it doesn't take long for me to put two and two together.

"You were checking to see if Miles was there."

Kane looks away abruptly, confirming my assumption.

"So you two do still talk?" I ask.

Just like a rubber band, the air is tight again. Kane opens the car door with force and slams it shut in my face.

I jerk in the driver's seat, regretting that I tried to find some normalcy between us. I know I should heed the warning he's giving me, but I don't. Instead, I open the driver's side door and follow him.

The truth starts to crawl through my blood. With every quick step after him, I become more and more outraged.

"You don't get to do that!" I shout.

Kane straightens when I follow him onto the elevator. The door slides shut, and he spins around to level me with a glare. "Do what?"

Why is he so much hotter when he's angry? His jawline sharpens, and his navy eyes darken.

"Act like I'm nothing but an annoying little nuisance to you but then get angry when you think I'm jeopardizing my safety. You're hot and cold. One second, you're acting like you care, and the next, you're slamming the door in my face. That isn't fair, Kane."

His nostrils flare, and I keep going, too riled up to stop.

"In case you've forgotten, you didn't put up much of a fight when we went our separate ways. Remember?" The elevator doors close us off from the rest of the world, and it's all the push I need to keep driving my point further. "If we could go back to that night, I never would have asked you to take my virginity! You clearly hate me for it."

Kane storms me, and I lose my footing. His arm winds around my lower back, and he pins me to the front of his firm body. His close proximity steals the rest of the thoughts from my head.

"Don't get it twisted, Daisy." His alcohol-scented breath wafts down into my face, and I inhale it like he's a drug. "I don't regret having you in bed, even for a second."

The elevator pings, and the door opens up on my floor.

He makes no move to let me go.

When the elevator door closes again, it's like he has a grip on my heart, and he's squeezing it until I burst.

"Fine!" I shout frantically.

Kane's eyebrows shoot down with confusion.

"I lied to you."

His eyes narrow. "Yeah, I fucking remember."

I swallow past the lump in my throat. "You don't get it."

I suddenly feel dizzy.

"When you came back to my room that next morning. I acted like it meant nothing to me, but I lied."

Kane, the most stoic of them all, jerks backward with shock.

The elevator door opens to his floor, and I gulp in a breath.

"If I would've said yes to there being an us, you wouldn't have left, or you at least would've come back to visit. So much would have been at stake…" Unable to meet his eye any longer, I turn and press the button to my floor. I grab onto my stomach when nausea hits me and keep my back to him.

We say nothing when the doors open again.

I step off and turn before the door closes us off from one another.

"You had to get away from Miles. The only way for that to happen was to cut off all ties…including me."

I rush into my apartment with my stomach rolling. Exhaustion hits me, and I shake all over.

I'm not much of a gambler, but in the spirit of things, I think I just laid all my cards out on the table for Kane.

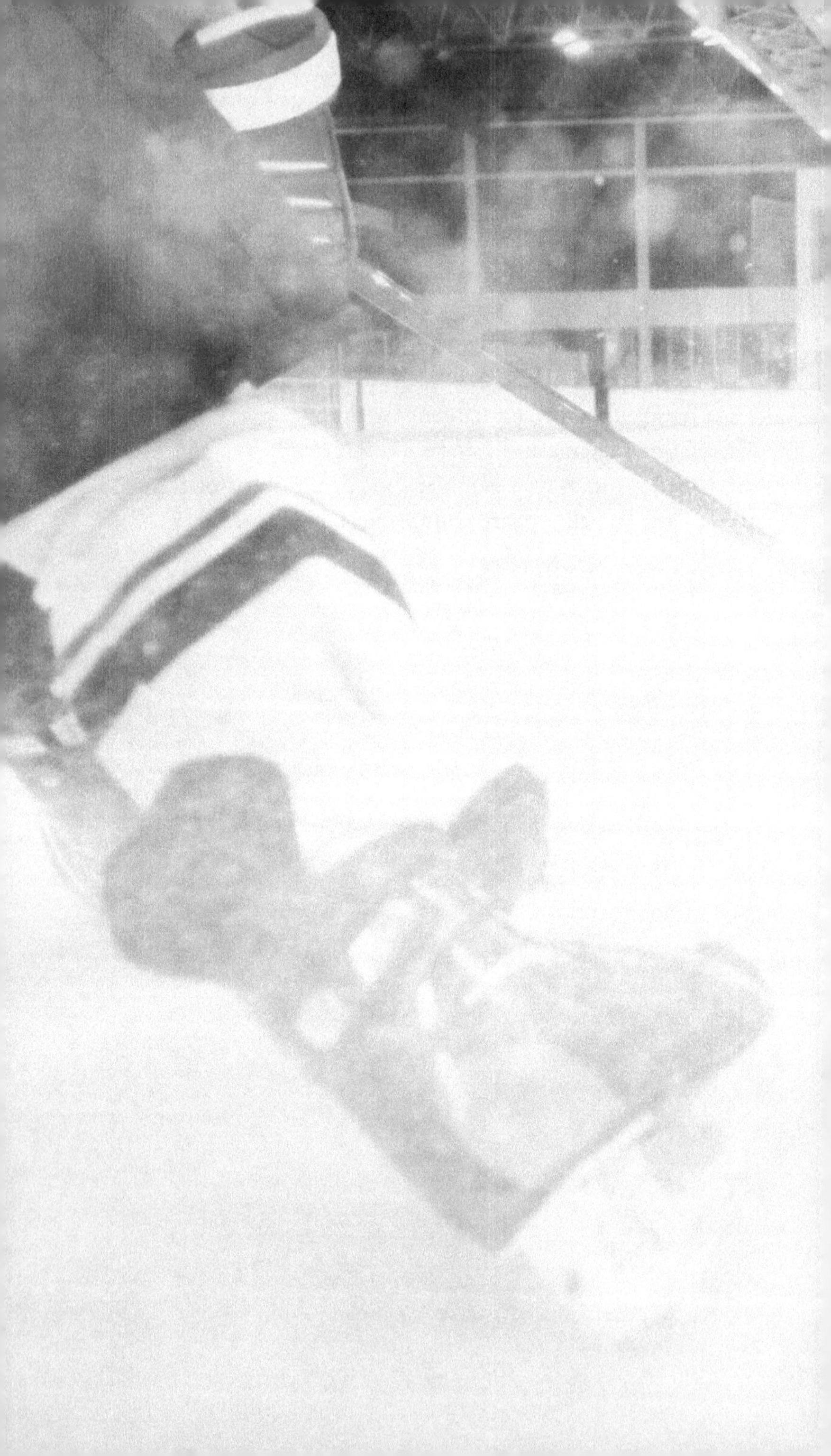

Twenty-Eight

KANE

I SOBER UP AS SOON as the elevator closes me off from her. My apartment feels miles away, but somehow, I'm standing right in front of the door. I unlock it and step inside, tossing my keys onto the counter next to the Tylenol bottle that Malaki has apparently laid out for me. I bypass it and head to my room. There's no medicine in the world that will relieve the headache Daisy has caused me.

I'm in a daze. My apartment feels emptier than usual, even with Malaki tucked away in his room.

My slow steps echo on my way to the shower.

I shed my clothes and step into the hot water with my head replaying the memory of her that I've had to block over the years.

Her rejection so long ago was a cut to my skin that I've had to live with. I've been through all the proper steps of grief, all the way down to acceptance.

I'd managed to convince myself that it was for the best— she always did have a way of looking at the bigger picture—so in hindsight, when she said there couldn't be an "us," it eventually made sense.

Too much was at stake for me.

I was vulnerable.

My thoughts were messy, and my life was spiraling out of control.

My desperation for her was an obvious tell that I was just trying to grasp onto the one constant I had. She was the only person who knew me down to my core and who learned of the truth behind the fiasco that led my mom to practically disown me.

Yet, hearing her admit that it wasn't all that I had made it out to be is a total mind-fuck.

The truth remains, though: She's still River's little sister, and her family is the only family I have left. If there is one thing that hasn't changed over the years, it's my loyalty. In fact, it has only grown stronger. If you have me on your side, that means something.

The shower runs cold, and I finally turn it off.

Exhaustion should be setting in, but the longer I lie in my empty bed, the more awake I become. I grab my phone and pull up my texts. I glare at Miles's *thank you* text. At least he has the decency to do that.

I delete it so I can avoid the regret that'll soon come and stare at Daisy's name.

Even with me being a complete fucking asshole to her, she's still showing up to bail me out of trouble.

I glance at the clock.

It's late.

She should be sleeping. There were bags underneath her eyes, evident beneath the brim of her hat.

I read that with Lupus comes exhaustion, amongst other things.

Maybe I should check on her.

Should I apologize for the hostility?

I scoff.

No. I'm not apologizing. Who's to say she's even telling the truth, anyway?

Fuck, why do I even care?

My heart hammers behind my ribs. There's a terrifying glimpse of losing her again in the distance that I can't ignore. I don't even have her, and yet, the thought scares me enough to fling the covers off my legs.

I'm shirtless but make no move to put a one on. My pulse thrums as I snag her key from the drawer beside my bed. River asked me to keep the spare, which is a true tell that he trusts me way too much.

He shouldn't, now that his sister is back in the picture.

He really shouldn't—not if he knew what was good for her.

Two minutes later, I'm standing in front of Daisy's apartment door. Instead of knocking and potentially waking her up, I insert the key and give it a twist.

An earthy smell mixed with something warm hits me square in the face, and suddenly, I'm back to feeling drunk.

I search the area for signs of River, blindly coming up with an excuse if he were to catch me sneaking around, but with his ID badge gone and keys missing, I know Daisy is alone. I chuckle at the sight of her wild plants with their green leaves and let the door latch quietly behind me.

I creep through her apartment like a stalker. Better me than someone else, though, 'cause then I'd really end up in prison. I evaded it once. I won't be so lucky the second time.

When she's nowhere in sight, I move toward her bedroom.

My dick twitches, and the dirty thoughts that slip in tell me that I'm royally fucked. That's what Daisy does to me, though—she drives me crazy to the point that I'm picturing myself slipping into her bed, pressing against her, and coaxing her to open up those smooth legs for me.

I swallow thickly and shove the thoughts away.

Act like a fucking man, not a teenager.

Slowly, I push on her bedroom door. The breath whooshes from my lungs. She's curled on her side in a ball, on top of her covers, with her wavy hair shielding her face from me, like she knew I was going to break into her apartment to watch her.

She's defiant, even in her sleep.

I chuckle quietly and shake my head.

What am I doing?

I should leave.

She's clearly fine, even if my gut tells me she's not.

I turn and put my back to her. I grip the top of the door jamb and pause. *Leave.*

I peer over my shoulder and trace the curve of her body through the darkness, but that's when I hear her.

The smallest whimper falls from her lips.

I turn and stare.

She shifts and pulls her knees up higher, giving me a better view of the tiny shorts she's wearing.

I walk closer and really give her a look. I wouldn't put it past her to fake a wet dream just to throw me off my game.

As if I can wake her with my stare, I drive my attention onto her. My worry heightens from the wince on her face. I scan her from head to toe.

She's shaking.

Without the intent to wake her, I place the back of my hand on her cheek. I pull my hand away just as quickly. *Fuck.* She's burning up.

Another faint whimper hits my ears as I move to her bathroom. I pull open all the drawers, and naturally, there isn't a thermometer anywhere. I know for certain that I don't have one lying around upstairs.

I never get sick, and I surely never take care of anyone who's sick.

Landing on her bedside table, I pull open the drawer in hopes that it'll be in there.

It takes a second for my head to catch up with the rising of my dick.

Does River know about these? *Jesus.*

Several condoms in various sizes are scattered around and not one but *two* vibrators. As if one isn't enough for her?

Goddamn it, focus.

Jogging back to the bathroom, I wet some towels like my mom used to do when I was sick. I wring them out so they're damp with cool water. With a steady hand, I push back her soft hair until her face comes into full view. I place the rag onto her forehead, and her nose scrunches immediately. That plump bottom lip of hers steals my attention when it plops out with a pout.

"Mom, stop," she whines, brushing my hand away.

I chuckle under my breath. She makes a whiny noise in response.

"I'm fine," she mutters.

"You've really gotta quit saying that, Daisy-Petal."

Daisy jerks awake with a gasp. Her eyelashes flutter several times before our eyes connect in the dark.

I raise an eyebrow. "You're not fine," I say. "Now move over."

Twenty-Nine

DAISY

IS THIS A FEVER DREAM?

Kane Barlow, in nothing but low-hanging sweats, standing beside my bed in the middle of the night seems like a ruse.

He mutters something under his breath before his arms glide beneath my back, shoving me toward the center of my bed. Something cold and wet falls off my forehead, but he's quick to put it back in its rightful spot before lifting my blankets and covering us both up.

Another chill racks my body, and my teeth suddenly start to chatter.

"Come here," he whispers.

One arm goes under my head as he pulls me in closer. The weight of his hand rests over the dip of my hip, and although I'm still frustrated from earlier, I can't refuse the warmth he's giving me.

I rest my cheek against his bare chest.

He hisses. "Goddamn, you're hot."

A small smile twitches against my lips. "I sure am."

His amused breath wafts against my hair. "You know that's not what I meant."

I shrug. "Doesn't mean it's not true."

"Where is your thermometer?" he asks.

"I'll be okay," I reassure him. "The fever will run its course. This happens sometimes with Lupus." It usually indicates a flare-up, but I'm hopeful it'll pass without any other symptoms.

Kane grunts. "I didn't ask."

Silence fills the room. It doesn't take me long to break from the rising tension. "The batteries are dead in my thermometer," I admit.

From the way Kane tenses, I prepare myself for a reprimand.

"Well, you could always use the batteries in those vibrators you have in your bedside table."

I gape at him in the dark. "Did you look through my drawers?!" *Wait.* "And you broke into my apartment?"

I growl quietly but move closer to him for warmth. "Did you come back to insult me some more? Tell me how I'm a liar?"

The grinding of his teeth is barely noticeable over the clacking of mine. "Maybe," he whispers.

A chill wracks through me. My body aches, my energy depleted. I want to keep sparring with him, but it takes too much out of me. *He* takes too much out of me.

Kane's fingers faintly brush against the skin of my arm, leaving a trail of goosebumps behind. He pulls me in closer, and I don't fight it.

"If I wasn't shaking like a leaf, I'd kick you out of my bed," I threaten.

He chuckles darkly. "No, you wouldn't."

My nose scrunches. I reach up and pinch him.

"Was that supposed to hurt?" He snickers. "You should

know by now that there are other ways to hurt me, Daisy-Petal."

I stay quiet and try to understand his words. The rubbing against my arm becomes more consistent, and—I won't lie—it feels good. With my head against his chest, I count his heartbeats to distract me from waves of nausea. A shaky breath clamors from my mouth, and his lazy fingers freeze against my flesh.

"Are you okay?" He sounds worried.

I barely raise a shoulder. "I've been worse."

"Wow." He exhales heavily, warmth coating my skin. "This is the first time you haven't lied to me and said you were fine."

A faint laugh slips from my mouth. "I'm too tired to play games with you tonight."

Kane pulls me in closer and removes the rag from my head. It flops to the floor, and suddenly, a new one takes its place. "Go to sleep. I've got you tonight."

My eyes close right away. If I were on my A-game, I'd get back at him for the other night on the ice when he tricked me into letting him strip me bare, but I can't fathom it right now.

Lying here wrapped in his arms feels too familiar, too comforting.

We can pretend things aren't messy for tonight.

But for tonight only, because even if he wants to play nice right now, I know it won't last long.

———

My alarm rings, and I curse groggily. It cuts off a moment later, and confusion slips to the surface. I pull one eye open and wince at the sunlight pouring in from the windows. The sun peeks through the tall Chicago buildings, and I glance to my herbs sitting nearby. It's the perfect window for them to thrive in.

A breathy sigh falls out of my mouth, and I turn on my side with a wince.

Let's play the game: *Is Daisy achy from a flare, or is Daisy achy because she has suddenly taken up ice-skating?*

I reach for my notebook. I need to write down my symptoms so I can try to backtrack and figure out what's flared me. The triggers are endless. Instead of landing on my notebook, I land on a soggy towel. I pull my hand back immediately, and the night rushes in.

Kane. Is he still here?

Through the throbbing in my temples, I force myself to sit. The covers fall to my lap in a lumpy pile as I glance to the doorway of my bedroom.

A swallow gets stuck in my throat. He's still here, alright.

If any other girl woke up to Kane Barlow standing in their doorway, shirtless, with a cup of steaming coffee in his hand, they'd think they were in some sort of fantasy. Me? It's like a nightmare.

A hot nightmare, but still.

"Your fever broke around four." He's so nonchalant, standing there in the doorway.

Steam billows out from his mug as he places it up to his lips and takes a sip. The bobbing of his Adam's apple catches my eye as he swallows. I gulp in response.

"How are you feeling?" he asks, glancing out at the skyline instead of my face.

Terrible.

I swallow the truth and lie because the sooner he's gone, the better. "I'm fine—"

Kane snaps a glare over to me, and as if it has a mind of its own, my mouth snaps shut.

"Told you." My heart stops from the sound of my brother's voice behind Kane.

Kane rolls his eyes over his shoulder at River, and my body

flares with heat. Are they chatting about me behind my back? A threat almost flies out of my mouth toward Kane, because I don't like the way he's suddenly banding together with River regarding my health. Just a mere twelve hours ago, he was hurling insults at me.

"I am fine," I repeat. "This is completely normal for someone with Lupus. It's just the inflammation." I sit up a little taller and lean to the left, putting my attention on River. "Something you should know...Dr. Sullivan."

He narrows his gaze before glancing back to his phone. His hair is damp from a shower, but instead of looking like he's about to collapse onto his bed as usual after a shift, his ID badge hangs off his neck, and he's dressed like he is heading back in.

"Are you going back to the hospital?" I ask.

"Yeah, they're short-staffed." He turns to Kane. "Can you stay with her and make sure she's good?"

I huff. "I do not need Kane to stay here with me. I'm fine. I know my body."

The moment the words leave my mouth, there's a shift in the air that only Kane and I can feel. River is going on about how I didn't even have batteries for my thermometer—*thanks for ratting me out, Kane!*—and attempting to persuade me to go get another round of blood work, but all I can do is glare at Kane's cocky smirk.

I thought too much time had passed between us for me to be able to read his mind, but I know exactly what he's thinking: that he knows my body too, especially after the other night.

He follows my brother to the door, chatting quietly about something. *Me* probably. I sit and stew on my bed until Kane suddenly reappears and takes up space in my bedroom.

"Up," he demands.

He turns to the skyline and sips on his coffee casually, like he expects me to just follow his command. I sigh loudly, and I see just enough of his face to notice that his mouth turns up on the side, which only irritates me more.

Kicking the covers off my legs, I move to stand with my arms crossed. "I'm not a dog!"

That chiseled jaw of his turns toward me. "You sure? You followed my command pretty well."

My nostrils flare.

"Maybe I should reward you with a treat."

Part of me wants to bark at him, but then I picture myself biting him.

"Maybe I should reward you with a *bite*," I snap.

He turns around, flexing his abs in my face. "Wouldn't be the first time a woman has bitten me."

Ugh.

I storm through my bedroom and head for the kitchen. If I'm going to be forced to talk to Kane this morning, I'm going to need my matcha latte as backup. Once I reach the island, I pause mid-step.

My tense shoulders drop slightly.

There's a mug of matcha already waiting for me.

"One drop of honey," he says, having followed me out of my room. "And I added a little turmeric. I saw it next to your vitamins, and I read that it's supposed to help with inflammation."

Unwilling to let him see my confusion, I grab my mug and take a sip before slowly turning to face him. I rest my back against the island and eye him closely. "Interesting," I note.

He squints. "What is?"

I shrug. "I didn't know you could be kind."

The taste of matcha remains on my tongue, and I *hate* that it's better than when I make it. The hint of honey bursts through the bitter tea taste, foamed to perfection.

Unfair.

Kane turns and walks toward the windows, keeping a distance from my plants. He stares at the skyline as I stand back and watch him from the kitchen with a pit in my lower stomach.

"Why are you here?" I finally ask.

I refuse to be blinded by one small, kind act from him.

I'm not naive enough to think that just because I let it slip that I cared more for him than I admitted back when we were teenagers that it'll be some new beginning for us. There's too much tension lingering in the air. It brushes against my skin like electricity. I bet if I look closely enough, the hairs on my arms are standing erect.

"What do you mean?" He keeps his attention on the city while sipping his coffee.

"I mean..." I place my mug down. "Why did you come over last night?"

He inhales deeply. His chest expands before answering me. "River asked me to check on you."

Oh.

Why am I disappointed?

I shouldn't be, but there was definitely a little prick of disappointment to my skin. Did I want him to come over on his own?

I glance to the floor and stare at my bare feet. I count my toes to keep me grounded, but then, Kane's feet end up next to mine. He grips my chin gently and tips my face to meet his. I do my best to cover up my thoughts by flattening my lips and evening out my furrowed brow.

"I knew something was off last night when you stormed off into your apartment. I called River, and he asked me to go check on you."

My eye twitches with skepticism. "You don't know me that well, Kane."

Is he lying? Did he come over to continue our fight? Or did he come over because he was worried about me?

His heavy sigh hits me in the face. "Yeah, I do."

A knock on my door causes his hand to fall, and he instantly puts space between us like he's been caught doing something wrong.

Even though it's my apartment, he's the one who walks over to the door and swings it open.

"What are you doing here?" Kane asks someone.

"Just making sure you made it home, high roller."

I peer off to the side and spot Malaki.

He walks inside, bypassing his roommate. "Thanks for bringing him home. I owe you."

"I didn't need her to bring me home," Kane grumbles.

With his mug still in his grip, he walks past Malaki. "Come on, let's go."

Before Malaki follows Kane back to their apartment, I fleetingly catch his eye. It's obvious from the way he flattens his lips that we're both worried about Kane gambling at the casino.

Thirty

KANE

MY FINGERS TINGLE, and my legs ache. Usually, when we're playing on the road, it's hard for us to come together on the ice. We're all a little disoriented, especially during the first period, but if I'm being honest, I'm more focused right now than I am at home.

I know it's because Daisy isn't here in that tight blue devil's outfit, waving her stupid trident around, stealing everyone's attention.

Malaki sits down and shakes out his sweaty hair like a dog, hitting both Rhodes and me in the face.

"I'm going to put you in a fucking cage if you ever do that again," Rhodes grumbles.

He stands up quickly with his phone in hand and stalks off toward Emory while half the team chuckles behind his back.

We're already gearing up for our last period. Lars and Crew, our new guys, are watching one of the iPads with furrowed brows while some of our veteran players are quiet and focused.

Things are tense, and with Malaki breathing down my neck, it puts me on edge.

"Back up," I snap.

He ignores me.

Typical.

"What's up with you and devil girl?" Malaki bends at the waist to retighten the laces on his skates. I do the same, except I start with my left, as always, because we need all the luck we can get.

"You really want to know?" I peer over at him, and the surprise is almost enough to make me feel bad for fucking with him.

Almost.

"Give me all the dirty details." He wiggles his eyebrows up and down. If I were going to tell him anything, I would have changed my mind immediately.

I stand and push back my damp hair. Malaki has a gleam in his eye, waiting for me to spill all my secrets to him.

There's only one person I've ever trusted enough to tell my secrets to, and it isn't him.

"Alright." I lean down and lower my voice. For dramatic effect, I pause for a few seconds and then say, "None of your fucking business."

"Oh, come on!" Malaki stands and throws his arms up. "You're no fun."

"Says the guy who called a woman to come get me," I quietly snap.

I take off toward the ice, not wanting to hear any bullshit from anyone else on the team.

They think I'm unaware of their little group chat and how they take turns keeping a watch over me if I'm ever feeling antsy and need to let some steam off. The last thing I want is for anyone else to learn that Daisy is the real gatekeeper when it comes to me.

A few laps around the ice, and Malaki is at my back.

"Listen"—he taps his stick on the ice as we wait for the game to start—"I did it for your own good. The casino is the last place you need to be."

My jaw aches with pressure. I skate around, pushing my blades into the ice with force.

"You just got out of the hole because of your brother's gambling," he says quietly as I pass by. "Don't end up there again because of your own gambling."

He'd be beyond pissed if he knew I was there to pay off another debt of Miles's, and I wouldn't blame him. Malaki saved my ass before, and I understand why he's concerned that I may have my own gambling addiction, but that's far from the truth.

In fact, I'm addicted to something far worse.

Coach gives us a warning before heading to his hotel room. *If you go out, don't fuck up.*

Noted.

Lars asked me to go out with him, and I know it's because I'm the only one who never refuses. He's out on the dance floor, wearing some girl's cowgirl hat while swinging her around, and I'm over here, sitting at the bar with my phone in my hand.

I glance at it for the fourth time since getting my beer. I keep River's text on unread, not wanting the notification to disappear, because it's a silent warning not to text his sister.

Back in my pocket it goes. I glance around the bar to find someone to fill my time with.

If I can't beat 'em, join 'em.

More like, if I can't be with Daisy, be with someone else.

The malty beer flows down my throat as I force thoughts of her and all the texts I've typed so far, only to delete a moment later, out of my head.

She's survived several years without me—something she made sure to point out when I attempted to check on her earlier in the day.

My now empty beer bottle clanks onto the bar top after I catch the eye of a blond.

There's a pull in my chest—and not the kind that is pulling me toward her.

I stand up because there is no way I'm letting Daisy get in my head to ruin this.

Instead of being a gentleman and asking the woman to dance, I wrap my arm around her waist and drag her onto the floor. The music is some kind of twangy country song, but it has enough beat to it that she can half-grind on my dick.

"What's your name?" Her voice reminds me of someone who'd be on one of those housewife reality shows.

"No need for names," I say.

Her hips don't fit right in my hands, and the smell of her perfume is too crisp.

I sigh angrily.

I know what my problem is, even if I refuse to admit it.

Little Miss Wannabe Dolly Parton moves easily when I swing her around to face me. She's flush against my body, and I pray that a spark ignites. My fingers wrap around her cheeks, and I lose them in her hair. I slip my tongue into her mouth, hoping she has some mystical kiss that'll sweep me off my feet.

My phone vibrates, and I eagerly pull away.

Since when am I thankful for a distraction during a make-out session?

The woman gasps for air, and I don't wait to see if she gets any.

Daisy's name appears on my screen, and the hottest thrill enters my blood.

I step into the parking lot to hide from Dolly and open the text in private.

DAISY

And here I thought you were done playing games.

My brow furrows.

One, I'll never stop playing games with her because, trust me, I've fucking tried. And two, I'm not sure what she's referring to.

ME

Winning gives me a high, so it's unlikely that I'll ever stop.

Unfortunately, she gives me a high too.

I type another text while leaning on the side of the building.

ME

What game are you referring to? The hockey game?

The thought of her all alone inside her apartment, watching me dominate the ice, shouldn't excite me like this. Why do I want her to watch me play? I'm used to playing for myself and no one else. It's not like my mom is tuning in to cheer me on, yet the thought of Daisy watching me has my palms itching to practice for our next game.

DAISY

The game where you take the batteries from my vibrator!

I pop up from resting against the wall. My fingers tighten around my phone with thoughts of Daisy and her vibrator.

ME

Didn't take you long to find that out. Feeling naughty tonight, are we?

My pulse skyrockets.

Time slows as I stare down at my phone screen.

The anticipation of waiting for her to text back is killing me. Little bubbles pop up when she types, but then they disappear, only for them to appear again.

DAISY

Where are they?

They're in her thermometer—where they'd be better use. I didn't steal them from her vibrator to be an asshole. It's not like I'm jealous of her vibrator or something... Okay, fine. I am.

ME

Mmm. I don't know. Guess you'll have to get off the old-fashioned way.

Or wait until I can do it for you.

Wait, no. Do not fucking say that.

I press myself against the side of the building and duck off into the darkness of the alleyway. The city is alive and well, but tucked in this alcove is just the amount of privacy I need to continue teasing Daisy without someone daring to interrupt me.

ME

Or you can wait until I do it for you.

I couldn't help myself. I just couldn't.

I get antsy when she doesn't reply, so I type another message.

> **ME**
>
> You didn't answer my question. Are you feeling a little naughty tonight?

> **DAISY**
>
> Fuck off.

My chuckle echoes all around me.

> **ME**
>
> Answer me, and I'll give you a hint on where the batteries are.

It takes her a few minutes to text back, and I can picture her now, looking for the batteries in the cabinets and under her couch cushions. It's either that, or she's actually touching herself.

I freeze with my fingers hovering over the call button.

She better not be.

> **DAISY**
>
> How do I know you'll actually tell me the truth? I don't trust you.

> **ME**
>
> You can say you don't trust me, but deep down, you do.

Daisy texts back right away, and I'm more engaged than ever.

> **DAISY**
>
> You seduced me the other night just to win your stupid little game. I most definitely don't trust you.

ME

You think I seduced you just to win?

Couldn't she see how wrapped around her finger I was? Or how wild I became with her taste on my tongue?

ME

That isn't the only reason I did what I did, Daisy. Now answer my question.

Time moves slowly. I swear it takes eons for her to message me back.

DAISY

I'll answer your question if you answer mine.

I'm intrigued.

ME

What's your question?

I call for an Uber and text Lars that I'm leaving. He clearly doesn't need me here anyway.

The Uber shows up before Daisy texts back.

I'm sure she's still searching around for the batteries.

By the time my driver arrives at the hotel, my pulse is flying. Visions of Daisy alone in her apartment, doing unspeakable things to herself instead of texting me back, has me on edge.

I choose the stairs instead of the elevator, too eager to be alone in my room with Daisy on the other line, rather than be caught by a fan waiting in the elevator.

The door latches, and my phone goes off at the same time. I'm so eager for the text that I fumble with the device. I accidently click on River's name, and it's a swift punch to the gut. I swipe his name and delete our entire message thread.

There. Problem solved.

DAISY

> You said there was another reason why you seduced me. What was it?

I flop onto my bed.

ME

> Seduced? I'm not sure I like the sound of that word.

I eagerly watch the bubbles pop up on the screen while she types and try to remember a time where I felt so captivated with something as simple as texting. The last time I felt this way was probably with her.

DAISY

> Lure? Corrupt? Deceive?

Corrupt. Why does that make my dick hard?
Corrupting Daisy Sullivan. *God yes.*

ME

> Corrupting Daisy Sullivan. I like the sound of that.

My dick does too.

I blame my sudden lack of rational thinking on the buzz the beer gave me. I've been forcing Daisy far from my mind since the other night and focusing on where my loyalty lies. Right now, though? I can't seem to find that steady ground I was on earlier.

DAISY

> Wouldn't be the first time. 😊

Oh, she wants to go there?

Me: If I remember correctly, you came on to me that night. In fact, I recall you begging.

I'd bet my life that Daisy is rolling her eyes at me through the phone.

ME

Stop rolling your eyes. You know it's true.

DAISY

How did you know I rolled my eyes?

ME

Because I know you better than you think.

Even with our time apart, I still know her like the back of my hand.

DAISY

Whatever. Answer the question.

The more we text, the more surprised I become. I would've thought she'd give up on the conversation by now, but maybe she's enjoying this as much as I am.

ME

Reason number one: To win, obviously. There's no way I was going to lose strip hockey and discuss Miles with you.

My jaw flexes with the mere thought of diving into that fuckery.

ME

Reason number two...

Fuck, I shouldn't be texting her this.

ME

Because I still can't resist you, Daisy.

And that's the whole truth and nothing but the truth.

DAISY

I don't believe that even for a second. Bye.

Afraid she'll slip right through my fingers for the night, I impulsively video chat her.

The phone rings once, and my chest grows tight.

It rings a second time, and my pulse races.

By the third ring, I'm contemplating taking an early flight back home.

But then, on the fourth ring, she picks up.

Thirty-One

DAISY

I SHOULD BAN myself from talking to Kane, because I clearly can't be trusted when it comes to him.

Butterflies fly to my stomach when his name appears on the screen. My finger hovers over the decline button. I teeter back and forth with an impulse I can't seem to escape from and eventually hit accept.

His face appears, and the breath whooshes from my lungs.

Perfectly tousled hair, steely-blue eyes staring at me through the screen, and a flexing jaw that my fingers beg to touch.

Even with exhaustion settling into my bones, one look from him and I'm wide awake.

"You don't believe me?" He shifts his attention all around my face. "Let me show you something."

Dangerous thoughts slip into my head, a trail of fire left behind from each one.

He pops up from his hotel bed and walks through his room until he stops and pans the camera. A lit-up city comes into view through the windows, and I suddenly feel insane for thinking he was going to show me something else.

"See how awake the city is?" he asks.

"Yeah?" I answer with hesitation.

The camera moves back to his face, and he has a determined look in his eyes—the same one he wears on the ice.

"Tell me what I'm doing in my hotel room on the phone with you instead of being out there with everyone else?"

I say nothing, so he continues after sitting on the bed and scooting up to rest against the headboard.

"When I say I can't resist you, I mean it." His eyes flare. "Something you know deep down."

A soft swallow moves down my throat as I repeat his words in my head. "I think you can't resist teasing me," I argue.

There's an uptick in my pulse the longer we talk. The tension bundled in my lower stomach tightens with his lopsided smile. This is exactly why I needed to take care of myself. I'm full of pent-up sexual tension, and it's forcing me to think hot...err, I mean *horrible* thoughts about Kane.

"Of course I can't resist teasing you, little devil."

I raise an eyebrow. "Is that why you stole the batteries from my vibrator?"

Kane shrugs. "Sure."

My lips flatten. "That wasn't very convincing."

His hot smirk slowly disappears. He sighs loudly and looks away from me. I stare at the sharp curve of his jaw as it flickers back and forth.

"What?" I ask quietly.

I watch him closely. Silence settles between us, but the energy is buzzing, even through the phone. My heart pounds, and my palms tickle with sweat. "Kane—"

He snaps his blue eyes to me suddenly, his pupils dilating. "I should get off the phone."

The disappointment hits me like a freight train. I open my mouth to accept his suggestion, because he's right. What are we even doing right now?

A second passes and then another. My finger creeps toward the end button.

He exhales loudly. "Too late. You win."

His temples flicker back and forth with the grinding of his jaw. He seems fed up with something.

Me?

Himself?

"What do you mean, I win?" My voice is quiet and raspy.

Why do I suddenly sound like a porn star?

Kane's tongue slips out of his mouth, and he swipes it quickly against his bottom lip. "I took the batteries because, yeah, I love irritating the hell out of you..."

An insult is on the tip of my tongue, but he interrupts me before I can get it out.

"And because I'm selfish as fuck." Now, his voice is raspy.

Our eyes catch. My bedroom fades, and the only thing I see is his face through the phone.

"How so?" I squeeze my legs together slowly.

A frustrated noise leaves him, and it's annoyingly hot. "I didn't want you to get off..."

My jaw falls open with a silent gasp. Kane is bold, arrogant beyond belief, and I'm highly attracted to it. "So you took my vibrator batteries?"

He shakes his head. "I didn't want you to get off without me there to watch...or help."

I close my mouth and stare at him. Oh. *Oh.* With blood rushing to the apex of my thighs, it's obvious that I like the idea more than I should.

He makes a noise, eyes focused on something other than my face. I glance at my shirt, and my cheeks grow warm. *Thanks for giving me away, boobs.*

"You like knowing I want to watch you?" His voice is seduction wrapped in a pretty bow that I'm suddenly desperate to untie.

With him alone in some hotel and me tucked away in my bedroom, I'm safe. There is nothing quite as enticing as Kane Barlow growing all hot and bothered, knowing he can't touch me.

"Answer me," he says.

I bite my lip before answering. "I wasn't aware it was a question. You seemed pretty certain in your assumption."

His jaw becomes even more defined as he leans back farther onto the headboard. "I still want to hear you say it."

Oh, how badly I want to give in.

"I'd rather not admit something you can hold over my head when you decide to remember that you hate me." *Or worse, when you remember that I'm your best friend's little sister.*

"I'll tell you where the batteries are," he says eagerly. "Or you can just wait until I get back, and I'll help you with your little problem."

That's enticing.

Too enticing.

Heat pools in between my legs, and I snap.

"Fine," I rasp.

Kane's eyes widen, full of hidden excitement.

"I..." My mouth runs dry because I know I'll regret this later.

"Go on." His tone is throaty, the words lingering.

My other hand, the one not holding the phone with a death grip, starts to play with the waistband of my shorts. "I like the idea of you watching me..."

His tongue slips out between his lips again, wetting them. "Finish the sentence."

Desire floods me, and I follow his command right away. "I like the idea of you watching me get myself off."

Sharp breaths filter through the phone, and Kane's chest is heaving. "And?"

I swallow. "I like the idea of you helping me too."

Kane clenches his eyes closed, and my teeth sink into my bottom lip. Either he's really good at messing with me, or he's truly just as turned on as I am.

"Thermometer." He forces the word through tight teeth. "The batteries are in your thermometer."

I exhale without even realizing I was holding my breath.

His eyes quickly open, the blue a stormy color filled with lust. Unable to handle the hold he has on me, I hang up in search of my thermometer.

When I get back to my bed with two batteries in the palm of my hand, I see his text.

KANE

I hope you're thinking about me, Daisy. Because I'm most definitely thinking about you.

———

The stands are full tonight.

Rival games always bring in a lot of energy. The crowd's enthusiasm is contagious, and for the first time in weeks, I'm less exhausted and more lively.

Though, I'm not sure if it's the fanbase that is giving me a sudden zest for the game or if it's a certain player that I can't help but follow on the ice.

I trap my lip in between my teeth as I think about the dirty images I fed myself while touching myself. If he asks, I'm totally denying that it ever happened.

My cheeks burn.

He needs to get out of my head.

"Go ahead, devil girl," someone says from behind.

I turn before stepping onto the ice. It's Wes, dressed in his white-and-black-striped shirt with a lopsided grin.

"I see you've improvised." He checks me out from head to toe, eyeing me a little too closely in my new-and-improved Blue Devils mascot costume.

I look down at the sparkly blue material and smile. "No more pesky zippers."

"Darn." He steps closer to me. "I was hoping you'd need help shedding it like the last costume."

"Wes." An older referee gives him a disapproving look before flicking his chin to the ice.

Wes winks at me before skating toward the other men dressed in black and white.

There's no time to rehash the conversation in my head, because as soon as my skate touches the slick floor, ice shavings rise like the tide, and two stormy-blue eyes are staring at me beneath a Blue Devils helmet.

"What was that all about?" There's a bite to Kane's tone that drives me wild.

A girly laugh leaves me. "Wouldn't you like to know?"

I attempt to skate past him with my foam tridents in tow, but he falls right in line with me.

His chuckle sends goosebumps to my skin. "You should feel violated by the way he was looking at you when your back was turned."

Like an addiction, I crave to keep the conversation going.

"No more than how I felt after you stripped me bare on this very ice, just to win a game." I catch a glimpse of his expression and wish I hadn't.

His furrowed brow smooths, and that smug mouth of his

quirks on the side. His gaze skips over his teammates and lands on the spot where he all but stripped me down to nothing.

"I don't think you can consider it violating when you enjoy it..." He's so confident, and it drives me crazy.

I fake my smile as I throw tridents over the glass to fans, all while keeping up the conversation with him. "Who said I enjoyed it?"

"Your cum on my fingers..." His whisper silently touches every intimate part of my body, and I grow antsy.

"Go away," I urge. "I'm trying to work."

"Yeah, she's trying to work," Wes enters the conversation, and I can sense Kane's blood pressure rising like it's my own.

The glare he sends Wes would make any man shake, but Wes stands tall with a haughty smirk in Kane's direction.

A rush of protectiveness burrows itself into my chest, and I grit my teeth. Kane glances at me briefly, and I suddenly worry he can read my mind.

Aiming to hide the truth, I skate a little closer to Wes. Kane flicks an eyebrow, and the muscles against his jaw flicker back and forth with a warning.

He narrows his gaze, focusing directly on me. "That's how you wanna play this?"

I remain ignorant. "Play what?"

His lip curls, but there's a hint of amusement there. "Just remember you asked for it, Daisy."

I should be worried, but instead, my stomach fills with anticipation, and my lips beg to curve.

Thirty-Two

KANE

IS this her way of getting back at me for making her admit out loud that she liked the idea of me watching her come? If so, I've gotta say, I'm not a fucking fan.

My fingers tingle as they wrap around the handle of my stick. I stare at Wes with the puck in his hand, and the only thing I want to do is hit him instead of it.

Can I really blame the guy for being interested in Daisy?

Just look at her—pretty, wavy locks of hair perfect for pulling, soul-wrenching baby blues, and a smile that is sweeter than any dessert I've ever tasted.

Actually...I do blame him. *He's officially on my shit list.*

A growl revs in the back of my throat. When the puck drops, I already have a plan brewing.

Two plans, to be exact.

I focus on the game, and it isn't until we're nearing the end of the first period that I find an opportunity to get my point across. I've got one eye on Wes and one eye on the puck. It slips out to the right, and I quickly race to it alongside one of the Bolts. Seeing that Malaki is curving around the back of the net to snag it for a breakaway, I turn because there's a ten-out-of-ten chance that number seven is going to slam into me.

I brace myself for the impact by angling my shoulder to take the brunt of it.

The crowd roars in the background, banging on the glass while they follow Malaki down the opposite end of the rink.

The connection my shoulder makes with number seven jolts my spine, but the pain is long forgotten when he flies into Wes, knocking him right off his skates.

A horn is blown when Malaki scores, and the fans erupt.

I smirk, mainly because there's a heap of black and white on the ice that's awfully slow to get up.

I skate over to him, like the good guy that I am, and help him to his feet.

"My bad," I say, voice hinting with feigned remorse. I brush him off, knowing the cameras are on us. "Sorry about that."

Wes's glare makes my mouth twitch. I lean in close before letting go of him. "Stay away from her."

It must give him some confidence without my grip on his shirt, because he scowls. "Or what?" he asks.

I shrug just enough for him to notice. "Targeting on the ice goes both ways, Wes. That was just a glimpse of what I can do."

He turns and glances off to the side, his jaw grinding with hidden anger. I follow his line of sight, and Daisy is standing off to the side with a silent warning on her face I've seen too many times before.

Unfortunately for her, I feed off it like a predator.

I skate toward the bench and grab some water, keeping my attention on her.

She crosses her arms against her blue sparkly outfit, and I wink at her.

Her glare isn't the least bit intimidating. In fact, it's sort of…cute.

Addiction comes in all forms, and mine is her.

I slowly skate past her to get into position for the last minute of the period.

"Was that really necessary?" she seethes.

I shield myself from the cameras, in case they see me talking to her when I'm supposed to be focused on the game of hockey instead of my game with her. "If you want to play games, you've gotta be prepared to lose, baby."

Those perfect lips purse with annoyance, and I chuckle on my way toward my position.

It doesn't take much longer for us to sweep the Bolts. They pull their goalie to add another player onto the ice, but with a quick steal, I send it flying into the net from center ice, and the buzzer sounds twenty seconds later.

I'm pulled to the side for Daisy to do her player-of-the-game announcement. Standing beside Emory and Malaki, I watch her take the ice with a microphone in hand.

I hate that outfit.

With her quick skating, the thin material hardly covers her from behind as it flies up to reveal her perfect curves. A hot pull in my groin gets my attention, but it disappears the second I hear catcalling from the side.

A group of horny college guys are staring at Daisy, as if they actually have a chance with her.

With jealousy swimming inside my veins, I take my stick and bang it on the glass. Their attention swings to me. At first, they're shell-shocked, in complete awe. But then, they get a glimpse of my glare, and their unhinged jaws snap shut.

I nod to Daisy on the ice, who just announced Malaki, and then back to them. I shake my head. *Don't even think about it.*

She's mine to play with, not theirs.

Which brings me right back to our little game.

Daisy probably thinks my *accidental* hit to Wes is the end of what I have up my sleeve, but she's wrong.

I scoot closer to the ice and catch the eye of a woman with a press badge wrapped around her neck. Knowing that Daisy is about to look in my direction when she calls my name, I lean in real close to the brunette and smile. "Hey."

She immediately straightens, and her cheeks turn red. "Oh! Hi."

"Did you enjoy the game?" I ask, moving a piece of hair out of her face.

She bats her eyelashes, clearly surprised at my close proximity. "Um—ye...yes."

Staying close to the woman, I wait for Daisy to call my name.

"Next up is Kane Barlow for the last shot of the game."

I laugh to myself.

Without even looking in her direction, I know she's irritated with me by the sound of her tone. I step onto the ice with my left skate and raise my arm toward the crowd. I make a circle around her while they cheer before casually slipping my arm around her waist to escort her off the rink.

Her peppermint scent fills my senses, and I refrain from inhaling because I know the cameras are on us. "Jealous?" I mutter, barely moving my lips.

"No," she hisses.

As soon as we disappear down the hall toward the locker room, she shoves my arm away from her waist with as much force as she can muster up.

I keep up with her angry stride. "Oh, good. You can find your own ride, then?"

She stops walking, so I do too.

"Something wrong?" I ask with a teasing tone.

Come on, admit it.

I'm desperate for her to tell me she's just as jealous as I am. I want her all to myself, even if I can't technically have her.

If I can't have her, no one can.

My shoulders tense. *What a fucking possessive thing to say.*

Yet...I said what I said.

Daisy waits for the equipment manager to pass before popping her hip. "Nothing's wrong."

She's lying right through her white teeth.

"You'll find a ride home, then?" I glance backward, and sure enough, the woman with the press badge I flirted with for a total of three seconds is waiting for me. When I turn back toward Daisy, she's staring in the woman's direction with pursed lips.

"Daisy," I muse, "you're showing all your cards."

Her chest heaves, and she exhales. The air surrounding us grows tight, my own breathing labored. I have the sudden urge to wrap my hands around her shimmery cheeks and pull her in to kiss me.

"Well, you're the gambler out of the two of us. Sorry I don't have a poker face," she snaps.

My lips twitch. *Mm, she must be really irritated.*

"Just admit that you're jealous." I take a step closer to her, and to my surprise, she keeps herself planted in the same spot.

She rolls her eyes, and my dick twitches.

I've gotta get this cup off immediately.

"Why? Does it even matter?" she asks, fully exasperated.

I nod.

It matters to me.

She sighs. Her hot breath against my face makes my knees weak. "It's not like anything will happen between us if I admit it. I'm still River's little sister."

My hands trap her waist. I drag her around the corner of the hall and gently push her against the wall with enough force to shut her mouth. "You don't think anything will happen between us? Just because you're off-limits?"

I glide my hand over her curves slowly, embracing the way she feels against my callused palm. The moment I touch the outer part of her breast, her breathing changes from annoyed heaves to ragged gasps.

She's out of her mind if she thinks I won't cross the line with her again.

I drive my stare into hers. "If you're off-limits to me, you're off-limits to everyone."

I've said some insane shit over the years, but this has got to be one of the most unhinged things I've ever said to a woman.

What am I? A fucking caveman? Am I going to bang my chest every time a man looks at her?

This is exactly why we were better off separated. I can't control myself when it comes to her.

"That's crazy," she whispers.

It takes every ounce of strength I have to pull away from her. "You make me crazy," I admit. "Now go get your things. We're going home."

Thirty–Three

DAISY

THE PARKING LOT IS EMPTYING, and the inside of Kane's car is becoming darker from the disappearing head-lights. If I was still in the mood to play games with him, I'd lock the car and make him figure out a way to get inside.

Or better yet, I'd drive home without him and make him find his own way back to the apartment.

But jealousy outweighs my need for revenge.

If I were to do that, who's to say he wouldn't get a ride from that woman he was flirting with?

I recross my arms.

Kane irritates me more than anyone, yet I find myself hungry for each interaction. Every time we're together, whether we're arguing or not, I become needier than the time before.

I shut my eyes and rest my head against the glass window. The idling of the engine calms my rushing blood, and within seconds, heavy exhaustion slips in.

Flares have a way of sneaking in and catching me off

guard, and the fear is in a constant loop inside my head when my body feels this fatigued.

I lied to my mom earlier when she called and asked if I was feeling okay. There's no need for her to worry about a disease that is here to stay, and the less she knows about my random fevers or bouts of exhaustion, the better.

The revving of Kane's car catches my attention.

My eyebrows furrow, and I readjust against the glass window.

Is the car moving?

A masculine scent hits my senses, and I relax. Still, after all this time, he smells the same.

"I know you're awake," he says quietly.

Just to be defiant, I remain silent.

After a few seconds of silence, he chuckles. I fall in and out of sleep for the next few minutes. By the vibrating beneath the tires, I know we're entering the parking garage. The thought of having to walk to my apartment sends a roll of nausea into my stomach.

I'll sleep in here.

"We're home, little devil."

Home.

A calmness settles over me like a blanket with the thought of us having a home together, but just as quickly, a wave of nausea hits me.

I make no acknowledgement to move.

Not even a twitch on my face.

Kane's door opens and then closes. *Ah, alone at last.*

Just when I think he's leaving me here, my door opens. I'm suddenly scooped into two strong arms and pressed against something hard.

His heartbeat pounds against my ear as I rest my head on his chest. I find myself wanting to smile.

"Again, I know you're awake..." he grumbles.

This time, I can't stop the curving of my mouth. "I'm too tired to walk," I admit.

His chuckle rumbles against me. "I think you just want my hands on you."

I should deny it.

I want to.

But in the end, I don't. I grow even more comfortable in his arms, and I swear I fall asleep on the elevator ride up.

The door unlatches, and Kane continues walking me through the apartment.

"Just throw me on the bed," I mutter. "I'm too tired to shower."

"Throw you on the bed?" There's a hint of seduction in his tone. "Don't tempt me like that."

His innuendo gives me just enough energy to pull my eyes open. The room is blanketed in dark shadows as he places me down onto what feels like a cloud.

"Thanks," I whisper, eyes fluttering closed again.

I press myself into the bed happily. I inhale deeply, but then my eyes fly open.

"Wait." I quickly sit up and ignore my achy limbs.

Kane blends in with the shadows as he stands over me. "Something wrong?" I can tell he's smiling by the sound of his voice.

"This is not my bed!" *This is not my room.*

My legs drag with exhaustion, but adrenaline gives me enough strength to swing them over the side of his bed. Unfortunately, he's standing right there to trap me. Kane creeps forward and leans in close, hovering above me. His hands fall to the bed beside my thighs, where he bundles the blankets in his tight fists.

The faint light from the window behind me shines directly on the side of his face, illuminating his tight jaw. "Lie down."

"I'm not sleeping in your bed," I refuse.

Kane dips farther toward me, and I remain still. When I realize he isn't going to stop, it forces me to move backward. Otherwise, his lips would end up on mine, and that would be...hot.

I mean...*bad*.

It would be bad.

He lingers above me as I lie flat against his bed. His strong arms move toward my head, where he cages me, as if he doesn't trust me to stay put.

"Go to sleep. You're exhausted."

What is the point of me sleeping in *his* bed? Does he enjoy torturing us both?

"Well...are the sheets at least clean? Or am I sleeping where millions of other women have been?" I ask.

His chuckle cuts through the tension. "As if I let women in my bed."

Vivid thoughts play out in my head of Kane fucking women in other places in his house. The couch? The kitchen counter? The *shower?!*

My mouth runs dry.

"I'm a woman, and I'm in your bed," I rasp.

Kane finally backs away, and I think I'm in the clear, but then he slips his arms underneath me. "You're not just a woman," he whispers, scooting us to the middle of his bed. He drapes the covers over my body, and to my surprise, he lifts his hand and gently brushes my hair away from my face. "You're Daisy."

His words surround my heart with something unfamiliar. I ignore the faint feeling of butterflies in my stomach and stay quiet.

"Go to sleep," he says again, but this time, it's a whisper that floats against my skin like a feather. I force my eyes closed and fall asleep within minutes.

Thirty-Four

KANE

I WAKE to my phone pinging and groggily trap it within my tired grip. Squinting from the light, I wait until my eyes focus and instantly dread the words following the random number.

UNKNOWN

It wasn't enough. They're saying I still owe.

My heart thuds inside my rib cage.

What does he mean it wasn't enough?

I skip my gaze all around my room, like the answer is written on the walls somewhere.

I paid the amount Miles said he owed, so either he lied to me, or he gambled again and added more dollar signs to his debt.

I click my phone off with anger. The morning sun is close to shining over the buildings, but for now, I decide to bask in the darkness of my room and ignore the pit in my stomach.

Daisy shifts beside me, and just like that, I'm distracted.

A yearning flies to my fingertips, but I've been on my best behavior all night.

Each time I stirred awake, I kept my distance, knowing she needed rest. Sure, I stared at her a few times and traced the curve of her delicate jaw, but as if there was an imaginary line drawn between us, I stayed on my side of the bed.

That isn't to say she has stayed on her side, though.

Her body heat pricks my skin, and if I move a breath in her direction, we'll be touching.

It's like high school all over again. The most innocent touches from her turn into wicked thoughts and insane desires. Nerves eat away at my stomach, which is insane because I rarely get nervous.

Especially with a woman.

Daisy moves again, and every hair on my body stands erect. Out of my peripheral vision, I watch her turn toward me with an outstretched arm.

My heart pounds.

One of her legs wraps around mine, and I die a silent death when she uses it as an anchor to pull herself closer.

Fuck me.

If she were awake, she wouldn't be doing this. She'd probably scowl at me and say something to irritate me, so I take this for what it is and wrap my arm around her and trap her.

There is no reason for my behavior other than it feels too damn good to have her body heat mingling with mine.

Daisy makes a noise, and my dick is the first to notice.

Her chest brushes against my side, and I'm on edge. I squeeze my eyes shut until...*is she shirtless?*

I snap to her torso playing peek-a-boo with the covers, and my life flashes before my eyes.

She has nothing covering her breasts.

My mouth parts as I continue to stare at her teasing curves

while realizing that her bare nipples are what's grazing my chest.

Is she trying to kill me? I think for a moment. Actually, yeah, that's probably likely.

"Daisy." Her name squeezes out between my clenched teeth.

She makes a noise right before a breathy sigh floats against my skin.

"Where the hell is your shirt?" I sound calm, but I'm raging just as much as my dick is.

She snuggles further into me. "I was hot," she says groggily. "Probably had a fever or something."

I shut my eyes. "So you took your shirt off? While in *my* bed?"

Daisy tenses, as if just coming to.

Before she can scurry away, I flip her onto her back and hover above her. Those pretty eyes flutter open, and I silently wish the sun would rise a little more so I could get lost in the blue of them like I'm out at sea.

"I..." Her slow, shallow breaths catch my ear. "I forgot I was in your bed."

I chuckle darkly. "Or do you enjoy tempting me?"

I'm turned on, irritated from the warnings in my head, and seconds from showing her how I really feel about her being in my bed.

This is bad.

I should have never even brought her here, but I was worried about her after she fell asleep in my car. After the fever incident and River's constant checks on her, I thought it was best.

"I do like irritating you," she whispers. "But I really did forget I was here."

Silence nestles in between the space I've purposefully put between us, but the longer I stare at her from above, the more my eyes adjust. Perfect bow-shaped lips, high cheekbones, soft hair intertwined in between my fingers.

"Are you going to tell me to get off of you?" *Why hasn't she yet?*

Her head tilts. "Will you actually listen?"

Heat erupts in my groin from the movement of her legs. I'm too afraid to see if she opened them up for better access, because if she did, I'll take it as an invitation.

"I'll listen," I answer. "If you want to leave my bed, I'll let you."

This little game we've been playing needs to end.

I'm already too sucked in, thinking about her every second of the day, watching her from the ice when I should be paying attention to the game, forgetting that her brother is my best friend who I made a pact with years ago not to touch her.

I broke it not once, but twice. I shouldn't break it again.

Unless...

"Do you want to leave my bed, Daisy?"

Silence.

All I hear is my raging heartbeat.

She opens her mouth, and I think I might die if she says yes.

"If you don't want to leave my bed..." I unbury my hand from her hair and gently brush the strands away from her face. "Then tell me."

Her sweet gasp hits me in every hidden spot as I brush my fingers against her delicate neck. I desperately crave her soft skin against my lips, so much that I'm starting to spew lies to myself.

Maybe if we give in to the tension, just this once, we won't be so tempted the next time. The chemistry will simmer; the pull will lessen.

"No."

My head jerks to the side. "No?" *No, what?* No, she won't tell me, or no, she doesn't want to leave my bed?

She pouts quietly, and I detest that I have no idea what she's thinking.

I drag my fingers achingly slow against her neck and let them brush over her collarbone before skimming past the curve of her breast. I land at her hip bone and pause. "No, what?" I ask. "You don't want to leave my bed? Or are you refusing to answer my question?"

Daisy's ribs expand, and I bite my tongue.

God damn, she is irresistible.

"Just say it," I beg.

"Say what?"

I'd give up my last breath to hear her say she wants me as much as I want her.

"That you want to stay right here in my bed." I lean down and brush my lips against her ear. I inhale her scent, and goose-bumps rise to my skin, just like they do hers.

My fingers get lost in her hair, and I tug on the strands to ground us both. "Tell me you want me to make you feel good. That even though we bicker and irritate each other on purpose, you still trust me enough to have you like this."

Somehow, my hand ends up in between her legs. I keep it steady on the inside of her thigh, but all I want to do is pull the thin boy brief panties from her body and toss them to the floor with the rest of her clothes she shed throughout the night.

"Kane." The heat behind my name coming from her lips is hot enough to burn the entire complex to ashes.

"Do you still trust me, Daisy?" I ask, hope obvious in my tone.

I glide my fingers up farther and play with the fabric of her panties.

We're both out of breath, desire pulling in every direction. *Say yes.*

"You can go back to hating me after," I say, in hopes it'll encourage whatever the hell we're doing. "We can go back to remembering that you're River's sister and never speak of this again."

I glide one of my fingers beneath the cotton of her panties. *Ah, fuck.* I shut my eyes from the heat pooling. My dick throbs, and my palms tingle. Touching Daisy feels right. *So fucking right.*

"I trust you," she whispers.

Her head tips backward against my pillow the moment I give in.

My fingers brush against her arousal, and the room spins.

"Fuck, you're soaked."

A breathy whimper falls from her lips while her hips flex forward for more pressure.

"Patience, little devil." *I need this to last.*

I slowly push a finger inside of her, and the heat travels through my bloodstream.

She moans, and it's the hottest sound I've ever heard. Eager to hear it again, I slowly pull my finger out only to glide it back in. The morning light begins to cast a glow throughout the room, and I watch her pretty lips part with pleasure.

"So fucking beautiful." I'm talking to myself more than I am her.

I add another finger and angle my palm so it skims against her clit. Her sexy whimper fills my room, and all I want to do is catch it on my lips.

Kissing her would be endgame for me, though.

I'd be trapped for life. Just watching her come apart from my touch is addicting. Feeling her lips on mine? I don't know if I'd be able to recover.

Daisy's breasts are on full display. They bounce slightly

with the shifting of her hips as she meets my fingers halfway. My mouth waters when I glance at her pretty, pink nipples. They deserve to be touched, sucked, and fucking worshiped.

I bend and suck the tight bud of her breast into my mouth.

A curse slips out of her, and I love the dirty word falling off her pretty lips.

My tongue sweeps against her nipple, over and over again, until I think it's had enough attention, then I move toward the other one, repeating the motion.

Daisy's hips work against my hand faster and faster. I eagerly pull her panties off, letting those perfect, smooth legs spread open wide, giving me the best view of my fingers slipping in and out of her.

"Look at how needy you are." I slow my movements and gaze between her thighs.

Daisy's eyes are full of lust as she looks down. We make eye contact a moment later, and I nearly burst. Her lip is trapped between her white teeth, and although she's the sweetest thing I've ever laid eyes on, there's a naughty glint in her eye that has my spine tingling.

"Jesus Christ," I mumble.

Her eyelashes flutter closed, and I pump in and out again. Her moans grow louder, and I know she's close.

"That's it," I encourage, brushing my lips over her ear. "Show me what you've got."

Her hand wraps around my wrist as I tease her pussy, nails digging into the skin, leaving the most delicious bite behind. "Kane," she whispers my name seductively.

"I'm right here, little devil. Come for me."

"Yo Kane, you up?"

Daisy sucks up all the air in my bedroom. Her entire body clenches, including her pussy.

You've got to be fucking kidding me.

"Don't move," I warn.

I quickly pull the covers up over my back as I hover above her, fingers still deep inside. My door flies open, and it takes River all of two seconds to figure out that I'm not alone.

"Oh. Shit. My bad." I expect the door to shut, but it doesn't. "Since when do you let girls in your bed?"

Daisy's eyes are wide, like she's just now realized that she has a brother and that he's my best friend. She tries to wiggle away, but there's nowhere to go. My free hand clamps to her hip, and I shoot her a warning look. If she thinks she's getting out of this bed without coming all over my hand, she's sorely mistaken.

"What do you want?" I'm agitated. "I'm a little busy."

"Yeah, I can see that." He snorts. "It reeks of sex pheromones in here."

I clench my eyes. If only he knew those were his sister's sex pheromones.

"I was just wondering if you knew where Daisy was...but apparently not. I just got home from a shift, and she's not in the apartment."

Daisy's lips roll together. We make eye contact, and I can't help but move my fingers inside of her. "Fuck if I know. I've been preoccupied most of the night."

Yeah, by watching his sister breathe and now watching her come.

Daisy's fingernails dig into my wrist again, and I raise an eyebrow.

"Finish," I mouth to her.

Her eyebrows cave. It's obvious she thinks I'm crazy. And I am...*for her.*

River sighs. "Alright, well, carry on. I'll see if Malaki knows anything."

Can I count that as having his permission to finger-fuck his sister?

Only someone demented would say yes, so I guess that means I'm fucking insane, because as soon as the door latches, I get right back to where we left off.

"Kane!" Her quiet scold pushes me over the edge.

"You're going to finish what we started," I say. "I didn't lie to your brother and pretend you were some random woman in my bed for nothing."

That addicting defiant look is in her eye, but her legs fall open as soon as my thumb swipes against her clit.

"There you go," I encourage. "Don't tell me you can't finish just because your brother interrupted us for a few seconds."

A challenge flares in those pretty baby blues. I grin at her with so much desire flowing through my blood that I may be hard for days.

Maybe even weeks.

My cock is rock solid, pulsing harder with each tilt of her hips.

Daisy's eyes flutter shut when I rub her clit faster. My two fingers are deep inside of her when her pussy squeezes me tight before she breaks in my hands like a dam.

Remembering that River could be just outside the door and hear his sister's hot little whine, I do the only thing I can think of.

I put my mouth on hers and seal my own fate.

Thirty-Five

DAISY

THE PLEASURE INTENSIFIES beyond anything I've ever felt. Kane's mouth traps mine as waves rock me from the inside out, dragging out every hidden desire and thought I've ever had about him.

It's too good.

Too addicting.

I suck his tongue into my mouth, led by hot impulses and dirty thoughts. Once I let go, his teeth clamp onto my lip before he goes back in for another scorching kiss. My hips continue to move, reaching new highs as he explores every inch of my mouth.

It's the best kiss I've ever had.

It's the best orgasm I've ever had too.

I'm tingly all over, and the only thing I can think is *more, more, more.*

Kane pulls back and balances himself above me. His pupils are dilated, lips swollen and wet from mine.

"Fuck," he groans, coming back for more.

I smell my arousal on his fingers beside my head as he grips my hair. I want to be embarrassed, but with the hungry look in his eye, I can't be.

It's animalistic and wild, like he can't get enough.

For the first time in a long time, I feel desirable.

Our mouths seal again, and this time, I'm the one to do the exploring. I deepen the kiss, sucking on his tongue, getting lost in the way it moves against mine.

His hard length presses against my throbbing clit, and even though the fabric of his pants separates us, my breasts grow heavy again.

A noise frees from my mouth, and he presses into me hard. I meet him halfway, rubbing against his pants to feel the roughness against my clit. "Daisy—"

I'm too lost in the sensation to say anything.

I'd let him have me right now if he asked.

"Fuck." Kane squeezes my chin and pulls my mouth up to his. He thrusts his tongue into my mouth at the same time he presses his hips forward. I let him kiss me to the point that I can't breathe. When he lets me go, I gasp for air and meet his dark gaze.

"What the fuck?" he grunts.

His heavy browline, always furrowed with anger, smooths. I look at his mouth when his tongue slips out to lick away my kiss.

"Never in my life have I done that."

"Done what?" I'm in a daze, my voice sounding like I'm drunk.

He looks at his sweats. "Came from a fucking kiss."

Wait, what?

Kane swallows roughly. He shakes his head back and forth, and I notice the red splotches on his chest from our heated moment. "Guess I can't hide from what you do to me anymore."

Unable to stop it from happening, a small smile curves against my mouth.

"Daisy Sullivan," he warns. "If you look at me like that after coming all over my hand, it won't be the last time."

Kane climbs off the bed, and glances over his shoulder at me when I remain quiet. Those blue eyes hit me right in the chest, and he shakes his head at the sight of my barely concealed smile. "Get dressed," he demands, "or else you're not leaving my room."

Before I can make an outlandish comment to tempt him, he spins and glares at me. "Don't tempt me." he warns.

The look he gives me sends the hairs on my arms upright. It's dangerous and sexy all in one, but I know a warning when I see one.

We can't do this, and we both know it.

I sigh and flip the covers off my legs to get dressed.

Surprisingly, my joints aren't as sore as they have been the last few days. I'm lighter on my feet. It's as if I'm walking on air.

Kane better be careful, or he's about to become my new cure.

"Okay," he says, walking out of the bathroom with new pants on. His lazy gaze watches my every move as I pull my clothes over my naked body. "I'll distract your brother, and then you'll slip out and go back to the apartment. Just tell him you were out with a friend."

I cross my arms. "At seven in the morning?"

Kane shrugs and runs a hair through his perfectly messy hair. "Say you stayed the night."

My eyebrow rises. "That'll go over well. I mean, at least it'll explain the fresh orgasm glow I'm sure I've got going on right now."

A faint growl echoes around his room.

I pull back in surprise.

Did he just get jealous over a fictional scenario where I got an orgasm from someone other than him?

"Say you were with a *female* friend," he adds.

I quietly laugh and roll my eyes. "Yes, sir."

His hot glare drops to my mouth. His jaw flexes before he walks out his bedroom door.

I grab my bag that he must've snagged in the process of hauling me into his arms last night and glance over at his bedside table.

His phone is lighting up.

Unable to look away, I quickly read the text message on the screen.

UNKNOWN

Can you meet him here for another exchange?

Another exchange? That sounds...*suspicious*.

River's and Kane's voices carry over the landing and into his room. I quickly stop snooping and head over to the door.

"I can't believe you brought a girl home," my brother laughs. "Are you in love?"

"Fuck off," Kane grumbles.

Coffee brews, and it reminds me that I'm in desperate need of a matcha latte. Anything to clear the brain fog I have that persuaded me to let Kane in between my legs.

What was I thinking?

I totally gave in to the enemy.

"So who is she?" River asks, clearly probing for information.

I bite my lip. How is Kane going to spin this? I press against the wall and wait until the coast is clear.

"Just some puck bunny."

I cross my arms. I am *not* a puck bunny.

My brother snorts. "You and your slutty puck bunnies. I

hope you wore protection or else you'll be seeing me in the ER for crabs."

Kane chuckles, and my face burns.

Slutty puck bunnies?

Just how many puck bunnies has he brought home?

Jealousy rushes to my fingertips. I glance at my legs. *Stay closed from here on out!*

"Did you find Daisy?" Kane asks.

He is completely nonchalant, knowing very well that my brother didn't find me, considering I'm upstairs now, regretting letting his best friend touch me.

"No. Her phone must be dead. Was she okay at the game?" River sounds worried.

"You should check the roof."

I pop up from resting against the wall. The roof?

"Why would she be on the roof?" River snorts. "Did you lock her up there or something?"

Wouldn't surprise me.

"She goes up there every morning. Probably to check on her soil," Kane says.

How does he know that?

I move closer to the stairs to get a better listen.

"Are you surprised? It's Daisy we're talking about." I sort of hate that Kane is acting like he knows me still. Maybe I was on the roof to...bird watch.

My brother sighs, and suddenly, his voice is even closer.

I dart backward to hide.

"True. Alright, I'll check up there."

I step out from behind the corner to glance below the landing. Kane is standing there with his arms crossed over his sculpted chest with his eyebrow raised in my direction.

"You're welcome," he calls out, walking back toward the kitchen.

I hurry down the stairs, feeling more stupid than ever for

staying in his bed last night. I make it all the way to his front door before his voice hits me from behind.

"What? No thank you?" he asks.

My hand freezes on the doorknob.

I glare over my shoulder at him. "For what? The orgasm or for making it seem like I'm a slutty puck bunny?"

Kane's mouth twitches. "Did I strike a nerve?"

No.

The thought of you with puck bunnies did!

I spin toward him angrily.

An insult taunts me, threatening to slip out to hurt him so I can hide the jealousy I feel.

Kane leans his bare hip against the counter, showing off his tight abs and low-hanging sweats. He's dangerously hot, but I refuse to be swept off my feet from the flirty look he's giving me.

"I should've known you'd never change," I grumble.

Kane places his mug down and eyes me closely. "Meaning?"

I pause.

The text I accidentally saw lingers in the back of my head, and I want to bring it up in the worst way, just to heighten the tension, but...I can't. I'm not even sure what it means, or who it's from.

"Ah..." Kane's lopsided grin makes me crazy. "I see. You're jealous at the thought of me being with puck bunnies?"

Irritation pricks at my scalp.

I mean, he's right, but there's no way I'm telling him that.

"I couldn't care less," I snap. "And thanks for the orgasm." I open the door. "It won't happen again."

"We'll see," he calls out, his voice carrying into the hallway and all the way to my apartment where I'll peacefully sip on my matcha latte...*alone.*

Thirty-Six

KANE

KEEPING my distance has been harder than I thought. Without there being a game for two days, I was counting on the fact that I wouldn't run into Daisy in that revealing devil's costume at the rink, but leave it to River to be fucking clueless and invite her to go out with us.

He rarely gets any time off, but whenever he does, he wants to go explore the city—something I'm fine being a wingman for.

Until he brings Daisy along for the ride.

Talk about a cockblock, and I can't decide if I'm referring to her or to him.

"Where are we going?" River asks. "I'm starving."

"Starving?" I chuckle. "What about thirsty?"

The only way I'm getting through this night is with booze. I won't overdo it, not with Daisy in proximity with that stupid dress hardly covering her ass, but one or two will at least knock the edge off.

"That too," River adds.

"A club downtown." I nod to the left, and they follow closely behind. "It's exclusive."

Daisy's annoyance skims my skin, and I grin.

"It better not be a strip club," she grumbles.

River laughs. "I wouldn't mind."

Daisy makes a gagging noise, and the filthiest thought enters my head.

I glance over my shoulder at her mouth.

Is that what she'd sound like gagging on my cock?

She glares at me, and I turn away with a tight jaw. *This is going to be a long fucking night.*

When we get to the club, music vibrates the soles of my shoes. I flick my chin to the bouncer, a long-time Blue Devils fan who lets us cut the line—something I don't feel bad about. The sooner we get in, the sooner we get out.

Every male on the other side of the red rope gives Daisy a once-over. My fist flexes by my side.

River leans in. "Get used to it." He chuckles dryly. "It's been like this for years."

It has?

It wasn't like this in high school.

Daisy was always preoccupied with other things—like *me.*

Her nose was either buried in a book, or she was out in the backyard, picking dead leaves off her plants and gathering pretty flowers for her mom. She's always been beautiful, but she wasn't like the other girls our age who stripped their sweaters off the moment their parents looked the other way. When teenage boys see a little skin, they're hooked. Daisy went unnoticed, except by me.

Now, though, everyone notices her.

I don't like it.

With Daisy taking in the vibrant colors of the club, I glance at River. "How many punches have you thrown because of guys looking at her like they're doing right now?"

He laughs and raises his voice so I can hear him over the music. "Only a few."

My eyebrows rise.

His heavy arm wraps around my shoulder as the other one goes around Daisy's. He pulls us through the crowd with a grin. "I don't have a temper like you," he adds. "That's why I wasn't surprised when I came across an article about you and how you're one of the biggest hotheads in the league right now."

I clench my jaw.

So what?

I'm a little angry at times.

Half the time, it isn't even because of the game, but when you're already on edge over something else, it doesn't take much to fall over it.

"Funny..." Daisy leans forward and looks me dead in the eye. "I came across an article about Kane too."

"What did it say?" River asks.

Here we go.

Daisy's claws are out, and I'm more than ready to be scratched.

Her flirty smirk itches something inside of me that is *just* out of reach.

"It said he was the biggest manwhore of the league, always pictured with a new puck bunny on his arm."

What a little liar. I sometimes bring them home, fuck them on the couch, and then they're off on their way. There is no time for photos in between all of that.

I chuckle. "Lying doesn't look good on you, Daisy-Petal."

She makes a sarcastic noise, stepping past her brother to spar with me. "I could say the same about you."

River puts his hands out and pushes us apart. "What is with you two? Apparently, we all need to let loose tonight."

He turns to Daisy. "Well, as much as you can I guess."

Daisy angles her chin and glances to the packed bar. "One drink won't hurt."

River drops his hands and shoots her a look. "Daisy."

She shoots him one right back, and I find myself wanting to stand up for her, even though I'm fully on River's side.

Her hip pops out, and three men behind her break their neck to get a look at her ass.

Like an animal, I bare my teeth at them.

"Moderate alcohol consumption can be good for Lupus," she argues. "That's something you told me and then was later confirmed by Dr. Gibson. Plus, none of my current medications have reactions with alcohol, so I'm fine to drink one, River."

I expect him to argue again. Maybe he'll even tell her to leave, which would probably be for the best.

"Fine," he says.

I snap my attention to him.

"Wait, what?" I ask.

He ignores me and continues with the conversation. "Only one."

Daisy plays with a lock of her hair and smiles mischievously. "Whatever you say, Dr. Sullivan."

Then she turns and takes off toward the bar to get her one drink.

River and I make eye contact, and I hate to admit that I'm the only one who seems perturbed by this. I quickly smooth my face to hide the fact that I'm filled to the brim with tension when it comes to her, even more after the other night. I rattle off my drink order so he can get the first round and find us a corner table to hang out at. I pull my phone out of my pocket and text for some reinforcements.

Slipping away for a few minutes to handle the rest of my brother's bullshit won't go noticed, but the more eyes on Daisy, the better. With her short black dress held up by nothing more than a few flimsy straps, some drunken idiot is bound to push the limits. I'd hate to throw him through a wall and show Daisy just how wildly possessive I am when it comes to her.

River returns with our beers after a few minutes with Daisy following closely behind. She's got this flirty look in her eye, and I can't help but ask what has her in such a good mood.

I stare at the side of her delicate jaw, the blush on her cheekbone catching the light above us. "I got a free drink."

My nostrils flare. I follow her line of sight and glare at a group of guys with hard-ons, looking at Daisy. She raises her fruity drink in the air, and they do the same.

"They just want in your pants." Malt flavoring coats my tongue as I take a swig of my beer, hopeful it'll cancel out the taste of jealousy.

Daisy's girly laugh fills the air. "Obviously." She shoots me a look that makes me want to wrap my hand around her neck and bring her mouth to mine. "This isn't my first time going out. I know how men work."

River, clearly oblivious to the raging war going on inside of me, shakes his head. "Daisy and Natalia were masters at getting free drinks in college."

"Well, they weren't always free." Daisy puts her glass up to her lips, but I can still see the outline of her sexy grin.

"Meaning?" I ask.

River clears his throat. "This is getting gross. Later."

With his beer, he heads toward the bar where a few women are standing. I should join him, just to put Daisy in her place, but I'm too interested in her answer to move even an inch.

"I mean, what do you expect when you buy a girl a drink?" She toys with the rim of her cup, licking the salt off the top. I know she's doing it on purpose. "Oh, wait." She laughs sarcastically. "You don't have to buy them drinks. I'm sure those slutty puck bunnies you're so fond of just open right up for you."

My beer clanks to the table with force as I set it down. I quickly lean in, and Daisy's knowing grin disappears right away. "Stop fucking with me."

The teasing glint in her eye disappears, and I know a challenge is coming. Her shoulders straighten, and she pushes her chest out so I get a direct view of her irresistible cleavage. "Or what?"

It's sort of sad that she thinks she can beat me at this little game. I tap my fingers against the table. "Or I'll really give you a reason to be jealous."

Daisy's lips part, but she keeps the charade up by acting unfazed. "The only person who is going to be jealous tonight is you."

My mouth curves. "You're going to regret saying that, baby."

Daisy snatches her drink, and I watch as she downs it in one gulp.

Ah, hell. Here we go.

"We'll see," she quips.

Before she can get too far, my hand winds around her waist briefly. I slip my mouth right next to her ear. "I'll win, little devil..." I move in front of her so she can't beat me out to the dance floor. "'Cause I always get what I want."

And what I want is *her.*

Thirty-Seven

DAISY

I BIT OFF MORE than I can chew.

Being alone in my apartment, filling my head with all sorts of empowering thoughts is one thing. Coming face-to-face with Kane and suffocating in the energy that surges between us is another.

My heart beats quicker every time he grabs a new girl to dance with. His palm, the same one that caressed my body like I was the most desirable thing on the planet, wraps around some blonde's waist, and although they're just dancing, I'm brimming with jealousy. It's not the good kind of jealousy either. It's the kind that will break my heart in two if I let it.

Searching for a good candidate to dance with, I spot a face I recognize.

Malaki? And Reese?

Relief slips down my spine at the sight, even if I am confused. I rush to them and envelop her in a hug that's more like a death grip. "I'm so glad to see you."

She pulls back, those honey-colored eyes softening. "You okay? What's wrong?"

I nod and smile. "I'm fine. I'm just happy to see a familiar face. Wait, what are you doing here?"

All of a sudden, Malaki slips into the conversation and puts his arm around Reese's shoulders. "I convinced her to come out with me."

Reese's face twists. "If requesting several Uber drivers until you get me as your driver is your way of convincing, then okay."

Malaki grins.

"I have to get back to work," she says, shoving Malaki's arm off her shoulders. "Malaki said you were in here, so I wanted to say hi real quick."

After giving Reese another hug, she heads for the door, where Malaki follows closely behind. They look to be in a heated conversation, except Malaki is half-smiling. I watch him open his phone to show her something, and before I know it, she's heading back over to me.

"What are you doing?" I ask.

She flips her warm brown locks over her shoulder and pulls me by the hand toward the bar. "I guess I'm staying."

A bartender appears in front of us, bypassing most of the other customers, and takes her order. I decline another drink and lean against the bar. "What about work?"

Reese sighs, glancing at Malaki from across the dance floor. I keep my attention far away, knowing that Kane is probably getting dry humped by now.

"He..." Reese purses her lips before leaning close to me. "He just paid me more than I'd make Ubering to stay."

My jaw drops. "What?"

She rolls her eyes. "It's a long story. But if I'm being paid to stay, I'd be stupid to leave, right?"

"Right. And not to mention…" I quickly glimpse over my shoulder, and a fire erupts in my stomach when Kane's steely jaw catches my eye right away. There's a girl dancing in front of him with her arm winding up his chest. "I could use an ally."

I turn back toward Reese, and she's smiling at me. "You've got it. Let's dance."

She pulls me onto the dance floor while scoffing at Malaki as he raises his glass to Reese, like he's proud of her or something. I laugh and put my back to my brother, who is clearly having no issues letting loose, and grab onto Reese's shoulders. We start to dance to the tempo of the song, and it doesn't take long for my gaze to snag Kane's through the sea of people.

My throat closes when I see him staring directly at me.

Not even a second passes before he skims his nose against his victim's neck. He whispers something in her ear, and suddenly, she grinds herself even faster against his front.

With my eyes still pinned to Kane, I reach my hand out and grab the first willing guy I can find. He replaces Reese, who happily moves to the other side of the bar to avoid Malaki.

I turn and press against the tall man behind me. His hands fall to my hips, and he moves them back and forth to the song. "You're gorgeous," he says, brushing his mouth against my ear. "I'm Nick, by the way."

I hate that his sultry whisper does nothing to my body.

The only thing I can think of is Kane. I'm desperate to see if he is watching me with a jealous rage, like I was just doing to him.

In reality, neither of us should care or even engage in this stupid game we're playing, yet here we are.

Too eager to catch his eye again, I spin and put my arms around Nick's neck. His green eyes are vibrant and stand out against his olive-colored skin, even beneath the strobing lights. But they do nothing to spark any excitement inside of me.

My attention slips off to the left for the briefest of seconds, and my heart crashes to the floor.

Kane and the girl are both gone.

I drop my hands and spin around. My shoulders fall.

"You okay?" Nick asks.

"Um..." I nod. "Yeah, I just..." I spin again, in search of the bathroom so I can berate myself in private for the way my chest aches with hurt.

A soft gasp slips from my lips when I spot him.

With his broad shoulder propped against the wall near the darkened hall beneath the neon bathroom sign, he raises an eyebrow at me.

He's asking me if I've had enough.

I'm scared to say no, but I'm afraid to say yes too.

Nick is waiting for me to finish my sentence, but I can't figure out what to say. I search for River in the crowd, and when I find his back toward me, I take it as a sign.

The moment I decide to head for Kane, a path opens up. My pulse quickens, thrumming in various places on my body. The closer I get, the faster it goes, only for it to stop altogether when Kane turns and disappears.

I continue moving in his direction, but there's fear in the back of my head that slows my steps. Am I about to stumble upon something I can't unsee?

Shit. What am I doing?

I've passed the line to the bathroom, darkness enveloping me the farther I move down the quiet hallway.

My hand skims the sticky wall as I turn the corner and ram into something hard.

"Good choice." Kane pins me against the wall, his warm, malty breath fanning against my face. "I would've hated to lead that girl on even further because you were too stubborn to call it quits."

The beating of my heart is louder than the thumping club music. I press myself farther into the wall, hoping it'll give me enough backing to think rationally, but it doesn't. Kane edges closer, his strong scent putting me in a daze. Sharp prickles of need are everywhere, but I'm afraid to make the first move.

Kane's hands find me in the dark. "That guy is lucky you decided to give up." His voice is throaty. "Otherwise, he'd probably be in the hospital."

My breathing is sharp and quick. He presses his knee in between mine, and all I want to do is sink down onto it. The rough calluses on his palm glide against my bare arm in featherlight strokes, leaving a trail of goosebumps behind. When his hand lands at the base of my neck, he pushes my hair behind my shoulder, and I let out a shaky breath.

"What are we doing?" *His touch feels so good.*

Without my permission, my head slowly falls to the side, giving Kane better access to my neck.

"I told you I always get what I want." His mouth hovers over my pulse, hot puffs of breath coating my skin. "And what I want is you."

Heat pools at the apex of my thighs. I push my breasts against his chest, desperate for the touch.

"Kane." Saying his name is the only warning I'll give.

"Do you know that I've never stopped wanting you?" he asks quietly.

My stomach dips, and without hesitation, I lift one of my hands and grab onto his scruffy chin. I bring his face to mine. "Then prove it."

Time slows.

Kane's movements are steady and sure as he pushes my hand from his face and grips my chin with force.

His mouth covers mine, and I open willingly.

I jump up, and he catches me with ease. I wrap my legs around his waist and give in to the pleasure. His tongue slips past my lips, and I make a noise that doesn't go unnoticed.

"You make me wild, little devil," he says before kissing me again.

I'm putty in his palm.

I make him wild. He makes me desperate.

His silent kissing demands I follow all his cues and commands.

"Open." Kane's palm nudges my legs farther apart, keeping one underneath me to hold me up.

I do exactly as he says. My dress bundles around my hips, giving free rein to Kane's fingers. One brushes against my slit, and my legs shake.

"No more games," he rasps.

Suddenly, my feet are placed on the floor, and Kane drops to a knee. Through the dark, I see how he angles his face to stare up at me. His hand slowly glides up my smooth leg, and I'm a mess.

Goosebumps fly to the surface, and my nipples tighten. Cool air floats in between my legs, brushing against my wet panties. Kane hooks a finger beneath the fabric and pulls them aside. "This is mine, Daisy."

A whimper falls free from my mouth when his finger runs against my seam.

"Look at how wet you are for me, baby."

His voice is low and gritty.

I move my hips against his teasing finger, wanting more.

"You're just as greedy as I am," he mutters.

His finger disappears, and I panic. I open my mouth to whine, but nothing comes out when I feel the quick flick of his tongue against my clit.

"God." I shiver.

He licks and sucks, placing soft kisses against my inner thigh every so often.

"Ride my face," he murmurs from in between my legs. "I've got you."

His hands grip me around the waist hard, hoisting me up so I don't fall. I move my hips up and down, chasing the high. One bite of his teeth against my clit, and I'm freefalling. A whimper slips from my lips as I rub against his scruffy face, still just as needy as before.

Kane pops up from his knees and wipes his face with the back of his hand. "You're so goddamn addicting," he groans. "Come on. We're leaving."

He pulls me by the hand after adjusting my dress back to its rightful position. He pushes on a hidden exit door, and the cool evening air washes over our heated bodies.

"Where are we going?" I ask, attempting to keep up.

"To my bed."

I pull on his hand when he's halfway out the door. "Wait! What about River? What will he think if we both just leave?"

Kane's chest rises quickly. The moon gives off its light to show me the carnal look in his eyes. I'm not sure he cares about River at the moment.

"Well, I'm not fucking you in the hallway of a club, Daisy. So leaving is our next best option."

The thought turns me on, and he notices.

Kane clenches his eyes and squeezes my hand at the same time. "Don't look at me like that. I'm seconds from filling you now, regardless of where we are."

I tug on Kane's hand.

We're playing with fire either way: leave and make River question our whereabouts, or stay and potentially have someone stumble upon us.

"I'm not that same innocent teenager you once knew."

The door slams shut behind Kane, hiding us in the dark. "I don't need some fluffy bed and a gentle hand."

"What exactly are you implying, little devil? You want me to fuck you filthy? Right here, right now?" He's calling my bluff.

My fingers find the button of his jeans right away. He makes no effort to stop me when I start to unbutton them.

"That's exactly what I'm saying, Kane."

Thirty-Eight

KANE

"I DON'T THINK you know what you're asking for," I
warn.

My pants pool at my ankles, and Daisy's warm hand rubs
against the hard ridge outlining my boxers. It feels so fucking
good that I can't help but flex my hips forward. I grab her
hand and help her rub against me until it's too much.

She's too much.

I can't help myself.

"Fuck it," I groan.

I grip her hips, turn her around, and shove her dress up for
the second time in ten minutes.

"Put your hands on the wall," I demand.

She does exactly as I say, which is such a turn-on. Instead
of slipping her panties down her legs, I pull on the thin fabric
until I hear a tear. They fall to the floor with a whoosh that
mixes with her hot gasp.

"Tell me if I hurt you."

It's not something I usually say to a woman, unless she's

tighter than usual, but it's different with Daisy. This isn't just a fuck, even if it's as hot as it is mind-bending.

I'm at her center, and she moves her legs even wider for better access.

It makes me wild. My jaw clenches tight when I push inside. There's a quick pause in time where my heart stops beating from the feeling. Energy flows to my fingertips as I grip her hips and glide in even farther.

We fit together so perfectly I can't help but believe that people are actually destined for one another.

"Goddamn, Daisy," I groan, short of breath.

I keep still, letting her adjust to me. A little whimper slips from her lips as I start to move inside of her. I grab a hold of her shoulder with one hand, while the other clamps to her hip.

"So good," she mumbles as I grind into her.

Letting go of her hip, I snake my hand around her belly and rub her clit. It's embarrassing that I'm ready to come after just a few thrusts, so I try to slow my roll. I need to feel her come apart on my dick like I need air to breathe.

Daisy coming might even be better than coming myself.

"You're so tight," I murmur.

Daisy turns her head and kisses me feverishly.

God, she's fucking hot. Having her like this brings that little devil nickname to life.

I circle her clit and push farther into her. I'm too lost in the moment to slow my thrusts any longer. I'm fucking her filthy, just like she wanted. Tugging on her hair, I bite down on her lip as she moans against my mouth.

"Mine," I hiss. "This mouth is mine." I kiss her again. "This body is mine." Her pussy tightens, and I'm seeing double.

I flick her clit, and it releases her orgasm.

"You're mine. You always have been." She pulses around me, and my world stops spinning.

I quickly pull out of her, swipe her panties off the floor, and come right into them.

An animalistic noise erupts from my throat, and the hand still on her hip will likely leave a bruise. She eventually turns and rests against the wall. The only things that fill the space are our heaving breaths and shock.

That was fucking unbelievable.

I reach for her, ready to kiss her again, but turn at the sound of laughter echoing down the hall.

Daisy sucks in air and hurriedly pulls down her dress.

My hand finds hers on the first try after I zip my pants. "We gotta go."

Her sweet giggle trails us as we take off toward the exit to escape outside. The gravel crunches beneath our fast strides, and we run until we're back to the front of the club where the line is still halfway down the street.

Daisy's sweet laughter is contagious. My chest rumbles with a chuckle that soon turns into a laugh that hasn't come from my mouth in years. Her hair is a mess, and her lips are a bright pink. They're a bit swollen too, which does nothing but give me a sense of pride.

I stare into the dreamy blue of her eyes that are bright with happiness. The apples of her cheeks are the prettiest shade of pink I've ever seen. I'll fuck her like that over and over again in any club if this is what she's like afterward.

"Oh my god." She covers her mouth. "That was close."

My smile is everlasting. I shake my head while I continue to gaze at her. I know I should feel guilty for fucking River's sister like that in a public place...but how can I?

Look at her. *Happy.*

"Hey, there you guys are."

Daisy and I both freeze.

My smile falls, and I catch the eye of Malaki a few feet behind River, looking at me with wide eyes. I'm not sure if he's looking at me because he heard me laughing or if he's looking at me because he knows I just fucked Daisy.

"Where did you go?" River asks us. He shifts back and forth between Daisy and me, and I pray he can't tell that she's just been fucked.

Daisy, thankfully, thinks fast on her feet. "I got overheated. Kane came with me to cool down out here."

River flattens his lips. "It was probably the drink. I knew you shouldn't have had one." He sighs. "Your face is flushed too."

They're mid-argument when Malaki comes to stand beside me. "Your pocket."

I can't take my eyes off Daisy. "What?"

"Your pocket, you fucking amateur."

My brow furrows. I know he didn't just call me an amateur.

Oh, fuck.

Daisy's wet panties are sticking out of my back pocket.

Malaki chokes on a laugh. "It'd be a shame if River saw his sister's panties in your pocket."

"Keep your mouth shut," I snap.

"I'm a little perturbed that you think you have to threaten me to keep another secret..." I watch as he shakes his head with disappointment.

I hurriedly shove her panties farther into my pocket with sweat trailing down my spine. River glances at me, and the group is silent, as if they're waiting for me to say something.

Malaki elbows me while chuckling under his breath.

"Sorry, what?" I shift my attention from Daisy, who still hasn't lost that little spark of life in her eye, even after coming eye-to-eye with River moments after coming all over my dick.

"You ready to go, or do you want to stay out longer?" I glance back to Daisy, like I'm waiting for her to answer for me.

Fuck, what am I doing?

Malaki clears his throat. "We leave for the road tomorrow afternoon, so we should probably go."

River nods. "Alright, that works. I have a shift tomorrow. I just didn't want to be the responsible one of the group."

Reese, who I'm pretty sure Malaki paid to stay with him the entire night, is mid-chat with Daisy as she pulls out her keys. "Let's go. Your chauffeur awaits."

"Later." He flicks his chin at me, and suddenly, I'm trailing River and Daisy.

With her taste still lingering inside my mouth, I move my attention to her swaying hips. I was a damn fool to think having her once would be enough. The only thing I can think about is how I know she has nothing underneath that dress of hers. I'm starting to conjure up ways I can get her alone again between now and when I leave tomorrow.

My phone vibrates. Still in a daze, I pull it out and glance at the message.

I stop walking.

All thoughts of Daisy vanish like quicksand.

Shit.

It takes me several times to fully read the text because I'm so shocked that I'd forgotten the real reason I'd come out tonight.

River doesn't notice that I'm no longer following them, but Daisy does. She peers over her shoulder at me, and I quickly look back at my phone. Guilt slams into my chest, and the thick wad of cash in my wallet is an anchor, holding me hostage.

"Hey..." *Shit, this is going to look bad.* "I'll catch you two later."

Daisy's spine straightens.

River turns with a lopsided smile. "Forget something...or someone?"

Somehow, by the grace of god, I am able to keep my expression in check. "You could say that," I say.

Don't look at her. Don't do it.

I look at Daisy.

Either she doesn't care that I'm not denying what her brother is implying, or she's even better than I am at keeping her emotions at bay. The best-case scenario would be that she knows there's no way in hell I'd go find another woman to be with after what we just did, but that's just a fantasy. What else would she expect from me? What else would *anyone* expect?

"Have fun, bro."

River and Daisy take off toward the apartment, and I'm left standing in the middle of the sidewalk with even more hatred for my brother than before.

I think I may hate myself more, though.

Thirty–Nine

DAISY

"THERE!" Reese stands back and admires her handiwork. The open container of blue sequins is at her feet, the needle trapped in between her teeth.

I glance at the row of sequins she replaced and run my hands over them. "Where did you learn to sew?"

Reese smiles. "My gram. I was her shadow when I lived with her. She taught me to sew and cook before I could even read."

"My gram taught me to garden." I step off the pedestal and fix my devil horns in the mirror. "I think that's why I'm so obsessed with plants now."

Reese laughs. "I think we are the same person, Daisy. Just two old souls."

"That's why we became friends in three seconds flat." I pause. "Or maybe it's because you were so invested in my mascot debacle."

She nods. "Well, that too."

"You good to go?" Cindy pops her head into my dressing room with her headphone piece on.

Today, I am tasked with working extra close to some of the hockey players for some media coverage. Select players are being interviewed by children with special needs to gear up for their annual fundraiser, and that calls for the mascot being in attendance.

Reese and I walk with Cindy down the quiet hall. I hear nothing but the violent beating of my heart.

"Which players are going to be present for this?" My high-pitched tone gives my nerves away.

I have avoided Kane since the other night. I didn't tune in for his away game on TV, half-afraid he'd somehow make eye contact with me through the screen. I triple-checked the apartment hallway before coming or going, and I even opted for the stairs instead of the elevator just to be safe.

It's not that I'm afraid of Kane, but to say I feel stupid is an understatement.

There was an obvious letdown the other night when he decided to stay at the club. I don't know what I expected, but it hurt.

We got caught up in the moment.

He said things he didn't mean, and I naively believed them.

It's not like anything was supposed to come from us having sex, other than orgasms, and we both got that, so end of story.

Cindy rattles off names, but I forget them all when she says *his*.

I make a noise, and Reese snags my eye. She looks at me funny. "I knew it," she whispers excitedly. "That's not hatred I feel between you two...it's...sexual tension!"

I shush her as we follow Cindy into the locker room.

For once, it smells clean and fresh. There's no stench of

sweaty men or their gear. Several kids, all ranging in ages, stand with their parents while waiting for the hockey players.

A few of them smile widely when they see me. One little girl squeals and lets go of her mother's hand. She has pink braces on her legs, but she doesn't let it stop her from rushing me.

"Devil girl!" she exclaims.

I drop down to get on her level and open my arms for a hug.

My heart swells, and I forget all about Kane and my wounded ego—for a second, at least.

"I'm Abby!" She giggles.

Before I know it, almost every child circles me like a shark. Hug after hug after hug. The cameras have shown up, but I pretend they're not there and keep hugging kids and posing for photos.

The air shifts behind me, and I notice the adults in the room all swing their gazes to the door. It doesn't take a genius to know that the players have entered the locker room. Still surrounded by the kids, I manage to peek through the crowd.

I see him right away. I'm pulled to him like a magnet.

A gust of butterflies fills my stomach.

There's a tiny hand that finds its way into mine. I look down and smile at the dark-haired boy. He smiles so widely I can see that he's missing both of his front teeth.

"Want a photo?" I ask.

He nods, his warm brown curls bouncing.

I laugh as he drags me through the locker room, the camera no longer paying any attention to us but instead on the players. "Where are we going?" I ask.

I realize exactly where we're headed after a few seconds, because, apparently, fate hates me.

The little boy's dad catches up to us. His hand lands on

my elbow, and I slow our pace. "Sorry." He laughs nervously. "Jonas is nonverbal."

I smile. "It's perfectly fine. Do you think he wants a picture with a specific player?"

Anyone other than Kane.

The dad shrugs shyly. "You. I think he has a crush on you."

I glance at Jonas. He puts his head down quickly. I give his hand a squeeze. "You're officially my favorite, but don't tell the others."

His dad chuckles. He tells me more about Jonas, and I'm fully engaged until a heavy presence appears, shadowing us like a storm cloud. Jonas tugs on my hand and leads me right into the thick of it.

Kane's body heat mingles with mine, awakening every nerve I've tried to cover up. Our gazes catch with Jonas in between us. His dad bends down to get on his level, and it takes everything I have to break eye contact with Kane.

"Jonas, do you want a picture with Barlow? Is that why you're dragging..." His father glances at me.

Oh, right. *Name.*

"Da–"

"Daisy," Kane interrupts.

He's staring at Jonas's father like he wants to murder him. Narrowed eyes, flexed jaw, stern stance. When he moves over to Jonas, his face softens. "Hey, little man. Let's get a photo with devil girl. Yeah?"

Jonas nods enthusiastically. His father steps back out of the way, and Jonas finally drops my hand. Just when I think he's going to stand in between Kane and me, he turns and puts his arms up.

Without giving it any thought, I bend down and scoop him into my arms.

His father apologizes, and I brush him off. "Please don't. I really don't mind." I wink at Jonas. "I told you he was my favorite."

Kane hums under his breath, scooting closer to us. I tense right away when his hand lands on my lower back. It's the only thing I can focus on.

I'm so screwed.

"Did you hear that, Jonas?" Kane leans toward him, meaning he's closer to *me*. "You're her favorite. What a lucky kid."

Unable to stop myself, I look at Kane.

His dirty-blond hair is pushed over to the side, revealing his soul-wrenching blue eyes fixated on mine. They speak a thousand words, but I can't decipher a single one of them. Seconds ago, he seemed irritated and maybe a little angry. Now his gaze is bright with something I can't name. Whatever it is, it zips right to my chest, warming me from the inside out.

I turn away abruptly after I hear the shuttering of a camera.

"Don't post that," I say to the pretty photographer.

Pulling Jonas in tighter to pose, Kane follows. His hand creeps around to my hip, and I feel it everywhere. "Look over there," I say to Jonas.

My smile stays steady regardless of Kane's fingers rubbing circles against my hip. The thin fabric of my costume does nothing to block his touch.

As soon as the photo is taken, I plop Jonas back down. He runs over to his dad, and I almost do too, just to get away from Kane.

Realizing he isn't removing his hand from my hip, I shoot him a glare disguised by a closed-mouthed smile. "What are you doing?" I whisper-seethe.

He doesn't bother looking at me. "Making a point."

What point?

That no matter how hard I try, my body can't help but react to him?

Jonas's father comes over to thank us before holding his hand out to shake Kane's. He slowly drags it away from my lower back and grabs onto Jonas's father's hand. He winces, and my eyes widen. "Not a problem." Kane's shoulders tense before he lets go. "Enjoy the game."

As soon as Jonas and his father disappear, I gape. "Are you serious?" I hiss quietly, well aware that there are many eyes and ears. I cross my arms angrily.

How dare he act possessive of me!

Also, how dare my body for liking it!

Kane lowers his voice. "Uncross your arms unless you want the entire hockey fan base to know you're a brat."

I do as he says and force a smile on my face. "If they think I'm being a brat, I wonder what they'll think of watching you nearly break that man's hand to make an insane point to him." The fake happiness doesn't reach my voice. Kane's peach-colored lips twitch with me all riled up.

"Insane?" he questions.

I turn my back to him. Hopeful to escape him, I search for another willing child to hang out with. I'll even take the one kicking and screaming on the floor over standing here with Kane.

"Yes, insane," I snap. "You make it seem like you're jealous!"

Kane grunts at my back as I make a beeline for the opposite side of the room.

"Jealousy doesn't even come close to what I feel when I see you talking to another man, Daisy."

My legs refuse to move any farther. I stop right where I am and repeat his words silently. I hate that the thought of him being jealous coats me with warmth. He stands too close for comfort, electricity buzzing so hot I wouldn't be surprised if there was a literal spark between us.

"I know why you've been avoiding me," he says.

I stare at him out of the corner of my eye.

"Barlow!"

We both jerk like we've been caught doing something wrong, when, in reality, it didn't even look like we were talking. Rhodes stands tall beside a boy who clearly wants Kane to join in on their photo.

"This isn't over," he says before heading in their direction.

I wait until Kane is far enough away before I say, "Yes, it is."

Reese comes and stands beside me, shielding herself away from the cameras. "What was that all about?"

"Oh, nothing," I say, feeling like I've won because I got the last word in.

Little does Kane know, I'm a master at avoidance. I managed to avoid him for several years. What makes him think I can't do it again?

Forty

KANE

I TRAIL HER EVERY MOVE. My attention to her angelic laugh never wavers, and each time she smiles at a child, I grow even more impatient.

How could I possibly be jealous of a fucking child?

I want her to smile at me like that. Instead, I get hurtful looks covered up by dirty glances and scowls.

Daisy makes a beeline for the exit as soon as the media leaves. She has to know I'm going to follow her, no matter how fast she walks. I openly ignore my teammates calling my name and chase her down.

You can run, little devil, but you can't hide.

The locker room door latches behind me, and I spot her turning the corner. My chuckle echoes within the narrow space, and she spins to face me in an outrage. "You know that just because we had a small slip in time, you don't own me, right?"

Own her. Those two little words shoot right below my belt.

Daisy is blazing with anger when I approach her. Heat fans from her body, making me sweat. "A slip in time?" I stand right in front of her, towering above her shorter frame. "Is that what you're calling it?"

Daisy makes a noise that resembles sarcasm. "No. I'm calling it a *mistake.*"

I sigh with impatience and take a step closer to her. That mighty chin of hers tips so she can keep her scathing glare on me. Before she can escape into her dressing room, I wind one arm around her back and rest my other on the door above her head.

"You're only saying that because you're hurt."

"Hurt?" The word races from her mouth with poison, but it's a poison I'd gladly take. "I'd have to care to be hurt."

My chest tightens, my stomach tensing.

"The truth is, I don't care. You're free to be with whomever you want to and do whatever you want. If you want to seduce every woman on the planet, then go for it. Sex meant—"

"Everything," I finish for her. "It meant everything."

Daisy's pink lips slam shut, but the furrowing of her brow is still there. I can't expect her to take my word for it, but I wish she would, because now I'm stuck toying with the idea of letting her in again.

"Did it hurt you when I stayed at the club? Were you up all night, wondering what I was doing and who I was with?"

Because I was up all night, wondering what I'd do if the roles were reversed. I came to the conclusion that I'd end up behind bars.

Before she can answer, I grip her chin tightly. "And don't lie to me."

Daisy exhales, and I have the urge to open my mouth so her breath lands on my tongue.

I wet my lip. "I've thought of nothing but you since the other night."

Actually, I've thought of nothing but her since the moment I stepped in the elevator weeks ago.

Daisy rolls her eyes, and my grip tightens in hopes that it'll drive my point further.

"I didn't stay at the club for the reason you think."

Silence lingers, and the longer Daisy peers up at me with her pretty blue eyes, the more I'm willing to come clean.

Nerves creep along my neck. "Despite what you've heard and what my reputation is, all I wanted to do was follow you back to the apartment and wait until your brother left so I could have you again."

"Get a room," someone jokingly shouts from down the hall.

Daisy and I both jerk.

Look at us, so lost in each other's presence that we can't even pay attention to our surroundings.

I grip the door handle behind her and shove us both inside her makeshift dressing room.

It smells like her in here, flowery and sweet like honey.

Having been snapped out of the stupor, Daisy immediately puts space between us. She's a thousand miles away, though I could reach out and touch her if I tried.

I watch as she furiously digs into her bag for her regular clothes.

"If you didn't stay for what my brother was implying, then why did you? I can't think of any other reason why you'd stay." Daisy rips the Blue Devil horns off her head and tosses them through the air. They land on my shoes. Her warm-blonde hair spills over her shoulders, surrounding her face. She's so goddamn pretty, even when she's angry.

I open my mouth, less confident than before. My pulse

thrums quickly as I prepare for her disappointment with the real truth behind why I stayed.

"You know what"—Daisy rolls her eyes—"it doesn't even matter. It's not like what happened between us will happen again. I won't let it."

"Miles," I blurt his name, and Daisy drops her clothes.

Her angry browline softens into confusion. "What?"

"I stayed because of Miles." My arms fall to my sides, and suddenly, I'm eighteen again. I nervously lick my lip and begin to pace in front of her, just like the last time I confided in her. "He owed money to someone. They were meeting me at the club so I could pay them the remainder. I'd forgotten all about it until we were heading back to the apartment."

I drag my hand across my face, suddenly hit with exhaustion.

"It hasn't stopped. The gambling. Every time I think it's the last time, and he leaves me alone for a while, he comes right back and asks me to bail him out again. The last time I refused, he was beaten to near death." My voice cracks, but I cover it with more of the truth. "I even moved him in with me for a while until he healed so he could hide it from Mom, with the promise of getting help, but turns out..."

I need to breathe. The room sways, and my lungs beg for air.

I'm in a state of panic, until I feel her arms wrap around my waist.

I raise my arms and stare down at her small frame pressing against mine. Her head rests against my racing heart, and her arms tighten even more.

"Just breathe," she whispers against my shirt. "In and out."

I do as she says.

When my chest settles and I can feel my legs again, I let my arms land on her slender frame.

We stand for so long I forget how we got here.
But unfortunately for me, Daisy has questions.

Forty-One

DAISY

"HOW LONG HAS HE BEEN GAMBLING?" I ask quietly.

I glance at the door behind Kane nervously, like we're back in time, tucked away in my childhood bedroom, afraid my parents or River will know he snuck inside.

Kane eventually drops his arms and pulls away from me. I release the grip I had around his waist, but I keep my feet planted in front of him. Adding distance between us feels wrong, especially now.

The last time he trusted me with the truth, I pushed him away, for good reasons. But this time, I'm staying put.

Kane's intense gaze never wavers. "It never stopped."

My thoughts freeze. "Never?"

His hard jaw tightens, the faint light enhancing the sharp edges of his face. "He didn't reach out to me for about a year after I left for the juniors..."

I glance away briefly, knowing the reason why. It isn't guilt that I feel for doing what I did, but I recognize the brief doses of fear, as if Kane will feel betrayed if he finds out that I meddled with a truth I never should've been privy to.

"But since then, it's been near constant." Kane runs a hand through his hair, messing up the perfect style leftover from the media shoot. "He bled me dry one time. That's why Malaki moved in with me. He covered the rent."

My mouth parts slightly. *Just how much money is Miles losing these days?*

"Who else knows?"

He glances away. "Just Malaki. Your brother still believes what everyone else does—that I'm the one with the gambling problem."

I stare at my devil horn headband on the ground—the same one that I threw at him moments ago.

"And now you."

My heart skips a beat when our eyes catch. He looks so vulnerable with his closed-lip frown but so resilient too. Broad shoulders, tense with frustration, but a heart that bleeds on the inside.

"I thought you said you'd never trust me again."

Kane takes a step toward me, and for the first time, I remain still. Surprise flickers against his features, only to smooth when he's less than a breath away. I'm lost in the quiet moment, my heart thudding.

I look at his mouth, tracing the perfect curve of his lips with my eyes.

I'm desperate for the feeling his kiss leaves behind.

My breathing slows when Kane buries his fingers into my hair. He cups the side of my face, and I grab onto his wrist. "I don't want to trust anyone," he admits. "Especially you..."

His words cut me, and I look away.

He quickly pulls me back to him by gripping my chin and

tilting my face. "That's only because being close to you leads to all the wrong things."

I watch as Kane's Adam's apple bobs slowly with a swallow.

"I wasn't man enough to ask you back then..." His words linger.

A noise leaves me when Kane's hand lands on the small of my back, pulling me flush against him. Our pounding heartbeats blend, and the room grows hot.

"Ask me what?"

"If you still feel the same undeniable pull between us. The unbreakable connection. The desperation to touch..."

Our warm breath mingles, my body craving him in the worst way. Tiny sparks of desire tingle against my skin as a flush creeps its way up my neck.

"Answer me," Kane says.

The room spins, and he brings my face closer to his, our lips nearly touching.

"Why does it matter what I feel?" I whisper. It's not like this can really go anywhere. Right?

"It matters because if you say yes, it gives me a reason to be good again. To be the guy I used to be before everything got fucked. You'd be my reason, Daisy."

He is good. He tries to hide it, but he is. The fact that he thinks he's not hurts me.

"Daisy." He is pleading with me, and I can't deny him, not when he's like this.

A second passes.

Then another.

My mouth opens. "Yes. But—"

"No buts."

My body ignites when his mouth seals against mine. The way his tongue slips inside to explore should be a crime. His kiss is possessive and untamed, bringing out a side of me that I didn't know existed.

I make a noise when he tugs on my hair, kissing me so hard that our teeth clank against one another. We break apart, and his eyes flip back and forth between mine, like he can't believe that we're doing this again.

"Shit," he mutters.

He picks me up in one fluid movement and wraps my legs around his waist.

I grab onto his face, his scruff scratching my palms. I kiss him again and again, my hair falling around us like a shield of protection.

"I want to kiss every part of your body," he murmurs.

The stuffy air of the dressing room blankets my sweaty skin as Kane pulls my costume down and over my shoulders. He peppers my neck with soft kisses before moving down to my collarbone.

Chills rush to the surface, and my head falls back with pleasure.

"Take me," I whisper.

Kane stills, his mouth hovering over my flushed skin. Before I know it, he's spinning us around and flicking the lock on the door. My back presses to the floor, and I'm stripped bare. The trailing of his sultry gaze over my curves has my stomach flipping. It's a thrill I never knew I'd like.

Kane's shirt flies over my head, and he quickly pulls his pants down. He's at my center before I have a chance to think and pushes into me slowly.

"Oh my god," I sigh.

Kane's mouth moves to my breast. The warm flick of his tongue against my nipple sends my legs open farther. "So perfect," he whispers, taking turns between each breast. "Do you know how perfect you are?"

My soft laugh is full of sarcasm. Perfect? I have an autoimmune disease.

"My body literally attacks itself," I remind him. "I'm far from perfect."

Kane freezes above me, hauling himself to his forearms. I furrow my forehead and move against him, wanting more, but his hand falls to my hip to stop me.

My bottom lip pops out.

"Take it back," he demands.

I inhale, searching for air. "Take what back?"

"You said you were far from perfect." He narrows his gaze. "Take it back, Daisy."

Kane starts to pull out of me, and I panic. "Fine!" I quickly say. "I take it back."

His face smooths, and a cocky grin replaces his grimace. "Good girl. Now take that perfect pussy of yours and show me how much it wants me."

Heat strokes my insides, and my eyelashes flutter with pleasure. Kane quickly flips us over, and suddenly, I'm on top of him. He hits a new angle, and it steals the breath from my lungs. His knuckle presses against my clit, and pleasure flows to my toes. I moan. My hips grind against him on their own as an orgasm rips through me suddenly.

"Fuck, Daisy." Kane's voice is strained, though I can barely hear it.

"It's...so..." I move again, and suddenly, another orgasm surprises me. My legs quiver around Kane, refusing to let him up.

"Don't hold back, baby." His husky voice and wandering hands send me over the edge. "I've got you."

I do as I'm told. I throw my head back, and Kane's fingers dig into my thighs. Suddenly, I'm lifted up and hovering over him as he comes. My lips part as I watch his hand glide back and forth over his hard length. The veins in his hand strain with the movement, and a groan tears from his mouth.

Jesus Christ. My lips part from the sight.

As soon as he's done, our eyes catch.

The dark-blue color lights up, and I'm back to staring at the boy who stole my heart years ago.

Forty-Two

KANE

MALAKI SKATES behind me and hums under his breath. "Someone is awfully chipper this evening."

I don't even bother looking over my shoulder.

I know he's sporting a shit-eating grin.

"Must've been those delicious smoothies left on our counter for us."

I turn to glare at him but fail. Turns out, I am *chipper.* "You're not getting one next time."

He snorts. "Are you seriously that possessive over Daisy that you don't even want me to have the smoothie she made?"

Maybe.

Another pair of skates comes into my peripheral. "You know it's okay to share, Kane. Sharing is caring."

I bare my teeth at Lars, my grip on my stick tightening with force. From the tone of his voice, I know what he's implying, and he should know that I am not against knocking the teeth out of one of my own teammates' mouth.

Emory skates in between us. "Will you fucking relax, animal?"

"Relax?" I growl under my breath. "Do you know what he's referring to?"

Emory chuckles, and I want to tear his goalie's mask off. "Of course I do. But you deserve it. How many times have you messed with me about fucking my fake wife? Or Rhodes and his nanny?"

A few of the other guys chirp while skating their rounds, pleading their cases that I deserve every joke coming my way. Most of them don't even know about Daisy and me, but they're still coming together to poke fun.

I do my best to ignore their jabs, focusing more on the opening in the rink rather than my rising temper.

Malaki skates over again, tossing the puck back and forth. "Seriously, though, that smoothie has given me energy." I watch as he rushes down the ice and back. "See."

"You're like a child."

"Malaki! Save your energy for the fucking game!"

Malaki salutes the coach.

He replies with a curse under his breath.

"He's right," I say. "We win tonight, and we will secure our spot in the playoffs. Get your shit straight."

Malaki laughs. "You get *your* shit straight."

I steal the puck and send it flying down the rink into the goal. "Looks like I'm just fine."

"There she is. Our favorite mascot."

I spin so quickly I almost slip.

Malaki bursts out laughing while Rhodes, who rarely smiles, chuckles.

"Yeah, you're fine, alright," he jokes.

"Fuck off," I snarl.

Daisy is paying me no mind, which completely messes with my head. We didn't say much after the dressing room incident because Reese and Malaki were both standing outside the door, waiting for us with amused looks, like they heard every last moan fall from her mouth.

He and I stayed back for some last-minute drills before the game while Reese took Daisy home, which means we haven't seen each other since I was dick-deep inside of her, coaxing her to show me what her pussy could do.

Just the mere thought sends my dick erect.

I squeeze my jaw and adjust my cup before making my way over to her.

After she throws some merch over the glass to a few fans, I skate behind her.

"Was that a *thank-you-for-the-orgasm* smoothie waiting for me before the game?" I ask in a low tone.

I catch her sweet grin in the reflection of the glass. She skates off without answering me, as if I won't actually follow her on the ice.

"Quit following me, and go warm up," she chides.

"I warmed up earlier"—I lower my voice—"with you."

I zero in on her white teeth sinking into her plump bottom lip.

"Careful," I warn.

Where can we go so no one will see us?

"Careful?" She peeks at me out of the corner of her eye.

"If you keep biting that lip, I'm going to have to remind you who it belongs to."

A thrill shoots down my thighs as a blush spreads over her cheeks.

"You're crazy." She tries to hide her smile.

"Crazy enough to fuck my best friend's sister and not feel even a sliver of guilt afterward."

Daisy's skates come to a halt, almost sending her flying onto the ice.

My gloved hand wraps around the front of her waist, and I

haul her back up. She presses her back against my front, and I hum.

"Kane!" Her voice wavers with worry. "River is here."

Is that supposed to keep me from touching her?

"And?"

She huffs, putting space between us. "He's going to know."

I tilt my head. "Be honest. Do you really think he'll disapprove?"

I ask the question with full curiosity. It's not really something I've considered until recently. The more we cross the line, the more the unease slips from my mind. Back when we were teens, River would have been repelled by the idea. If any guy showed interest in Daisy, he shooed them away or made up some excuse as to why they couldn't hang out with us. But now we're adults, and if anyone is protective over her, it's me.

"I..." Daisy's gaze darts around. "I think he'll be concerned."

My shoulders tense. What she means is that he wouldn't approve of a guy like me with a girl like her. My reputation precedes me, and I have to admit, it isn't a good look, especially since he thinks I can't handle my own finances as a grown man.

"I see the look on your face, and that's not what I mean..." Daisy slowly skates away from me.

I ignore the fact that she just read my mind. "Then what do you mean?"

A flash of panic crosses her features, and she skates away again. I want to follow her across the ice, snatch her around the waist, go back to our little hiding spot, and work whatever it is she's thinking out of her mouth, but the buzzer goes off, and the lights turn down.

I catch up to her, and we both climb off the ice.

"Not going to tell me?" I whisper in her ear from behind.

She pauses but remains quiet.

Knowing I have to take the ice in a moment for the national anthem, I desperately attempt to make a deal with her. "If we win, you have to tell me…"—I pause—"while naked."

I mean, let's get real. I'll work it out of her one way or another, but at least this way, I have more than just the play-offs to fight for.

Daisy turns, and my heart stalls from the flirty smile on her face. "Too easy. You have to get a goal too."

I smile like a maniac with the challenge. "Done."

She rolls her eyes, and I hear my name being called.

I quickly poke her side, causing her body to jerk to the side. I take advantage of the move and let my lips graze her ear.

"Thanks for the smoothie." My chest grows tight from the thoughtfulness of her action. "Yours was better than my mom's."

I skate onto the ice with my usual, straightlaced face, but on the inside, I'm buzzing.

A goal, a win, and then Daisy underneath me?

I've never been more ready for a game.

Forty–Three

DAISY

HE'S SUCH A SHOW-OFF.

I stand beside my brother with pursed lips and crossed arms as Kane scores a goal. My brother brought some of the residents from the hospital, most of whom have bags under their eyes from lack of sleep. He asked that I come hang out with them for the remainder of the period, and without having much reason not to, I agreed.

Once I slid my way into one of the empty seats, I realized pretty quickly that the only reason he wanted me to make an appearance was because none of his co-workers believed that his sister was the mascot.

"So, like, was this your dream job or…"

I don't bother moving my attention from Kane while I answer one of them. "Oh yeah," I joke. "That's what every little girl dreams of…being a mascot when they grow up."

Everyone laughs.

My brother swoops in to vaguely explain the situation, leaving my Lupus diagnosis out of it, which landed me in this position, but I tune him out and watch the game. Kane is fierce on the ice. He always has been, but as a man with much more control of his body, he weaves in and out of clusters of players, shooting down the ice quickly.

The goal buzzer sounds again, and my jaw drops.

Is he serious?

Another goal?

My lips curve from the sight of his smile. His teammates meet him at center ice and clap him on the back. Warmth settles into my belly. It isn't often that Kane looks genuinely happy, but when he does, all feels right in the world. My world.

One of my brother's friends...Tom or Tim...Ted?...comes into my sight, blocking my view of the ice. He asks me how I'm liking Chicago. I quickly move to see the game and answer him blindly, not really paying much attention to the conversation. My sights are glued to Kane, who heads to the bench. He talks to Malaki before they both swing their gazes to me.

My stomach lurches.

Kane's lip curves with the crook of his eyebrow.

Yeah, yeah. I know. You got two goals.

He winks at me, and my face warms.

The guy to my left is still chatting away, but instead of continuing the conversation, my teeth sink into my bottom lip as I try to hide my smile. Kane jerks his chin and gives me a questionable look. It takes me a second to realize that he's silently asking me who the guy is beside me.

"A friend," I mouth.

Kane glares, and the thought of him being jealous twists something dangerous in my lower stomach. I know I shouldn't push the limits any further with him, but it's too fun not to. While keeping his attention, I reach over and grab onto Tim's arm to cease his endless talking.

"It was really nice to meet you, Tim," I say with a smile.

From across the ice, I'm sure it looks like flirting. But anyone in the near vicinity knows that I just shut Tim down as nicely as possible, considering he was still in the middle of a conversation.

My brother snorts.

"It's Ted." Tim—I mean, *Ted* corrects me, and I wish I felt bad.

"Told you not to hit on my sister," River jokes. "You're not her type."

I crinkle my brow. "And what *is* my type?"

River taps his chin a few times. "Cocky, arrogant, athletic—"

My heart races.

"Blond hair."

Is he describing Kane on purpose?

Does he know?

Better question...does he care?

"So assholes? Great," Ted mumbles.

"That's not true," I blurt.

Kane isn't an asshole.

I quickly try to cover my tracks with my brother. "I've dated guys with brown hair," I admit.

"Hooking up isn't dating," River says under his breath.

I scoff. "Says the guy who hooks up with a new girl every time he goes out."

One of his female co-workers furrows her brow. "You do?"

I smile deviously at my brother, who shoots me a *thanks a lot* look. I scurry down the stairs to get back to the Blue Devils' bench because now that it's almost intermission, I unfortunately have to get back to my job.

The buzzer sounds right when I make it to the opening in the ice. The team stands to head back to the locker room for their last break. I stay out of their way, smiling at the few that glance in my direction.

Until Kane comes into view.

Butterflies swarm my stomach.

He steps off to the side casually. "Friend?" he questions.

"Hmm?" I murmur.

He sighs impatiently.

Sweat trickles down the side of his face from his damp hair, and the most erotic thought pops into my head. *I wonder what he'd do if I licked the little bead?*

The end of the line is quickly coming to a halt, and we both know that he has to go into the locker room while I skate out onto the ice. I give him a playful smile while he relentlessly glares at me.

Once the last player passes, Kane steps in line with him.

I try to move past with my foam tridents trapped in my arm, but Kane stops me at the last second. His arm wraps around the front of my belly, and his warm breath coats the side of my face. "Feels like you're daring me to do something, Daisy-Petal."

My heart pounds. "What are you going to do, Kane? Claim me in front of everyone in attendance?" I laugh softly because the thought is completely outlandish.

"I could."

I roll my eyes playfully. "You will not. My brother is here. Not to mention, we'd be on national television."

"Seems like you've forgotten who you're dealing with." His voice is tight, and my grasp on the situation starts to slip.

My confidence starts to waver with the seriousness of his tone. Someone calls his name, and he slowly slides his arm away. I let out a breath that I didn't know I was holding as he flicks his chin to the ice, silently telling me to get out there.

I blink several times and move toward the rink. With the tridents still trapped in my arm, I skate quickly in an attempt to untangle my thoughts, but the entire time I'm skating and throwing merch to fans, I circle back to my biggest worry: that the thought of Kane claiming me in front of every single person in attendance, including my brother, makes me giddy.

345

Forty-Four

KANE

I'M ACTING IRRATIONALLY.

The thought of sticking my tongue down Daisy's throat in front of everyone does wild things to my body.

My fingers itch with the need to touch those perfect curves, possess her, and show her that I'm not playing around. The more I have her, taste her, *look* at her, the needier I become.

I'd be in deep shit if I went through with my plan of pushing her to center ice and kissing her in front of everyone during a game of this magnitude. We're two points from a spot in the playoffs, and I'm over here, picturing Daisy's parted lips with my name slipping off the end instead of focusing on winning.

Not to mention, River is only a few seats behind the glass. I'm man enough to know that this isn't the way to go about this. He's the longest friendship I've ever had. I respect him too much to declare my claim over his sister in front of millions without so much as a warning. Then there are his parents to think about too.

A streak of loyalty runs through me.

Fuck.

I'm not even positive that Daisy is on board with the thoughts in my head. If I alluded to them all, they'd probably scare the hell out of her.

"Six minutes."

I glance at the doorway to the locker room, and panic sets in. Six minutes?

My thoughts are all over the place.

I'm unfocused, and I know just the thing I need.

Six minutes is plenty of time.

With my freshly taped stick, I head to the doorway.

"Where're you going?" Rhodes asks, being the father of the team and all.

"To take care of something." I don't bother waiting to see his reaction.

The hall is quiet, the reporters still locked away until the end of the game. I peek into Daisy's dressing room, searching for her, but she's nowhere in sight.

Where is my little devil?

After a few more seconds of searching, I quickly move over to the hallway that leads to the ice. It's long and narrow and echoes with the sounds of fans. My lip curls with anticipation when I see her standing there, all alone, in her devil's costume.

I creep down the hall as quietly as possible. I rest my stick against the side of the wall and slide behind her. "There's my little devil," I whisper.

Daisy gasps as she spins toward me. Those wide eyes as blue as the sky lock onto me with a flash of excitement in them.

"What are you doing?" She peeks around me to see that we're all alone. "The last period is about to start."

I shrug. "We've got a few minutes."

Daisy's hip pops, and she flings those shiny waves over her shoulder. "For?"

"For me to remind you of something." I drop my gloves at her feet and grab her. A breath rushes into the empty space as I push her gently against the wall. Her gasp is heaven to my ears.

Our eyes lock, and the words on the tip of my tongue are dangerous. "I just wanted to remind you that you're mine."

"Oh?" Her playful smile sends me reeling. "Am I?"

"I almost stopped mid-game to pull that guy away from you." I don't care if that makes me sound insane.

Daisy's soft laugh calms me. "Your jealousy is showing."

More like insecurity.

Panic squeezed my lungs as I sat on the bench and watched that guy practically drool over her. Fear seeped in at the thought of losing her again, which is exactly why I need to remind her that she's mine, even if we haven't discussed the ins and outs of whatever the hell we're doing right now.

"That's the difference between you and me," I say in a low voice. My hand creeps past her hip, and I graze my knuckles against the inside of her thigh. She has on thin, sparkly, nude tights that I want to rip to shreds. "I'll admit when I'm jealous, and you won't."

Daisy's chin tips with my other hand cupping the side of her face. Her skin warms my callused palm, putting me into a daze. I zero in on her pretty mouth and watch her tongue jolt out to wet the plump bottom lip. A waterfall of heat works through me, and I pull her mouth to mine.

The world stops spinning. I'm calm and grounded when I have her like this but eager too. A sweet noise leaves her, and I swallow it whole.

"Turn," I say, separating our mouths for a second.

Her little brows crowd, and I don't waste any time. I spin her, the sound of the zipper blending in with my racing heart. She peers over her shoulder at me with pink cheeks and confusion.

"Kane," she warns.

"Little devil..." I repeat. "Let me remind you of something else."

I erase all the space between us, and Daisy's ass rubs against my front. My hand has a mind of its own, snaking around her and dipping into her loose costume. Her head falls back to my shoulder with a shaky sigh of relief.

"Remind me that you have a lot of experience?" she asks.

I chuckle against her neck and nibble on the skin. The moment my fingers slip lower, I realize she's not wearing panties.

You mean to tell me that she's out there, on the ice, in this tight outfit, pantyless?

I'll never be able to focus now.

"No." I rub her clit, getting her—and myself—all worked up. "This is a reminder that you were made for me." My dick is rock solid—something I'll regret the second the buzzer sounds. "Look at you." I blow a hot breath into her ear and watch in awe as goosebumps fly to her bare skin. "Letting me, your brother's best friend, touch you like this in a public place with fans only a few feet above us."

This better be the only time she's done something so dirty in public.

Daisy's attention rises to the bottom of the stands. No one can see us. I wouldn't dare let anyone watch her like this.

This is for me...and me only.

"You're so wet," I whisper. "You like being secretive in public with me?"

I slide a finger inside her and clench my eyes shut from the heat.

My plan was to get her all worked up, just to remind her that *I'm* the one who makes her feel good. Not some tall, nerdy guy her brother brought with him to the game. But not letting her come is torture for me too.

"I think I just like you." Her breaths are sharp and fast. I fucking love it.

"Tell me that you're mine." I'm desperate to hear it.

With my other hand, I grip her chin and pull her to peer at me over her shoulder. Our heated gazes lock, and *fuck*, I want her forever.

"Is that what you want?" Daisy rolls her hips, climbing toward an orgasm. "For me to admit that I'm yours?"

"Yes."

All I want is her.

My chest tightens with my silent admittance.

Daisy's sweet gaze turns grave, the moment between us turning weighty.

I hear a noise behind me. Stomping skates against the padded floor get louder.

Fuck.

A thick swallow works down my throat, and I hastily pull my hand away and spin her toward me. Panic rushes through my fingers, and the only reason I stop is because I refuse to let my teammates see her half-naked.

Daisy is mine and mine alone.

I'm not sharing.

"Reality calls." I pull her zipper up, and she pouts, sticking that bottom lip out.

I run my thumb over it. "I want you naked and waiting for me after the game."

"Oh, Barlow..." Malaki sings my name. "Come out, come out, wherever you are."

Daisy's mouth curves with a cute smile.

"Devil girl too," he adds.

A pink blush spreads across her cheeks, and I can't help but lean forward to kiss her.

It's a quick one, just enough to make me briefly hate the game of hockey for stealing me away from her.

"And don't think I've forgotten about our deal." I take a step back and grab my gloves off the ground.

Daisy rolls her eyes. "I know, I know. You scored two goals."

Leaving her standing there with a flushed face and wetness between her legs, I know I'm going to score again later on tonight too.

Forty-Five

DAISY

THE LAST PERIOD took years to end, and I have no one but myself to thank for that. I've always had a hard time resisting Kane, and now that we're adults, you'd think we'd be able to deny the impulses and ignore the hot tension.

But no, it's the complete opposite.

As soon as the game ends and I do my final rounds on the ice, I'm zipping back toward my dressing room to impatiently wait.

I want you naked and waiting for me after the game.

Anticipation flew to my toes with his parting words.

As I kick my skates off, the energy is still buzzing against my skin.

River's text goes unopened on my phone, asking me to come out with him after the game. I can't very well text him back and say, *sorry I have plans.* Because those plans involve his best friend touching every single inch of me—again.

I don't know what Kane and I are doing or what the plan

is after it's all said and done, but right now, I really just don't care.

This is my one indulgence.

Every other part of my life is micromanaged. It's detrimental to my health if I veer from the straight and narrow or step a toe out of line and forget to take a vitamin, or god forbid, I catch a cold.

Kane is my wild, my chaos. My dirty little secret.

My phone vibrates again, and I glance at it, figuring it's River.

But instead, it's Kane.

Heat sweeps over the back of my neck.

KANE

Are you waiting for me, little devil?

I nibble on my lip to hide my smile. Of course I'm waiting for him, but I wouldn't be me if I didn't torment him a little bit. After all, he left me wet and needy for the entire third period, so he sort of deserves it.

ME

I am. But you have to find me. 😈

KANE

I should have known. You always did like the chase.

He's right.

I lived for his lingering looks back in high school. The way his eyes would follow me around at a party if my brother dared let me go with them. Or how he'd always be the first to show up if I needed a ride, searching every room and sending scathing glares to guys until he found me. I loved when he'd find me in the stands at his hockey games too.

No matter where I sat, he'd find me.

KANE

> Ready or not, here I come.

A high-pitched squeal squeezes from my mouth. I head for the door, thankful the hallway is empty.

Jitters bounce to the bottom of my feet, pushing me to reach the stairs in record time.

The Blue Devils arena is gigantic, and there are plenty of places to hide.

There are multiple conference rooms, the equipment closet, the visiting team's locker room, the Blue Devils' locker room, and the penalty box.

A lightbulb goes off. I bite my lip and head for the stands opposite of the bench. The fans are long gone, not a single person lingering in their seats any longer. I push on the door of one of the box seats and let it close softly behind me. Glass surrounds me, cutting me off from any noise other than my own racing heart.

The anticipation is something I've never felt before.

I'm not a Goody Two-shoes like I was when I was in high school. I've had plenty of hookups and no-strings-attached flings, but this is something more. Nerves fill my belly, and my heart races. A flirty smile overtakes my face, and the fact that I'm doing this with Kane makes the entire situation that more insane.

KANE

> I'm becoming impatient.

I smile.

ME

> Here's a hint: I have the perfect view of the rink.

My phone vibrates, and I'm so excited it almost slips to the floor. I scrunch my nose when I see that it's a text from a random number, asking me if I'm coming to hang out. Then another text that says, **It's Ted. Your brother gave me your number.**

I have the sudden notion to send my brother a message that says, *Sorry I'm busy, getting fucked by Kane* just to get back at him for handing out my number like candy, but I quickly toss my phone and stride over to the glass.

The lights over the ice are low, only a few remaining on. Kane will have the perfect view of me all alone in the box seat with the light illuminating me beyond everything else.

I slowly begin to unzip my costume, pulling it away from my shoulders. I zero in my attention on the Blue Devils' bench, waiting for Kane to show up.

He's a smart man, so I wouldn't put it past him to know exactly where to look.

After a few more seconds of waiting and an increasingly alarming number of butterflies in my belly, I spot him.

My heart flips.

A small smile slips onto my lips as he strides casually down the long hallway toward the bench with his hands in his pockets. He has shed his hockey uniform and slipped back into something more casual. I shouldn't be surprised that he appears even hotter in his sweats and beanie, but I am.

Kane Barlow was all the rave in high school. His cocky smirk and dark-blue eyes had every girl labeling him as the bad boy. Now that he's all grown up, he's more like a sin. One that I'd gladly be punished for.

The closer he gets to the bench, the more I ache.

I'm nervous, eager, turned on, and on the very tip of my toes.

It takes him a few scans of the area before he lifts his gaze.

Once he sees me, his lip curves. I manage to keep my smile at bay while his hands remain in the pockets of his pants, like he's waiting for me to come to him instead of the other way around.

I crook my eyebrow.

As if.

Slowly, with my heart pounding violently inside my ears, I pull my costume the rest of the way off.

It falls in a heap at my feet.

I stare at Kane, and he stares right back.

The playfulness is still there on his features when his eyes drop.

My hair hides my chest perfectly, concealing my pebbled nipples, only showing off the bottom curve of my breasts.

I watch Kane's eyebrow hitch as he takes me in.

He digs into the pocket of his pants and pulls out his phone.

I glance at mine and see his name lighting up on the screen.

"You found me," I say as soon as I put it on speaker.

"Wasn't hard." He chuckles. "I can smell your arousal from here."

I snap my attention to him through the glass. An entire rink separates us, yet he can still irritate me with a few words.

At this point, I think bickering is how we flirt.

I pretend to squint. "If I look close enough, I think I can see your hard-on." I pause for a second. "Oh, actually. I think that's just a shadow. You *are* on the smaller side compared to the guys I've been with before."

His growl echoes around the empty box seat.

A laugh bursts from my mouth, and he sighs with annoyance.

"You love fucking with me, don't you?" His voice is low, and it hits all the right spots.

I bite my lip and lean closer to the glass. His eyes light up across the ice.

"I'm just trying to keep up with you," I admit. "I can't let you have the upper hand."

His chuckle is raspy. "It's funny that you think I have the upper hand when it comes to you, Daisy."

He stands in the same spot with his phone up to his ear, his eyes never leaving the box.

"I like the idea of having control when it comes to the unattainable Kane Barlow," I admit.

Have there been any other girls who have been able to bring Kane to his knees?

If only he knew that it was me who was wrapped around his finger and not the other way around. I mean, look at the situation I'm in—standing in a public place, completely naked, just to prove a point to him.

Never mind the fact that this is *Kane.*

"Don't get ahead of yourself," he says.

A spark rushes to the tips of my toes with a challenge.

"I know that look," his rugged voice interrupts my thoughts. "You're gonna try to prove a point."

He knows me too well.

His eyes follow me as I slowly push one side of my hair behind my shoulder to show off my breast. I smile to myself when his breathing becomes labored.

"Daisy, Daisy, Daisy," he rasps.

I giggle and catch his eye, but just as quickly as we lock gazes, his head snaps toward the other end of the rink.

"Fuck," he mutters.

I scan the ice. The Zamboni comes into view with a man behind the wheel. My stomach drops.

Rationally, I know I should take a step back so I'm out of sight, turn the light off, and quickly get dressed.

But the very second Kane's attention flings to mine while I stand naked in front of the glass, I smile like the little devil he keeps referring to me as.

"Daisy," he warns.

"Better hurry, Kane. Or someone other than you is going to get a nice view tonight."

Kane has officially made me lose my mind.

But if losing my mind means feeling like this, I'm perfectly content being thrown in a padded room.

Forty-Six

KANE

I'M out of breath by the time I make it to the other end of the arena, and that's saying something, considering I'm in perfect shape.

The Zamboni machine whirs in the background, mixing with the sound of my thrumming pulse.

Daisy has nestled herself deep inside my head, making me chase her all over this damn arena just for a taste. She's the only girl I'd be willing to do this for, and if that doesn't mean something to her, then I don't know what does.

I pull on the door handle eagerly and spot her immediately. "Found you."

I flick the lights off so whoever is on the Zamboni won't see us. She knows how wildly possessive I am of her by now, so it should come as no surprise to her when I make that *very* fucking clear in a few seconds.

"Now it's time for me to make a point." I'm driven by jealousy, but I admire her cheeky ways. She keeps up with me, and that's something no one has ever been able to do before.

The door shuts behind me, and I flick the lock.

My dick pulses with the idea of having her all to myself behind a locked door.

"What point is that?" Daisy's sweet whisper has a hint of excitement to it.

I swallow roughly as I stride over to her. Those glossy waves slip backward as she tilts her face to look me in the eye. It takes everything in me not to stare at her bare body.

"That even though you drive me crazy, I can drive you crazier."

There's no time to waste.

My hands clasp her curves to haul her against me. Her smooth legs wrap around my waist, and I sit in one of the seats. I glance at her sexy bedroom eyes and almost forget what I'm doing, but with the Zamboni getting closer to this side of the rink, I'm reminded pretty quickly that she was playing with fire just seconds ago.

"The thought of someone seeing you naked makes me lose my fucking mind."

A tiny smile curves on her mouth. *Oh, she likes it when I'm jealous?*

"Do you like knowing that I want you all to myself?" I ask, running my nose against her delicate jaw.

She nods slowly, breaths rushed and fast. I become unhinged at the sight of her breasts rising and falling with every one.

My mouth lands on her nipple, and desire pulls on my insides like a puppet. I swirl my tongue around, obsessing over the sounds leaving her. Daisy moves her hips, begging to feel my cock against her slick center, but I tap on the brakes.

"Not yet, little devil," I rasp, needing to drag this out.

I grip the insides of her thighs, my fingers biting into the soft flesh to keep her still.

She huffs with a pout, and I smirk with her nipple in between my teeth.

I let go and sit back farther onto the seat. I stare up at her furrowed brow. "You drive me crazy. I drive you even crazier. That's the way it goes," I say, smirking.

Her lips open with a soft gasp. "And don't think I've forgotten that you owe me an explanation for earlier. We had a deal, and I scored." My fingers run up and down the inside of her thigh. "Twice."

Daisy shivers, and I glance down to see how wet she is.

Blood rushes to my dick. *Fuck.*

"Needy little thing." I dig my hands into her hair and bring her face to mine. I glide my tongue past her lips, and she moans against my mouth. The kiss itself is hot, let alone the sexy mewing she's doing.

Driving her crazy drives *me* crazy.

"Are you all hot and bothered, Daisy?" I ask, our breaths mingling.

"Mm-hmm," she whines.

"I don't think I've made my point yet, though..." The whirring from the Zamboni grows louder.

"What?" Her breasts bounce as she sits back, rubbing that wet clit against my raging cock.

I smirk. "On your knees, Daisy."

Her parted lips zip shut. Those pretty blue eyes brew a fire that land against my skin like burning embers. I tilt my head, wondering if she'll continue with her bravery, and sure enough, she does.

My legs flex when she slips in between them and drops to her knees. Her small hands fall to my thighs, my hips jerking from the subtle touch.

The part of me that cares deeply for Daisy wants to pull her up by those arms and take care of her body like she's some delicate angel I have to be gentle with. But the other part of me is wild with desire, and I crave to do all sorts of dirty things to her.

Instead of waiting for her to pull my dick free, I lift up and shove my pants down. Surprise carves into her features, and I grow harder. She licks her bottom lip, and her gaze glazes over as I move my hand to squeeze my cock.

I've never been so desperate for a woman.

"So brave," I groan, watching her follow my hand up and down.

Those blue eyes flick to mine, and there's a tug on my balls.

"I'm not seventeen anymore," she whispers, moving her hand over me.

My head falls back from her soft touch on the tip of my dick. I move my hands and let her take over. She rubs up and down a few times before I feel the brush of her hair skim my legs like a feather.

I peer at her on her knees and drown in desire.

Her lips wrap around my cock, and my hand instinctively flies to the back of her head.

Warm.

Silky smooth.

Tight.

Fucking perfect.

The strands of her hair get tangled within my fingers as she moves her head up and down. She takes me so well, pushing me into her throat and never once wincing.

"Fuck, Daisy."

She smiles with me in her mouth. I tip my head backward so I can't watch her and try to control myself.

A few more thrusts of my hips, and I'm pulling her up by her shoulders. "Sit."

The Zamboni must be right up against this side of the rink, because it's so loud I can't hear the hissing coming from between my teeth when she slides down onto my cock.

I squeeze her torso with my palms. "Fuck," I groan. "You're fucking perfect."

Daisy moves her body like a stripper, fluidly and so precise. Every time I hit the end of her pussy, my balls tighten. She makes a noise I find myself suddenly consumed with.

Her breasts are right there for the taking, bouncing up and down in my face. I suck a bud into my mouth and move one of my hands to her clit. My thumb circles it over and over again, and her eyelashes flutter closed.

"Come for me," I beg.

I sit up a little taller and make her kiss me.

Our tongues move over one another as quickly as our bodies.

It's so easy to become obsessed with her. Having her like this is a sin and heaven all in one. I'm entranced by her, her body reacting to my touch right away.

"Ah," she moans against my mouth, stopping our kiss. She's right on the edge of her climax, tightening around my cock. Grabbing her by the throat, I kiss her through the pleasure and she comes so hard over my dick that I can't stop myself from coming too.

"Fuck," I groan, holding still.

I feel her everywhere.

In my head, my blood, my fucking bones. This girl carved a place for herself in my heart long ago, and she just nestled herself right back in.

Our breathing finally begins to slow, sweat drying against our flushed skin. With my cock still inside of her, I lean back and stare up into her eyes.

Her teeth make worry marks on her lip, indenting the swollen soft flesh.

"I'm obsessed with you," I admit, not caring if it scares her.

I'm so obsessed with her that I don't even care that I just came inside of her.

I've never come inside anyone.

I've never even entertained the idea. I had a condom nearby, but the thought didn't even cross my mind because it's *Daisy.*

I keep waiting for the guilt to show up, but it is nonexistent. River's sister or not.

"I came inside of you."

I wait for shock to cover her features. I expect her to get angry at herself for not realizing and at me for doing the act in the first place. But the longer I stare up at her, the more confused I become.

Her soft hands fall to my shoulders.

Is this when she breaks my heart again? Because this feels too much like the morning I left for the juniors.

She glances away, her face paling. "It may be hard for me to have kids...because of my Lupus and past medications. So, I'm sure it's fine."

I blink once, then twice, and then a third time. Daisy keeps her attention away from me, staring off to the side in a daze.

Being tender and sweet isn't my thing, but my subconscious seems to know exactly what to do when it comes to her. I reach my hand out and grip her chin to turn her back toward me. Those wild blue eyes are tamed with something sad, and it cuts me down to the bone.

"I don't like it when you look sad,"

She shrugs and tries to climb off me. I keep her pinned, my dick still inside of her.

"Do you want kids one day, little devil?" I ask, brushing a hair out of her face.

If she wants a child, I'll give her one. The thought should scare me, but it doesn't, which is even crazier.

She attempts to climb from me again, and this time, I let her go. I watch her jerky movements as she shimmies back into her outfit in a rush.

That's enough of that.

I quickly pull my pants up and stride over to her. I grip her wrists and make her stop. In her frazzled state, she freezes and glances up at me with glassy eyes and wild hair.

"Stop," I demand.

She blows a breath out, moving another strand of hair from her face.

I give her wrists a quick squeeze. "Talk to me."

She turns away to hide, but I refuse to let her. "Let me be here for you."

Who am I?

My heart moves inside my chest. It's reaching for something, and I think it's her.

"If you want children, I'll give you children." I rub soft circles on the inside of her wrist. "If you still want that little plant shop you've always dreamed of owning, I'll build it for you." It was what she wanted years ago. I've never forgotten.

Daisy swallows, and I watch her sorrow fade.

My lip lifts on one side. "I'll even compost...you know, for your soil."

Her attention flies to mine, and her mouth works into a crescent.

"There's my Daisy-Petal." I lean forward and kiss the tip of her nose. I pull her into my chest, wrap my arms around her, and exhale when she rests her head against my beating heart. I wonder if she can hear how fast it's racing toward hers.

She pulls back, and we lock gazes.

Just when I think she's about to say something crazy, like *"who cares if you're River's best friend"* or *"who cares if we hated each other a week ago,"* she looks me dead in the eye and sends me her best flirty smile. "Will you really start composting?"

I snort. "Not a chance."

But I think we both know I'm lying right through my teeth, just like I was when I said I hated her.

Forty-Seven

DAISY

"GOOD MORNING, DEVIL GIRL."

I spin around with my heart in my throat. In an attempt to cover my bare legs from Malaki, I spill half my matcha on the floor. The green foamy liquid lands with a splash in between us, and I stare in shock.

He chuckles behind the rim of his coffee mug. "Don't bother covering up in front of me." His smile grows wider. "I heard you and Kane going at it like rabbits all night long."

My face warms.

"Kane must've forgotten to mention that you were home," I say with a bitter tone.

"No, I didn't." His voice comes from behind me, and I'm swarmed with butterflies. "I just didn't care."

Malaki throws his head back and laughs loudly. "You're fucked up."

I turn and shoot Kane a dirty look. "Kane!"

He shows off his cocky smile before tossing a towel on top of the matcha beneath my feet.

"How loud was I?" I worry, watching Kane kneel below me to wipe up my mess.

It's a nice view—one that reminds me of last night after we left the arena.

We lay in the quiet calmness of his room for a while before he suddenly flipped me on my back and kissed me senseless. He took his time with me, caressed my curves, his lips everywhere, and massaged my sore muscles before lying me down and bringing me to the edge of insanity.

"Loud," Malaki answers for Kane.

"Loud enough for my brother to hear?" I ask, panicked.

I pray he stayed out at the bar until well after Kane and I were done.

"Hopefully," Kane murmurs from below.

I shoot him a look. "Do you want to ruin your friendship with him?"

He shrugs. "Do you really think he'll be that against the idea?"

"Of you fucking his sister so hard the bed creaked?" Malaki snickers. "Yeah."

Kane's lips flatten. He slowly stands and tosses the towel over to the sink. All I can stare at are his rippling muscles moving against his bare chest, thanks to me stealing his T-shirt. "I think we should tel—"

Suddenly, our attention is pulled to the apartment door.

My heart falls.

Malaki spits out his coffee, and Kane, as poised as ever, remains unbothered at the sight of my brother strolling into the apartment.

The moment River sees me, he does a double-take.

A line of confusion digs in between his eyebrows.

"I thought you worked today?!" I exclaim.

Oh my god. I'm in nothing but panties and Kane's shirt.

"What the hell are you doing here"—River looks at my

half-naked outfit—"in nothing but...*that*." His hand wafts up and down in front of him with disgust.

Shit.

He immediately turns to Malaki, who is sitting on the couch with wide eyes. "Are you fucking my sister?" he asks him.

Kane steps forward, but so do I.

"Yes," I quickly say, attempting to save the situation before things get hairy.

The tension rises in the apartment, but I can't tell where it's coming from.

River? Or Kane?

Malaki plays along because he's not living in a world of delusion by thinking that River will be completely unfazed by Kane and me having sex. It's a tale as old as time. Your brother does *not* want you to mess with his friends, no matter how old you are.

"Sorry, bro." Malaki stands from the couch and starts to head to the kitchen. "It was a one-time thing."

River quickly steps forward and blocks him from coming toward me.

Malaki stops mid-walk. He straightens his shoulders, unsure of what my brother is going to do.

"Are you about to punch me for having your sister naked in my bed? Should I brace myself?" There is a hint of amusement in his tone, and I'm pretty sure he's the only one who thinks this entire ordeal is funny.

River shakes his head. "I'm not going to punch you. I'm protecting you."

A laugh bursts out of Malaki's mouth. "From your sister?"

"From Kane," my brother answers.

I turn and lock onto Kane over my shoulder. His smooth expression is long gone, and in its place is anger. One would assume that Kane is playing along with our made-up scenario, but with the way his jawline is sharpening and his fists are flexing at his sides, I'm not so sure.

"See." River snorts. "Kane is more protective over my sister than I am. Never once in high school did I have to throw a punch. He was always there first."

Malaki's mouth turns up on its side. "But what if Kane was the one to fuck your sister? Then what?" he asks.

My brother spins to face Kane and me. With Malaki behind him, he looks at Kane and puts his hands in his pockets with his eyebrow raised.

"He wouldn't fuck Daisy."

River answers so confidently I almost choke on the taste of Kane still inside my mouth from last night.

"We made a pact years ago, and Kane is too loyal to break it." My brother chuckles.

A pact?

About me?

"What?" I ask. "A pact?"

River chuckles. "Well, yeah. I didn't want him fucking my sister..." He pauses. "I still don't."

Knife to chest.

In the worst way, I want to turn and yell '*See!*' at Kane, but I quickly move on.

"How many other guys in high school did you make a pact with?" I ask, fully invested now.

"I don't know..." He pretends to think and shrugs. "All of them."

"Oh my god!" I huff. "Are you kidding me?"

River tries not to laugh. His mouth flattens, and he glances at his partner in crime.

I spin and glare at Kane.

He doesn't look guilty at all. In fact, he looks pretty damn proud of himself with that arrogant smile.

"Anyway," River sighs. "I have the morning off because I made Ted take my shift."

I cross my arms. "You clearly didn't make a pact with him since you gave him my number!"

Kane steps forward. "Wait, what?"

River puts his finger up. "Actually, that's why he has my shift this morning. He asked for my phone with some bogus excuse, and instead, he looked up your number so he could text you like a fucking creep."

"Time to get a new number," Kane grumbles.

An irritated breath rips from my lungs.

"I'm fully annoyed with men today." I grab my mug of matcha and head for the door, bypassing all three guys.

"Where are you going?" Kane asks.

River leans against the counter with his hip, unbothered by my tantrum, while Malaki tries not to laugh.

I stomp the rest of the way to the exit and turn with my hand locked on the doorknob. "I made a pact with my plants!" I snap. "I'm going to go water them and tell them all about how irritating you three are."

"Hey!" Malaki scoffs. "What did I do besides give you multiple orgasms?"

River glares at him. "You're pushing it."

"I agree," Kane growls.

Oh, for fuck's sake.

"You know what..." I try not to smile with my sudden payback. "You're right, Malaki. You can come with me and learn all about plants."

Surprise washes over his boyish face, and he quickly strides forward. "Here...let me." He grabs onto the door and opens it for me while Kane and River remain in the kitchen.

"Put some pants on!" Kane shouts.

Malaki snickers as the door shuts. We rush to the elevator,

and when we're fully enclosed, he nudges me with his elbow. "So, tell me," he says, "was I good in bed?"

I can't hold back my laugh. "The best."

"Good. Tell Reese that, will ya?"

I roll my eyes, and we head into my apartment, where I tell him all about my plants *and* Reese.

———

KANE

Are you still mad at me, little devil?

I scowl at my phone as soon as the message pops up.

ME

Shouldn't you be getting ready for the game?

Away games are always a nice breather for me. It gives me a chance to relax in my own space without wondering what Kane is doing upstairs. I pull open my journal and scribble some less than ideal symptoms I've been having lately before flipping to the back to work on my *goals* page.

It's the same worn piece of notebook paper that I've had since high school.

New notebook but same piece of paper, just paperclipped in the back, splattered with matcha stains, filled with new and improved goals throughout the last several years.

I'm no closer to achieving them than I was before moving to Chicago, but my grandma always said dreaming was good for the soul, so I've never stopped.

My phone goes off again, and I put the journal down.

KANE

I'm not playing tonight.

I sit up a little taller. Worry sits on my shoulders.

ME

What? Why? Is everything okay?

Why wouldn't Kane play? Is he hurt?

KANE

We're seated for the playoffs. Coach is keeping a few of us off the ice so we don't get injured before the series starts.

I jump to my feet and furiously text him.

ME

Are you serious?! When did this happen? The playoffs?!

As the mascot, I should know this. But I'm too busy thinking about a particular Blue Devil instead of their record.

With the remote in my sweaty grip, I turn to the sports channel and wait until the commentators begin talking about the current seats.

Oh my god.

I cover my mouth with my hand.

There they are.

The Chicago Blue Devils are going to the playoffs!

The men in their pressed suits talk about how it's a miracle that the Blue Devils are going to the playoffs through the screen. They discuss the recent trades and how they've slowly become one of the most sought-out teams currently.

A gloss works over my eyes.

With my thumb and finger, I pull the paperclip from the thin, fading piece of paper and flip it over.

There, from several years ago, is Kane's messy handwriting.

One goal.

That's all he had written one summer night when he found me on the porch surrounded by bundles of flowers.

Make it to the playoffs as a pro.

I snap a photo and send it to him.

ME

You reached your goal.

I never had any doubt, and although the thought of living this close to him again sent me into a frazzled mess weeks ago, and how irritated I was that he got me the job as the mascot, I'm glad it worked out this way so I didn't miss this moment in his life.

KANE

I can't believe you still have that.

Of course I do.

KANE

Remind me to add to it next time I'm over. I have a new goal.

ME

Who said you're coming over? I'm still angry with you.

My attention is pulled to the TV when they cut to the Blue Devils game. The commentators list the players not playing in the game this evening, and sure enough, Kane is one of them. The buzzer sounds, and the puck is dropped.

I go back to my journal, knowing Kane isn't going to text back right away, except my phone vibrates again.

KANE

I'll make it up to you.

I look back to the TV and then my phone.

ME

How are you texting me? Aren't you on the bench?

KANE

There isn't much that'll keep me from you, Daisy-Petal.

Butterflies slip in, but I quietly push them to the side.

ME

Except for a years-old pact with my brother...

I smile to myself.

ME

He has no pact with anyone else on the team, though, so I guess they're fair game.

I would never do such a thing.

But it's awfully fun to mess with him—when he's states away, of course.

There's a sudden knock on my door, and I freeze.

With anticipation backing my every step, I slowly make my way across the floor and peek through the eyehole.

All I manage to see is a cute baby bundled in pink being held up to the peephole. I laugh and start to unlock the door. I push the disappointment away after realizing it isn't Kane. The fact that I thought it could be means I'm entering a state of delusion.

I open the door and pull Reese into a quick hug before scrunching my nose at Charleigh. "What are you two doing here?"

She's carrying a large bag over her other arm that swishes when she walks inside. I hurriedly take it from her and drape it over the couch.

"I have a gift," she says, excitedly. "And gossip."

"Oh?" I pull Charleigh from her grip and sit on the floor with her.

My muscles are sore, my joints a little more creaky than usual, but I'll sacrifice it for Charleigh.

"Sorry I had to bring Charleigh." She starts to mess with the large bag she brought. "This was sort of a last-minute... favor."

"Favor? What kind of—" I quickly close my mouth when Reese pulls out a dress from the bag she brought.

By the end, there are three of them draped over the couch with Reese smiling in their presence.

"What is this?"

My phone goes off, and we both look at it.

I open my recent text thread from Kane.

> **KANE**
>
> Take your pick. You're wearing it as my date to the charity function.

"His *date*?" I say aloud.

And how the hell did he know to text me that right this second? Also, I recall him being there when my brother very clearly stated he would not be okay with Kane fucking *his sister*.

"Yep," Reese sighs. "And I'm Malaki's."

I gape at Reese. "What?"

She bites her lip. "Yeah, and that's not all."

My phone goes off again and I glance down to see another text from Kane.

> **KANE**
>
> And your brother may not have some type of pact with anyone else on the team, but I sure do.

ME

Pact or threat?

KANE

Is there a difference?

I roll my eyes.

KANE

Anyway, it doesn't matter. I'll make sure to remind them at the function when you show up by my side.

"I am not going as his date," I announce to Reese, who is reading the texts over my shoulder. "Everyone is going to think we're together."

Never mind River. Surely this goes against workplace ethics.

Reese laughs. "I think that's the point he's trying to make."

The opposite team scores, the buzzer pulling our attention to the TV. Charleigh claps and bounces on the floor.

KANE

Pick a dress that's easily removable. I'll pick you up tomorrow when I get back to town.

My fingers race against the screen.

ME

I am not going as your date!

The cameras. The media. Ethics and morals. River!

Reese and I share a look and glance back to the dresses. "Might as well try them on," she says. "I'm learning that those Blue Devils are pretty persistent."

I sigh.

That they are.

Forty-Eight

KANE

I ADJUST my tie in the mirror and see my phone lighting up on the bed. I'm certain it's another text from my little devil, telling me once again that she isn't going to the charity function as my date, but she is.

She's worried about River, and I should be too, but what he doesn't know won't kill him. If he questions it, I'll feed him the same excuse I'm going to feed Daisy: She's the Blue Devils' mascot, and it's required that she go *with* an escort. Sure, I had to talk Cindy into that bit, but it worked.

Hence the reason I purchased...with Reese's help...three dresses the same shade of blue as her mascot costume.

I'm eager to see which one she picked, and even more eager to strip it off of her.

I'm so fucked.

River's response to Malaki's question wasn't quite what I'd hoped for, and now I'm not only in a state of denial, but there's a twinge of wrongdoing lingering in the back of my head too.

After running my hand through my hair and fixing the collar of my shirt, I shrug my suit jacket on and swipe my phone.

I don't bother looking at her text, because regardless of her refusal, she'll be by my side tonight.

The ride down to her floor takes longer than I'd like.

My hands itch to touch her. It's only been forty-eight hours, but the way I crave her drives me insane. Games on the road were never a bother to me because I'd get to explore the city after and usually end up with someone in a bar bathroom, but now the thought of sleeping in a building that isn't shared with Daisy makes me impatient and irritated.

I rap my knuckles on her door and glance at the camera in the corner of the hall. The red light blinks and calms me.

It's not that I'm a stalker or creep, though it does feel sort of controlling in a sense. I'm possessive, yes, and there's a jealous surge that winds through me when it comes to Daisy, but this is none of those things.

This is for protection.

River had one thing right: I am protective over Daisy.

When Miles was assaulted and moved in with me to hide —or *recover*, if you ask him—I installed cameras outside of my apartment door as a safety measure. It only felt right to install one on her floor too, especially with the increasing texts and calls from random numbers.

"Daisy," I call out. "Open the door."

I sigh impatiently when she doesn't answer.

I could go back upstairs and grab the spare key that River gave me, but then I'd really be invading her privacy.

Right?

I knock again before pulling my phone out to call her.

My hand tightens on the thin device when I see that it wasn't her who had texted me minutes ago.

The address isn't foreign to me.

I text Miles with anger brushing against my neck.

He gave them my fucking number? As if I'm his personal ATM?

You give Miles an inch, and he takes a fucking foot. Or in this case, you give him half a million dollars, and he wants a million more.

The door opens.

I'm still squeezing the life out of my phone when I lock onto her blue eyes lined with makeup. I trail my attention down her curvy frame, landing on a slit that hits mid-thigh. The heels she wears make her taller, and all I want to do is pull on the thin string tied around her ankle and throw them off to the side so I can strip the rest of that dress off her.

My heart beats out of my chest the longer I stare. Blood pools below my waist, and I reach my hand out to grip her around her hip so I can kiss her.

As soon as I go to do that, her palm touches my chest to keep me in place.

I scowl, not appreciating that she's denying me.

"River," she whispers.

I freeze, like I'm caught red-handed.

I want to go back to that state of denial, where I pretend he'll be fine with the two of us.

"You got your brass knuckles ready?" River's large hand

grips the door to open it farther. I drop my outstretched hand and adjust the collar of my dress shirt.

Why the fuck is he wearing a suit?

I smooth my expression. "For?"

He glances at Daisy and sighs. "For the necks she'll break wearing that scrap of a dress."

"Scrap?" Daisy huffs. "This one has the most fabric out of the three."

I'd like to see the others.

"You can practically see your underwear with how high it cuts," River argues.

Daisy crosses her arms, and that enticing glint of defiance sparkles in her eye. "What underwear?"

I cough to hide my real reaction. River turns to me, and I quickly change the subject, all while forcing myself to stop looking at her. "Why are you dressed up? Feeling left out?" I joke.

He gives me a look. "I'm going to whatever the hell you two are going to. Daisy said she needed an escort, and it was too late for her to find a date."

Slowly, I turn my attention to *my* date. "Is that so?"

She won't meet my eye, but that's okay, because by the end of the evening, she *absolutely* will.

I stroll inside the apartment, passing them both, and head for her bedroom.

"What are you doing?" She follows me with her heels clicking against the floor, driving my annoyance up to its highest level.

"Grabbing a dress for my date," I say nonchalantly.

A line of confusion digs in between her eyebrows. I glance through the crack in her door to see River still near the front door with his back to us, so I lean into her space, inhaling her warm earthy scent.

She jerks backward. "You're bringing a date?"

"Well, you were my date," I remind her quietly. "But since you've decided to bring a chaperone, I guess I'll have to find another."

Daisy blinks, her blue eyes filled with hurt. It's like getting a puck to the face. "Well, we need a chaperone," she says in a hushed voice. "You heard him the other day..." She glances away. "We need to stop before one of us gets too invested."

"Too late."

Daisy flicks her gaze back to me, but I don't waste my time dissecting her thoughts. I pull out my phone and text a woman I've taken to functions before, knowing she'll drop everything to be there, even if I preface it with a forewarning that she won't be in my bed tonight.

Once River, Daisy, and I load up in my car, I zoom out of the parking garage and head to the freeway. I manage to keep my gaze away from my rearview, too pent up with irritation to give in to her.

It's hard to be angry at Daisy.

I know what she's doing and why she's doing it.

It's the same thing she did years ago when we crossed the line for the first time, but doesn't she understand that things are different now? Doesn't she understand that I love her more than I could ever love anyone else?

My foot slams on the brake.

Daisy's palm hits the back of my seat, and I flick my gaze to the mirror. Our eyes catch, and I'm suddenly sweating.

I'm always cool, calm, and collected, but right now, I am in a state of chaos. *Did I just admit I love her?*

"You alright?" River stares at me with confusion. "Did you see a ghost or something?"

I force a chuckle out, because with his sister in the backseat with my heart in her hands, it feels like I'm in the presence of a ghost. The ghost of the fucking past.

I pull up in front of an apartment near the venue and beep the horn.

Paris comes bouncing out of the house with rollers in her hair, dressed in a bright-pink matching sweat outfit.

"I'm coming!" she shouts.

"Are you kidding me?" Daisy mumbles.

I unlock the door and catch her eye in the mirror. *This is your fault, little devil.*

I cock my eyebrow, and she smashes her lips together. I catch the roll of her eye, and it settles me because I know the look of jealousy when I see it.

"Hi!" Paris's high-pitched voice makes my ears ring as she gets into the car.

Daisy gives her a tight-lipped smile, and I speed down the road, sending Paris flying farther onto the backseat.

"Here." Daisy hands Paris a dress.

"Ah!" Paris exclaims. "I *love* it, Kaney!"

River snickers, and I squeeze the life out of my steering wheel.

I'm about to fake an illness.

One that will spread to Daisy so we can both leave together.

When we pull up to the venue, Paris is fully dressed and pulling the rollers out of her hair as we all climb out of the car.

One glance at Paris has me revolting against the idea of taking her arm instead of Daisy's. Her fake boobs spill out of the top of the dress, and she looks like a hooker the longer I stare at her.

My phone vibrates, and I thank the universe for giving me a small distraction, even if it is a text from my brother.

I had to give them some point of contact in case I didn't show with the money. I'm going to win it all back tonight, so don't worry about it.

I grind my jaw back and forth and click my phone off.

The small brush of Daisy's elbow against my arm as she walks beside River pulls me toward her. I expect to find her scowling at me, thanks to my choice of date, but instead, her lips are pulled into a frown as remorse slips onto her features. One slow shake of her head, and I know she's read my text.

My chest grows tight.

We keep a hold of each other's gaze for a few seconds. But then we're being ushered into the venue, and she's walking up ahead of me with River. Worry settles into my stomach, but I can't decide if it's because of Miles's text or if it's because Daisy isn't hanging off my arm where she belongs.

Forty-Nine

DAISY

MY PLAN COMPLETELY BACKFIRED, which seems unfair because it wasn't meant to be malicious.

If I wanted to stir things up between us, I would have brought some random guy as my date to the function, but instead, I convinced River to go, promising him a night of free food and drinks.

But then Kane just *had* to bring Paris, and now I'm regretting much more than my decision to deny Kane as my date.

"I almost didn't recognize you without horns," Emory chuckles, staring out at the party.

I grin. "I made a last-minute decision to tuck them into my purse. I can put them on if you'd like."

Emory *almost* smiles. He shakes his head and puts his hands into his pockets to rock back on his dress shoes. "I take it you haven't seen all the photos from the media shoot, huh?"

When walking into the charity event, I was in awe. The photos that Scottie took hang on the walls, showcasing all the children smiling with their favorite Blue Devils player. It's a great idea for the charity function, and I'm sure it has donors emptying their pockets.

"Why do you say it like that?" I ask Emory.

He nods to the left, and I follow him closely. I glance into the sea of people. Reese and Malaki are deep in conversation with their faces awfully close, while Coach Jacobs stands with his hand resting against his wife's lower back. I refuse to look any farther and keep my focus ahead. I'm too afraid I'll snag a glimpse of Kane with Paris—something I can only blame myself for.

The knot in my throat gets tighter the closer Emory and I get to the far-left corner of the room. When he stops, I do too. My heart slips, landing in the pit of my stomach, as I stare at a photo of Kane and me.

His sharp jaw is tilted to the side as he gazes at me over the head of Jonas, who is sitting happily in my arms. I'm staring up at Kane, and to the naked eye, it may not look suspicious, but a photo speaks a thousand words, and if River sees this, we're doomed.

"It's a good photo." Emory takes a sip of his drink. "And I'm not just saying that because my wife took it."

I force a laugh.

"It makes Kane look like he actually has a heart," he adds.

I'm quick to defend him. "He has a heart."

The broody goalie grins over the rim of his cup. "I know he does. But there aren't many that do."

I follow his line of sight when he looks toward the large room basked in warm light from golden chandeliers and hundreds of people dressed in suits and gowns.

I find Kane right away, and the breath whooshes from my lungs.

Kane's hand rests on his date's lower back, and I suddenly wish I'd worn her dress instead of this one. If Paris and I had traded, at least his hand would be on silky blue fabric instead of her bare skin.

"Excuse me." I rush off and leave Emory alone to stare at his wife mingling with her camera around her neck.

This is high school all over again—me watching Kane flirt with other girls from afar while dying a slow death of jealousy. Nausea climbs up my throat until I find a random door along the hallway just outside the venue space.

I'm desperate to be alone to clear my thoughts.

I shut the door and exhale. My shoulders drop with the quietness of the dark room, but they quickly tense when the door opens. I turn to see who it is, but it closes just as quickly.

It only takes me a split second to realize it's Kane. His scent envelops me, but I try to mask my emotions before he catches on to the hurt and confusion lying just beneath the surface. I square my shoulders and step backward, hitting something on my way. I can't see anything, but I can most definitely sense the shift in the air with his presence.

"Are you hiding, little devil?" His voice is smooth and confident, brushing against my bare arms like velvet.

"I'm not hiding, *Kaney*," I snap.

So much for not acting perturbed by his choice of date.

His gruff chuckle races against my skin.

"Where's your date?" I ask, the question full of utter disgust.

I hate myself for showing my jealousy.

"Nuh-uh," he says in a hushed tone. "You don't get to do that."

I cross my arms, though he can't see me. "Do what?"

His warm, whiskey-scented breath brushes against my lips. "You can't force me to bring a date and then act jealous. That's not how it works."

"I am not jealous," I stress, my body strung tight.

His sigh is heavy with something other than anger, and to

my surprise, he doesn't respond. My heart pounds when I take a step forward, the tip of my heel touching his shoe. He makes no move to get out of my way.

The small closet fills with tension, our attraction feeding off each other.

"Fine," I finally admit, too exhausted to fight it. "I'm jealous."

"I know you are." He sounds sad, his voice more of a breath.

I think back to the text I saw on his phone, the worry settling on my shoulders once again.

"You okay?" I whisper.

Kane sighs loudly. "I don't know."

"Do you want to talk about it?"

"No," he snaps. The air surrounding us grows even tighter. "Yes? Fuck, I don't know. What is there to talk about, really? It's Miles. I should be used to his bullshit by now."

A low growl rumbles from his chest, and a gust of hot air fans against my face. My eyes have adjusted slightly, and I can see that he's put his back to me. A sense of urgency pulls me toward him, afraid he's going to walk out the door and feel more alone than ever.

My arms wrap around his waist, and my head rests against his firm back. His chest heaves, his heartbeat thunderous.

It only takes a breath for him to place his hand on my arm. I pray that it grounds him.

"Talk to me," I whisper. "I'm here."

Silence fills the tiny room, settling into all the empty spaces around us. His heartbeat quickens before his deep voice hits my ears.

"Every time he comes around, I say it'll be the last..." He chuckles darkly. "Hell, he says it too."

"Why do you keep giving in and helping him?" I ask, softly.

"Because he's my brother." Kane's hand tightens against my arm. "Because I need to protect my mom from another tragedy. It's clear he isn't going to stop getting himself into these situations, and if he doesn't pay these people back, they'll probably kill him."

The heaviness in his voice pulls me in even further. Hurt washes over me, and I slowly slip around to the front of him. I glide my hand up his suit jacket and place it on his freshly shaven face. "Have you ever thought about the fact that it'd be a tragedy to lose you?"

He swallows loudly. "What do you mean?"

"Your mom," I say slowly, needing him to hear. "Did you ever think that maybe your mom thought it was a tragedy to lose you?"

He pulls his face away from my hand, like he can't fathom the thought. "My mom hates me."

"That's not fair to assume." I pull his face back to look at me, and even in the dark, I can see there's a slight gloss to his eye. "She doesn't know the truth."

This moment between us feels eerily similar to the one we shared the night before we parted ways. There's a quietness around us, a stillness that I think we're both afraid to disturb.

But I do anyway.

"You have to cut him off, Kane."

He knows it, and I know it. The endless pamphlets I'd gathered for Miles over the years flash inside my head like a jumbotron. The research and understanding of someone with a gambling addiction comes to the forefront of my brain. "You're enabling him by cleaning up the messes he finds himself in."

Kane's chest rises, and a tight breath floats between us. "I guess you and I are both enablers, then."

The briefest squeeze of his palms around my waist draws a

spark to every intimate part of my body. My thighs tingle, and my stomach flips.

"What does that mean?" I whisper.

Goosebumps cover my arms as Kane drags one hand up my back, gliding the pad of his finger over my spine until he reaches the back of my neck. I sigh wistfully as he curves around to cup my face, and the only thing I suddenly care about is his mouth on mine.

Kiss me.

It's torment to have him so close but to keep him at arm's length.

"You..." his voice is low and husky. "Standing here in front of me behind a locked door, showing me how big your heart really is..."

I swallow. "You call that enabling?"

"I don't know," he murmurs. "Let's see if you allow me to kiss you without pushing me away."

Kane gently grips me around the throat and pulls my face to his. His mouth is on mine, so wet and hot, sending warmth to the very tips of my toes. I open up for him, craving his tongue against mine and unconsciously letting out little noises of pleasure.

I pull away briefly, breathing heavily and glance at his shirt. My fingers work quickly. I pull the crisp linen shirt out of his pants and undo his belt. I tip my face back to his, and we're lost in each other.

His hands are everywhere.

I forget where we are and who we are.

It's just *so* right when he's touching me.

He breaks the kiss to shrug out of his suit jacket. "I want to be angry with you for pulling your little stunt of making me take another date." Kane hauls me up into his arms, and I wrap my legs around his waist. "But it's hard to be mad when I know how pure your heart is. I know you did it because you think what we're doing behind River's back is wrong. You're always trying to keep the peace."

The scruff of his face scratches my palms when I grab his cheeks to pull his mouth to mine.

We kiss again, our tongues starting off in a rush but slowing down as soon as he moves my panties to the side and begins to glide inside of me.

I throw my head back and push my hips forward to meet him halfway. "Ah," I breathe out.

"I think I know what it's like to be addicted to something," he admits.

I meet his gaze through the darkness and let him run the show. His thrusts are slow and deep, but he keeps me steady against him, never moving his fingers from my hips. I move along with him, matching his pace until I can't focus anymore. A bundle of warmth stirs in between my legs and shoots down my thighs.

I whimper, and Kane shushes me.

"You've gotta be quiet, baby," he whispers. "Bite me if you have to, but keep it down, or more than River will find me here, proving to you that we're impossible to keep apart."

I fall into a tailspin of pleasure. My body goes into overdrive, and I move up and down over his hard length, his fingers sinking into my flesh to keep us steady.

"No one compares," he murmurs against my mouth. "No one ever has."

I lean close and kiss him with every hidden thought I've buried over the years. I use the kiss to prove to him that it isn't just him that feels this between us. It's so much more than sexual tension and attraction. I've had chemistry with other guys, and he's right, nothing compares to this.

Kane kisses me with an urgency. An orgasm rips through me, the pleasure so intense I do what he says to do to stay quiet and bite him.

My teeth move to his shoulder, the muscle bundled tightly from holding me up.

"Fuck," he groans quietly.

He pumps into me one more time before his body stills with another grunt escaping him. He collapses to the floor with me still on top of him.

I rest my forehead on his sweaty chest, both of us gasping for air.

After a few minutes pass, I slowly sit up and attempt to climb off him. Kane's hands grip the tops of my thighs, and I stop.

"You may not have come to this function with me as your date...but you sure as hell are leaving as it."

I bite the inside of my cheek to hide a smile. "What about River?"

"I don't want to think about River right now...or Miles... only *you.*"

My lips part, an argument on the tip of my tongue.

"Please, Daisy," Kane whispers. "I've never admitted it before, but I just need you."

"You just had me," I remind him.

He shakes his head. "I don't mean like that." My cheek falls into his palm as he reaches for my face. "I just need *you.*"

"Okay." I exhale slowly and accept my fate. "Then you have me."

Fifty

KANE

IT'S the last game of the regular season.

Playoffs start in a week, and the team has never been more harmonious. Our plays are much smoother than they were at the start of the season, and our communication is clear, despite having a few new players on the team.

"You three are out tonight." Coach points to me, Hart, and Volkova. "Olson, you'll still play goalie, but our defense should be able to hold strong so you don't get plowed."

Emory nods, and Coach moves to Malaki.

"You're a fucking spring chicken. I'm not worried about you taking a hit, because I know you'll just get right back up."

Malaki grins.

We all acknowledge Coach's parting words and take the ice.

I immediately look for Daisy. Two smoothies were waiting for Malaki and me in the locker room before warmups, and I couldn't help but smile. The rest of the team felt cheated that they didn't get a smoothie, but that's what they get for making fun of my superstitions.

Though, I think I'm about to start another, and her name is Daisy.

With the playoffs on the horizon and Miles's constant texts and updates that I haven't asked for, I refuse to think about the mess she and I are in. Instead, I push it to the back of my mind and ask Daisy to do the same.

Just for now.

I don't have to think of the future or the repercussions that will come with it because, regardless, my future is her, whether or not she is willing to admit that yet.

I'm in deep.

She's a constant inside my head.

I lived six years without her and didn't find an ounce of happiness that didn't belong to a little black puck.

I won't go another six without her.

"Where's our devil girl at?" Malaki plops onto the bench beside me and squirts water into his mouth.

I grind my jaw back and forth. *I don't know.*

"Pst."

Malaki and I turn and glance down the bench to see Reese standing there.

A noise leaves Malaki that sounds an awful lot like a moan.

I roll my eyes. "Put your dick away."

I leave him behind to calm his boner and head for Reese. She has her daughter on her hip with one of those foam tridents that Daisy throws into the crowd. She's sort of cute, smiling up at me with big brown eyes. I wink, and her baby laughter fills the space between Reese and me.

"Hey…" Reese puts her daughter on her other hip. "So, Daisy told me to first tell you not to panic."

A knot grows in my throat. My hackles rise. "What's wrong?"

Fuck, did River find out about us?

Actually, that may be a load off my shoulders.

"She's at her apartment."

"Devil girl isn't coming tonight?" Malaki slides up beside me and starts to play with Reese's daughter. She bounces up and down in Reese's arms, pulling her hair in the process. "Hey. Hands off your mama!" Malaki laughs.

"Reese," I stress, trying to gain her attention.

After Malaki takes the baby for a lap around the ice, Reese glances back at me.

"Daisy is sick. Cindy said it was fine for her to stay home, especially since it's not a playoff game."

"Sick?" My stomach drops.

Is it her Lupus?

Reese nods while watching Malaki and her daughter closely. "I dropped off some medicine and soup before coming. She looked exhausted. I offered to stay with her, but she shooed me away, telling me she was just going to sleep. She wanted me to relay the message to you because you hadn't texted back. She also told me to tell you not to panic."

I hate to break it to her, but I feel panicked.

Malaki brings Reese's daughter back.

"Oh, and she said to stay put," Reese adds.

My chest tightens.

But does she need me?

She'd never admit it if she did, but what if she does?

I glance at the time ticking down until the game starts.

Malaki and I head back to the bench, and I'm as silent as a monk.

"You're not going to stay put, are you?" he asks.

"I'm not playing tonight." My mind is already made up. "Coach will let me go."

Malaki snorts. "You gonna tell him the reason?"

I shrug. "You got a better idea?"

Malaki thinks for a second. "Honestly, devil girl has made a pretty big impact on the team. He may just accept the real reason."

How could she not make an impact? Her smile alone stops everyone in their tracks.

I catch a glimpse of Malaki's growing grin. "Or he might collapse from shock that you are thinking of someone other than yourself for once."

I send him a glare. "Fuck you."

Rhodes, from down the bench, chuckles. "It's the truth."

It isn't.

I've always thought of her.

Even when I pretended I didn't.

I glance at Coach with his furrowed brow and ignore my teammates' snickers as I head toward him.

———

The apartment is quiet with only a few lights on. I eye the bag of medicine and Tupperware of soup on the counter, both untouched.

I walk past the coffee table, pausing when I see her journal. I flip it open to the last page she's written in. There's a long list of numbers beside a line of dates: *99.6, 99.8, 99.5, 100.2, 100.8*. Below those are a few symptoms that she must have been dealing with over the last week: *fatigue, achy joints, sore muscles, nausea, increasing fevers.*

I quietly close the journal and move to her bedroom. The door is cracked slightly, but the lights are all off. My heart is lodged inside my throat as I push it open.

Where is she?

I glance to the bathroom and stride over to the opened door. The lights are off. I reach my hand out and flip the switch. My eyes adjust right away, and the sight I see scares the shit out of me. There she is, body lifeless on the floor.

"Daisy?"

I scoop her up into my arms with my heart pounding violently. Her eyes flutter open, and I frantically search her face before giving her body a once-over to see if she's hurt. "What are you doing on the floor, baby?"

"Um." She clenches her eyes shut and winces. "I kind of fell and then just got tired, so I went to sleep."

"Are you hurt?" I ask, needing to know if she's okay. "I'm calling River."

"No!" Her eyes fly open, and she locks onto me.

There are dark bags beneath her bottom eyelashes and a pinkish hue to her nose and cheeks. I can tell she's not herself right now, yet she's still just as beautiful as ever.

"Why not?" I brush a few strands of hair out of her face and realize her skin is burning hot. "Have you taken anything for your fever?"

Daisy pulls her attention away from me. The wheels are turning in her head as she thinks about my question. "Daisy." I give her arms a little shake.

She looks back at me, her eyes red. "I can't remember."

"You can't remember?"

Well, shit.

Suddenly, she starts to shake in my arms, trembling with the chills, or exhaustion, or—

A forced swallow works down my throat as I stare at her wobbling lip. Two blue, glassy eyes stare at me from inside my arms, and I feel her pain like it's my own.

"Let's get you into a bath." I'm flying blindly, acting on pure instinct and nothing else.

I reach forward and turn the water on, making sure it's lukewarm. She's already hot enough, a steaming bath won't do her any wonders. She nods quickly, and I hold her in my arms until the water rises farther.

When it's finished, I sit her up to help shed her clothes. Her movements are slow and weak, which does nothing but worry me further. I keep my shorts on, discarding my shirt before I pick her up. It takes everything in me not to run my eyes past her shoulders to gaze at her perfect breasts, bare and ready for the taking.

Not now.

"What are you doing?" she quietly asks, eyes opening just far enough that she can see I'm still half-dressed but slipping us both into the tub.

"Taking a bath."

A soft laugh that comes out as a breath floats from her mouth. "Your clothes are on."

She shivers when we enter the water, and I hold onto her tighter. "There has to be some sort of barrier between us or else I might accidentally slip inside of you."

Her light laughter tells me she thinks I'm kidding.

But I'm not.

I wait until her trembling limbs calm before I move her so her back is resting against my chest. It gives me a perfect view of her body, my eyes moving directly below her belly button.

Smooth, perfect, and mine.

I shut my eyes, willing my dick to stay soft.

"Daisy?" I rub her thighs, massaging the muscles.

She breathes out the word, "Yeah?"

"How long have you been feeling bad?" And why didn't she tell me?

Her loud swallow catches my ear over the rippling water. "A couple of days."

"On and off fevers for about a week?" I ask.

She tenses. "How do you—" Her words fade, and her shoulders relax. "You looked in my journal."

I run my palms up her legs and grab onto her hands. I interlace our fingers and squeeze before massaging each knuckle with light pressure. She relaxes against me farther, her legs opening a little and her rising chest slowing.

"Why didn't you say something?" I ask her.

I notice the water stops dipping near her breasts. "Daisy."

She lets out a shaky breath, and I glance at her mouth. The trembling of her bottom lip cuts me in every which way.

"Daisy," I whisper.

She chokes on a silent sob.

"I don't want to be in a flare," she admits through a choking cry.

I'm quick to wipe her tears with my thumbs. I nod against the side of her face, trying to understand.

"I don't want to take steroids," she cries.

I read somewhere that, sometimes, patients with Lupus can come out of the flares on their own.

"Is that only if you can't come out of it on your own?" I ask.

She nods against my chest, sucking in deep breaths.

The bath is getting cooler, but so is she, which is good. The ends of her hair are wet as I brush them out of the way. "How do you come out of it on your own? Tell me how to help you."

"I just have to try to rest and manage my stress. When I get stressed or sick, it puts my immune system into overdrive, and then I go into a flare."

Guilt crashes into me.

Fuck.

"You're stressed because of us, aren't you?" I ask.

"Maybe," she whispers, relaxing into my chest farther. "It's hard to know."

Silence settles within the bathroom, nothing but my guilt filling the gaps.

"What can I do to help you?" I pray she doesn't say what I fear the most.

"This is a good start," she says quietly. "Baths reduce stress and inflammation."

I nod and go back to rubbing her muscles again. I softly knead her shoulders and biceps before reaching over and grabbing her body wash.

Jasmine and eucalyptus.

That explains her sweet, earthy smell that I continue to crave—that and all her plants.

The soap lathers between my palms, and I begin to rub her legs, smoothing the soap over each curve that I long for.

"That feels good," she whispers in a sleepy voice.

My mouth is right over her ear. "Good."

After her legs, I glide my hands up her arms and move to her shoulders again. The bath fills with sudsy bubbles, covering up parts of her body from me. I push my thumbs gently into her muscles, and she makes a noise that resembles her sweet moaning from just the other day when I had her wrapped around my dick.

"Feel good?" I ask.

"Mm-hmm." I watch with rapt attention as Daisy's legs fall open, as if they're inviting me to relax her even further.

"You know what else is good for reducing stress?" I move my hands into her hair and tug gently on the strands.

Her head flops to the side, giving me more access to the nape of her neck. I pull on her hair a few more times before my hand slowly descends beneath the water, disappearing from sight.

"Orgasms."

Daisy's eyes flutter open, the wild desire for my touch still bright through her sleepiness. She keeps a hold of my gaze as she grabs onto my wrist and slowly pulls it farther into the water, landing right in between her thighs.

"Open your legs," I whisper. "And let me take care of you."

Fifty-One

DAISY

KANE IS A GOOD DISTRACTION. His hands are an even better one.

My eyes close, and it feels like I'm floating. Water caresses my body, the waves of Kane's subtle movements gliding against my skin like a feather. I'm so tired, exhaustion keeping me unmoving, while his fingers play with the inside of my thigh.

I'm worked up in all the best ways, craving his touch instead of sleep.

A soft breath slips from my mouth when his hand moves closer to the apex of my thighs. With the water, he easily slips a finger inside of me, only to pull it out slowly a moment later.

He does this several times before my breathing turns from slow and steady to ragged and uneven.

"Feel good, baby?" He nuzzles his nose against the side of my cheek.

I answer with a whimper and relax farther into his hard chest.

"You're so beautiful," he mutters, spreading me wider with another finger. "I love watching you come undone from my touch."

I lick my lip, my eyes remaining shut. His slow strokes feel so good I can't focus on anything but the way my body is curving to meet him halfway. The water laps the sides of the tub, the splashing mixing in with my heavy breathing.

"That's it," he encourages, his voice raspy.

The brushing of his teeth against my earlobe pulls a moan out of me, and when he adds his thumb to my clit, I turn my face and find his lips.

The kiss is lazy and slow. Our tongues move in sync, his fingers working their magic. My toes begin to tingle, and water rushes over my breasts. I arch my back with the first touch of pleasure bundling low in my belly and then break completely with a powerful orgasm.

"My god," Kane groans against my back, a low rumble deep in his chest.

My eyes flutter open, the bathroom in a hazy glow. I'm sated, but with his rigid length digging into me from behind, I know he's far from it. I try to turn, ready to rub my hand against him, but he stops me with a firm grip on my wrist.

Our gazes crash, and he studies me with a furrowed brow. "What are you doing?"

I inhale a shaky breath. "Taking care of..." I nod at his wet shorts stuck to his body like glue. They outline how hard he really is, but before I can do anything, Kane is climbing out of the tub while picking me up in the process.

We're soaking wet, water falling to the rug beneath his feet. "Absolutely not." His voice is pulled tight. "I'm here to take care of you. Nothing more."

After wrapping me in a fluffy towel, he walks me over to my bed and lays me down before going back into the bathroom.

I don't know how long it takes him to return, but we're both fully dry when he pulls me underneath the covers with him. He kisses my forehead softly, and I snuggle closer to his warmth. I know I should be worried that River will walk in after his shift and see us like this, but I just don't have the energy.

———

I wake to a tiny sliver of sunlight streaming through my window. I sigh wistfully, my muscles less achy and my mind a little clearer. I know my body enough to know that things are still feeling off, especially as I glance at the clock and see that it's almost lunch time.

How long did I sleep?

I groggily sit up and try to remember the night prior. My gaze is pulled to the bathroom. I flush, and a small smile slides onto my mouth.

Kane Barlow taking care of me is my new favorite thing in the entire world.

His tender touch, soft kisses, and talented hands...no one would believe me if I told them.

I guess I'll just add that to my list of secrets that have been continuing to pile up.

After steadying my feet and taking care of my needs in the bathroom, I quickly run my fingers through my hair and splash water on my face.

My temperature is normal, which is a good sign.

Walking over to my window, I pull back the curtain and let the sun shine onto my plants.

"There," I whisper.

A deep voice catches my attention from the living room, and butterflies pull me toward the door.

"You know she's going to be pissed," River says, voice hinting with humor.

"So?" Kane scoffs. "Plus...who's to say I don't know how to take care of plants?"

I gasp and head straight for my bedroom door.

Both Kane and my brother look like they've been caught red-handed when I push open the door and step into the living room.

My brother holds one pot steady as Kane grips my green watering can in his hand. Water trickles out of the spout. "Stop right there." I place my hands on my hips. "What are you two doing?"

"Well, good morning, sleepyhead." My brother lifts a brow. "Kane here thought it would be a good idea to water your plants."

Kane peers at me from across the room. "The soil was dry. They're thirsty."

He's probably right. Exhaustion has won lately, and with the fogginess of my Lupus settling in, I can't remember to water them. I'm going to have to start a chart again, just like I used to do.

My brother sets the pot down on the ground, and a little bit of soil plops onto the tile. "Careful!" I shout.

He ignores me, putting his hands on his hips. "So when were you going to tell me about being in a flare?"

I immediately gape at Kane. His jaw flexes, but he keeps a hold of my stare until River interrupts us.

"Don't be angry at him." River walks over to the coffee table and snags my journal. "I forced it out of him when I found you two in bed together."

The blood drains from my face, but I make sure to keep my attention on River instead of Kane.

River flips open my journal, landing on the page where I'd

been writing my fevers down. "I'll admit, I thought he was in your bed for a completely different reason." He chuckles sarcastically, as if he's saying, *what an absurd idea, right?* "Once he told me that he found you on the floor after you didn't show at the game and then showed me this"—he holds up my journal, but I don't bother looking at it—"I knew he was telling the truth when he said he was making sure you were okay because you were in a flare."

Whew.

The nerves in my stomach fizzle when I see that we're in the clear.

"I'm calling Dr. Gibson."

Even though I know it's childish, I stomp my foot. "River. Let me try to regulate myself before jumping to conclusions that I need a steroid or something long-term. This may just be an acute flare."

He turns his back to me. "Blood work won't hurt. If Dr. Gibson agrees that the homeopathic route is the way to go, then so be it. But you know what this disease can do, so you're going in for labs."

My shoulders dip.

I'm not one to jeopardize my health, and I know deep down that he's right. This is something I should discuss with Dr. Gibson. It's one of the main reasons I'm in Chicago. I have to get a better grasp on my life, even when I'm in a flare. I've been trying to keep things under control and the same as before, but since I've moved here, things have gotten to be too much.

Once River is on the phone, talking to his *friend*—my doctor—Kane makes his way over to me. My watering can is still in his grip, but it lowers when he dips his head closer. "I'm sorry," he whispers. "I had to give an explanation as to why I was in your bed."

I try to grab the watering can, but he doesn't let go.

"I thought you'd use it as a good excuse to tell him about..." My words fade because do we put a label on this?

"Us?" he finishes for me.

He pulls on the watering can, and I stumble toward him. "Because there is an us, Daisy."

My mouth remains closed.

I won't argue, not after the last few times we've crossed the line.

"I'm letting you lead." Kane's finger brushes mine, and I swear it leaves a trail of heat behind. "If it lowers your stress to keep this between us for now, then okay."

With River's back to us, Kane's hand slips up my arm and around my neck for a brief second. His messy hair flops onto his forehead as he tilts his head toward me. "I'll keep you a secret forever if you need me to...as long as I get to keep you forever too."

A blush spreads over my face.

He pulls the can from my grip, and I willingly let go. He takes his time inspecting each of my plants with as much care as he showed me last night and waters them with a steady hand.

When my brother comes back, informing me of Dr. Gibson working me into his schedule, I hardly hear a word he says because, instead of paying attention, I'm too busy falling head over heels for his best friend.

Fifty-Two

KANE

I LEFT Daisy with a quick kiss and wink behind River's back this morning before practice. We've officially gotten our playoff schedule, and our first game is in two days at our home rink. We always play better here, but that means nothing when it comes to the playoffs. Every team comes prepared with their skills sharpened and their focus impermeable, which is admittedly something I've had to work hard to reach as of late.

I have other things on my mind, like Daisy.

Her appointment with Dr. Gibson is today, and I'm eager to know what's going on. This is new territory for me, but caring for her comes naturally, unlike keeping my touching to a minimum when her brother is home.

Do you know how hard it is to keep my hands to myself when we're in the same room? The other day, I followed her up to the roof of the apartment building just to get a taste. I watched her mess around with her compost container and stood back with a grin until she was done.

She yelped when she saw me, but I quickly caught it in a kiss, which led to a fast fuck that only left me wanting more.

With my focus bouncing between Daisy, keeping a secret from River, and the playoffs, I've hardly had room to think about Miles. His texts have come and gone, and though the worry is there, something Daisy said to me stuck.

I'm enabling him.

I've heard it before. Something my mom used to say to my father before he up and left us long ago. She was *'done enabling him,'* afraid her sons would turn out like him if they continued being raised by a gambling man.

Unfortunately, Miles was already locked in by the time he left—not that anyone knew other than me. I still remember the two of them sitting at the kitchen table when Mom was away at work, flipping cards and betting with cold peas from Dad's untouched dinner. *Like father, like son*, he'd say.

It's time that comes to a stop, though. Now that I have something worth having in my life, I can't very well continue feeding my brother money and supporting his habits.

"I'm stopping to run an errand. I'll see you in a few," Malaki says as we both head out to the parking lot.

I shake my thoughts away and acknowledge him before slipping inside my car to head home. It isn't long until I'm parked in the parking garage with the engine idling, phone in hand as I research another article about Lupus.

I may know more than River about the disease, and he's the doctor genius.

The more knowledge I have, the better I can take care of her.

I surprised her, River, and their parents just yesterday. While on FaceTime, I showed some of my cards, which caused River to furrow his brows and her parents to enter into an hour-long discussion over medication.

Daisy sat quietly, staring at me with confusion.

I shrugged. What does she expect?

After waiting impatiently for her call, I head up to my apartment to shower before she gets home. I'm not even halfway up the stairs before River comes through the door without knocking.

I pause, hand on the rail, and raise my brow. "Everything okay?"

My heart rate speeds up the longer I look at him. His heavy browline deepens as he looks around my place.

Is he looking for her?

I swallow my thick spit. Ready or not, here we fucking go.

"Where is Daisy?"

I walk back down the stairs slowly as I think about my next choice of words. River is my best friend, the one I've been closest with for almost my entire life. Loyalty to our friendship runs deep, not to mention his family's ongoing support over the years. They were the ones to dust me off after everything happened in the past and the only true pillar of stability I've had for the last six years.

I mean, they send me a good luck text before every game.

Even when I was in the juniors.

"Have you seen her?"

I pull my attention back to River. Have I seen her? So he isn't specifically looking for her at my place?

"No." Something doesn't feel right. "Doesn't she have an appointment?"

River runs a hand through his sweaty hair. "Yeah, but I was on a run when Dr. Gibson called me to ask where she was. She didn't show."

My chest screams for air. "What do you mean she didn't show?"

Without waiting for his explanation, I dial her number while heading out the door. We're both in the elevator a second later, Daisy's soft voice from a years-old recorded voice-mail hits my ears, and I clench my jaw.

River and I walk through their apartment door.

"I've already searched here," he says.

"Well, did she take an Uber?" I shake my head and call Malaki for Reese's number. Unsurprisingly, they're together, and Reese says she hasn't heard from Daisy all day.

"I've already called her best friend from back home too, just in case," River adds. "She has no idea where Daisy is."

"Well, we need to go search the route she would have taken to the appointment. I thought you were going with her?" I ask.

It's hard to hide the anger in my voice. My worry is coming out in all sorts of different shades of red, and if River can tell, he doesn't mention it.

"I don't know if you've forgotten," he snaps, "but Daisy is pretty independent. She didn't want me to tag along."

A frustrated growl tears from my chest as I pull up the cameras. It'll show me what time she left at least, and then we can figure out if she was heading to her appointment.

River comes and stands over my shoulder. "This isn't creepy at all," he mutters. "Do I even want to know why you have access to the security cameras?"

"They're mine," I answer.

"Wait, what?"

I go back through the footage until I see the elevator open, ignoring River's questions. He's always believed that the cameras were security from the apartment building, and I let him believe it, unwilling to dig into Miles's shit.

Daisy appears on the screen with her lip tucked in between her teeth as she steps off the elevator towards her apartment. She nibbles on it worryingly, and as soon as the next person comes into the frame, I know exactly why.

My heart stops.

There's a cracking sound from the bones in my hand with how hard I squeeze my phone.

"Is that Miles?" River pulls the phone from my grip. "I haven't seen him in years. What the hell is he doing with Daisy?"

Fuck.

"What the hell?" River mumbles beside me. "Are they together? Like a couple?"

I'd kill my own brother over her.

Without answering, I pull the phone back into my hand and quickly switch the footage to my apartment. I scroll further back in time until I see him walk off the elevator toward my apartment. He knocks twice, and the door opens.

"Why is Daisy at your place?" River asks, glancing at the time on the footage. "At six in the morning?"

I press the sound button.

"With nothing but an oversized T-shirt on? Did Malaki fuck my sister again?"

"Will you shut the hell up?" I snap, already on edge.

I'll admit, the thought pisses me off, even if I know it's not true.

Her voice is soft and sleepy as it flows out of my speaker. "Miles?"

"Daisy?" Miles rocks back on his feet and puts his hands in his pockets. "It's been a while."

She rubs her eyes. "What are you doing here, Miles?"

He gets right to it, attempting to push through the door. Daisy slams it shut and blocks the doorknob from my brother.

"Um, what the hell do you think you're doing?" he seethes.

My teeth grind with obvious anger from the way he's talking to her. *How fucking dare he speak to her like that?*

"Kane isn't here," she says.

He scoffs and sends her a scathing look that does nothing

but pull my attention to his skinny face. His clothes are wrinkly, and he looks as if he hasn't slept for weeks. "And you expect me to believe you?"

"Why wouldn't you?" Daisy crosses her arms.

"Because you've been protecting him for years. Now I know why he hasn't been texting me back." Miles leans in close to Daisy, and my shoulders tense. "It's because of you."

When Miles pokes his finger into Daisy's shoulder, I curse under my breath.

"What is he talking about?" River asks me. "Protecting you for years?"

I shake my head and brush him off. We both put our attention back to the scene unfolding.

"You promised you'd never ask anything of him again." Daisy shakes her head. "All those times I checked on you, dropped off pamphlets, made sure you were staying off online gambling sites, you've been lying?"

Wait, what?

"How could you, Miles? After everything? Do you know that you basically wiped him clean? He makes millions, and he didn't even have enough to pay his rent!" Daisy's voice rises with anger, and all I want to do is reach through the phone and separate them. "And to think that *you*"—Daisy pokes his shoulder just like he did to her—"knew this entire time that he hasn't even spoken to your mother because she still thinks *he's* the one who turned out like your father, and you're still coming around to ask for money?"

I feel River's stare.

The air shifts with the whipping of his head, but I refuse to look at him.

"You should be ashamed of yourself."

Fuck, fuck, fuck.

"Let's go," Daisy says.

"Go?" Miles repeats.

"I know exactly why you're here. You're here for money. I've seen your texts on his phone."

Daisy, what the hell are you doing?

River tenses. "What the hell is going on?"

"Are you going to come up with the money, Daisy? Because if we show up without anything, they'll probably kill me and then take you for their prize."

My throat closes with the thought. Too many thoughts filter in, and I'm seeing red by the time I take my next breath.

"I have money," she says. "But I'm only paying off your debt on one condition."

"Money?" River repeats. "She can't have that much. She's a mascot."

"What's your condition? That I go back to rehab? You going to pick me up and take me to those stupid gambling anonymous classes again?"

Again?

Daisy shakes her head, and I almost miss the next thing that comes out of her mouth from the ringing in my ears.

"We're going home."

Miles squints. "Home?"

"And we're telling your mother the truth. Kane took the fall for you, Miles. He hasn't been home in six years because of *you.*"

Miles stares at her for a long time, and River stares at me.

By the time I settle my thoughts, Miles is agreeing with Daisy, and they're stepping onto the elevator to head back to her apartment for clothes.

I click my phone off and rush over to my keys.

I know exactly where they are, and when I get there, I'm going to fucking strangle my brother to the point that he passes out.

"Wait up." River moves in front of my door, and the

confusion on his face stops me in place. "What the hell is going on?"

With my blood pressure rising to the point that my fingers tingle, I decide it's now or never. Too much is out in the open. Going back is impossible.

"You know you're like a brother to me." I grip the keys tightly in my fist. "We've grown up side by side, your parents giving me more support than my own."

River interrupts me, seemingly becoming more confused by the second. "What is Daisy talking about? Taking the fall for him?"

"I took the fall for Miles when all that shit went down six years ago. He begged me to throw the game of poker that led to me in handcuffs, being charged with illegal gambling. It was all so he could get off the hook with some high roller that was wanted by the police. I covered for him to protect my mom. If I ratted him out, he would've ended up in prison. It was easier for me to take the fall." *Something he begged of me.* "Mom was able to avoid the judgmental stares at the grocery store, and instead of both of her sons being involved, it was just one."

River's eyebrows furrow deeper the more I talk, but I keep going because there's no way I'm going back on the truth now. It's not a secret I'm worried about any longer. I'm much more worried about the other secret—the one with pretty blue eyes and a heart of fucking gold.

"Kane. What the hell, man." River sighs. "Why didn't you tell me?"

I hate that he's showing his concern, because after I tell him the rest of the truth, that concern is going to morph into something much worse.

"That doesn't matter," I say, moving on quickly. Every second I'm not with Daisy is a second too long. "I need to tell you something else."

"Alright, what?" He wipes the sweat off his forehead with his shirt, and I prepare myself for a sucker punch.

"You know I'd never do anything to jeopardize our friendship." I clench my jaw. "Not purposefully."

"Uh, yeah?" He shakes his head. "What the hell is going on? Is this where you tell me that Miles and my sister were secretly together at some point or something?"

My stomach knots. "Not Miles."

"Then who—"

River's mouth shuts suddenly. A look of betrayal flashes in his eye, and I hope he hears my next words and believes them before he decides to punch me.

"I've never loved anyone," I admit, "but her. It's only ever been her."

I don't wait a moment longer to move past River. I tear open my apartment door and head for the parking garage.

Daisy is with Miles, and I know exactly where they are.

If River wants to hate me, that's fine.

If Miles wants to refuse to believe he has a gambling problem, then so be it.

If my mom wants to continue to disown me, let her.

All I care about is Daisy, and I refuse to hide it any longer.

River's anger is nothing compared to the anger I have for Miles for dragging Daisy into his mess.

Fifty-Three

DAISY

MY HEART BEATS AS QUICKLY as the shuffling of cards. The bells on the slot machines go off every other second, and I never thought I'd wish to be at a doctor's appointment, but I'd much rather be in Dr. Gibson's office, getting stuck with a needle, than beside Kane's older brother, who is the most selfish person I've ever met.

"Well?" I glance to Miles, who swings his gaze around the smoky room. "Where are they?"

I hope they left, thinking that Miles stood them up. After taking the train because neither of us has a car, we're way later than expected.

Casinos have a way of shutting out the real world. There are no windows or easy exits. Clocks are nonexistent, making reality so far out of touch you forget that it exists. I can see why Miles is sucked into this lifestyle, as the casinos don't necessarily make it easy to climb out.

"There." He nods up ahead, angling his lean jaw toward a

group of men smoking cigarettes. They're staring directly at us, shuffling their attention between Miles and me.

My head pounds with each step we take toward them, the smoke clouding my lungs, making it hard to breathe.

"Where is it?" one of them asks, not bothering to stand up from their chair.

A card game is unfolding behind the man's back, the dealer glancing at us a few times before putting his attention back on the table.

"And who is this?" A tall man with a sleek, black mustache slides around in his chair and eyes me up and down.

I cut right to the chase. "How much does he owe?"

"More than you can offer," the large one muses. His belly hangs over his high-end belt buckle, but I bet if I looked hard enough, I could see the utter disgust on my face within its glossy reflection. "But I'll take some off what he owes me if you come back to my room with me."

"Not a fucking chance, Al."

I'm surprised when Miles steps forward to defend me. I gape at him from the side, wondering if he dug down deep to find a smidge of guilt for what he's done to Kane.

"Oh, possessive, are we?" Al's lips curve, his round cheeks rising with amusement.

Runs in the family, I think to myself.

"How much does he owe?" I repeat, wanting to get this show on the road.

I don't have a ton of money saved, but since I've been working, money has been accumulating in my account, especially since River has refunded my rent both times I've tried to pay it. Being the Blue Devils mascot pays more than one would think, and although I was going to put it toward getting my own place and maybe, *possibly*, opening my own plant cart one day with soil, plants, and composting materials, this is more important.

"Seventy-five thousand."

My lips part.

Oh.

Al cackles, throwing his head back with loud laughter.

Attention is drawn to us, Miles and I catching each other's eye immediately.

"How much do you have?" he whispers.

"Not that much." Not even close.

Panic sets in. *This was a terrible idea.*

I glance to the table behind the men.

I've played poker before. Kane taught me, and Miles taught him.

It's a gamble—no pun intended—but I don't see any other option.

"My offer still stands," Al says. "Let me have you for a while, and I'll take some money off the table."

Miles's jaw clenches, and he looks eerily similar to his brother, despite him taking after their mother's features as opposed to Kane, who must've taken after their father.

Miles stands in front of me, blocking me from their view. "You're not touching her, Allen."

All of a sudden, two hands wrap around my waist from behind, and my back straightens. A breath rushes past my lips when Kane's voice hits my ear. "And you're not gambling with anything else today, little devil."

I peer back at Kane, relief rushing my veins like a waterfall.

"I haven't gambled yet," I whisper.

He chuckles deeply while spinning us around. I stare up into his eyes and zero in on the bruise forming on his cheekbone. River is standing off to the side with his hands in his pockets, and it doesn't take his brains to know what happened.

"You have too," he argues.

His hands cup my cheeks, and he shakes his head back and

forth. "You've been gambling with my heart from the moment I met you, Daisy. Today is no exception."

My eyebrows furrow.

"Risking your safety to protect me? Are you crazy?" A touch of anger flickers within Kane's blue eyes.

I shrug, and he clenches his jaw.

"You make me crazy." He shakes his head. "But I love you."

My heart flies behind my ribs.

"Even more now, knowing how much you've done for me over the years without ever letting me find out."

My eyes gloss over, my bottom lip trembling. "I did it because I love you. Not because I wanted you to love me."

Kane crushes me to his chest and places a kiss to the top of my head. "Go with your brother," he urges, pulling away from me. "I'm going to handle this once and for all."

"How?" I ask, watching him head toward Miles, who is pleading his case with the men behind us.

"Exactly like you said. Pay off his debt and then take him home."

"Home?" I ask.

"Not our home."

Our home?

"I'm taking him back to Lakeview, Daisy. Where it all began."

I try to hide a smile because Lakeview *is* where it all began. It's where I fell in love with him, despite the silent warnings not to.

As if he can read my mind, a slow smile spreads on his face. "Me too, Daisy-Petal. *Me too.*"

Fifty-Four

KANE

IT'S late by the time I get home. Coach is pissed that I missed afternoon practice, but since it was a *family emergency*, it's unlikely I'll have repercussions—not with our first playoff game tomorrow.

After dropping seventy-five thousand into the hands of someone I'd like to rip to shreds, Miles followed me out to my car and remained quiet until we crossed the state line.

That was when the silence broke.

I'd heard his sorry excuses before, going in one ear and out the other. But this time, things were different. Miles could take me down with him, but the moment Daisy was involved? That was where I drew the line.

And to think, she'd been involved from day one.

I didn't need another apology from him, or confirmation that Daisy took him to and from Gamblers Anonymous meetings before leaving for college, or how she checked in on him from time to time during the one year he was apparently clean.

Instead, I need him to change, and if he's not willing to change, then he's out of my life.

I had never let myself think about the moment I'd show up on my mom's doorstep again, but for the sake of Daisy, I went with my brother with his head hung low beside me.

I didn't waste any time cutting to the chase.

It was a hard pill for her to swallow, but the moment Miles nodded, confirming the actual truth, a tear slipped over her cheek, learning that she'd been fooled all these years. I left without a goodbye, too pent up with nervous energy and mixed emotions.

Those emotions are wired even tighter now as I head to the thirtieth floor back at the apartment complex.

I rap my knuckles on Daisy's door, having no idea what I'm walking into.

When the door swings open, I tense. River narrows his eyes, unmoving from the doorway.

I flex my jaw. "I let you hit me once. That's all you get."

He flicks his eyebrow. "You didn't *let* me hit you. I saw the surprise on your face."

I put my hands in my pockets. "Actually, I was surprised at how much it stung. Who taught you how to throw a punch again?" I think for a second, knowing very well that I was the one who taught him. "Oh, wait. That was me."

"River." Daisy's sweet voice hits my ears from somewhere in the apartment, and my nerves calm.

He surprisingly moves to the side, and I walk inside.

I find her right away, sitting on the couch with a blanket wrapped around her. Strawberry-blonde tendrils of hair frame her face from the high ponytail on top of her head, and those sleepy eyes hit me right in the chest.

Forgetting all about River behind me, I stride directly over to her and squat down low so I'm on her level. "How are you feeling?"

She barely lifts a shoulder. "I'm okay."

I'm not convinced.

"Are you okay?" she asks quietly.

I shoot her a look. "Don't worry about me. Did you make it to Dr. Gibson's? Did he do blood work?"

The smallest smile hints against her lips. "Yes, but I'll be fine. I've been dealing with Lupus for a couple of years now. You don't have to worry."

I furrow my brow, ignoring the looming presence of River, who is probably plotting my death. "Well, I haven't," I argue. "I am worried."

River makes a noise, and I flick my attention to him. His jaw is set, his gaze narrowed.

Daisy sighs with annoyance. "River, we talked about this."

"Well, I'm still angry," he grunts.

I slowly stand up and stare at him. Daisy, sitting quietly on the couch, is the only barrier between us.

"I'm sorry," I say.

My apology lingers. It's not often that I apologize or that I'm sincere, but I think River knows me well enough to know that it's true. Just like he has to know that my feelings for Daisy are genuine. If he thinks hard enough and takes a brief peek to the past, how could he not?

"I don't think you understand why I'm angry." River shakes his head and sits on a barstool in the kitchen.

I stare at him from across the apartment, ready for this overdue conversation. "I understand exactly why you're angry. Why would you ever want someone like me with your sister?"

It's not like I've been a saint over these last few years. In fact, I've been trying my very hardest to be anything *but*. The only thing I've got going for me is my career. At this point, I don't even have a load of money in my account.

I have to start all over again.

"That's not why I'm angry," River snaps. "I'm angry because

you two hiding your fling has caused unnecessary stress for her. She just got things under control after two years of medications, lifestyle changes, and constant doctor's appointments. She's been with you for three seconds, and she's right back to where she was. You're selfish, Kane. And sure, a little part of me is upset that you two hid this from me. I thought we were friends?"

The blanket falls to the floor as Daisy springs up from the couch. She quickly turns to her brother, her rigid back to me. "That is not true, River."

He scoffs and follows it with a sarcastic chuckle. "Which part?"

"Kane is not selfish," she argues.

My jaw aches as I clench my teeth together. I hate that she's trying to stick up for me. She doesn't have to plead my case to her brother. He knows me, almost as well as she does.

"He risked his future and reputation to protect his family. He saved his brother from going to prison by taking the fall for something that was selfishly asked of him. He was practically cut out of the family, not having seen his mom for years, because of something he didn't even do."

Daisy is shaking by the end. I erase the space between us, putting my hands on her arms. I rub my palms softly over her warm skin. "Hey, calm down. It's okay. You don't have to defend me."

She peers backward at me, those blue eyes filled with worry. "Yes, I do, because even you don't see it. You're selfless and beyond loyal."

"Loyal?" River repeats.

Daisy turns to him. "Yes, loyal. It's part of why neither of us has said anything to you. Do you think Kane wanted to risk your friendship? Do you think he wants Mom and Dad to feel cheated by him?"

It's true. The thought has been there, starting out in the

forefront of my brain, only to get more and more buried by what I feel for Daisy.

I clear my throat and pull Daisy behind me. The anger is dying down against River's features, his furrowed brow smooth and his expression blank.

"I've always loved her, River. If you think hard enough, you'll remember all the times you caught me staring at her from across the dinner table." I swallow the emotion clogging my throat, confused from the way my neck tightens with the thought. "She's the one I went to when things turned dark. She's the reason I left and went to the juniors, which led me here. I owe her everything," I admit, laying it all out. "My life, my future, my heart."

River stares at me long and hard.

My pulse thrums behind my skin from my confession. I don't think I've ever said it aloud. Not even to Daisy.

"Well, fuck." River runs a hand through his hair, tipping his head back to stare at the ceiling. "Fine!"

My heart does a fucking backflip.

"Fine?" Daisy repeats.

River stands and puts his hands on his hips. "Yes, *fine*. You two can be together."

Daisy snorts with a quick roll of her eyes. "As if we needed your permission?"

River shoots his attention to me. He points to Daisy. "Good luck with her."

My lips lift, and I grin.

"Where are you going?" I ask him when he heads for the door.

I'm not necessarily sorry to see him go, but I'm still playing nice, relieved to have everything out in the open.

"I'm going to your apartment. There is no way in hell I'm going to watch you kiss her as if she's not my sister."

Daisy gives him a look. "You've never really cared before when I've been kissed in front of you."

Before River leaves, he peers back at us. "Yeah, well, I know how he is, so..."

Daisy's cheeks turn a bright shade of pink.

"See!" He shakes his head at her.

The door latches shut, and Daisy pouts. "How rude." My heart is beating a million miles a second, my palms suddenly tingling to have her in my grasp. "He acts like you're going to strip me bare right in front of him or something."

I thought about it. Now that everything's out in the open, nothing can keep us apart.

"After today, I don't think anyone could stop me from doing just that." I pull her in close and her breath catches.

"Bad day?" she asks with a barely-there smile.

"Not all bad." I skim my nose against hers, breathing her in like she's my oxygen. I creep my hands past her curves, landing on her cheeks. "Say it again."

"Say what?" she whispers, her mouth lingering right in front of mine.

Damn, I really do love her.

I have no idea how I went six years without her.

The devastation I felt the day she turned me away sent me to the edge of insanity. I cared about nothing.

Then she came back, and now I'm on edge whenever we're not together.

"Tell me you love me." Our lips are almost touching, our bodies buzzing.

She smiles against my lips. "Make me."

Anticipation flies to my fingertips. I grip her thighs, and she's jumping to wrap her legs around my waist with her faint laugh filling the quiet apartment.

I peer into her eyes before gazing at her mouth. "You know I will."

I walk us to her bedroom and shut the door. I lay her back on the bed, and those blue eyes have me trapped.

"I love you," she whispers.

I hover over her, wind my hand through her hair, and press my mouth to hers. I deepen the kiss, my insides pulling on my heart until I can't breathe.

"I love you too," I say, just in case she didn't get the gist. "Now instead of all those rituals I do the night before a game, let me take care of you, and make sure to scream extra loud...so your brother can hear."

I wink and catch the laugh right off the tip of her lips with mine.

Epilogue

DAISY

"I'LL TAKE THAT, thank you very much." My brother swoops in between Kane and me to steal the chocolate cake placed on his plate.

Kane stares at his empty plate but reluctantly nods when he remembers that he made a pledge that he was going to cut out all the same foods that I have, in solidarity, now that it's the off-season.

"Too sugary for you, and there's gluten," River mumbles with a mouthful of cake.

I glare at him, but Kane's hand falls to my leg to calm my irritation.

"I made you something special." My mom comes around with a dish that looks like pudding. "There's enough for Kane too."

"Thanks, Mom." I give her a quick hug while Kane hands me a spoon.

Dr. Gibson put me on a small dose of steroids after my

levels came back higher than usual, despite how much I hate taking them. Thankfully, after a week, I was feeling more like myself, and with another round of blood work, my levels plateaued, so I was only on them for a short period.

Now that Kane is well versed in Lupus, he's taken it upon himself to make sure I get enough rest, eat all the right foods, and practice various forms of stress relief...all of which involve him.

River has sort of come around to the idea of us. He's no longer making vomiting noises whenever we kiss in front of him, and he's stopped taking his blood pressure, which he only did to prove that Kane touching me raises it.

When I told my parents, with Kane nervously pacing in front of me while I was on the phone, they laughed. At first, I thought they were laughing because they assumed it was a joke, but then my dad said, *"What took him so long?"* and I realized right then that Kane and I weren't as sly as we thought when we were teenagers.

We're not so sly now either, considering River is acting disgusted at Kane's arm beneath the table, resting his hand on my thigh. There's a twinge of awkwardness at the kitchen table that has nothing to do with Kane and me touching, though. Kathleen, Kane's mom, is quieter than I remember her being. There was some major tension between her and my parents the summer they took Kane in that has now switched to discomfort and maybe even a little embarrassment.

Kane and his mom have only talked a handful of times since he dropped Miles off on her doorstep.

Which is why I thought it'd be a good idea to clear the air once and for all—no less on Mother's Day weekend.

"I'll be right back," Kane whispers in my ear, scooting away from the table.

I nod and continue eating my pudding.

It's not chocolate cake, but it's good enough.

As soon as Kane leaves the room, my brother following after him, Kathleen's bundled shoulders relax. She asks me questions about Lupus and then brings up how cute I am in my mascot costume during the games.

I tilt my head. "You watch the games?"

"Of course." She glances in the direction Kane and River went. "I never stopped."

I shoot her a small, reassuring smile when she looks back at me. Things may be awkward now with Kane, but I know it'll get better. I know him, and I know his heart.

My mom makes small talk with Kathleen until our attention is drawn to the guys walking through the kitchen with something behind their backs. I raise an eyebrow and put my spoon down. *What's this?*

"Happy Mother's Day." River pulls out a bundle of flowers and leans down to kiss my mom on the cheek.

"I told you that you coming home this weekend was my gift!" She's beaming while gazing at her flowers.

I sit up a little taller. "Are those from my garden?"

River pretends not to hear me, but I know my peonies when I see them.

Kane steps forward, and he, too, pulls out a bouquet of flowers, one in his left and another in his right. He hands one to my mom, who gives him a *'you shouldn't have'* look, and the other to his mom.

"Oh." Kathleen blinks back the surprise, the flowers clutched in her tight grip.

Neither of their bouquets are from my garden. My mom's is full of daisies, which is no doubt because of me, and his mom's is full of daffodils.

I know Kane well enough to know that he's uncomfortable with the gesture, so I glance at River. He gives me a swift nod, swooping in to save the day.

River clears his throat, stealing the attention in the room, and looks at Kane. "I thought you were taking flowers from Daisy's garden too."

Kane shakes his head, chuckling. "I know better than to do that."

I hum and give my brother a look. "You're doing the dishes."

He scoffs. "Isn't that the second part of your Mother's Day gift to Mom?"

I smile. "It was. Now it's yours."

My dad chuckles off to the side, my mom busying herself with finding a vase for the three bouquets of flowers now resting on the table.

Kane and his mom talk quietly. I take the opportunity to give them privacy since they've only chatted briefly since Kane came clean, and it was to give Kane an update on Miles, who is at a gambling addiction treatment facility for the next several months.

I disappear upstairs to escape River's complaining about the dishes and end up in my childhood bedroom. In the past, I refused to linger in here for too long, afraid it'd bring up too many hidden memories of that summer.

With my back to the door, I stare out the window. I smile softly with the memory of Kane across the yard, staring at me out of his own window. Even back then, when we were too young to realize anything was happening between us, I was drawn to him. Seeing his boyish smile, that later turned into a bad-boy smirk, was the highlight of my evening each night.

"Should I go over there and wave at you from my old bedroom?"

I spin quickly with a yelp. My hand moves to my racing heart. "God, you scared me."

Kane gives me a lopsided smile and shuts my bedroom door behind him. The noise of it latching shoots a thrill down my spine. Heat pulls on my core as Kane strides over to me, his tall frame taking up so much space in my small bedroom.

I peer up at him. "It was nice of you to give both of our moms flowers."

His tight jaw flickers when he glances away. For someone as arrogant as him, he doesn't take compliments very well.

"Did you purposefully give your mom daffodils?" I question, knowing his heart goes so much deeper than anyone realizes.

He eyes me out of his peripheral vision.

"You did, didn't you? I was wondering why you were reading my floriography book." I smile.

Daffodils represent new beginnings—something that's very fitting for him and his mom.

"You can be awfully sweet when you want to be," I say quietly.

Kane finally turns to me. "Don't tell anyone that."

I laugh quietly, but it fades when he starts to dig into his pocket. "I got you something too," he says.

"Me?" I observe his face before glancing at my belly. "Do you know something I don't?"

His laugh makes me smile. "This isn't a Mother's Day present." He turns serious. "Not yet, anyway."

I try to hide a smile at the thought of us having a baby one day. It may be a struggle because of my Lupus, but with him by my side, I know we'll be able to handle anything that is thrown our way.

"Then what is it?" I ask.

I study the way his fingers move against the screen of his phone, as if he's searching for something. He sharply flicks his blue eyes to me when he stops swiping.

"Hear me out," he starts. "When you're ready to move on from being the mascot..."

I pretend to be outraged by the idea. "Never. You're stuck with me."

Kane grins, softening his tight masculine features for a second. His hand lands on my hip, and he brings me in close. He spins me next, pulling me backward to rest against his hard chest. When he places his phone in front of my face, it takes me a couple of seconds to realize what he's showing me.

My eyelashes flutter as I attempt to clear my blurry vision. I grab onto his phone and zoom in on the photo. In blue typography, the words **The Blue Devil Gardener** appear above a shovel, rake, and hoe graphic with a tagline underneath that says, ***Soil so good it's devilishly strong.***

"I had a logo made for you whenever you're ready for that plant stand you've been dreaming about since we were kids."

I bite down on my lip to keep from crying—or squealing. Maybe both.

The room fills with silence, and Kane shifts behind me.

"Uh, do you like it? Or..." His words fade, and he shifts nervously again. If I wasn't so blown away by the gesture, I'd make him sweat it out a little longer, because it's not often that Kane Barlow gets flustered.

His phone falls to the floor as I spin around in his arms. I take him by surprise when I push him onto my twin bed, his blue eyes gleaming with something enticing.

"I love it." I climb over his legs and straddle him.

That bad-boy grin spreads on his face, and he leans back on my flowery blanket to relax.

"You gonna show me how much you love it?" he asks, voice husky.

I nod with a smile. He lets me kiss him deep and slow before needing to take charge. He flips me around to my back, like I weigh no more than his pinky finger, and hovers over me.

"The first time I had you on this bed, I went slow."

I bite my lip from excitement.

His hands roam, caressing each of my curves. I squirm beneath his touch, eagerly waiting for another secretive moment with him.

"But this time, I'm going fast, little devil." He smirks. "So hold on tight."

What's next?
Get ready for Malaki and Reese!

Book 4 in the Chicago Blue Devils Series releases fall of 2025!

Head to sjsylvis.com for info!

Heartless Boys Never Kiss

Pretty Girls Never Lie

Standalones

Three Summers

Yours Truly, Cammie

Chasing Ivy

Falling for Fallon

Truth

S.J. Sylvis is an Amazon top 50 and USA Today bestselling author who is best known for her new adult sport romances. She currently resides in Arizona with her husband, two small children, dog and cat! She is obsessed with coffee, becomes easily attached to fictional characters, and spends most of her evenings buried in a book!

Stay up to date at: sjsylvis.com

Acknowledgments

First, as always, I have to thank my husband for always being so encouraging and supportive. I wrote this book for my autoimmune girlies because it's been an uphill battle for me. What started as some strange muscle pain in my legs turned into something much larger with more symptoms, lots of doctor's appointments, blood draws, etc., and I'm *still* trying to find answers. My husband has refused to let me quit searching, and all but demands someone pay attention to what's going on so, in the spirit of having the majority of the same symptoms as Daisy, I decided to incorporate that into this book.

So again, thank you to my husband for taking care of me, and I'm sending all my love and patience to those who struggle with an autoimmune disease or something similar. <3

And of course, thank you to each and every person who had a part in making sure this book was up to par. Emma, Bri, Kari, Ratula, Sahara, Jenn, Mary, Sarah, Ashlee, VPR, my agent, TU group chat, my besties, family, and every reader who shares, makes content, reads, etc. I am so thankful for you all and wouldn't be where I am with you!!

xo

SJ